THE YEAR OF THE COBRA

THE YEAR OF THE COBRA

Paul Doherty

headline

GW 2863849 2

Copyright © 2006 Paul Doherty

The right of Paul Doherty to be identified as the Author of
the Work has been asserted by him in accordance with the
Copyright, Designs and Patents Act 1988.

First published in 2006 by
HEADLINE BOOK PUBLISHING

1

Cataloguing in Publication Data is available from the British Library

ISBN 0 7553 0342 3 (hardback)
ISBN 0 7553 0343 1 (trade paperback)

Typeset in Trump Mediaeval by Palimpsest Book Production Limited,
Polmont, Stirlingshire

Printed and bound in Great Britain by
Clays Ltd, St Ives plc

Headline's policy is to use papers that are natural, renewable and
recyclable products and made from wood grown in sustainable forests.
The logging and manufacturing processes are expected to conform
to the environmental regulations of the country of origin.

HEADLINE BOOK PUBLISHING
A division of Hodder Headline
338 Euston Road
London NW1 3BH

www.headline.co.uk
www.hodderheadline.com

In memory of Caroline Mary Fox, a remarkable and gifted woman, who died on 18 April 2004

PRINCIPAL CHARACTERS

PHARAOHS

Sequenre
Ahmose
Tuthmosis III
Hatchesphut:
} war-like Pharaohs of the Eighteenth Dynasty (1550–1323 BC) who founded the great empire of Ancient Egypt and cleared the Kingdom of the Two Lands of the Hyksos invaders

THE ROYAL HOUSE (OF AMENHOTEP III)

Amenhotep III, 'The Magnificent': Pharaoh of Egypt for about thirty-nine years during which time the Kingdom of the Two Lands reached its pinnacle of power

Tiye: Amenhotep III's Great Queen and Great Wife: a native of Egypt, daughter of Thuya and Yuya, from the town of Akhmin

Crown Prince Tuthmosis: heir apparent of Amenhotep III; he died in his youth

Prince Amenhotep: the Veiled One (also the Great Heretic; the Grotesque) – known to history as Akenhaten, younger son of Amenhotep and Tiye

Sitamun: daughter of Amenhotep III and Queen Tiye

CHILDREN OF THE KAP (ROYAL NURSERY)

Horemheb: general

Rameses: Horemheb's great friend and fellow general

Huy: leading courtier/envoy of the period

Maya: treasurer during this period

Mery-re: Principal Priest of the Era, a fervent follower of the Aten Cult

Pentju: Royal Physician, friend of Princess Khiya, guardian, for a while, of the baby prince Tutankhamun

Sobeck:	Chief of Police in Thebes

THE ROYAL HOUSE (OF AKENHATEN)

Akenhaten/Amenhotep IV:	Pharaoh
Nefertiti:	Akenhaten's Great Queen and Wife, daughter of Ay

Meketaten
Meritaten
Ankhesenaten
Ankhesenamun } children of Akenhaten
Tutankhaten
Tutankhamun: } later Pharaoh of Egypt

Khiya:	Mitanni princess, one of Akenhaten's 'junior' wives, mother of Tutankhamun

THE AKHMIN GANG

Ay:	First Minister of Akenhaten, father of Nefertiti, brother of Queen Tiye
Mutnodjmet:	younger daughter of Ay, married to Horemheb
Nakhtimin (Nakhtmin/Minnakht):	half-brother of Ay, commander of Palace troops

OTHERS

Amendufet:	royal scribe
Nabila:	Theban lady
Mahu:	Chief of Police under Akenhaten, senior official under Tutankhamun
Djarka:	Mahu's lieutenant
Suppiliuma:	Hittite king
Zananza:	Hittite prince
Nebamun:	colonel in the Egyptian Army
Mert:	Djarka's wife

Introduction

The Eighteenth Dynasty (1550–1323 BC) marked the high point, if not the highest point, of the Ancient Egyptian Empire, both at home and abroad; it was a period of grandeur, of gorgeous pageantry and triumphant imperialism. It was also a time of great change and violent events, particularly in the final years of the reign of Amenhotep III and the swift accession of the 'Great Heretic' Akenhaten, when a bitter clash took place between religious ideologies at a time when the brooding menace of the Hittite Empire was making itself felt.

I was very fortunate in being given access to an ancient document which alleges to be, in the words of a more recent age, 'the frank and full confession' of a man who lived at the eye of the storm: Mahu, Chief of Police of Akenhaten and his successors. Mahu emerges as a rather sinister figure responsible for security – a job description which can, and did, cover a multitude of sins. This confession seems to be in full accord with the evidence on Mahu that has been recovered from other archaeological sources – be it the discoveries at El-Amarna, the City of the Aten, or the evidence of his own tomb, which he never occupied. A keen observer of his times, Mahu was a man whose hand, literally, was never far from his sword (see the Historical Note on page 307).

Mahu appears to have written his confession some considerable time after the turbulent years which marked the end of the Eighteenth Dynasty. He kept journals, which he later transcribed, probably during the very short reign of Rameses I (c.1307 BC). Mahu's original document was then translated in the demotic mode some six hundred years later during the seventh century BC, then copied again during the Roman period in a mixture of Latin and the Greek Koine. His confession, which I have decided to publish in a trilogy, reflects these different periods of translation and amendment; for instance, Thebes is the Greek version of 'Waset', and certain other proper names, not to mention hieroglyphs, are given varying interpretations by the different translators and copiers.

In the first part of the trilogy, *An Evil Spirit Out of the West*, Mahu described the rise and fall of Akenhaten: that Pharaoh's mysterious disappearance, the attempt by his Queen Nefertiti to seize power, and her brutal and tragic end. In the second part, *The Season of the Hyaena*, Mahu reflected on the mysteries surrounding such dramatic events. He and others of the Kap, now Lords of Egypt but bound by the close ties of childhood, were still haunted by what had happened and fearful of what might come. Mahu's fears were more than justified. A great usurper, pretending to be Akenhaten, appeared in the delta to raise the spectre of civil war. Mahu had to deal with this as well as search for the true fate of his former Pharaoh. In doing so, he discovered secrets which were highly dangerous to Egypt's future, as well as scandals about Khiya, Akenhaten's second wife, and was drawn into a deadly political rivalry with the cunning Lord Ay. In the end Mahu paid the price for such opposition, being placed under house arrest for years. He was recalled to court for very sinister reasons: the young Pharaoh, Tutankhamun, was suffering from a serious mental illness . . .

The Year of the Cobra now resumes Mahu's tale:

Tutankhamun is unwell, but there is no heir apparent. Egypt's enemies, the Hittites, are advancing through Canaan, and Ay still plots, like the spider he is. The web is woven, the traps set . . .

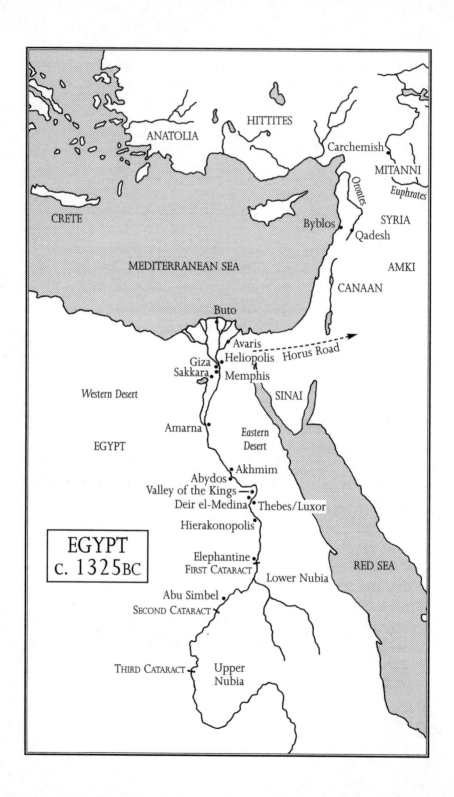

ANATOLIA

HITTITES

Carchemish

MITANNI

Euphrates

Orontes

SYRIA

CRETE

Byblos

Qadesh

MEDITERRANEAN SEA

AMKI

CANAAN

Buto

Avaris

Horus Road

Giza

Heliopolis

Sakkara

Memphis

SINAI

Western Desert

Amarna

Eastern Desert

EGYPT

Akhmim

Abydos

Valley of the Kings

Deir el-Medina

Thebes/Luxor

Hierakonpolis

EGYPT
c. 1325 BC

Elephantine
FIRST CATARACT

Lower Nubia

RED SEA

Abu Simbel

SECOND CATARACT

THIRD CATARACT

Upper
Nubia

Aakhu-t: the fiery cobra on Pharaoh's crown

Prologue

She who lights the fire to stir the embers
with sharp flames, quick in killing without hesitation.
She against whom there is no protection.
She by whom no one can pass without harm;
the one that rears up towards her Lord.

She sharp as knives,
Mistress of the Two Lands,
who destroys the enemies of the tired heart,
who arouses trembling before the Sinless One.

I often quote these verses from the Book of the Dead. They describe the soul's progress through the Am-duat, the underworld, past the Devourers, the drinkers of blood, the gobblers of flesh. I don't believe a word of it, yet I do like the poetry, its description of fiery lakes which lap desolate shores on which the cities of the dead rise in ghastly splendour. Why do I like it? Well, it seems to describe my life, or at least most of it. True, I have walked through the Fields of the Blessed where the blue and white lotus opens and shuts at your command, where the air is sweet with hyacinth and the fresh green smells of spring. Where the white ibis soars beneath blue, rain-washed skies, where the sun and moon, and all the blossoms of the night, hang in perpetual glory. Such blessedness is mine. I have drunk from gold cups heavy with precious stones, sipping the wine of Charou and Canaan. I have eaten the most succulent meats, the freshest honey-drenched bread and the choicest fruits. I have known the bodies of the most beautiful women with their perfume-drenched wigs and sloe-eyes, ringed with blue, green or black kohl, all bright and sparkling with passion. I have held them in my arms, their glittering jewellery flashing and tingling as they turn and twist in the Netchenet, the sexual paradise.

I have strolled in palaces and been adorned with all the regalia of power as a servant of four Pharaohs. I have been spy, traitor and warrior. I have eaten the dust-clouds of battle as the chariot squadrons thunder in. The hideous clash of the Menfyt and Nakhtu-aa and Maryannou, the strong-arm boys, the braves of the king, as they fought with spear, sword, shield and club out in the Redlands or along the marshes of the Nile: such bloodshed is no stranger to me. I have fought in the cold blackness of the desert nights and under a sun so searing the rocks have splintered and cracked. I have wandered across battlefields where the dead bloat, burst and stink and the earth seems carpeted with feathery winged vultures. I have known the terror of being hunted by night prowlers, by assassins, the disciples of the redhead Seth, with blades snaking out of the darkness or the unexpected arrow whipping through the air. Why? Because I am Mahu of the Medjay, formerly Chief of Police under the great heretic, he whose name is proscribed for ever, Akenhaten.

See, I have proclaimed his name. The Great Heretic! Now he is gone, him and the rest. I am an old man brought back to Thebes with my journals written in my own *terf shta-t*, secret writing. The Divine One, Rameses, Mighty Bull, Most Fitting of Forms, Horus in the South, Smiter of the People of the Nine Bows, wishes my life to be told, for his own secret purposes or, perhaps, not so secret. I am Pharaoh's bridge to the past because the rest have all gone into the never-ending darkness. Only old Mahu remains from the glory days of Egypt's past. I am to write what I know.

I use my journals but I also call on the dead. The Ancient Chronicles describe how, many decades ago, before a Pharaoh died, he had a priest strangled and sent before him to prepare his journey. I heard of a similar story during my exile, which reminds me, I've met some eerie characters on my travels. One in particular springs to mind, a scholar from the kingdom of Punt, which borders on the Great Green to the East. He had wandered south, past the Cataracts, before turning west into the great jungles to meet the tribes who live along the far coast. He told me of one chief who, when he wished to communicate with his dead father, had a dozen slaves strangled and sent into the netherworld to ask for advice. I asked this scholar why the chieftain had a dozen slaves executed. The man smiled, wrinkling his face in amusement.

'Just in case one of them got lost in the darkness; out of twelve, one of them was bound to find his or her way.'

'And how was the advice brought back?' I asked.

'Ah,' that teller of great lies replied, 'the chief would have a dream, and if he didn't, twelve more would be sent.'

A droll story, yet all I can send into the eternal night is my soul, even though I doubt I might have one. If I have, will the other souls be waiting for me? All my companions: Huy, Maya and the rest?

They have taken away what I have written, yesterday. The Chief of Scribes, Overseer of the House of Secrets, came down to interrogate me: a fat, arrogant fellow, puffed up with his own importance, like a cobra is with poison. He brought his personal secretary to take down the words from my mouth, a young fellow who stared at me in astonishment. He may well do so! My eyes are sunken, my teeth blunted, my skin yellowing and coarse. My black hair is now white as a lily pod. I suppose he hasn't met many men in their eighty-sixth year who can recall so vividly the sterling days of the Great Heretic. The Chief Scribe, I forget his name, calls himself the Eyes and Ears of Pharaoh. I was about to reply how blind and deaf his master must be, but I bit back the reply. He wants to summarise what I've written. He settled his fat arse on a cushioned chair and gazed sorrowfully at me. I lounged on cushions, half drunk from a goblet of wine, head slightly turned, as if I was more concerned about a rat-hole, the one the servants had tried to block with roasted cat fat mixed with snake oil.

'You are Mahu of the Medjay,' he began. 'Your mother died when you were young? Your father was a colonel in the desert police? You lived with your aunt Isithia; you hated her and hired another to kill her?'

'I hate rats.' I glanced away from the hole in the wall and peered at him.

'Mahu, you must answer my questions.'

'Why?'

'Because the Divine One, may life, health and blessing be upon him, may he enjoy a million jubilees, may Osiris anoint him, wishes it.'

'Why does he wish it? Oh ripest of pork?'

'Insults are chaff in the wind, Mahu.'

'Lord Mahu to you.'

'Those were the old days.'

'Those were my days, fatty!'

'The Divine One could have you impaled.'

'I have been threatened with worse.'

'You are a heretic.'

'Don't insult me.' I made to rise. 'Don't threaten me, fatty!'

'So you are not afraid to die?'

'I didn't say that.'

'But Pharaoh would reward you. More wine – perhaps a *heset*, a temple girl, to warm you at night?'

6

'What about two?'

'It's possible.'

'I'll answer your questions, fatty, and I'll try not to insult you.'

'Good – then to repeat my first question—'

'There is no need. You are correct about my mother and father. Yes, I did hate Isithia – she killed my mother—'

'You have no proof?'

'She was a bitch. I told Sobeck, my old companion, that it was she who betrayed his love affair with a royal ornament, a concubine from the imperial harem. He was exiled to a prison oasis, and his lover torn alive by a wild animal.'

'She was a concubine of Amenhotep III, the Magnificent, father of the Great Heretic?'

'Yes.'

'And Sobeck had grown up with you in the Royal Nursery?'

'Like me, he was a Child of the Kap in the House of Residence at the far side of the Malkata Palace outside Thebes. Sobeck later escaped from the prison oasis. He became Lord of the Underworld, King of the Slums of Thebes before he was restored to favour.'

'And the other children of the Kap?'

'Huy later became Overseer of the House of Envoys, Fan Bearer on the Right of Pharaoh, King's Son in Nubia.'

'Yes, yes, and the others?'

'Maya – the man who wanted to be a woman, lover of Sobeck, the most brilliant financier the land of To-Mery ever had.'

'You must remember other names.'

'Mery-re the priest.' I shrugged. 'Horemheb, mighty as Montu in war, and Rameses, his lieutenant, soldiers through and through, killers to the bone.'

'As you were?'

'Still am; you'd better be careful.'

'So you all grew up together in the Kap with the Great Heretic?'

'No – I met him by chance. His father banished him to an isolated mansion in the palace grounds and forced him to hide his face. I called him "the Veiled One".'

'Yes, you did.'

'That was before his older brother Tuthmosis was poisoned,' I added.

The fat one lifted his hand. 'And the Great Heretic,' he declared, 'became Pharaoh. He owned the double doors of the Great House.' He paused, wafting his fan before his plump, sweaty cheeks. 'This nonsense of his about one God, the Aten, his rejection of Egypt's gods, particularly of Amun-re, the God of Thebes? He moved from the Waset to build a new city hundreds of miles to the north. You supported all this?'

'Read my confession.'

'I have read your confession. You said it was all due to the influence of the Heretic's mother – Queen Tiye – and what you call the Akhmin Gang.'

Ah, there he had it! What they were all searching for: the real truth.

'The Akhmin Gang.' I smiled. 'Many years ago the Hyksos were driven from Egypt.'

'I know my history.'

'Shut up and you'll learn more. Anyway, among the Hyksos invaders were the Apiru – shepherd kings – and one tribe in particular, Israar. They had a notion of One God who had chosen them to produce a Messiah.' I shrugged. 'The Apiru, with its clan of Israar, were eventually driven from Egypt with the rest of the Hyksos. However, they returned, peacefully, by way of the Valley of the Shadows in the eastern Redlands. They used its caves to bury their dead and draw pictures of their history.'

'Ah yes – you destroyed all that, didn't you?'

'I had to, to protect the people I loved.'

'That would be Djarka, your servant, and Mert, his wife. They were of the Apiru. Where are they now?'

'Dead, I hope, well beyond your reach.'

'Let's return to the Akhmin gang,' the fat scribe declared smoothly. 'The Apiru settled down in the city of Akhmin. They became wealthy nobles, more Egyptian than the Egyptians, dedicated to the city's god. What was it now? Ah yes, Min, the God of Fertility. Though secretly,' he narrowed his eyes at me, 'though secretly they nursed their dreams of One God and a Messiah who would deliver them and give them their own land flowing with milk and honey.'

'That's true of some of them,' I replied, trying to curb my panic. 'Particularly Tiye, a truly beautiful woman who caught the eye of Amenhotep III, the Magnificent. He refused to marry any foreign princess, so besotted was he with her. Tiye became his Great Queen. She produced two sons and three daughters, of whom only Ak—' I stopped myself just in time. 'Only the Great Heretic survived into adulthood. Amenhotep's father had always been against his son's marriage with Tiye, as had the priests of Amun at Karnak and Luxor. They knew all about the legends of Apiru, their One God and this mysterious Messiah.'

'And Tiye brought all that with her when she married Amenhotep?'

'Yes, disguised behind the idea of the Aten, the Sun Disc rising in splendour. The Aten was already accepted as a god in Egypt; Tiye simply developed the idea. Amenhotep kindly indulged her in this as he did in everything else.'

'And then the Great Heretic was born.'

'Yes, he was born with a strange face and limbs – the priests called him the Grotesque.'

'He *was* strange,' the Chief Scribe mused. 'That long face and jaw, those peculiar eyes, the woman's breasts and thighs. I've seen the paintings.' He sighed. 'Or the few that still exist.'

'I thought they'd all been destroyed – like his statues, his inscriptions, his prayers, even his city?'

'All dug out,' the Chief Scribe replied,' though a few escaped.' He picked up a cup of apple juice and sipped carefully. 'As did a few individuals, like yourself. Do continue. You were talking about the Grotesque.'

'The priests wanted to kill the Great Heretic at birth. Tiye successfully pleaded for his life and raised him, instructing him in the secret knowledge about the One God.' I pulled a face. 'It wasn't hard. The Great Heretic hated the priests of Amun as well as the father who'd rejected him. I became his friend. I helped destroy his enemies and, yes, I supported him as Pharaoh.'

'And the attack on Thebes – the priesthood of Amun? The disgrace and fall of his father's ministers? The move to the city of Aten?'

'Yes, yes, yes.'

'But there is more to it,' the Chief Scribe lisped, 'than what you've said. We know that from the other Children of the Kap. Oh, by the way, you missed one name out when you listed them.'

'Horemheb, Rameses, Huy, Maya, Sobeck, Mery-re – which one?'

'Pentju the physician.'

'Ah yes,' I replied offhandedly. 'I'd forgotten him.'

'Had you, Mahu?'

'At this moment in time, yes.'

'But there was more to the Great Heretic? His wife?'

'Of course . . .' I let my voice trail off and peered at the window, watching a fly crawl along the sill. The wooden shutters were closed, the sun pouring through in rays of light, like in one of Akenhaten's paintings. Of course, I reflected, there was always her – there always had been, there always would be: part of my soul, part of my heart, the beautiful woman, Nefertiti, with her red hair like a cloud about her golden face, those strange blue eyes, lips so sensuous, her languorous walk, head tilted back, heavy eyelids half closed.

The scribe leaned over and touched my knee.

'Did you love her, Mahu? You confessed as much.'

10

'Yes, I loved her.'

'Even though you killed her?'

'I didn't kill her!' My voice rose to a shout. The mercenaries lounging at the door stirred; the Chief Scribe waved his fingers and they drew back.

'I carried out her legitimate execution,' I explained, 'at the command of the Royal Circle – the very people she'd plotted to destroy.'

'Such scheming!' the Chief Scribe wondered aloud. 'Even her father?'

'Ay!' I interjected. 'The source of so many problems.'

'Why is that, Mahu?'

'Ay was leader of the Akhmin Gang. He joined the Great Heretic when the Heretic married Nefertiti. Ay was Great Queen Tiye's brother. When the Akhmin Gang swept into Thebes, Hell must have been emptied of its demons.'

'Why do you say that?'

'They all came to work for Ay,' I replied. 'He became the Great Heretic's First Minister, his vizier, his chapel priest, anything his son-in-law wanted. Ay plotted with a skill and panache second to none. I'll say his name – I cannot keep calling him the Great Heretic: Akenhaten became Pharaoh, Nefertiti his Queen. They tried to convert Egypt to the worship of the Aten – the One God. They shook off the dust of Thebes and founded a new city. You know what happened next: Akenhaten had five daughters by Nefertiti.'

'They say Ay, her own father, was responsible for them.'

'So they claim. However, Nefertiti's downfall was that she failed to produce a son; that and her arrogance in believing she was equal to Pharaoh.'

'And Khiya,' the Chief Scribe whispered, leaning forward. 'The Mitanni princess, small and plump, Akenhaten's refuge – you must remember her, Mahu? Nefertiti blocked her womb with poisonous potions. Your friend Pentju the physician purified her, and she conceived a son by the Great

11

Heretic.' The Chief Scribe shrugged prettily, like Maya would have done.

'Khiya also,' he continued evenly, 'conceived an illegitimate son by Pentju, a son whom they hid amongst the Mitanni. Ay hunted him down and brought him back to Thebes to die. He lies buried somewhere out in the Valley of the Kings, doesn't he?'

I just stared. Some secrets they would have to discover for themselves.

'So Khiya drove the Great Heretic and his wife apart.' The Chief Scribe flailed his fly whisk. 'Nefertiti was exiled to the northern palace in the city of the Aten, and then it happened . . .'

'Oh yes, then it happened!' I recognised what the fat scribe wanted to know: the true fate of Akenhaten. Was he murdered by his wife or his daughter? Did he escape into Canaan from where an imposter emerged claiming to be him?

'So,' the Chief Scribe moved restlessly on his cushions, 'Akenhaten went into the dark, and you and others killed Nefertiti; even her own father, Ay, gave his assent.'

'Yes.'

'And you all settled down to rule Egypt in the name of the young Tutankhamun, the Great Heretic's son by Khiya. He was betrothed to his half-sister Ankhesenamun, the daughter of the Great Heretic. Was she so like her mother Nefertiti?'

'As one lotus to another,' I laughed. 'Oh, by the way,' I gestured with my fan, 'I never ruled Egypt – Ay and the rest did that. I was simply the guardian of the young Tutankhamun.'

'Until Ay sent you into exile. He summoned you back when . . . ?'

Ah yes, I reflected: when Tutankhamun had reached his sixteenth year and developed alarming and disturbing changes of mood, lapsing into the actions of a child rather than those of the Wearer of the Two Crowns, the Holder of the Flail and the Rod, the Beloved Son of Amun-re.

'What happened next?' the Chief Scribe asked softly.

'What happened next?' I rocked backward and forwards on the cushions. 'You know what happened! Ay and his gang had been busy destroying the devotions to the One; Akenhaten's city was left to rot. The old gods of Egypt, led by Amun-re, were restored. Egypt's armies crossed the frontier to fight their enemies. The gold and silver, the tribute of foreign princes, poured back into Egypt.'

'What happened?' the Chief Scribe repeated meaningfully. 'What happened . . . you know, towards the end?'

'That is what you want me to confess, isn't it?'

The Chief Scribe, his eyes never leaving mine, nodded.

'You will write.'

'Oh yes,' I rasped back. 'I shall write!'

Aarutankhuat: the cobras of the underworld who burn up
the souls and shadows of the dead

Chapter 1

Yes, I shall write! I shall call up all the ghosts as if this place, this time was the Gerh-en-srit-sapt; the night of counting the dead. I shall drink wine and, on its power, flow back down the years to the second week of Parmouthi – the first month in the season of the planting, the ninth year of Tutankhamun, Horus in the South, Strong Bull, Pleasing of Birth to the Two Ladies, the Effective of Laws who Placates the Two Lands, Golden Horus, Young of Appearance who Pleases the Gods, Son of Re, Beloved of Amun, the One who Appeared in that Other Throne of the Living Horus, Smiter of the People of the Nine Bows, Owner of the Great House, Lord of Jubilees . . .

I remember the herald proclaiming such titles as the Royal Circle, the Supreme Council of Egypt, met in the beautiful mosaic Dolphin Chamber at the heart of the Malkata Palace. All were present: General Horemheb, Chief Scribe of the Army, and his lieutenant Rameses, both powerful men of war, dressed in light half-armour, with their swagger sticks, their precious collars and medallions winking in the light; Huy and Maya in costly gauffered robes; Pentju, Royal Physician, Guardian of the Left and the Right Ear, who had arrived late, much the worse for drink; and, of course, Ay, with his dark patrician looks, beside him his *rekhit*, 'shadow god', or, as Ay secretly called him, Hui, which means 'he who is ready to shoot venom': Chief Scribe of the Armies of Thebes, Ay's younger brother Nakhtimin, ever ready to do his brother's will, a killer to the heart, a slayer to his very soul. Finally there was Sobeck, Chief of Police of East and West Thebes. He had dressed elegantly for the occasion, a green cornelian necklace around his throat, with matching rings and bracelets, and a gauze-like linen robe over his padded kilt and sleeveless vest. Like the rest, he had left his sandals in the antechamber. Sobeck was now very much the man of leisure, even betraying a small paunch, his hard face made gentler by lines of fat. The truth was, he had married and found some measure of happiness.

No soldiers were present, none of Nakhtimin's killers. Horemheb had insisted on that. Everyone, including myself, had left their retinue sunning themselves in the courtyard or gardens around the chamber. I had told my lieutenant Djarka to keep our mercenaries well away from those other great lords. No one trusted anyone. We were hungry hyaenas padding around making sure no individual became more powerful then the pack. The meeting had been summarily called and I could tell from Ay's clever face that there was mischief being planned and plotted. A stole priest of the Royal Chapel intoned a desultory hymn, incense was burnt, and rosewater scattered on the floor. Afterwards the chamber was emptied of all except for the Royal Circle and its confidential scribes.

A trumpet blared in the corridor outside. Tutankhamun, garbed in white robes and a blue and white head-dress, a floral collarette around his neck, came into the room resting on a silver cane. Beside him, gorgeous and resplendent, the voluptuous Ankhesenamun, dressed in snow-white linen, coloured braid in her wig, which was bounded by a gold jewel fillet. A string of precious stones shimmered around her beautiful neck and a multicoloured sash emphasised her narrow waist. She walked languidly, carrying a small, half-finished floral wreath in her hand composed of hyacinth and other early flowers. She swung this backwards and forwards, looking slightly cross as if she was more interested in her flower-arranging than in business of state.

Our young Pharaoh looked in good health, clear-eyed and composed, with that serene, smiling look I shall never forget. Oh yes, he truly was the innocent surrounded by the guilty. The gentle protected by the cruel, the child in the midst of killers. He took his seat on the throne in the centre of the dais, Ankhesenamun squatting beside him. I went and sat on his right just below the dais. Tutankhamun came swiftly to the point of that council meeting. Of course, we'd all heard the rumours. Ay, as Overseer of the House of Secrets, had listened to the dusty pedlars and merchants as they flocked into the city with a litany of stories and tales. All of Thebes had grown alarmed as the news spread like some invisible smoke through the streets. A great battle had been fought in Canaan. The Hittites, under their leader Suppiliuma, had brought their lumbering war chariots, hordes of spearmen and archers on to the plains near Amki and enticed Egypt's ally, Tushratta of the Mitanni, to battle.

'A dreadful defeat for our allies,' Ay declared at that meeting. 'Tushratta and all his chiefs and princes were either killed or captured. Those who survived were led into the Hittite camp, captives in the dust of the enemy's victorious chariots, their tongues pierced with rings. All were later decapitated or impaled.'

'So,' Horemheb had declared,' the Mitanni are no more.'

'The Hittites will sweep south,' Rameses predicted. 'They have allies amongst the chieftains of Canaan, not to mention—'

'Not to mention,' Maya interrupted, 'those heretics who worship the Aten, exiles in Canaan under our former companion and high priest Mery-re.'

Ay did nothing to silence the hubbub which broke out as

19

we turned and discussed the news with each other. Mery-re had been a Child of the Kap, raised with us, a treacherous, slithering priest who had toadied to Akenhaten and become Chief Priest of the Aten cult. He had not accepted Akenhaten's fall and fled Egypt, stirring up trouble wherever he could.

'You're forgetting someone!' Horemheb shouted. 'You know who I am talking about.'

Pentju, who'd sat swaying backwards and forwards, glanced up.

'I know who you are talking about,' he snarled at Horemheb. 'Our glorious Pharaoh Akenhaten. You still fear him, don't you, General?'

'We must invade Canaan,' Horemheb replied, ignoring the insult. 'We must check Hittite influence, and yes, if necessary, seek out and destroy those heretics of the Aten, whoever their leader is.'

'We were all heretics once,' Pentju retorted. 'Don't you remember, General, years ago when Akenhaten ruled the Great City to the North, we were part of his circle, we all supported him, we all grew fat and rich.'

'And drunk.' Rameses smiled back.

'Egypt is now restored.' Nakhtimin, usually quiet, now spoke up. Horemheb lowered his head to hide his grin. If Nakhtimin was going to urge war, then Ay had already agreed to it.

'Our treasuries are full,' Nakhtimin continued. 'Our granaries replenished. Thebes is strong. Lawlessness has been suppressed. We should send troops across Sinai.'

'Is that the will of Pharaoh?' I glanced up at Tutankhamun, who had already been rehearsing his reply.

'It is the will of Pharaoh, the command of my father Amunre that my sword be drawn, that the vile Asiatic,' the young king's voice grew stronger, 'and all the People of the Nine Bows feel our strength.' Tutankhamun finished, eyes fixed on the mosaic of silver boats on a golden sea at the far end of the chamber.

'Pharaoh has spoken,' Ay declared. 'It is now the Season of the Planting. Our troops should be across Sinai very soon, but first we shall talk. Let us discover what the Hittites intend. Whom shall we send?' Ay stared malevolently at Pentju. There was deep rancour between them for a myriad of reasons, ranging from Pentju's hostility towards Nefertiti to the fact that the physician owned the Cup of Glory once held by Amenhotep the Magnificent, an object much coveted by Ay. For a while Pentju held Ay's gaze, then he belched loudly. Ay smirked and gestured at me. 'I propose we send Lord Mahu, Overseer of the House of Scribes, to the Hittites. What say you all?'

His Majesty proceeds as he is the male of masculinity
He slid from the outflow between the Goddess's thighs,
That is why his name is Jackal of the Light.
He broke from the divine egg,
He oozed out like the godlike essence, beautiful is he like
the Ibis of Thoth . . .

The choir of twelve Kushites, three male, three female, three eunuchs and three children, sang the refrain of the hymn from under the shade of the outstretched sycamore in the Garden of the White Lotus at the edge of the Malkata Palace. Nearby, an orchestra of Nubian dwarfs, under the direction of their overseer, played liltingly on oboes, lutes, lyres and harps. Across from them, under the shade of blue-dyed ostrich fans, Tutankhamun and Ankhesenamun, dressed in all their finery, were hunting on the edge of the artificial canal dug in from the Nile. The broad strip of water, purified and filtered, had been fashioned to represent all the beauty of the great river with its marshy, grass-filled edges, hardy bushes and papyrus groves. The stench from the oozing mud was hidden by the perfume of every type of flower, as well as the gusts of incense, cassia, frankincense and myrrh, burnt around the gardens, not to mention the fragrant kiphye in which the sheltering fans had been soaked.

Pharaoh sat on a chair fashioned out of ebony and ivory with a cushioned footstool for his sandalled feet. Beside him lounged his tame lion cub Khonsu, sleeping and twitching whilst his master readied to shoot his bow, waiting for the beaters in the grove to flush out the moorhens nesting there. Ankhesenamun, resplendent in her coloured robes and ornamented head-dress, her necklace of the sun dazzling in the light, was trying to help him. A short distance away her confidante and principle lady-in-waiting, Amedeta, was holding up gold-fringed parasols against the sun. Tutankhamun ordered the fan bearers to move away as a flock of birds burst from a grove in a flurry of sound and colour. Ankhesenamun handed her husband an arrow. Tutankhamun loosed the one he was already aiming, turned to grasp the next, but caught sight of myself and Djarka standing with the chamberlain in the shadowed portico leading into the garden.

'Uncle Mahu, Uncle Mahu!'

The hunting was forgotten, both bow and arrow dropped from his hand as if he had become totally oblivious to his quarry now whirling and shrieking in the sky above the canal. Ankhesenamun grimaced in annoyance but Tutankhamun was already gesturing us across. The chamberlain, an official of the Golden Chamber, waddled forward pompously, white wand in hand. Tutankhamun was already shouting stridently for his throne to be moved round, cushions brought and both choir and orchestra to be quiet. Djarka and I knelt on the cushions, pressed our foreheads against the footstool then sat back on our heels. Tutankhamun gazed down at us, his beautiful almond-shaped eyes bright and hard. He was smiling though he looked distracted. Pentju should have been there:

Tutankhamun looked pale, heavy beads of sweat coating his brow beneath the blue-gold head-dress. Ankhesenamun leaned against the throne, sensuous lips pouting, eyes watchful, her beautiful head tilted back, a gesture so reminiscent of her mother.

'Uncle Mahu, are you leaving? Will you meet with the Hittites?' Tutankhamun began. 'Do they grow their hair long and have cruel, parrot-like faces and talk like chirping birds?' He clicked his tongue in imitation.

'So they say, your Majesty, but more importantly,' I urged, 'are you well? Djarka and myself have come to say farewell.'

'Djarka!' Tutankhamun beamed down at my lieutenant. 'You are of the Apiru, are you not? General Rameses often questions me about your people, so I have asked Uncle Ay all about them. They say,' he continued, blinking furiously, 'that's where my father learnt,' his voice dropped to a whisper, 'all about the Aten. Is that true, Uncle Mahu? Is my father still alive, hiding in some cave in Canaan after he learnt he was not the expected one?'

'Hush, hush,' Ankhesenamun quickly intervened.

'No, no.' Tutankhamun raised his fly whisk imperiously, then, lifting his head, ordered the fan bearers, the holders of the royal sandals, the King's Perfumer and other flunkies to stand even further back.

'God's Father Ay,' he whispered, 'claims my father left secret knowledge about the Aten, the One God, as well as the Great Messiah who is to come. He left it with people called the Watchers – who are these, Uncle Mahu, who are the Watchers?'

Djarka moved restlessly beside me. Tutankhamun may have had lapses, and sometimes his soul might drift, but he could also be sharp and decisive. He had placed his finger on the heart of the problem. Akenhaten had turned everything on its head, proclaimed the new God, built the great city, and shaken Egypt to its very foundation. However, after the great plague had swept through his new city and his queen had been disgraced, he had disappeared. Had he survived in Canaan? Was he plotting a return? Years earlier, Generals Horemheb and Rameses had certainly supported him. Once Akenhaten had fallen, however, they had returned to the old ways. More importantly, they wished to destroy any idea of the Aten, both root and branch.

I knew General Rameses was quietly compiling records on the Apiru and their legends about a Messiah. I too had studied these. I had learnt the stories, how the Apiru and Israar tribes would one day leave Egypt to occupy that land flowing with milk and honey, Canaan! Of course, Egypt would never allow that. Any attempt to snatch Canaan out of Pharaoh's rule would be fiercely resisted. From Canaan flowed a veritable river of tribute, precious stones, metals and, above all, timber for Egypt's buildings, palaces and ships. My nightmare was that if General Rameses learnt everything, he'd argue that Egypt was nursing a viper to its bosom. A purge would be launched to destroy the Apiru and Israar, pull them up by their roots and wipe them from the face of the earth. If that happened, Djarka, his lovely wife Mert and their children would be no more. Little wonder that at that meeting in the Garden of the White Lotus, Djarka betrayed his agitation; even Ankhesenamun's sullenness had disappeared. All members of the Royal Circle knew what was going on but few dared voice it. How could they? Ay and his family were of the Apiru tribe themselves, whilst General Rameses would never be strong enough to launch any challenge, not as long as Tutankhamun ruled.

'Your Majesty,' I kept my voice light, trying to dissipate the tension, 'I too have heard similar stories,' I hid my lie behind a smile, 'but I do not know, truly, whether they are fact or legend. Yes, I've heard that your father left knowledge with people he called the Watchers, but who they are,' I continued in a rush, shaking my head, 'I do not know.'

Tutankhamun leaned back, caressing the side of his head, his boyish face crumpled with disappointment. 'Then you must go, Uncle Mahu. Pharaoh wishes you well.'

'Life, health and blessing, O Divine One.' I pressed my head against the footstool and rose to my feet.

'Goodbye, Uncle Mahu.'

'Take care!' Ankhesenamun smiled brazenly at me.

I backed away, then glanced up at Tutankhamun. He sat staring sadly at me. I bowed and turned away. As the scrutineer of hearts knows, I left him a doe among the jackals. It was the last time I saw him alive.

'Where are we going?' Djarka, sallow face sharp with anger, posed the question as our war barge, with its lion-headed prow and raised stern carved in the shape of the Horus falcon, turned midstream. The oarsmen chanted as they rested on their oars watching the great blue sail being unfurled to display the golden ram's head of Amun-re. The stench of the river mud mingled with that of the fish drying on the skiffs and other small craft which bobbed around us like leaves. Across the river drifted odours from the monkey and gazelle pens on the quayside; beside these, a group of Danga dwarfs, garbed in coloured rags, indulged in a vigorous dance to the music of lyre and cymbal. I thought of Horemheb, who always loved to have dwarfs in his retinue, though not so publicly now he was Great Scribe of the Troops, Commander-in-Chief of Egypt's Army.

'I asked where we are going,' Djarka repeated crossly.

I leaned against the taffrail and patted his hand. 'You needn't have come.' I smiled at him. 'You left Mert and your two children. I could have taken Sobeck.'

'Too fat,' Djarka scoffed. 'Too slow. He is going to end up a plump, pompous Theban merchant, just like his wife's family.'

I laughed and turned to lean against the rail, pretending to watch the last glimpses of the sun dazzling the cornices and gold-capped obelisks of Thebes. In truth, I was more keen to observe Iputer and his gaggle of high-ranking scribes, a gift from God's Father Ay. Iputer was bald, with a bland face, opaque eyes and an ingratiating manner; in fact, the perfect spy. I had my own plans for him, as I had for Ay, that beautiful cobra! If he could plant his spies amongst me and mine, the least I could do was respond in kind. There was the scribe Amendufet, not to mention the Dog-Man of Lower Thebes.

I abruptly became aware of a small skiff pulling alongside, one of those prophets of doom, proclaiming his poem. I've heard the words since; they still create a sombre echo in my heart:

For your great crimes, oh Egypt, the gods have issued their
blood-soaked decrees.
Because you have sold the innocent man for silver and the
poor beggar man for a pair of sandals.
Because you trample on the heads of ordinary people – and
push the poor out of your path.
Because father and son have both resorted to the same girl.
Because they have profaned the holy name.
Because they have stretched themselves out before
every altar.
Because they have drunk the wine of the people who will
be destroyed, both fruit above ground and root below.
You are going to be crushed to the ground and the fleshing
knives will be clogged with blood.
Flight will not save even the swift.
The strong man will find his strength useless.
The mighty man will be powerless to save himself.
The bowman will not stand his ground, the spearman
will retreat.
The horseman and charioteer will not save themselves.
The bravest warriors will run naked on that day.

Does the lion roar in the jungle if no prey has been found?
Does the young lion growl in his lair if he has captured
nothing?
Does the bird fall to the ground if no trap has been set?
Does a snare spring up shut if nothing has been caught?
Does the trumpet sound in the city and the people not
become alarmed?
Does misfortune come to the city unless you have brought
it upon yourselves?

I was about to intervene, tell the skiff and its cowled occupants to sheer off, when a voice spoke, clear and carrying.

'Lord Mahu, Baboon of the South!'

I gazed over the rail. A second skiff had approached our barge, now riding midstream as we waited for our escort to gather about us. This skiff was expertly managed by the speaker, whose face was hidden under a grotesque temple mask displaying the features of a snarling monkey. In the prow, a squatting figure pulled a veil across to hide his own head and face.

'Lord Mahu, we bring messages from the other world.'

The captain and his officers were elsewhere, waiting for orders; only because we were leaning against the rail was our attention caught.

'Lord Mahu,' the voice repeated, 'we bring messages from the other world.'

Djarka bent down for the bow and quiver lying at his feet.

'We come in peace,' the harsh voice warned, and the figure threw something towards us. The copper scroll-holder twinkled in the sun as it fell to the deck. I picked it up and glanced down, but the skiff had already pulled away, hidden by the myriad of craft around us. I pulled the stopper off and, with Djarka staring over my shoulder, shook out the papyrus roll. It was a chart, a map cleverly executed to show valleys, a river, an enclosed lake or sea, but nothing else.

27

'Do you recognise it?' I asked.

Djarka shook his head. 'A valley, a river and a plateau,' he moved his finger, 'and an inland sea. Somewhere in Canaan, I think, but who sent it? And why?'

I could not answer. I could do nothing but walk across the barge and stare out over the teeming river. On the far bank rose the peak of Meretseger, She who Loves the Silence, above eerie rocky cliffs which overlooked the City of the Dead, so busy with its embalming houses and coffin shops. From where I stood, I could smell the pungent odours from that ante-chamber of the other world. I moved the map from hand to hand and wondered why the mysterious messengers had been sent. That voice was so familiar. Akenhaten?

The captain of the barge bellowed out orders and our craft, its escort clustered about, began its journey. In those first few hours Djarka pestered me about the scroll and what it could mean. I could tell him nothing. Eventually we settled down to the daily routine of our voyage, and four days later, put in at a small village quayside, where I promptly ordered Iputer and his scribes ashore.

'Go tell my Lord Ay,' I shouted down at their surprised faces, 'that I have no need for his scribes.'

'Or his spies!' Djarka muttered.

We left the surprised scribes standing on the wharf, the laughter of our soldiers and marines bellowing across the water.

We reached Avaris, that bustling city-port, by the end of the month. Here the Hyksos had set up camp so many years before, during the Season of the Hyaena, when they'd brought fire and sword to the Kingdom of the Two Lands. Now it was a busy military camp. Already Pharaoh's writ had arrived, ordering a mustering of troops in preparation for Horemheb's planned invasion of Canaan. The governor of the city had his Nubian police patrolling the streets dressed in their foxskin loincloths, feathers in their crimped hair, all armed with spear, club and khopesh. They were fierce-looking fighters, eager to impose order on the mercenary horde of Canaanites, Amorites, Libyans and even fair-skinned, blue-eyed Shardana from the islands across the Great Green.

We, of course, the official Shems-Nesu, envoys of Pharaoh, were received most royally, processing along an avenue of gold-capped obelisks into the labyrinthine royal palace with its old rooms and new quarters, its narrow corridors and whitewashed courtyards smelling of roses and jasmine, cooled by fountains of water ingeniously brought in by canals. We were given chambers high up in the palace, their doors and woodwork inlaid with lapis lazuli and malachite and decorated with gold and silver panels. The pillars of the rooms were painted to look like trees with giant papyrus stems, the walls light-coloured, their paintings picked out in vivid reds, blues and greens. I remember them well because all their welcoming beauty was spoilt by hideous screams. Djarka went to discover what was happening and came back to report that a horde of beggars were being beaten.

'The Governor has ordered them to be gathered together, then lashed to encourage them to leave the city.'

I went down to the great outer courtyard. It was packed with a throng of the hideous with their disfigured faces, open sores and fly-infested eyes. Governor Pinnakht, one of Horemheb's henchmen, an old military scribe with a face like granite, stood on a dais supervising his mercenary police, who moved up and down the lines of kneeling beggars, lashing them with canes. After a while the punishment ended. Each of the beggars was given a small goatskin of water and a loaf, and told to be out of the city by nightfall. I watched them hustled out through the gate, then hastily withdrew myself when Pinnakht ordered two women caught in adultery to be brought up from the House of Chains and burnt in the far corner of the courtyard. The smell of burning flesh lingered long in the air and could only be dissipated by perfume-

29

drenched ostrich plumes carried out into the courtyard by a host of page-boys. One of these breathlessly informed me that it had to be done before Lord Pinnakht hosted us at a feast in the Jasmine Garden, which lay at the centre of the palace.

On the evening in question, the second day of our stay in Avaris, Pinnakht spared no expense. Djarka and I were the guests of honour, the banquet being held by torchlight in an exquisite flower garden. We dined under red-gold awnings, squatting on feather-filled silver cushions, square ebony-inlaid tables placed before us on which platters of delicious meats, fruits and bread had been piled. We each had three goblets so different wines could be poured. Singers, musicians and sinuous, scantily clad Babylonian dancing girls entertained us. I distinctly remember the latter, whirling and turning, black hair flying to the rhythm and clash of cymbals and sitars. Afterwards, two stick fighters, faces protected by cloths, with leather armguards and gauntlets, put on a breathtaking display of whirling canes. They were skilled combatants who could display their prowess without really hurting each other.

Only afterwards, when Pinnakht thought we had drunk enough, did he draw us into conversation, describing the military preparations, the hiring of barges and ships, the opening of storerooms in the House of War, and the need to have everything ready before the Great General himself appeared in the Delta.

'That's why we've cleaned the streets of undesirables,' he declared.

'So more can arrive!' Djarka joked. 'The mercenaries.'

'Chief Scribe Horemheb is offering good terms,' Pinnakht replied, signalling to his master of music to stop playing. 'All these preparations,' he grumbled, 'as if we haven't got enough problems dealing with the Apiru.' He glanced sideways at Djarka, who gazed stonily back.

'What's the problem?' I asked quickly.

'Little problem,' Pinnakht chattered on drunkenly, 'except

that General Rameses now takes a great interest in the Apiru. He's been here scouring our libraries and archives. He's their patron—' Pinnakht paused as Djarka choked on his wine.

'Patron?'

'Yes, patron.' Pinnakht smiled, tapping the side of his nose. 'He is offering the Apiru land and houses here in the Delta, giving over stone quarries to them as well as a licence to trade. I thought you knew. Anyway,' he droned on, 'you are to seek out the Hittites and negotiate with them.' He turned to other business and the banquet ended shortly afterwards.

I had to help Djarka back to our chambers. He sat for a while cleaning his belly with generous draughts of spring water.

'You know what Rameses intends?' he asked at last.

'Yes, I do.' I was standing on the balcony, staring out into the night. In the far distance pinpricks of torchlight moved along the ever-busy quayside of the port. 'Two reasons,' I added quietly, almost to myself. 'First Akenhaten's mother. She instructed him in the religion of the Aten, the One God of the Apiru clan, of the tribe of Israar; that was the source of the great heresy, the vision of a chosen people, of a Messiah, the Suter, the Saviour Man who would shake the power of Egypt. Rameses wants to ascertain if such a vision still lives. If it does, will it harm Egypt yet again?'

'And secondly?'

'Rameses is acting on behalf of Horemheb. He wants to discover what truly happened to Akenhaten. Did he really escape the City of the Aten; is he alive? If he is, where is he?'

'And?'

'So they can kill him,' I replied wearily.

'And my people?' Djarka asked. 'What is being plotted against them?'

'Horemheb and Rameses are gathering them together,' I glanced over my shoulder, 'like a fowler does – birds into a net. You should warn them.'

'They'll pay no heed,' Djarka slurred. 'They'll be consumed with visions of plenty. Perhaps,' he shrugged, 'one day they might see. Ah well.' He stretched out on the couch.

'Tomorrow we leave for Tyre and our Canaanite princes,' I murmured. 'Egypt's so-called allies. I call them the Vermin Lords. They protest loyalty yet betray us blithely.'

'If they can.' Djarka picked up a fan and started wafting his face. 'As for the Hittites, they'll soon realise we are no more interested in peace then they are. I wonder,' he sat up, 'what that message was about. The one we received on the barge before leaving Thebes. I also wonder,' he walked across to stand beside me, 'if Rameses has found the secret knowledge entrusted by Akenhaten to the Watchers. Who are these, master? Priests? Wise men of our people? What is the secret knowledge?'

'I don't know.' I paused. 'Something about the Suter,' I said, 'the Saviour Man, but who is he? Where he will come from? What will he do?' I shook my head. 'Legends,' I whispered. 'As for the Watchers, they, and what they hold, are hidden. I doubt if Rameses will be successful.'

Djarka continued to fan himself, grumbling that he was exhausted and wished to write a letter to Mert. He retired to his own chambers. I remained on the balcony, listening to the sounds of the palace. I wondered who the Watchers really were. Faintly, on the breeze, I heard the opening words of a hymn to the resurrected Osiris.

Oh beautiful Prince come into thy house
Let thy heart be glad, full of joy near the Goddess . . .

I glanced up at the sky: stars gleamed, the moon was full and strong. The hour was not late. I wondered who was singing the hymn. I recalled Pinnakht telling me how strolling players were visiting the palace, preparing a great drama celebrating Osiris's brutal death at the hands of his red-headed brother Seth, and his eventual resurrection through his sister goddesses Isis and Nepthys. I had glimpsed the players earlier in the day wearing the masks of the gods: the jackal of Anubis, the cruel face of Seth and the half-moon masks of Isis and Nepthys with their cow-horned crowns. I moved off the balcony and, as I did, something clattered to roll on the hard polished floor. I cautiously picked it up and took it over to one of the oil lamps. It was a scarab beetle bearing the sign of the Aten, the Sun Disc rising in glory above the eastern mountains. I hurried back to the balcony and glanced down. Three figures stood in a faint pool of torchlight. The one in the centre wore the gold mask of the resurrected Osiris.

'You are the players?'

'Hush, my lord Mahu.' Osiris stepped forward. He must have been about two yards below me. His voice was deep yet carrying, like the sound of rocks falling into a pool.

'You are the Watchers?' I asked.

'We are not the Watchers, nor are we the players, but messengers from the other world.'

'Why not show yourselves?'

'We could but we may not – these masks will not be used again.'

'Who *are* you?'

'Messengers from the other world. Listen, Lord Mahu, for we must be gone soon. Remember what we say. *Beware of the Kheb-sher of the Hittites*.

'Kheb-sher?' I retorted. 'A magician?'

'Hush, now. Beware of the Kheb-sher and his Vesper Bats. On your return south, go to the Valley of the Sea of the Dead. Indeed, you will have no choice.'

'Where? Why?' I asked.

The figure retreated back into the darkness.

'You have the map, Lord Mahu. You have the map, Baboon of the South.'

The figures disappeared. I hurried into Djarka's chamber,

but he was fast asleep, head lolling over the writing desk. I ran down into the garden. In the darkness beyond the pools of light I heard the clatter of weapons, and glimpsed a flare of torchlight through the trees. A voice called out and the captain of the palace guard, sword drawn, swaggered from the line of trees.

'Peace,' I called. 'This is the Lord Mahu.'

The captain of the guard stopped, squinting through the darkness.

'My lord,' he called. 'You are well?'

'As ever I can be.'

'Lepers,' the Nubian spat out the word, 'lepers have been seen in the palace grounds. Three men: they have stolen masks from the players.'

My foot touched something. I looked down and saw the gold-painted mask of Osiris glowing through the darkness.

'My lord, have you seen anything?'

'No,' I replied, 'but,' I pointed into the night, 'I was on my balcony and I thought I saw something over there, rustling among the bushes, so I came down.'

The captain of the guard, now joined by his companions, hurried away. I was about to pick up the mask when a disembodied voice chilled my heart.

'Don't do that, Lord Mahu. Do not touch something we have worn; it is unclean.'

I stepped hastily back. 'Lepers?'

'Aye, my lord, lepers – yet messengers.'

'Are you the Watchers?' I asked again.

'No, we are not. They are in Thebes. They contain the vision.'

'Why not tell me now?'

'Because you have a task to do. You must kill the Khebsher of the Hittites. Journey south to Irunet, the Valley of the Sea of the Dead, then you shall know.'

'Is your master Akenhaten alive?'

'And your master too, Lord Mahu. Journey south and find out.'

I heard a rustling, a night bird shrieked, an eerie piercing sound, and I realised they were gone.

I returned to my chamber and took out the map. I failed to recognise any of the contours. North and south were indicated; grassland, desert, the inland sea, but nothing else. I grasped a piece of papyrus and a reed pen, pulled across an oil lamp and wrote down the questions which concerned me:

Is Akenhaten alive in Canaan?

Who were those messengers?

What is the secret knowledge?

Who are the Watchers? According to what I have learnt, they are in Thebes, but where?

What will I find out in the Irunet region of Canaan?

Why is General Rameses, certainly on the orders of Horemheb, inviting the Apiru into the region of Avaris?

Who is the Kheb-sher?

Why should I have to kill him?

Why have I been given a map of Canaan, when I planned to return by sea?

Why, why, why?

I wrote the last word several times, then, throwing the pen down, listened to the sound of the night.

Aarati: the two cobras or serpent goddesses

Chapter 2

We boarded the imperial warship *The Glory of Isis* the following morning and left the harbour, hugging the coast-line through the mist, sailing north-east to the port of Tyre. This was my first time on a warship in the Great Green. I was fascinated by the sea: the roaring chaos of the water, the changeable sky, the brisk winds, the rhythm of the ship packed with soldiers, sailors, scribes and marines. *Isis* was the pride of the Imperial Fleet; it had a long, low hull with raised defensive bulwarks through which the oars were pierced. The prow ended in a lofty, snarling golden-headed lion; the stern was also raised to give the helmsmen a better view as they managed the great tillers. Offensive platforms ran across either end for the archers, with a raised gangway going the full length of the ship for the rest of the fighting men. A soaring mast rose from the double-roofed ornamented cabin. At the top of the mast was another fighting platform for bowmen just under the insignia of the silver-winged royal Horus falcon, a sign that the ship was under the direct command of Pharaoh.

Once we were clear of the harbour, the great square sail with its bracing ropes was unfolded to flap in the breeze and display the glorious silver Nekhbet – the Vulture Goddess – and the protective glaring red *wadjet* eye against a blue and gold background. The ship turned in a sickening judder and screech of wood and rope which sent me trotting back against the rail. At first I felt a little sick, though this soon passed. The ship made good time and I could only stand, stare and admire. The captain rarely joined us, but paced up and down, constantly shouting at the lookouts to watch for any sign. I asked what the matter was.

'Sea people,' he replied. 'Savage warriors from the islands further north. They have been seen along the Libyan coast and cruising off the Delta. They wouldn't attack us, but,' he coughed and spat, 'it's good to keep a weather eye open and murmur a prayer to the Searcher of Souls.'

The captain's lieutenant, a rather wizened old man with a profound knowledge of the sea, was more phlegmatic. He talked of the islands to the north, and beyond them, vast rolling grass plains where men rode horses and drank the milk of mares. He'd travelled beyond the Cataracts and visited the tribes, even those who fed on human flesh. He talked of chieftains who painted themselves yellow, blue and red, and who, when they died, were lowered into a pit along with young men and maids who were buried alive to escort them into the afterlife. He was a most entertaining old man, and described a human meat market in the jungles of the south where, according to him, prisoners were chained to a pole while customers chose which piece they would like. Once the entire body was sold, the victim was lowered into water up to his or her chin for a day and a night before being dragged out and killed, and the corpse chopped up for the customers! A droll fellow! I half listened to his tales as I watched the gulls swoop and dive or the sea monsters playing on either side of the ship.

I only mention the lieutenant because he was a great traveller and had spent some time in Canaan. In fact, he claimed to be of Apiru descent, and chattered about their legends and history: how the Apiru had passed through Canaan into Egypt, and how one day they would return. At first I thought he was a spy, but he gabbled too innocently, ever ready to share my wineskin. He knew all about General Rameses' so-called patronage of the Apiru, and quietly confided that members of that tribe had been given unfair promotion in the Imperial Fleet. I decided to trust him, and showed him the map. He examined it carefully, grunting under his breath.

'Yes,' he declared. 'It's Irunet, an area of Canaan out in the Redlands. There is a dead sea, a huge lake of salty water, where nothing sinks, everything floats. They say it's the abode, the house of the Teshu-Redfians, demons.'

'Do men live there?'

'Yes,' he replied, squinting at the sun. 'The unclean and the Khenru.'

'The recluses?' I asked.

'That's right, sir, recluses, hermits, holy men. Oh yes.' He laughed. 'I've heard all about it, the clean guarded by the unclean, the pure guarded by the impure.'

I grabbed the wineskin from him. 'Don't talk to me in riddles!' I snapped. 'I'm not in the mood.'

'Then listen,' he replied. 'There's a valley there so hot they call it the Gateway of Hell. Holy men go there who have withdrawn from the world. They beg for sustenance and grow their own crops. They support the lepers. Many of the latter are soldiers, sailors or marines, travellers who contracted the disease on their journeys. Yet,' he shrugged, 'they are still fierce fighters, as violent as the Nakhtu-aa . . .'

Our conversation ended as the lookout sang out a warning. A ram's horn wailed and a drum began to beat as the crew hurried to battle stations. Archers climbed on to the platforms. Marines collected their shields and curved swords from the stores. The captain donned a leather jerkin and helmet; I did the same and stood by the rail. At first I could see nothing, but straining my eyes and following the direction of the captain, I glimpsed dark curling smoke, a sinister

41

smudge against the blue sky. The wind dropped. The rowers hurried to their benches and oars were pushed out. The helmsmen sang a line from a battle hymn:

Glorious is Montu, Shatterer of Souls.
Glorious too is Horus who broods over the Great Green.

The oarsmen chanted back, and the warship moved like an arrow through the water. I gripped the rail, quite frightened. One moment I was on a ship on a calm sea beneath a breath-catching blue sky; the next I felt as if I was riding Seth's spear, a weapon sliding through the water to confront some unknown danger.

A fierce discussion was taking place between the captain, his lieutenant and the other officers. The captain kept shaking his head, but the old lieutenant argued heatedly until the captain changed tactics. The chanting stopped. The oars were rested and the sail was rolled tight like a scroll. The royal Horus standard was removed. The soldiers and marines were told to hide their weapons from the glint of the sun. More surprisingly, pots of fire were readied over which oil-soiled rags were placed. Smoke billowed out in black, throat-catching clouds which stung the eyes. The captain ordered the rowers to take us silently and slowly forward, and *The Glory of Isis* became hidden in smoke as it moved to where that black plume grew against the far horizon. At last we reached the scene of destruction. A small galley lay low in the water, nothing more than a floating, burning raft with bodies bobbing around it, traces of blood from their cut throats colouring the water. They floated like straws, hands bound behind them. Sea monsters with dark triangular fins were already gathering to feast. Our captain whispered orders, and grappling hooks were issued and used to pull in the floating mast, to which a man had been lashed; huge nails, hammered through his chest and throat, pinned him against the wood.

'Who did this?' I asked.

'Barbarians,' the captain replied. He coughed on the smoke and shouted at the lookouts to keep constant watch. '*Aiau.*' He spat out the word. 'Sea brigands.'

'No,' the lieutenant replied. He pointed to one copper-coloured corpse rolling near the boat. The headless body was soaked in water, its linen kilt floating loose. 'Sea people,' he declared.

'Master.' Djarka leaned over the rail and pointed to the corpse nailed to the mast. 'He is from the *Morning Star.*'

'I agree,' the captain declared, and pointed to the hulk. 'The *Morning Star* left Avaris a day earlier than us.'

'Master!'

Djarka clutched my arm and pulled me away. I followed reluctantly.

'The corpse on the mast,' he whispered. 'It's not the captain of the ship, but Huaneru.'

'Who?'

'One of Ay's personal scribes. You may remember him from meetings of the Royal Circle; he always sat in the centre.'

I recalled the slender, graceful man, sharp-featured, with thin lips, sallow cheeks and deep-set eyes. I walked back to the taffrail, coughed, waved away the smoke and peered down. The horror of death always shocks me, but despite the cruel wounds and empty, staring eyes, I recognised the scribe.

'Where was the *Morning Star* bound?' I asked.

'The same as us.' The captain, coming up behind me. 'Its cargo was wine.'

Djarka drew close. 'Why was Ay sending his own envoys?' he whispered. 'What business did Huaneru have in Tyre?'

I could not answer. As I stared down at the corpse, the lookout screamed.

'They are here, two ships!'

I glanced up. Two long craft, similar to our own but smaller and lower in the water, were heading towards us. The wind, which whipped smoke past me, billowed out their broad-striped square sails. They reminded me of hunting wolves closing fast. Our captain's strategy was to draw them in. The *Isis*, with all its crew hidden and weapons concealed by the smoke, could be taken for a merchant ship, arriving on the scene in order to help but experiencing its own difficulties due to a fire.

I clambered on to the lookout platform in the poop and stared out at the ships. Our oarsmen bent over the oars. Orders were issued and *The Glory of Isis* swerved abruptly to the left, streaking towards one of the enemy craft. I became aware of a hideous smell, the odour of closely packed bodies; the stench of latrines. Our warship, oars now pulled in, hit the enemy in the bows, pushed hard then quickly pulled away, oarsmen straining fiercely as the orders were screamed out. During this manoeuvre our prow and central gangplank became thronged with archers who loosed a hail of arrows into the packed ranks of the enemy. The speed of our assault, the violence of the ramming and the hail of shafts created havoc and devastation. The enemy's ship keeled to port and the sea rushed in even as its crew either spilled out or were hit by our arrows.

The sun, the sky, the peaceful calm of the sea disappeared. It was as if we had sailed into the gloomy lakes of the underworld where the water boils and the air is filled with pungent smoke, hideous cries and the horror of battle. Beside me Djarka was busy with his great bow. He was a master archer, a leather armguard on his left wrist and goatskin coverings on the fingers of his right hand. He loosed shaft after shaft, choosing his targets carefully as he braced himself against the movement of the ship.

The Glory of Isis swiftly manoeuvred to confront the second enemy craft; caught off guard, its crew tried to pull away, but, due to the chaos on board, its captain had not decided whether to flee, fight or go to the rescue of his comrades. Whether by chance or design, our craft caught the enemy ship a resounding blow, ripping away part of its stern. Sea water poured in. The ship lay so low to the water, so packed was it with men, that it immediately listed and the sea created further havoc.

Isis pulled back. The master oarsman now had the measure of what was happening. The sea, in fact, did our work whilst our archers simply loosed shaft after shaft, that heart-chilling sound of a horde of angry wasps as the arrows blackened the sky. Our captain would have liked to have boarded and taken both ships, but they were now wrecks disappearing beneath the surface, leaving the survivors threshing in the water. Some clasped at oars and tried to climb aboard *Isis*, only to be clubbed or axed. Our captain, however, was eager to take prisoners amongst the enemy officers, easily distinguishable by their great feathered head-dresses and ornamented body armour. A number of these were pulled aboard, coppery-skinned, with square-cut beards, their faces garish with smeared war paint. They shouted and resisted but eventually they were forced to kneel, their arms bound behind them. The archers pulled off necklaces, bracelets, even rings from their earlobes so the blood poured out.

The Glory of Isis pulled further away from the destruction, leaving the two wrecks nothing more than a tangle of timber spars. Clothing, half-opened chests and coils of rope bobbed amongst the corpses; many of these, feathered with arrows, rolled and turned like dead fish. The quickening wind blew away the last tendrils of smoke and stench from the place of slaughter. No more cries were to be heard, only the sound of the sea, the creaking of our ship, that silent moment after every battle when you become aware of what you have done, what has happened, of life being snuffed out as easily as an oil wick.

One of our officers, sword aloft, turned towards the sinking sun.

Glorious are you, Amun-re.
The rays of your purity stretch from the far horizon, man
cannot live without them!
Glorious are you in your cunning.
Glorious are you in your going out.
Glorious are you in the strength of your heart.
Glorious are you in the aftermath of the battle, in the
sharing of spoils.

The refrain was taken up by the crew, a thundering roar to the heavens. The captain was cheered and he ordered the wine casks to be broached. The battle orders were revoked, the normal routine restored. A quick survey showed that our prow was damaged and some oars on the port side bent; otherwise *The Glory of Isis* was unscathed. The crew had suffered some minor casualties, and three were missing, fallen overboard. One of them was the old lieutenant.

'He must have slipped when we collided with the second craft,' the captain commented sadly. 'Come.'

We went to the rail, poured our libation and sprinkled some incense. I was sorry for the lieutenant; he was a good companion and could have told me much more about Canaan. *The Glory of Isis* nosed forward. On either side, corpses and scraps of wreckage banged against the ship as sailors manned the bulwarks looking for survivors now the lust of battle had cooled.

'There.' One sharp-eyed lookout pointed to where the setting sun sent a path of light rippling across the sea. 'Look, a woman in the water.'

I followed his direction but could see nothing. The ship moved forward, sailors gathered at the sides with hooked poles stretching out. One of them, urged on by the captain, climbed over, scrambling down an oar, and pulled the young woman out of the sea. I'd thought it was a bundle of rags; now I glimpsed straggling black hair, a bloodied face and soaked robes. She was dragged aboard and the captain felt for a pulse at the side of her neck.

'She's alive!' he declared. 'She's been struck on the back of her head.'

The unconscious woman was dragged across the deck, greedy hands ever eager to grope her full body, and lowered on to a piece of green matting. The ship's leech wiped away the gore, leaving her nose and mouth clear. He pulled up her robe to show long, slim legs, broad hips and a narrow waist. Blood glistened between her thighs but there was no other wound. The man sniffed and shrugged.

'If she's kept warm she should be in no danger.'

The captain ordered the woman to be taken into his cabin, then stared across the water, shading his eyes against the sun.

'Let's leave!' He roared his orders and the ship echoed with the sound of running feet. We stood and watched as the Horus standard was raised, ropes cascaded down and the sail billowed out.

'I lost a good man, the lieutenant,' the captain murmured. 'He was right: the pirates thought we were a merchant ship in distress. What I would like to know is why they were so easily fooled.'

He had a special chair, a small throne with curved legs ending in the shape of rams' feet, brought out and placed before the cabin. Then he donned his collar of gold and silver bees, put on a pleated robe and took his seat like any Pharaoh come to judgement, sandalled feet resting on a footstool carved in the shape of a crouching panther. I stood beside him as the enemy officers were brought before him. At first they just stared blankly, then sneered, muttering in their own tongue, ignoring the interpreter. They spat at the captain, and one turned and tried to break wind in his direction. The captain had him lashed by his wrist to a beam and his stomach was split open, the insides spilling out like coils of rope, blood spurting. The prisoner screamed, the stench of this horrid sight making us all gag. The captain had a fire prepared, and the unfortunate's entrails were dipped in oil and set alight. The captive writhed in agony as the flames crept up.

Eventually the captain had the man cut down and tossed like a rag over the side. The rest of the prisoners now agreed to talk in return for a speedy death. They confessed they were from Pussam, north of Canaan, part of a fleet the Hittites had brought south. They had captured the wine galley and used it as a lure, only to be tricked themselves.

'They hadn't seen an Egyptian warship before,' the captain turned to me, 'or realised how strong one is.' He smiled sourly. 'We too know the tricks of the sea. They were apparently on patrol; their main fleet is still far to the north, clustering like vultures over a fat corpse. Lord Mahu,' he sighed, 'you are supposed to be negotiating with the Hittites while the Divine One prepares for war. I tell you this, the Hittites will smile at you but secretly prepare to fight.'

'Ask them about the woman, and the man nailed to the mast,' I demanded. The interpreter did so but shrugged. 'My lord, they know nothing. The woman was with the Egyptian who was carrying the cartouche of the Divine One.'

'Anything else?'

The interpreter asked the same of all the prisoners, but they shook their heads: they knew nothing, except that they had captured an Egyptian official. They had killed him as they had done the rest, but they knew nothing of what he carried or why he was there.

At last the sun finally set in a blaze of fire, transforming both sky and sea. The captain ordered the *naos* of his local patron god, Horus the Pilot, to be brought from the cabin and placed prominently on the poop. Wine bowls were filled and given to the captives, who drank greedily. Darkness was falling as the incense bowls were lit, their fragrant, pungent smoke curling across the warship where the crew massed to watch the proceedings. The captain washed his lips and hands in water mixed with natron, covered his face and prayed. Afterwards, grasping his war club and in full view of the ship's company, he executed each of the prisoners. One by one they were led before him, arms tied behind their back, the hair on the crown of their head arranged in a sacrificial tuft. The captain grasped each of these, whispered his prayer to Horus and dashed their brains out.

Night fell, silent, dark, no sounds except the murmur of the sea, the creak of the ship and a grunt from the captain followed by that deadly bone-crunching blow. The prisoners died bravely; none asked for mercy. Afterwards the captain gulped a goblet of wine and trickled the drops across the corpses before ordering them to be thrown overboard and the decks swilled clean.

I went up into the stern.

'Master.' I turned. Djarka stood grinning from ear to ear. 'You'd best come and see this,' he explained. 'Our young woman has woken from her sleep.'

That night, after such a fearful battle and gruesome ceremony, I crossed another river in my life. Nabila, the woman from the sea, looked comely enough in her makeshift tunic, long legs drawn up on the captain's sleeping mat. She had done her best to make herself presentable, and held her goblet of wine as elegantly as any lady of Thebes. The smell of burning lamp wicks made me cough as I entered, stooping under the low door. The captain was squatting before her, a look of puzzlement on his grizzled face.

'Are you the Lord Mahu?' She pointed the cup at me. 'Yes, you must be, and this is only the captain.' She gestured with her cup. 'I complimented him on his work, a very clever trick. I did warn the sea pirates, but,' she sighed, 'like many men, they wouldn't be told.' She nursed a sore on her mouth. 'I fell against a ladder.'

'Did the sea pirates ravish you, my lady?' The captain's voice was nothing more than a squeak.

'Violated me, no.' The woman pulled her hair back. 'It's my

monthly courses. I told them I didn't couple with monkeys.'

'And?' I asked, squatting beside the captain.

'They roared with laughter. They said I was brave so they would save me for one of their chieftains.'

'And?' I said again.

'I told them they were pigs and smelled. They felt my hair and face; they were as stupid as pigs. I warned them that an imperial warship was nearby.'

The captain turned to me and winked. 'I've heard this before,' he whispered.

'How did you know that?' I asked.

'Huaneru told me. I was with him.'

'Was he your husband?'

She made a rude sound.

'Who are you?' I asked.

'Nabila, daughter of Snefru. I am almost seventeen summers.' She lifted her head, beautiful eyes staring hard at me. 'I hated Huaneru!' She spat the words out. 'He tried, quite often, to get between my thighs, but failed.'

'Why were you with him?'

'To keep him pleasant and sweet towards my mother, not to be violent to her. He always lived in hope.' She sniffed. 'A stepfather in nothing but name.'

I pointed to the tattoos on her arms.

'My stepfather wanted me trained in love. I was a heset, a temple girl in the Sanctuary of Isis. I hated it, but, as I said, I had to keep Huaneru honey-sweet. I am glad he is gone. The sea people didn't like him. He begged for his life. You don't do that with such men. If you face death, you might as well keep your face hard as flint.'

Behind me Djarka snorted with laughter. The captain seemed completely bemused. I was astonished and amused at this young woman's impudence, the mischief sparkling in her eyes. She leaned forward, finger pointing at me.

'Narkhentiu.'

'That is what they used to call me, Baboon of the South. Now it's Lord Mahu, Overseer of the House of Scribes, Pharaoh's personal emissary to the Hittites. So, where was your stepfather going?'

'To Tyre.'

'To do what?'

'Only the Nine Gods know.'

'To meet whom?'

'Only Nas-ra, the intercessor between God and man, knows that, my lord Baboon.'

'Don't be impudent or I'll smack you.'

'I'd rather like that.'

I smiled. 'I can see why the sea people respected you.'

'I didn't say that. They respected my courage; warriors generally do.'

'Tell me about your stepfather's mission.'

'Highly secretive, commissioned by that snake of snakes the Great Lord Ay.'

'You don't like the Divine One's First Minister?'

'Anyone my stepfather liked or served I distrust.' Her face become serious; this time she bowed her head without any mockery. 'My lord Mahu, I thank you for saving me. I would like to help but I know nothing of my stepfather's mission except that it was highly secretive. He was to land in Tyre and meet someone: he had to do so before you arrived. He carried some documents in a small sealed coffer, but,' she shrugged, 'the Great Green now has those. Well,' she pulled a face, 'I am free of him, and so is my mother.'

'Why did you come with him?'

'I have told you, to keep him pleasant for my mother's sake. He always thought that one day he would seduce me. Now he can wander the underworld gnashing his teeth, if he has any left! By the way, where is his corpse?'

'We had to bury it at sea.' The captain spread his hands. 'We have no *wabet*, no place of purification.'

51

'Of course.' Nabila smiled. 'As in life, so in death. Anyway, he'd only stink.' She smiled dazzlingly at me. 'I'd like to wash again, Lord Mahu, and then we can talk.'

We withdrew from the cabin. Djarka burst out laughing. The captain, shaking his head, went off to check the night watch. I stood by the rail, looking up at the stars. I wondered what treachery Ay was plotting and drew some comfort from the fact that he hadn't succeeded. I kept thinking about Nabila, her hard, beautiful face, her laughing eyes, her undoubted courage. The captain came back and asked what we should do with her when we reached Tyre.

'She'll enter my household,' I replied without thinking. 'Yes, I will take care of her.'

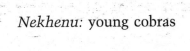

Nekhenu: young cobras

Chapter 3

We reached the port of Tyre just after dawn the following
day, and docked along a busy quayside which stank of fish,
spice and above all the pungent purple dye that was the
staple industry of that city. I was pleased to reach land. I
welcomed the bustle and the noise of the city. News of our
victory against the sea people soon spread, and the quayside
become thronged with a river of colour as the citizens flocked
down to see an imperial war galley, a rare sight in itself
during those days of Egypt's weakness. Eventually, the
governor of the city dispatched an escort to bring us up to
the palace. I went accompanied by Djarka, Nabila and about
thirty mercenaries.

A strange city, Tyre: it had yet to grow to a great power,
but the seeds, already sown, were thrusting up. Its princes
were building forts and palaces, strengthening the harbour
defences and sending their small fleet across the deep. At the
time I arrived, Tyre was just a jumble of houses, palaces and
temples enclosed by a lofty reddish wall and defended by a
gate and makeshift towers above a wine-coloured sea. Inland,
it boasted reservoirs, canals and deeply dug cisterns which
they used to water gardens and crops, so corn and wine pressers
were in abundance. The houses of the poor near the quayside
were the same as the houses of the poor anywhere: a mass of

entwined branches covered with thatch and cemented with mud, dingy places clustered along narrow, evil-smelling alleyways. The mansions of the merchants stood in their own grounds with walls of baked brick, enamelled in different colours, and palm-wood roofs, their doorways painted red to fend off demons. In the courtyards were half-sunken pots filled with water to keep the stones cool. I also noted that all food was placed in pots and baskets to be winched high above the beams, well away from the rats and mice which seemed to swarm through the city.

I visited many such mansions as I met the petty princes and tribal chieftains of Canaan, the Vermin Lords whom Pharaoh had summoned to meet me, his special envoy, in the city of Tyre. They all arrived with their shabby retinues, each acting like a great king. They were garbed in long tunics, hair and beards heavily scented, in one hand an ornamented walking stick, in the other their personal seal or cartouche which they loved to display as a mark of high office. Others were more barbaric in their splendour, ever drunk on palm wine, garbed garishly, their boorish retainers carrying brilliant, eye-catching banners. These were Egypt's so-called allies. I didn't trust them, and they didn't believe me.

I met these Vermin Lords in hot, stifling chambers, the walls draped in coloured hangings, ceilings blackened by fire, sheep and goat skins covering the floor. We sat on chairs and stools fashioned out of coarse palm bark and used fans to protect ourselves against the cloying heat and marauding flies. Terracotta bowls of charcoal spluttered, oil lamps shaped like slippers and displaying the symbol of Nusca, the God of Fire, glowed against the dark. Servants and retainers in fringed robes crowded the doorways as I repeated my promise that I had come to muzzle the mouth of the insolent and bind the halter on the overbold. I was Pharaoh's envoy. I was a display of his authority. I was there to make sure that if Egypt and the Hittites clashed, our allies would support the power of Horus.

The Vermin Lords, of course, acted their part. They listened, black eyes gleaming, as I declared that the power of Egypt would return, that Pharaoh would bare his arm and display his strength. They smiled at this and stretched out crooked fingers for gold, silver and precious jewels. They reminded me how, during the days of Pharaoh's great-grandfather, such revenue, so many prizes and gifts were commonplace. Of course, I had nothing to give but threats and promises. I told them to wait until Egypt's army made its presence felt. They nodded reassuringly, then wondered loudly why, if Egypt was so strong, I was there to treat with the Hittites. I replied that Pharaoh wanted the path of peace where all accepted his sovereignty, the Hittites included. Again the wise nods, but the Vermin Lords were not convinced. Akenhaten's long reign, followed by the policy of peace and retrenchment under Tutankhamun, had cost Egypt dear. Of course, I could hint that Horemheb was preparing armies in the Delta, of correspondence between Egypt and its allies in both Babylon and Syria. Indeed, the Vermin Lords themselves had heard such rumours, but was Egypt's power strong enough? It had to be seen to be believed.

In the past, these princes and chieftains of Canaan had been bought with gold, but that precious river had dried up. More significantly, serious revolts and coups had removed some of Egypt's strongest allies. The Vermin Lords were quick to point out how the Hittites now possessed a sea of chariots and hordes of troops, and were offering their advisers to many of Egypt's allies in the area. The defeat of the Mitanni had caused everyone to reflect.

In the end, such meetings produced little and achieved nothing. They became empty rituals where toasts were offered, promises made, assurances given and accepted, but it was all chaff in the wind. Djarka became busy in the city trying to meet Egypt's agents, the merchants and traders, but even here there was a sinister wall of silence. Some had disappeared, others had slunk into hiding; the more Djarka searched, the more uneasy both he and I became. We discovered that some of our agents had been found dead in their chambers, throats cut. Others had been attacked by robbers in alleyways or had been the victim of some unfortunate street accident.

I sent my own chief scribe to seek assurances from the Hittites, now camped further north besieging the city of Lachish, that I would be received as an accredited envoy. He returned pale and agitated.

'Oh!' he sighed, rubbing the side of his face. 'The Hittites under Zananza, that's the king's eldest son, will receive you most hospitably.' He took his fingers away from his face. 'But Lord Mahu, their power is very great. An armed camp stretching for over a mile, a host of chariots and a mass of foot soldiers and mercenaries from countries I have never even heard of.'

'Did you hear about their Kheb-sher?' I asked. 'A great magician?'

'Whispers and rumours,' the scribe replied. 'But nothing substantial.' He undid his leather bag and pulled out clay tablets, written in the Akkadian script and sealed with Prince Zananza's own cartouche. 'We have our passes.' He thrust them at me. 'The Hittites await us.'

'Did you,' I asked tentatively, 'hear any rumours or stories that Akenhaten may have survived and be sheltering either amongst the Hittites or somewhere in Canaan?'

'My lord,' the plump scribe wailed, 'I heard nothing. The Hittites are polite, but they realise that Egypt is asking for peace yet planning for war.'

'I keep hearing the same.' Djarka spoke up once the scribe had left. 'I have been amongst the Vermin Lords as well their retinues and the merchants and traders who serve them. Nothing but silence! Nothing about Akenhaten, just a certainty that war will come.'

Later that same day I went to see Nabila. She had her own small chamber which she had cleaned herself and made fragrant with flowers, borrowed, as she put it, from a nearby garden.

'Djarka wants to come with me to meet the Hittites,' I declared as I sat on a low stool. Nabila, squatting on a pile of skins, put down a small carving she was working on and pushed back her long black hair. She looked more beautiful than she had done on board ship, though just as impudent.

'And I suppose,' she fluttered her eyelids, 'I am to stay here with the Vermin Lords because it would be too difficult for me?'

'Exactly.'

'Well, I don't want to stay here.'

'You can't come,' I replied. 'You have no place.'

'I could be your wife.' She laughed at my surprise. 'Are you astonished? I'm young, I am nubile, I am to inherit property in Thebes. I am of good and noble birth. I like you, you like me. You may even lust after me, for all I know. I think you do, I can tell that by the way you are looking at me. Well?' She spread her hands. 'I'm not ugly, am I?'

'But you hardly know me.' I was intrigued by her boldness.

'Oh, I know you very well, Lord Mahu. My stepfather kept extensive records on you. I know all about your youth, your aunt Isithia, your friendships with Sobeck and Djarka, your devotion,' again her eyelids fluttered, 'to the glorious, but infamous, Nefertiti. I know you keep journals, as well as your love of gardening, your knowledge of potions, and how you bed your maids. Anyway, my lord Mahu, why haven't you married?'

'Because until I met you,' I snapped, 'no one had asked me!'

Nabila threw her head back and burst out laughing.

'How do I know,' I continued crossly, 'that you're not a spy?'

'Oh, it's true what they say about you, Lord Mahu. You look like a baboon and you're as suspicious as one. I suppose,' she sniffed, 'I arranged for my ship to be attacked so I could be thrown into the water and be rescued by you.'

Now I laughed.

'However,' she continued softly, 'to show you my good-will, let me tell you, my lord, that you're in great danger. Ah,' she raised an eyebrow, 'I have your attention.'

'I'm always in danger.'

'Lord Ay hates you. No,' she shook her hand, 'for some strange reason he fears you; he claims that you cannot be bought.'

'Oh, I can be.'

'No, not in the important things. He knows the Divine One holds you in great affection, close to his heart, in the palm of his hand.'

'How do you know of such matters?'

'I read.' She grinned impishly. 'I also stand at doorways and listen, especially at supper parties when my stepfather, Ay and Lord Nakhtimin have drunk too much.'

'You said I was in great danger: did you learn of it here, amongst the Vermin Lords?'

'No. At a dinner party held in the third month of the Inundation. I had decided to stay up and listen.' She folded her legs beneath her. 'They were talking of the future, about those who will suffer.' She waved a finger. 'Oh, that's it, the Tems.'

'The decree of doom,' I whispered. 'The sentence of death. When will that occur?'

'Ay and my stepfather used temple language, phraseology from the sanctuary. They talked of,' she stumbled over her words, 'the Day of Judgement, that's right, the Day of Weighing the Words, when you and others would meet your death.'

'Why?'

'My lord Mahu, I do not know.'

'And your stepfather's mission?'

'As I have said, I do not know, except for one thing, and over that I might be mistaken. Listen: at their supper parties, they were secretly joined by a Hittite merchant. I listened to his speeches. The Hittites will be expecting you, Lord Mahu. You may meet them, but I am not too sure what will happen next.' She smiled. 'Now do you trust me? Now will you marry me? Anyone whom Lord Ay resents so much must be interesting. Well?' She tried to look impudent but I could tell from her eyes that she was speaking the truth. 'I have followed your exploits from afar, Lord Mahu. When I realised who was on board that warship that rescued me, I thought it was fate, the workings of the gods.' She looked me up and down. 'In fact you're quite personable for someone who has not reached his fortieth summer.'

'Thank you, madam. I'll bear that in mind.' I rose to my feet.

'My lord Mahu, an answer?'

'Madam, you have yet to convince me.' I left the chamber pretending to be angry with the minx; secretly, I was deeply amused by her impudence and attracted by her beauty.

Djarka was waiting with an imperial envoy, a small wiry man with a leather strap on his wrist displaying the personal seal of Pharaoh.

'Great news,' the envoy declared. 'Lord Horemheb and Rameses have arrived in the Delta. The Isis, Horus, Ptah and Amun-re regiments are following, as are supply carts and mule trains.'

'How long,' I asked sharply, 'before they are ready?'

'A few weeks, my lord. Envoys have been dispatched to our allies, Assyria and Babylon.'

'In other words, they need more time,' Djarka scoffed, 'and we must find it.'

'What news from Thebes?' I asked.

The emissary chattered like a monkey, giving me all the gossip and rumours.

'Of course,' he concluded breathlessly, 'the news about Great Queen Ankhesenamun is now common knowledge. My lord, she is pregnant.'

I walked to the window. The room was stuffy, the night breeze most welcome.

'You're sure of that?' I called over my shoulder.

'It has been officially proclaimed.'

'And what further instruction do you bring?'

The emissary took a deep breath. 'There will be no warship to bring you home.'

'What!' I spun round. 'I am to travel overland back to Egypt?' I paused as I recalled my secret visitor and that map. Ay must have planned this from the start, and those mysterious figures had guessed what might happen.

'Why is there no warship?' Djarka asked. 'The land route back across Canaan is dangerous; we have enemies.'

The emissary shrugged. 'The captain of *The Glory of Isis*,' he mumbled, 'must have carried sealed orders. I went to the harbour but he was already gone.'

I groaned and turned away. Djarka continued to question the messenger but the man had delivered all his news so he was dismissed.

'You know why, don't you?' Djarka asked.

'Of course I do.' I picked up a leather belt, drawing the dagger in and out of its sheath. 'Lord Ay will have us followed,' I continued. 'He still thinks Akenhaten will emerge to meet us.'

'Why blame Lord Ay?' Djarka laughed sourly. 'The warship is returning to Avaris, where it will come under the command of Horemheb and Rameses.'

'I don't know.' I gestured. 'When our business with the Hittites is finished, we will be walking home whatever the cause.' I paused. 'What concerns me, Djarka, is that our secret friends, as well as our enemies, knew we would not be returning by sea; that we'd be forced to take the land route.'

'The Governor of Tyre has promised us chariots.'

'Then, Djarka, we shall arrive in the Hittite camp like princes.' I smiled thinly. 'And probably die like them.'

Djarka left. I wondered what poison Lord Ay and the rest were brewing. Were we to return by land so as to entice Akenhaten, or, indeed, any remaining Atenists, out into the daylight? If so, who would kill them? Would we be followed by a cohort of assassins through that wilderness? I ceased my pacing, the sweat turning cold on the back of my neck. And what about us? The Hittites would never dare to harm sacred envoys, so if there was no cohort of assassins to kill us, that must mean that some or all of my mercenary escort had been suborned, bribed to carry out secret orders. A few of these mercenaries I knew from days of old, but others were fresh recruits. I turned to the other problem, the Kheb-sher, the mysterious magician: why did he have to die?

I closed the shutters of my window, stripped and climbed into bed. I lay there for a while and was about to drift into sleep when the door opened and a figure slipped into the room.

'No need for the dagger beneath your headrest,' Nabila whispered as she slid naked into bed beside me.

Within a week Nabila and I were married. We clasped hands and exchanged vows and flowers over a bowl of burning incense in the sombre shrine to the goddess Astarte – which lay at the heart of the temple precinct in Tyre. An old priest with milky eyes and slavering gums gave the blessing, whilst Djarka stood beside me trying not to laugh at him. I looked the same as always, but Nabila was exquisitely beautiful in her pure linen robes and multicoloured sash, gold slippers on her feet, a floral garland about her neck. Her face was framed by a gleaming oil-drenched wig, her eyes kohled, her wrists and fingers glittering with the rings and cornelian bracelets I had taken from my treasure box. When I close my eyes, I can still remember her perfume, the juice of the blue lotus, the pure mother-of-pearl rings in her earlobes and the flower wreath about her brow.

We feasted afterwards in the courtyard on heaped platters of meat and fish whilst Assyrian dancers entertained us to the tune of the horn, pipe, lyre and harp. Happy days, sensuous nights! Ay and his mongoose ways seemed an eternity away. I felt as happy as if I was with Osiris, Foremost of the Westerners, and Hathor, Lady of Glee and Drunkenness, in the evergreen Fields of the Blessed. The only reminder of the truth, the harsh reality rather than the opiate of dreams, was the refugees from the fighting in the north whose cries I could hear from behind the palace walls. Even during my nuptials I took time off to go out and meet some of them. They told stories of fire and sword, about the sky being blackened by smoke, of fields a-flame and a great army moving like a swarm of locusts, of villages being razed, cities burning, of execution stakes stark against the sky each with its gruesome burden.

The Hittites were still moving south, and the great city of Lachish was caught in the snares of death, bound tightly by the ropes of Hell. Increasingly Djarka, Nabila and myself were left to our own devices as the governor of Tyre turned to deal with the swelling river of refugees, whilst the Vermin Lords decided that discretion was the better part of valour and quietly disappeared.

We often discussed the situation as we sat on cushions on the flat roof of the palace whilst the colour of the sky turned a purple-blue, the moon moved in a great circle of light and all the flowers of heaven blossomed in their beauty. The evening breeze was always cool and refreshing. Djarka was our news bringer; he listened to the chatter of our entourage as well as that of the governors. One grim truth was emerging: the Hittites had broken out of their northern fastness and were advancing south not just to invade but to occupy. Nothing was being left to chance. No hilltop fortress or city of the plain could be left unscathed to threaten their rear and the route back to their kingdom. King Suppiliuma and his eldest son Grand Prince Zananza were skilled warriors and astute politicians. They openly declared how they were defending their borders against incursions and accused the kings of Assyria and Babylon of encouraging such incursions.

'Nonsense,' Djarka whispered over his wine. 'They will move south until they are stopped.'

'Across Sinai?' Nabila asked. 'Along the Horus road?'

'Perhaps.' Djarka smiled dazzlingly at Nabila; that always sparked a little jealousy in me, but that was Nabila. She and Djarka were not as cynical as I was: a fire burned in their souls, unlike mine, which was chilled and hard.

The conversation turned back to Ay and what he intended. Undoubtedly he had sent Nabila's stepfather ahead of us, but for what? We also scrutinised our list of scribes and mercenaries.

'One or two of them must be Ay's spies.'

'Or assassins,' Djarka added.

'It mightn't be them.' Nabila spoke up. 'What happens if the Hittites kill you?'

'No.' I shook my head. 'Too dangerous, we are accredited envoys. The same is true of the Vermin Lords: they wouldn't dare raise a hand. No, Ay wants us to be here so that we can stumble on something, then he will kill us. The gods know from which direction the arrow will come. Or . . .'

'Or what?' Djarka asked. 'Does Ay simply want us out of the way?'

I stared out across the garden, a small paradise created by the governor. As a keen gardener I loved to walk there with Nabila, describing the different herbs and aromatic shrubs. I always did so distractedly, because as the days passed, my heart became fixed on Ay and what plots he was nurturing. Of course we could have fled, but where to? There were no warships back to Egypt. Whatever happened, it was the land route, through Canaan and across Sinai. Whilst we remained accredited envoys we were safe, but what then?

Two days later Hittite messengers arrived on the outskirts of Tyre. We donned our travelling clothes, marshalled our scribes and mercenaries and went out to an oasis a mile from the city gate, the usual meeting place for merchants, sand dwellers and desert wanderers who wanted to sell their ill-gotten gains before approaching the city. The Hittites had taken it over, a terrifying band of warriors and braves with their sharp, parrot-like faces daubed in war paint under feathered head-dresses adorned with brilliant plumage. Veterans, those warriors tried in battle, also fixed a silver comb in their oil-drenched black hair which was shaved at the front and allowed to hang down at the back, either to the shoulder or twisted into a coil behind their heads. They were muscular and sinewy and, as Djarka whispered, smelled like the kennel, despite the perfumed robes pulled over the gleaming leather armour.

I was not so dismissive of them. They brought with them the stench of war, the camp, the latrine pit, the rigour of siege and wounds inflicted during fierce hand-to-hand fighting. Despite their oils and perfume, these warriors were from the main army besieging Lachish. Their chariots were clean and oiled but the leather-bound wheels were marked and cut and the quivers and javelin pouches dark with sweat stains, clear indications that these war chariots had been in the heat of battle.

Their hard-bitten commander, a cunning-eyed, grizzled individual with a luxuriant moustache and beard, introduced himself as Negeven, or so it sounded. He was dressed in leather cuirass and coloured kilt, a war belt looped over his shoulder. A staff officer carried his dark plumed helmet with its red spray crest. Negeven's Egyptian was no better then my Hittite, so we conversed in the lingua franca of the mercenaries. As he talked, I studied his hard and unblinking eyes; they were like those of a dead man. He scrutinised me, then his gaze moved to Djarka, who stared coolly back, fingers tapping the bronze hilt of his dagger. Negeven blinked as if dismissing him and glanced at Nabila, pursing his lips, looking her up and down. She was garbed in a pleated travelling robe and hid her beauty beneath hood and veil. Negeven smacked his lips and continued to do so until Djarka's finger's drummed a little faster. Negeven remembered himself. He stretched out his hand and I clasped it in friendship, matching his firm grip. He squeezed my fingers, grinned and asked what presents we'd brought for the Hittite king.

'Since time immemorial,' I replied, 'Pharaoh, the Beloved of Amun-re, Horus in the North and Horus from the South, Strong Bull, Fitting of Created Forms, the Living and Lordly Manifestation of Ra, sends presents to no one. Has Lord Suppiliuma gifts for him?'

Negeven gave a crooked grin and placed his hands on his hips, head going from right to left, imitating a city merchant considering a purchase.

'Your lord,' he was staring at Nabila, 'often sent gold and silver to the lords and princes of Canaan.'

'Gifts to his subjects,' I replied. 'If the Lord Suppiliuma . . .'

Negeven laughed mockingly and waved us deeper into the shade of the oasis, where his chariot squadron was stationed. The horses had been unhitched to be watered; others were being walked round to cool off. Negeven led me amongst the chariots. They were like carts in comparison to our Egyptian ones, with their central axle and four heavy wheels. Nevertheless, the Hittite chariots were powerful, each capable of taking three fighting men into battle. In a mass formation they'd be deadly against foot soldiers. Negeven indicated our chariot and introduced its driver, a lithe, dark-skinned mercenary from the islands in the Great Green. Negeven's own chariot stood beside ours. My gaze was drawn by the decorations around its rim and I turned away in disgust: what looked like ragged cloths pinned to the sides were, in fact, the scrota and testicles of executed enemies. Djarka and Nabila also glimpsed these and recoiled in horror. Negeven laughed out loud and gestured us to follow him to where strips of tender lamb, coated in herbs, were sizzling above a fire.

We ate and drank, Negeven and his officers laughing and talking amongst themselves. They all seemed very much taken by Nabila. They did not talk about politics or our reasons for being there but asked us a stream of questions about Egypt's cities, its gardens and above all the glory of Thebes. They reminded me of children, hungry children being promised a good meal and looking forward to it with relish. Afterwards we returned to our own makeshift pavilion, rolls of leather stretched out across poles, and settled down to an uneasy sleep.

Nesemekhef: cobra fire god

Chapter 4

Our journey began the next morning, a long convoy of huge creaking war chariots interspersed with foot soldiers, servants and slaves. My mercenaries and scribes travelled in carts behind us. We crossed a strange-coloured landscape, heading north towards the Hittite army. An eerie journey, like that in a reverie, across country where thorny, pale-leaved mimosa flourished alongside sweet-smelling gorse. I was surprised by the abrupt changes in light as the sun caught the various rocks: white limestone, dark dashes of basalt, or the rose-coloured shale rising above stagnant pools where legions of flies hovered and buzzed.

Now and again we entered small villages with whitewashed house walls, roofs blackened by fire and a few sheep and goats nosing amongst the rubbish. The inhabitants came out in their unbleached, undyed robes to stare at us and plead for food with long hooked fingers. Sometimes we stopped in these hamlets to eat and rest. I could now understand the Hittites' hunger for richer places. This land was so different from the lush greenery of the Nile, with its fertile meadows, plains and garden estates where asphodels flowered next to barley fields ripening under the sun. All that place held was mud huts, rocky outcrops and steep green valleys where olive trees flourished alongside oaks, pines, cypresses and majestic cedars. It offered plenty to build with, but little to plough.

Of course, the signs of war were everywhere. Streams of people were fleeing south, black plumes of smoke stained the horizon, and, increasingly, we encountered patrols of Hittite foot soldiers with their conical helmets, or troops of horse moving in clouds of dust. I tried to learn as much as I could. The Hittites were being clever: they were not harassing the refugees but moving south amongst them with orders to seize strategic ports, towns and forts.

We entered the plain of Lachish the day after the city had fallen. The Hittite camp sprawled to the far horizon, circling the city's fire-blackened walls, a sea of tents, makeshift bothies and stately pavilions. The air reeked of smoke, blood, ordure and horse dung. Gusts of grey smoke rose from behind the cracked city walls. The Hittite camp itself was protected by a palisade, its gateways closely guarded by garishly armed mercenaries, chariots standing at the ready.

We crossed the bridge into a place of horror, as if all the demons of Hell had come pouring out of the sand and rocks, red heads blazing, black eyes gleaming with mischief. Captives were being led shrieking and screaming to a marketplace in the centre of the camp, to be auctioned to the highest bidder. The old were plucked out and cruelly strangled. Women were stripped and pawed, families divided, their goods piled high before the tents of the Commanders of One Thousand Warriors, to be later divided amongst the troops. Three mercenaries caught stealing from the common store were being crucified on poles, their tormentors oblivious to the hideous screams which pierced the air. Cooking fires crackled and burned. Drunken soldiers lurched about, though order was being imposed by the guards from the royal regiments in their distinctive pointed helmets, chainmail shirts, leather kilts and coloured boots. No one approached our retinue of thirty mercenaries and a dozen scribes. I heard the occasional curse and had to draw my sword when some horse dung was flung at us, but little else happened.

We entered the royal enclosure; at its entrance, the Prince

of Lachish and his principal courtiers had been stripped naked, tongues plucked out, eyes burned to water in their sockets. They sat crouched, tied to poles, dead men in all but name, their glory and power reduced to being licked by the yellow-coated camp dogs. Inside the royal enclosure reared a huge altar of stones taken from the city walls, drenched in blood and ringed by the horse-tail standards of the Hittites. Corpses, male and female, had been slung before it, throats cut, naked bodies dirty and bruised, macabre offerings to the Hittite storm god, Shraruma. Booty and plunder – precious cloths, silver and gold plate, jewelled goblets and costly armour – was piled in heaps. Nearby, grooms were exercising a string of captured horses, whilst scribes seated at low tables sifted the manuscripts plundered from the temples and libraries of Lachish.

Guards pulled back the flap of the royal tent and we were ushered into a perfumed darkness lit by oil lamps. We stood for a while, dazed by the contrast, until a voice invited us forward. More guards squatted deep in the shadows, though my gaze was drawn by a group of men sitting on cushions before tables at the far end of the tent. I looked around. More plunder lay there, caskets and coffers, chests and leather panniers opened up and spilling out their precious contents: ivory figurines, alabaster bowls, silver-gold pectorals, collarettes, embroidered cloths, precious gems and pearls. A group of young women, naked except for their loincloths, huddled together like frightened fawns, hands and feet bound with golden cords. Our retinue was not allowed in. Djarka's objection to this broke the silence.

'Do you not trust us, Lord Djarka?' a voice called. 'I invite you to come forward. You are the accredited envoys of the King of the Two Lands. Come, we have been waiting for you.'

Servants hurried up to take our cloaks. Djarka and I refused to surrender our war belts; this provoked a chuckle from our unseen host, though nothing was done about it. We were invited forward, all three of us, to a line of tables where places had been prepared. I took the centre cushion. Servants hastened forward with dishes of kid cooked in cream, tender lamb coated in herbs, and jugs carved in the shape of pelicans brimming with red wine. Our goblets were strange copper bowls.

'Eat, drink,' the voice commanded.

I ignored him, my hand going to my belt. I heard the hiss of a dagger being drawn from its sheath. I opened my wallet and took out small clay tablets in leather coverings, and scrolls of papyrus wrapped in linen sheets.

'Why must we do business in the dark?' I snapped.

Again the chuckle. A servant brought oil lamps, large alabaster jars, and their strengthening flame illuminated those around us, warriors, counsellors and priests. I concentrated on the figure in the centre, a tall, grey-haired man, clean-shaven, with a harsh lined face and strange blue eyes. He was dressed in knitted robes and adorned with rings, bracelets and brooches which proclaimed him to be the Hittite leader. King Suppiliuma introduced himself and those around him. The one I turned to was Prince Zananza, sitting on Suppiliuma's right, the king's heir and eldest son. The likeness was obvious: he too had those light blue eyes, but his face was olive-skinned, the moustache and beard neatly clipped, and his black hair, shaved above the forehead in the Hittite fashion, gleamed with oil. Suppiliuma inspected our tablets and scrolls, kissing the imperial cartouche.

'You are surprised I speak Egyptian, Lord Mahu? I was raised at the court of Amenhotep the Magnificent, a time when, if Pharaoh bared his arm, the People of the Nine Bows trembled like dust under his heel.'

'They still do, my lord,' I answered.

'Do they?' Prince Zananza spoke up, his voice cultured as any courtier from Thebes. 'Do they really?' he repeated. He lifted his goblet. 'You are most welcome here. We congratulate you on the beauty of your bride. We hope your journey back home will not be too rigorous. We have heard about the war galley.' He paused at the laughter his remark provoked. 'We shall make sure that Pharaoh's envoys are safe.' He pointed to our brimming bowls. 'They are copper-lined, but the metal holds the skulls of my father's enemies.'

Nabila quickly put hers down. I drank greedily from mine and so did Djarka.

'Are you threatening us?' I asked. 'Talking of Egypt's past glories, of your enemies' skulls in your drinking cups? A sword,' I continued, 'slips easily from the sheath, as will Pharaoh's to cut down his enemies.'

'Now you are threatening us.' Suppiliuma raised his head.

'We do not threaten,' I retorted. 'We have come to ask what is your intention.' I gestured round the tent. 'Lachish has fallen, its princes humiliated, their wives and daughters the slaves of your soldiers.'

'We are protecting our borders.'

'A long way from home,' Djarka intervened.

'As are the armies of Egypt.' Suppiliuma's voice turned harsh. The hum of conversation around him died. He clicked his fingers. A servant hurried into the circle of light and placed an earthenware pot on the ground. At Suppiliuma's order he lifted the lid and took out a head, pulling it up by the hair, the jagged skin of the severed neck a few inches above the rim. I stared at the face with its half-closed eyes and mud-caked mouth, and recognised one of the Vermin Lords I'd first met in Tyre.

'We captured him,' Zananza explained, 'coming back to Tyre. He bore letters from your General Horemheb. Did you know your general is already marching along the Horus Road?'

'No!' Djarka protested. 'Impossible!'

I agreed. The atmosphere in the tent turned ugly.

'So what are you doing here?' Suppiliuma hissed. 'Why did you come?' He waved his hands mockingly. 'To talk of peace? To discuss our policies? To assure us? You're wasting our time!'

'You say,' I gestured at the severed head left resting on the rim of the pot, 'that he carried information from General Horemheb, but that's impossible!'

'About twenty-five thousand men,' Suppiliuma intoned as if he was chanting a hymn. 'They arrived in the Delta, where the air is cool and the land still soft. They took the Horus Road, supplies being sent before them.' Suppiliuma then listed the oases which lined the royal road across the Sinai Desert.

'He rests at the Oasis of Great Green Shoots. He has twenty-five thousand men,' Suppiliuma repeated. 'Three crack regiments of the line, the Isis, the Horus Red-eye and the Ptah, six thousand chariots and about the same number of mercenaries. He is supported by his old friend and colleague General Rameses.'

'I did not know this,' I stammered, genuinely afraid. We were now exposed as envoys of a Pharaoh who clearly no longer wanted peace. If Horemheb and Rameses were already crossing Sinai, I wondered what had happened. Was Ay's hand behind this?

'My lord.' Nabila raised her head. 'On our way to Tyre, an Egyptian merchantman was attacked by pirates.' I moved my hand to urge caution, but Nabila was insistent. 'One of those who died was Huaneru, envoy of the Lord Ay, the Eyes and Ears of Pharaoh.' Nabila paused. 'Were you expecting him, my lord?'

Suppiliuma shrugged and spread his hands; Zananza looked quickly over his shoulder.

'Let us withdraw,' Djarka hissed into my ear. 'Let us ask for time to reflect.'

'My lord.' I spread my hands, palms up, in the gesture of peace. 'What you have told us is truly disturbing. We need to consider.'

'The cords of Hell stretch out to ensnare you. The traps of the grave lie hidden before you.' The voice, strong and carrying, rose from behind Suppiliuma's line of counsellors.

'To whom shall I speak today? My brothers and kinsmen are shallow; the friends of yesterday are enemies today.' The voice stirred memories, though I was still shocked by Suppiliuma's revelation. A figure rose from behind the line of Hittites and came round into the light, squatting down next to the pot bearing the severed head, its eyes still gazing sightlessly at us. The new arrival edged forward. He wore an expensive thick linen kilt edged with red stitching; leopardskins covered the upper part of his torso. On his hands were red gloves like those given by Pharaoh to his favourites. A rough shawl of hyaena skin was draped over his shoulders; his face and head were hidden by a lion mask. Around his neck were silver chains with a small gold beetle hanging like a pendant. In truth a hideous apparition, exuding menace and threat. I glanced away. Suppiliuma and Zananza were fully enjoying our consternation.

'Lord Mahu! Baboon of the South!'

The grotesque mocked me. I immediately knew who he was.

'Mery-re,' I breathed. 'Mery-re, former High Priest of the Aten, traitor and rebel. I thought you were dead.'

My old enemy removed his mask to reveal the familiar monkey-like face, smooth and round like a pebble, malicious black eyes and that protruding mouth, lips slightly pursed as they always were in perpetual disdain.

'You have aged, Mahu, Baboon of the South.'

I still stared in shocked surprise. Mery-re! Who had been raised with me as a Child of the Kap, a priest from birth with an innate belief in his own superiority. He later became High Priest of the Aten under the Great Heretic whose name cannot be mentioned. After Nefertiti's fall from power, Mery-re and his supporters attempted a coup but were scattered across the desert. He had disappeared, emerging now and again as a threat, a man like me who believed Akenhaten was still alive, sheltering amongst the Vermin Lords.

'You are alive.' I grinned to hide my surprise. 'Mery-re, you are as quick on your legs as you always were. Now,' I taunted, 'you hide like a *hekau*, a sorcerer, amongst those who have not seen the Nile, bathed in its waters or felt the cool breath of its gods.'

'Insults, Mahu, insults.' Mery-re leaned forward and breathed noisily in my direction, what sorcerers and scorpion men call the venom of death. 'I know the names of the Devourer,' he chanted. 'I can call on the battle ghosts of the dead who ride through the night in chariots pulled by purple-maned horses.' He tapped the small silver box on a chain round his neck. 'I hold the key to the place of the departed spirits.'

'Oh yes,' I retorted. 'And I walk amongst the blossoms of heaven and ride clouds which sweep me into the evergreen fields of Osiris.'

My reply provoked muttering amongst the Hittites. Mery-re slid the cord off his neck, opened the box and sprinkled some of its contents over one of the oil lamps. As he did so, he rocked backwards and forwards, chanting curses from the Book of the Dead.

'Whom do you look for, Mahu?' He broke off and grinned at me. 'The dead surround you, so whom do you call upon? Nefertiti?' he whispered. 'The beautiful woman? Or what about your aunt Isithia, any of those who've gone before us into the Eternal West?' He shuffled sideways and, stretching out a claw-like hand, grasped my goblet and pushed it towards me.

'Drink, Mahu, Baboon of the South, drink deep and you will see the shades amongst the shadows.'

I did so, gulping the wine, watching the smoke curl and shift as I listened to Mery-re's chanting. At first nothing but my stomach jittered, then my heart skipped a beat as if something sinister had crept into that tent.

'Look into the smoke, Mahu.'

I did so. I saw faces: Nefertiti, Isithia, men I'd killed, women I'd loved. The longer I stared, the firmer they became. I felt I was being dragged into the smoke. Tears stung my eyes. I raised my goblet to toast these ghosts of my life but Djarka seized my wrist, shouting at Mery-re in a tongue I could not understand. It was Apiru, their sacred words, or so he told me later. I keeled over and woke in my own tent with Nabila crouching over me, Djarka kneeling at the foot of the bed. I struggled up and thirstily drank the watered beer, clenching the beaker firmly in my hands. Nabila coaxed me to sip more slowly. I felt feverish, my head slightly pained, my eyes smarting.

'Drugged.' Djarka smiled. 'Mery-re knows all the little tricks. The wine and smoke were mingled with dream dust. You fainted and we carried you here.' He pulled a face. 'I think the Hittite lords were impressed.'

'Not by us.' I grasped the wet rag Nabila offered and dabbed my face and neck. I felt as hot as you do when you drink too much unwatered wine. 'They are not impressed by us,' I repeated.

'True.' Djarka gestured with his thumb over his shoulder. 'We are to be gone by dawn tomorrow. We are to take our mercenaries and scribes; the Hittites will sell us chariots and pack-ponies. We are to make our own way south. They haven't even offered us scouts.'

'How many men do we have now?' I asked warily. I held my hand up for silence and grew aware of the sounds outside.

'The Hittites are breaking camp,' Djarka declared.

'Where to?' I asked. 'South with us?'

'No.' Djarka narrowed his eyes. 'Surprisingly, east.'

'They're marching east,' I exclaimed. 'Why?'

'I don't know, just gossip around the campfires collected by our chief scribe. Suppiliuma has apparently decided to deal with the Assyrians, but that is not our problem. My lord, we must be gone by tomorrow morning.'

I had no choice but to agree. I sent Djarka for a second interview with Suppiliuma and his son but he returned shaking his head. 'They'll have nothing to do with us; they are polite but firm. They do not wish to see us any more.'

I left my bed, washed and changed, and went to stand at the entrance of the tent staring out over the camp. Lachish was still burning, black plumes of smoke spiralling up to the darkening sky. The cries and the stench of the camp only emphasised my feeling of unease. We were at the heart of an enemy horde with little choice but to travel south through rugged, dangerous country back to Egypt, and what then? What had been the purpose of our journey?

Djarka and Nabila became busy supervising our departure. We had about three dozen mercenaries and fourteen scribes. Our treasurer had been busy buying chariots, carts and sturdy-footed donkeys. Supplies and possessions were piled outside our tent. The Hittites, in the main, ignored us, limiting themselves to catcalls; though now and again a group of drunken soldiers would lurch across and bawl insults before officers armed with white wands drove them away. Evening came and a cold breeze sprang up. I decided that we would eat in our tent, Djarka, Nabila and myself. Nabila was calm and assured; just gazing at her serene face gave me some hope that we could overcome the dangers facing us. I tried to close my ears to the screams and yells of the camp as the Hittite soldiers enjoyed the captured women.

'No mercy was shown,' Nabila murmured. She sat cross-legged, a platter of meat and vegetables on her lap, her long hair framing her face. She looked younger than her years, though I could see something was on her mind. For a while we chattered about the Hittites.

'They are using terror,' Djarka observed. 'That's what they are doing, my lord. They are making examples of certain cities and princes as they advance further south. They don't want to leave any enemy in their rear, nothing to block their communications. It's war by fire and sword.'

I thought of such an enemy moving down the Nile towards the various cities of Egypt. Surely that would be impossible if Horemheb and Rameses were already across Sinai, with massed chariot squadrons and crack regiments of foot?

'My lord?'

I glanced up. Nabila edged closer. She stroked my arm. 'I have been thinking of our own journey.'

'Yes, so have I.' I smiled, touching her hand affectionately. 'We are well armed.'

'That's what worries us!' Djarka's voice was harsh. He moved closer, whispering like a conspirator. 'My lord, you drank dream dust but you are still Lord Mahu, Baboon of the South, cunning and sharp. You must have reflected on why we came here.' He gestured with his hands. 'To negotiate peace? Lord Ay has put an end to that. Egyptian troops are now in Canaan, and the Hittites will fight. Were we sent to buy time?' Again he gestured. 'There was no need to buy time.'

'Why then?' I asked. 'Why were we sent?'

'To be killed,' Nabila declared softly.

I glanced at her.

'My lord, I know we are accredited envoys,' she said warily. 'The Hittites will not touch us, but now we must journey south through dangerous, rugged terrain.'

'And?'

'Oh . . .' She took a deep breath. 'Lord Ay does not want you to return to Egypt. I believe Huaneru was sent to arrange your deaths.'

'To negotiate with Suppiliuma over our murder?' I asked.

'No.' She shook her head. 'The Hittites would have nothing to do with that. I keep thinking of that loathsome creature in the tent, the magician, the Kheb-sher, Mery-re.'

From outside a conch horn wailed; some signal to the Hittites, for the din in the camp subsided.

'But Mery-re wouldn't act whilst we enjoy the Hittites' protection.'

'I don't think he needs their permission to do anything.' Nabila half laughed. 'He is dangerous enough and does not mean us well.'

'And yet,' I intervened, 'that's only half the mystery. We received that secret message before we left Egypt. Nabila, I told you about it. Now I understand why we were given orders to kill Mery-re.'

'Yes, so do I,' Djarka agreed. 'We are travelling south, through the hill country of Canaan.' He paused. 'If Pharaoh Akenhaten is still alive, he may try to communicate with us. I have a feeling he will, and that others, like Mery-re, will be watching.' He let his words hang in the air.

I took a piece of lamb, dipped it in the pot of herb sauce, and popped it into my mouth. I sat for a while, eyes half closed, chewing carefully. Djarka and Nabila were right. I had a reputation for cunning, yet I felt like a fool who had blundered from one trap into another. Ay simply wanted us out of Egypt, but for what? We were now between two armies, facing a perilous journey south. All those rumours about Akenhaten sheltering in Canaan. Did Ay truly believe his former son-in-law would reveal himself? And then what? Capture? Assassination? I glanced sideways at Nabila; she, too, was lost in her own thoughts.

'If Ay wishes to strike,' she declared, 'and I have said this before, the assassin must be one of our own company. If the Hittites offer scouts, we refuse them; the same goes for any escort.'

'Continue,' I urged.

'I believe . . .' She lifted her wine cup and coughed, then turned and spat elegantly into the small bowl beside her. 'I have given this deep thought, my lord Mahu, and not just about our pleasures!' She grinned impishly. 'I want to return as your wife. I want to go back to Egypt. I do not want to die in a foreign land, to leave my bones whitening to be gnawed at by jackals and lions. If Lord Ay wanted you out of Egypt, that means he has also decided you shall never return. Yes, Akenhaten may manifest himself. If he does, something terrible will happen. Now, any one of us . . .' She gnawed at her lip, a gesture which reminded me of Nefertiti. Indeed, I'd come to realise how much Nabila resembled that long-dead queen: beautiful, playful, flirtatious, with a wit as sharp as any knife. I caught Djarka's eye and his glimmer of suspicion. He trusted so few people. I could read his mind. He was considering the possibility that Nabila herself might be the secret assassin. My wife, allowing her hair to hide her face, glanced quickly at Djarka, pushing her hair back. 'Any of us,' she repeated,' could be the traitor, and that includes me, does it not? You must accept my reasons for travelling to Egypt. I would take any oath that I am no traitor; I would also take a second oath, to any god you name, that there must be a traitor, an assassin, in our midst, but who he is I do not know. Except . . .'

'Except,' Djarka finished the sentence, 'what can one man do against so many?'

I was about to reply when the tent flap was pulled back. My senior scribe, his wizened face all concerned, lips puckered, scrambled in like a dog. The noise outside the tent had subsided.

'My lord, you have a visitor. The Kheb-sher.' He spat the word out. 'He is here with his retinue.'

I told Nabila to stay and, followed by Djarka, came out of the tent. It was that moment before night; Mery-re had chosen his time well. The sky was a dark blue, still scored by the rays of the setting sun. The black plumes of smoke from Lachish were wafting across. Mery-re was squatting some distance away, behind him a horde of fierce-looking tribesmen, war paint on their faces, moustaches and beards thickly oiled. They all wore animal skins, and their hoods were long flaps raised at each end so that they looked like bats, an impression heightened by the long leather shields on their packs which resembled wings. These shields, slightly concave, rose high above their shoulders and were pierced with holes to peer through. When the men wearing them moved, as we later discovered, they created an eerie whispering sound, a sinister fluttering like that of a flock of macabre winged creatures swooping round a lonely courtyard. These were Mery-re's retinue, the Vesper Bats, named after those malignant shadows which fly through the sky between dusk and night. Mery-re was always one for show. He sat silently, his face hidden by his hideous mask, supported by those orderly, silent rows of tribesmen, squatting or kneeling, armed with curved swords, clubs and maces. Their very silence was terror enough.

I swaggered over, deliberately scratching my crotch in a gesture of contempt. I picked up a handful of sand as if wishing to fling it into Mery-re's eyes. My old companion, my former fellow scholar, grinned back as he pulled the mask from his face.

'Greetings, Lord Mahu, you feel better?'

'Naturally.' I came as close as I could and squatted down before him, not kneeling as he was but legs apart, as if I was preparing to relieve myself. I was pleased at the low moan of protest this insult provoked amongst Mery-re's entourage. 'Who do you think I am, Mery-re?' I whispered, pushing my head forward. 'A little boy to be frightened by phantoms of the night? So you have fierce warriors to protect you and do your bidding. What do you think I am going to do? Let my bowels turn to water? Squat and beg for mercy?'

'You're travelling south, Lord Mahu?'

'Yes.' I bared my teeth like a dog. 'We are travelling south tomorrow. Do you wish to join us?'

'We might accompany you,' Mery-re smirked, 'just to make sure you're safe on the way.'

'Oh, I'm sure you will.' I let the pile of dust in my hand trickle through my fingers. 'Mery-re . . .' My head was so close I could smell the various perfumes on his body; strong as they were, their fragrance didn't hide that rottenness, that smell of death, of dried blood. 'Mery-re,' I repeated, 'you and I . . .' I gestured with my finger, 'this cannot go on.'

'We'll meet again, Lord Mahu.' Mery-re rose abruptly to his feet, towering over me, war club in one hand, dagger in the other. I heard a sound and turned. Djarka was standing in the entrance to our tent, his great horn bow in one hand, an arrow in the other.

'Until we meet again, Lord Mery-re.' I also rose, spat to one side and walked back into my tent.

We rose early, before dawn. It was still bitterly cold as we hurriedly ate some oatmeal mixed with milk, warming ourselves before the campfire. All around us the Hittites were stirring, camp marshals and officers going along the avenues and paths, accompanied by trumpeters, enforcing a discipline Horemheb would have envied. We concentrated solely on leaving as quickly as possible. I summoned my scribes and mercenaries, who squatted in a semi-circle as I addressed them. I told them of the coming journey and its dangers. I offered, especially to the elderly, the chance of returning to Tyre, where they could wait for the next Egyptian merchantman. No one accepted. They too had had enough of the Hittites and were fearful of being delayed for months, even years, in some foreign city. They all assured me they were ready to leave. I studied their faces, recalling Nabila's words, and wondered if any or all of them might be assassins, just waiting for the opportunity to strike. I made them retake their oaths of loyalty. I promised we would move as swiftly as we could, and assured them I had an accurate map to guide our path. I informed them that the Hittites were falling back, marching east, whilst we would hurry south and, if the gods favoured us, meet the Egyptian troops who were crossing Sinai. My retinue had already heard the rumours and many nodded, smiling, clapping their hands softly.

A few hours later, our possessions piled high in the five chariots and carts our treasurer had managed to buy, along with a string of sumpter ponies, we left the Hittite camp, heading out along the dusty track into the wilderness. For a while we were escorted by a group of Hittite war chariots. Their officers were simply determined to make sure we left; they had little care for our safety and well-being. It was early summer; the best time for armies to march and envoys to travel. The ground underfoot was firm. My scribes had also bought rough charts of Canaan, and with the help of my map we planned our route through the Jordan river valley. We carried only what we needed – foodstuff, a change of clothing, and water jars – and everyone wore the stout leather marching boots we'd purchased in the markets of Tyre.

The first few days were pleasant enough, a string of men, ponies and rattling chariots marching in the early morning under the strengthening sun. Towards midday we'd seek shade, a cave or some oasis, and lookouts would be posted in the trees. We'd rest until late afternoon then resume our march, not stopping until the scouts brought back news of a suitable place to camp for the night. We followed the same military routine as if we were soldiers in hostile territory, using our chariots as a defensive wall, and ensuring that we had a ready supply of water. Djarka and some of the mercenaries were good hunters. We ate well on fresh meat, and once we were free of the Hittite camp and its pervasive stench of rotting flesh, blood and smoke, our mood improved.

We must have been on the road five days before we met the Silent Ones. We were about to enter a valley when two of our scouts, bows in hand, came scurrying back, feet pounding, stirring up flurries of white dust.

'My lord,' they gasped

I was walking beside the chariot where Nabila crouched, her head and shoulders covered by a thick striped cloak against the heat of the sun. She had once owned a parasol, and had spent the first hours of our march cursing the Hittite who had stolen it.

'My lord.' The scout pointed back down the road. 'Strangers are waiting for us.'

'How many?' I asked. I was about to sound the alarm when the scout intervened.

'No, no, sir, they mean peace: their hands are raised, but they will not speak to us.'

Hui: to spit venom

Chapter 5

I went forward to investigate. As I approached the mouth of the valley, two men leading a donkey came out to a rocky culvert, silent as shadows slipping under the sun. They were dressed like sand dwellers in striped robes with long straggling hair; one had a thick moustache and beard, the other was smooth-shaven. The elder one handed the reins of the donkey to his companion and came forward slowly, hands raised, palms forward in a gesture of peace.

'I seek the Lord Mahu.' He spoke throatily the lingua franca of the mercenaries.

'I am Lord Mahu,' I replied. 'What do you want?'

'I have been sent.' The man gestured for me to approach. I drew my sword; Djarka strung an arrow to his bow, and we walked forward warily, fearful of an ambush.

'No danger; Lord Mahu, we come in peace.' The stranger knelt on the ground, and opening the wallet on the cord around his waist took out a scarab and handed it to me. Black, smooth and polished, the scarab showed the Aten, the Sun Disc, rising between the Sacred Peaks. I turned it over and read the hieroglyphs of the Great Heretic Pharaoh. I balanced it in my hand.

'You may look at me.'

The man lifted his head. His face was rugged, burned dark

by the sun. He had grown a moustache and beard to hide the wounds on his face, particularly the thick cut to his lower lip. I walked round him, staring at his ankles, and, stretching forward, pulled down the back of his robe to reveal scars.

'Once a soldier,' I said. 'A mercenary? You've been beaten badly, scarred in the face. What is a mercenary doing out here in the dry lands? Who sent you?'

'I am a messenger from the Hall of Shadows.' The mercenary kept his head down. 'I have been sent by the one who lives there.'

'Who is the one who lives there?'

'My lord,' the man's voice turned into a plea, 'all I am is the envoy who brings the messages. I am told to lead you.'

'How can I trust you?' I asked.

'My lord, you've seen the token I bring, the cartouche of the Aten, may his name be blessed for ever more. I and my son.' He gestured at the young man who stood holding the reins of the donkey.

'What are your names?'

'We have no names,' the young man called out. 'We are what we appear to be, a mercenary and his son.'

'Wait a moment.' Djarka knelt beside the mercenary and, gently putting his hand under the man's chin, tipped his head back. 'I know you.' Djarka spoke quickly in the Apiru tongue, and the stranger, without thinking, replied immediately and looked guilty; his head would have gone down but Djarka forced it back. 'I know you,' Djarka continued. 'You were once captain of the guard in the royal palace. You served Akenhaten. You were one of those who disappeared with him.'

'I am a mercenary,' the man replied, spreading his hands, not flinching at the way Djarka kept pressing his head backwards. 'I come in peace. I am here to lead you through dangers. Whom you meet along the road is not for me to decide, but I tell you this, master.' Djarka relaxed his hand, and the mercenary twisted his head to relieve the tension. 'My lord, we are what you see, a man, his son and their donkey carrying our own possessions, our own supplies. The journey south is dangerous; you need us.'

'We are well armed and protected.' Djarka gestured back at our retinue.

'You are being followed,' the mercenary continued. 'By the Kheb-sher, the man you should have killed. He and his Vesper Bats follow you as swiftly as any wolf pack does a wounded deer.'

'I have seen nothing,' Djarka replied.

'You're not meant to see them,' the mercenary replied. 'They slip like shadows. There are many, at least three times your number.'

'We haven't seen anyone,' Djarka insisted.

'You'll only see them,' the mercenary replied, 'when they want you to see them, and that could be too late.' He edged forward on his knees, pushed by Djarka, and stared beseechingly up at me. 'I bring messages from the Hall of Shadows, my lord. You are in great danger from both without,' he glanced around me at the retinue, 'and within. You must follow me.'

I hid my own fears. I had dispatched scouts back on a number of occasions to see if we were being followed, but they had reported nothing. Now these strangers had appeared. I also felt a thrill of excitement. Years had passed since I had last seen Akenhaten. Were the rumours true? Was this man going to lead us to the Hall of Shadows, where the Great Heretic now sheltered? I bent down, clasping the man's face between my hands.

'I swear,' I repeated, 'by he who lives, that if you're traitors or mean us harm you will scream for death.' The man blinked back at me.

'And if you don't trust me, my Lord,' he whispered, 'you'll never return to Egypt!'

I made my decision: the mercenary and his son were

admitted into our company. Nabila was anxious about what I told her, openly distrustful of the strangers, but they soon proved their worth. One night, shortly after they joined us, father and son, together with three of my mercenaries, slipped from the camp. Dawn had broken before they returned, bloodied and cut, but they carried the head of one of the Vespers. I took the grisly token by its tuft of hair and placed it on a boulder for all my retinue to see. I studied the half-closed eyes, the ugly painted face, the snarling blood-caked lips, the strange hood still knotted under the chin.

'We found him sleeping,' our new-found guide declared. 'They are swift and they are silent, but they've grown lazy and careless. As with all hirelings, they do like to drink.' He held up a small wineskin. 'He was a scout sent forward before the rest. We caught him in a gully and killed him silently.'

'Now they'll know,' Djarka declared, 'Mery-re and his parasites, that we've realised we are being followed.'

'Who cares?' Nabila retorted. 'We've struck first.'

Our journey continued. Time and time again I would stride back down the column, or take a chariot and go rattling out in clouds of dust, searching for any sign of our pursuers. However, they'd learned their lesson: if they were silent and unseen before, they now became ghosts, following us relentlessly but showing no sign.

How can I describe that journey? Canaan is a strange land, cut by dark stone valleys of limestone and basalt cracking and crumbling under the relentless sun. These places of terror would lead us out on to plateaus of lush grass and clumps of holm oaks, where game and birds were plentiful. The local tribes glimpsed our imperial standards, our well-armed mercenaries, and posed no threat. Sometimes they came out from their hilltop villages to offer supplies, trade and barter, or just share the gossip. We learnt two important facts: first, the great Hittite army seemed to have disappeared. Second, a large Egyptian force was crossing Sinai and would slowly advance north. We took heart at this news and continued our journey untroubled.

At times I felt as if I was in a mirage, cut off from the luxury of Thebes with its broad imperial avenues and the rushing Nile. The scenes and places which had shaped my life disappeared. There was nothing but the open sky, rocky valleys and fertile green plains, whilst the calls of birds or the hum of insects in the grass along either side of the track were the only alien sounds. I was at peace, yet it was that peace which precedes a battle. Sometimes at night, lying entwined with Nabila, I would suddenly wake in sweaty fear, throat gasping, heart pounding. I'd scramble to the mouth of the tent and look out, only to be greeted by a blast of icy air and the stars shining bleakly against their dark, empty background. I'd go back to bed calming my own fears, wondering what might happen. Of course, I'd question the mercenary and his son about the future, but they had told me what they could and would say no more. I also asked them if they'd seen their great Pharaoh. They just gazed blankly back, shook their heads and turned away.

Both father and son proved to be valuable scouts. They knew the tracks, the short cuts, where water could be had, the best places to camp, which towns to approach, which villages to avoid, and where we had to be most vigilant. They grew excited, telling us about a great inland sea where the water was thick with salt. Eventually we began to descend from the hill country into scorching desert. The contrast was striking. One day we were in a region where wheat, grapes, pomegranates and other fruits were plentiful, where farmers and merchants would sell us fresh meats as well as new leather bottles full of water or wine. The next we entered what the mercenaries called the 'Barren Lands', of rearing dark limestone cliffs and dusty tracks, rocky plateaus, stony hills, and shadow-filled canyons. The only birds were the hunting buzzards and vultures hovering above us; the only plants the occasional acacia tree or thorny bush clinging desperately to the hard soil. There were very few places to rest.

Now the mercenary and his son proved their worth. Water was essential, and they knew the whereabouts of hidden cisterns which collected the winter rains. In the distance glinted what our scouts called the Sea of the Dead. The track beneath our feet became dangerous and shifting, our attention distracted by the way the rain, when it did fall, had weathered the rocks into antic shapes like images from a nightmare. The air, almost too hot to breathe, was laden with salt, which stung the eyes and choked the throat. Many of my scribes began to object, and even a few of the mercenaries loudly demanded if there was another route, but our guide was insistent. I realised we were not only travelling south but journeying to meet someone. The heat grew intense. The sun beat down like a hammer; yet our guide led us on even when it was at its peak. We followed the track around a bend in the cliffs and the mercenary pointed down.

'The Oasis of Zorar.'

It was a welcome sight: tamarind, date palm and balsam trees sprouted around a pool of sweet water. We hurried down to this relief from the torrid heat of the sun, to bathe our faces and wet our throats. Two of our donkeys, desperate for water, buckled and broke free; one damaged its leg and had to be destroyed. At last we reached the oasis, men and animals desperately seeking the shade, filling their stomachs, lapping the water into their mouths.

We sheltered for days at Zorar, bathing in its water, lying under its shade. I was aware of the danger – Mery-re and the Vesper Bats were not far behind – but I didn't care. The mercenary and his son had changed, becoming even more watchful and silent. I could see they were studying me, but when I stared back, they always glanced away.

In such circumstances the little things of life fascinated me:

the beauty of the olive or the ever-green cypress; Nabila's sweet smile, the way she would anoint herself with perfume, tie her hair or go out and stretch, breathing in the fresh air, rejoicing in the green-filled shade. I relaxed. I was reluctant to move from the oasis, at least not until man and beast had refreshed themselves. I didn't care about our pursuers. I enjoyed the moment, the escape from the relentless sun, the dusty track, the hot air pressing in on us. However, we were there for a purpose. One fateful night I sat beside the campfire and shared a jug of wine with Djarka, Nabila, the mercenary and his son. We didn't discuss the great things of life but shared jokes and stories; no one talked of what was to come, and, half drunk, I staggered to my bed and fell asleep. I was awoken by a gloved hand across my mouth. I always remember that touch, soft and smooth yet pressing against me, the disembodied voice warm and reassuring.

'Lord Mahu, Baboon of the South, do not struggle! Come with us!'

I pulled myself up. Shadows surrounded me. I stared around. Nabila was fast asleep; Djarka also, where he sprawled near the entrance to the tent. I remembered that wine jug going round and wondered what opiate it had contained, for both my companions were lost in the sleep of dreams. All around me clustered figures hooded and cowled. I didn't resist. I was pushed quietly out of the tent into the cold night air, away from the trees, across the sandy shale. The blossoms of the night gleamed down, whilst the ruffling breeze carried the roars of the night prowlers. I glanced to the left and right, almost in a trance. Shadows hurried beside me, pushing me forward, not like a prisoner, but gently, urging me on as if the place they intended was one I had always wanted to be.

So we hastened through a night full of sounds and eerie sights. I was not frightened. I realised whom I was going to meet. We climbed a rocky shale to where a fire glowed before the entrance to a cave. Three people sat there, hidden by the shadows. Hands seized me; they were gloved in lambskin, soft as the touch of a mother on your skin. I was taken up towards the fire and made to sit; the flames were merry, crackling the thorn twigs. The three figures sitting opposite me, cowled and hooded, did not move. A bowl of wine was thrust into my hands and I heard that voice, the one I'd heard so many times throughout my life.

'Well, Mahu, Lord Mahu, Overseer of the House of Scribes, close friend of Pharaoh, Baboon of the South, how fare you?'

I fought back the tears as I stared across the fire at the figure in the centre shrouded in darkness.

'My lord,' I stammered. 'So many years!'

'Not your lord, Mahu, not your lord,' the voice whispered, weary and sad.

As I edged a little closer to catch a glimpse, the figure turned and I caught the whiff of corruption, the scaly whiteness of the skin. I was amongst lepers; that was why they'd worn the gloves.

'Are you frightened, Mahu, Baboon of the South? Are you so fearful of confronting the reality, of escaping from the dream?'

'My lord, you are Akenhaten, Pharaoh of Egypt.'

'Mahu, Baboon of the South, I am nothing but a leper, a hermit of the valley, and now you sit before me. So listen.' The voice grew harsh. 'You did not kill the Kheb-sher, the magician, Mery-re, the traitor.'

'I could not,' I stammered. 'I had neither the means nor the motive.'

'Listen, Mahu.' The voice echoed, hollow, as if from beyond the grave.

'My lord,' I interrupted. 'I have so many questions, so many things have happened.'

'Silence! You do not know to whom you speak. I have changed. I am no longer the Grotesque. I am no longer the Veiled One, no longer the son of the Aten, but his slave. I sinned and I was punished. I know my true worth. I am not the Son of the One. I am not the Messiah, I am not the Chosen Child; he is yet to come. I was simply to prepare his way. I was his voice, his herald. I cried in the wilderness and no one heard; now I am being punished. Ah well, Mahu, Mery-re and his Vesper Bats pursue you. They are dangerous. They wait for something to happen in your camp. One person amongst you means to do great evil. I do not know whom, so you must be vigilant.'

I raised my hand to speak, but the voice across the fire turned harsh.

'Time is short. Mery-re and his Vesper Bats draw close. Soon they will attack. Now you have come here they will know where I am. There is no reason, Lord Mahu, Baboon of the South, for them to let you live any longer.'

'But my lord . . .' I protested.

'Listen, Mahu, and listen well. Suppiliuma and his Hittites have advanced east. They will shatter the power of the Assyrians and return stealthily like the jackal, crossing rivers and valleys to seal off Horemheb's return to Egypt. They will trap the Egyptian army in Canaan and destroy it. At the appropriate time you must tell Horemheb and Rameses, much as I hate them, that they have to retreat.'

'Why?' I asked. I was no longer Mahu the accomplished politician, the skilled intriguer, but the boy in that grove of the Malkata Palace, talking to the Veiled One, who was so full of wonder and secret ideas. I wanted to reach out, touch his hand, clasp him close, call back the days, evoke the memories, summon up the past, the glorious past, of Nefertiti, of the great City of the Aten, the power and the glory, the conspiracy and intrigue, the friendships and alliances which had forged us so close. The voice cut through such thoughts like a knife.

'Mahu, it is all over.' His tone was mellow but solemn. 'I am a leper. I am tainted. I have come to this place to hide, to reflect and make preparations, yet I watch what happens in Egypt. The future is not about kings, about who holds power, but the will of the Divine One. Oh, Mahu,' the voice trembled with emotion, 'you must return to Thebes. You must survive. My son is dead.'

My throat constricted, my heart pounded, the blood throbbed in my ears. I glanced around. Here I was in the middle of the wilderness; above me the stars glittered. A fire burned between me and those three figures sitting opposite. I recalled Tutankhamun's beautiful oval face, his brilliant smile, his full lips, his gentle eyes.

'My lord,' I gasped. 'You must be wrong.'

'My lord is not wrong.' The figure on the right spoke up. 'Tutankhamun, Fitting of Forms, Horus of the South, is no more. Tutankhamun is dead.'

'Murdered?' I asked.

'Might as well be,' the voice replied evenly. 'He has gone into the Far West; the divine seed is no more, the flame is quenched, the fire is out. Egypt will go into darkness but the Messiah will still come.'

I felt my stomach pitch. Just for a heartbeat I felt like leaping to my feet, running into the darkness, screaming, shouting, escaping from the burdens piled upon me, but that voice across the fire, gentle and seductive, drew me in.

'Mahu, Baboon of the South, your task is not yet finished.'

'It is!' I shouted back. 'Tutankhamun is dead! If the Beloved of Horus, Fitting of Forms has gone into the West, then why am I here? What need of me is there now? I shall go back and be a farmer, till my fields and tend my garden! Love my wife, raise sons and daughters! I will have no more to do with the men of power.'

'Listen, Mahu, you are at the heart of the power. You do not know what is happening. Tutankhamun is dead; what happens in Thebes now is the dust of history. You should have killed the Kheb-sher! He has to die. You must kill him, Mahu! When you strike, be ruthless. There is also that traitor in your midst. We do not know who it is, but he intends great malice against you. We can only do what we can; the rest is in the hands of the One. He is merciful and compassionate. He plots his plans and devises his own schemes, well above the thoughts and deeds of man. Remember, Mahu, I left wisdom for my son. I left it with the Watchers.'

'Who are they?' I shouted. 'You deal in riddles, enigmas and mysteries. Who are the Watchers?

'They were with you all the time, my lord Mahu: the statues, the *shabtis*.'

My hand went to my mouth. I recalled the two statues, life-size figures guarding Pharaoh's tomb; they represented smiling young men dressed in head-dress, kilt and belt. I had found them in the City of the Aten.

'The Watchers,' the voice declared. 'The secrets were always with them: the manuscripts, the predictions, the prophecies, the way things will be. The Watchers contain them. Didn't you realise that, Mahu? Didn't you have the sense? We thought you and our other friends in Thebes would have found them without our help. It was too dangerous to send a messenger.'

I closed my eyes. Of course! The Watchers were the two *shabtis*!

'Search them,' the voice continued. 'Search them and you'll find the knowledge. Time is pressing, Mahu, matters swirl on like a rushing river. You must play your part.'

'Why have you brought me here?' I asked. 'Simply to be told of the way things are?'

'No, Lord Mahu,' the figure on the right declared. 'You may not know it, but you are the vengeance of God! You will dispense justice to the left and to the right. People will realise that there is a truth, there is a way, there is a law, and that law must be followed. You will be our vengeance. You must survive. If you survive, so will the dream and the vision.'

'How do I know this?' I asked.

'My son is dead.' The figure in the centre replied. 'Lord Mahu, you know who I am. I was Akenhaten, Pharaoh of Egypt, Lord of Lords, the Glory of Horus, Fitting of Forms, Beautiful in All His Aspects. Now I am a leper, sheltering with other lepers here in the Valley of the Sea of the Dead. I have tasted the dregs of my pride. I have feasted on the ashes of my arrogance. I know who I am and what I am to be. Lord Mahu, I am not the way, I am not the truth; I was simply directed towards it. Now you must take over and finish what I cannot accomplish. You must return to Egypt. You must seek vengeance for my son.'

'Was he murdered?' I asked again, recalling once more that gentle face, the almond-shaped eyes, the affectionate touch.

'Do what you have to,' the voice replied. 'Do what you think is right. Discover the truth and act upon it. Remember this at all times: what you do is not what you think but what is planned; the river has set its course and flow it will, and you must play your part.' Then the figure in the centre began to sing, low yet vibrant, a beautiful psalm exulting the beauty of the One, of the Glorious, of He who cannot be seen, yet guides the thoughts of every man. A gentle but powerful hymn thrilling out into the darkness. I sat, flesh tingling, till the song ended and the figure in the centre slumped like a man exhausted.

'Do you remember the glory days, Mahu?' His voice came as a whisper. 'Do you remember her, the most beautiful, most fitting, the Glory of Hathor, the Pride of Egypt?' His voice became chill. 'Nefertiti the Glorious! I have sinned, Lord Mahu. I have sinned against heaven and against earth and my sins weigh like a rock between my shoulders. Bowed down I groan under the pain. All I can seek is pardon from the One. I thought I was he, but I am nothing, no more than dust beneath his sandals. Mahu, the memories of the past gather round me like ghosts; they cluster and cling, grasping my heart, invading my soul. They stop my mouth and cause

my breath to halt. So many memories, Mahu, so many things.'
The voice grew weary. 'I cannot touch you or embrace you.
You have a task to do, a mission to finish.' He gestured with
his hand and rose, a long, gaunt figure hobbling back into the
cave.

Hands rested on my shoulders, gloved fingers touched my
face. I rose to my feet; the two other figures still sat staring
at me through the darkness. I could not make out their faces,
though I grasped their sadness. I knew I'd reached the end.
The story was done, the glory was gone. What I had to do
now was finish whatever had to be finished, like you would
skin a dead animal and stow its hide away. I withdrew into
the darkness, down the shale-strewn bank, across the rocky
desert, back towards the oasis. I was pushed gently into the
trees and my escort left. I stumbled towards my tent, where
I picked up the wine bowl resting on a rock outside and drank
from it greedily. Then, slumping down on my bed, I fell into
a deep sleep.

The next morning I woke late and struggled to rise. Nabila
was already busy, glancing strangely at me.

'What happened last night?' she asked.

'I do not know,' I replied wearily. 'The wine, I think the
mercenary and his son drugged it. I saw visions in the dead
of night.'

'What visions?' she asked.

I gestured at the tent flap. 'Bring Djarka.' He joined us a
few moments later and, squatting on the bed, I told them
what had happened. Djarka sat open-mouthed.

'You saw him?' he gasped. 'You met Akenhaten?'

'No longer Akenhaten,' I replied. 'No longer Pharaoh of Egypt,
but a leper, a hermit, doing reparation for his many sins.'

'And the news?' Djarka demanded.

'Tutankhamun is dead.'

'The boy Pharaoh! It's not true, it can't be!' Djarka gasped.
'He was hale and hearty . . .'

'Everything,' I replied, 'everything we have done here, everything that has happened in Thebes, is the work of Lord Ay. We know that. We recognise that now. I was sent from Egypt so Ay could be free to play his games. Now we're here in the heart of the wilderness, unable to do anything.' I clenched my fist and shook it. 'If we escape, there will be a settling.'

'Were you followed last night?' Nabila asked. 'Mery-re and his Vesper Bats, they must have seen some movement if they have our camp under scrutiny.'

'They are not close,' I replied. 'Akenhaten, as always, is cunning and astute. Who would notice a figure being bundled secretly out of a camp at the dead of night? Whatever, Akenhaten has gone. What we must do,' I stared at both of them, 'is survive. We have a traitor, an assassin amongst us. He will strike soon. Once we leave this valley, and I am sure of this, danger will be lurking to the right and to the left. We must be prudent, vigilant.'

'So easy,' Nabila murmured, 'so very easy. We drank that drugged wine last night yet none of us noticed. We could have been drinking our own death.' She rose to her feet, walked to the entrance of the tent and stared out. 'Will we survive?' she asked. 'Do you think we will?'

I glanced at her lovely figure, hair tumbling down, and I recalled that voice in the night proclaiming its warnings. Nabila was clearly agitated. A woman, faced with danger, she concentrated on the small things of life. Thanks be to the lords of light, such dedication saved us.

We had rested enough time in the oasis so we spent the next few days preparing to move. Nabila confided in me that, although I'd been taken in the dead of night, she believed that others outside the camp may have seen it, so the danger was very close. She had taken to sitting at the entrance to our tent staring out across the camp, lost in her own thoughts; after darkness, she'd wander out amongst the men, talking and chatting. I was more concerned about what might be happening in Thebes. Tutankhamun suffered seizures, strange fits when he would regress to be a mere child, soiling himself, playing with toys or, worse still, indulging in tantrums, yet he was healthy enough. Nabila had been shocked by the news but was distracted by her own anxieties. Djarka grew even more pensive and reflective.

'If Tutankhamun is dead,' he declared, 'the line of Amenhotep III is extinguished, with the exception of the Princess Ankhesenamun. Do you think she'll be proclaimed Queen Pharaoh?'

I'd sit listening to Djarka going through all the possibilities, listing other princesses and princes related to the royal house, wondering loudly whether any of them would succeed. What role would Ay, Horemheb and Rameses play, not to mention my old companions Huy, Maya and Sobeck, as well as the powerful courtiers and merchants in the capital and the provinces? I could not answer but decided that we should leave the oasis, climb back into the highlands of Canaan and travel south as quickly as possible. In the end, we spent five more days at the oasis following my strange encounter in the middle of the night, before I gave the order to leave.

At first the climb out of that rocky, burning valley was a nightmare. We truly experienced all the horrors of the underworld. As one of the scribes said, it felt as if we were going across fiery lakes through one of the gates of Hell. Those who could, silently prayed as we toiled, sweated and bruised ourselves climbing the rocky escarpment, urging our donkeys on. At last we left the horrors of that Valley of the Sea of the Dead and entered the meadowlands and soft hill country of southern Canaan. On our second day out, the mercenary and his son demanded an audience.

'We are still being followed,' they declared, 'by Mery-re's Vesper Bats. They waited in the entrance to the valley until we moved; now they are coming through in close pursuit.'

I stared at both of them. Neither they nor I had mentioned my secret meeting at the dead of night. I had not discussed the wine or the opiate it must have contained. I fully accepted there'd been no malice in them.

'The past is the past!' the mercenary whispered, as if he could read my thoughts. 'My lord, look to the present!'

I did. That night I ordered camp to be pitched, our chariots and carts arranged so as to provide a defensive wall around the small oasis where we sheltered. During the day we often ate dry rations: biscuits, salted meat, hardened bread, and whatever fruits we could collect from the countryside. The lands we now entered were desolate, no wisp of smoke on the horizon to indicate a village. We were eager for fresh meat, so I sent hunters out to bring back quail, partridge, a deer, a hare and, if they were more fortunate, fresh fish. On our third night in the grasslands we slaughtered enough game for a feast. Our cook built up the fire to boil the usual potage, meats of all kinds mixed with sauces, vegetables, even slices of fruit, in two large cauldrons. Nabila, on that particular evening, sat under the tent awning, staring out, watching the cook tend the fire and place the heavy pots over the flames.

'My lord,' she called over her shoulder. I was busy mending a strap; I put it down and joined her. The men were occupied with various tasks: watering the horses, cleaning equipment, sitting under the shade of the tree playing knucklebones or some other game favoured by soldiers. The scribes, of course, were always concerned about their precious papyri, pen caskets and ink pots, as well as the lists of stores and other goods: officials are the same wherever they are, be it the heart of Thebes or some lonely highland in Canaan.

'What's the matter, light of my life?' I nudged her gently. 'You've been sitting here staring at that cook. Are you so hungry?'

'I was, but not now. I have thought, Mahu, about our assassin. One man against so many could do no damage, yet when we were in the Valley of the Sea of the Dead, the mercenary and his son, for the right reason, served us drugged wine.' She sniffed. 'I began to think how an assassin could deal with all of us in one fell blow.' She gestured across to the pots. 'Poison!'

'Nonsense,' I whispered, though I felt a deep unease. A prickly sweat courses down my back whenever I'm in danger; when you have encountered as much peril as I have, such premonitions are not lightly ignored. I was no longer concerned about the oasis, the wind bending the grasslands before us, whispering like some ghost. I kept my composure and studied the cook more closely. I recalled what I knew of him, a squint-eyed Assyrian, a mercenary, who had always served as quartermaster. He'd proved himself to be an able cook, serving up food which at least we could eat and enjoy. No one had ever complained; he was a man who apparently enjoyed his work. I watched him, armed with a copper ladle, stirring the two cauldrons very carefully.

'If one man,' Nabila spoke my thoughts, 'wished death for us in a single throw of the dice, what better way? We take our platters and he serves us one after the other, very quickly, no longer than it would take me to walk from one side of this oasis to the other. I have sat and watched him every night, nothing suspicious until this evening. He mixed herbs with the meat and sauces.'

'So?' I asked.

'Since then he has never tasted what he's stirring.'

I recalled the chefs in my kitchen: they were constantly tasting, nodding in appreciation, and inviting others to do the same. Our mercenary cook seemed most intent on what he was doing, stirring the pot quickly, pulling the ladle out, allowing the meat and sauces to mingle, but never once did he take a spoonful, a mouthful, even a sip. Intrigued, I walked over, Nabila behind me. Squint-eyes turned, peering up at me.

105

'Good evening, my lord, you are hungry? Soon it will be ready.'

'It looks ready enough now.' I pushed the ladle towards his mouth. 'Take a sip, have a taste; the cook always samples what he prepares.'

Squint-eyes' face betrayed everything, his hand immediately falling to a knife resting on a stone. This I kicked away. Again I thrust the ladle at him, 'Eat, I said, eat as much as you can.'

'I'm not hungry, my lord.'

'What do you mean, you're not hungry? You've had the same rations as us, you've been toiling all day, but you're not hungry enough to take even a sip of what you're preparing? Tell me,' I squatted down, 'where are you from?'

'My lord,' he stuttered. His lips were dry; he had difficulty speaking. A narrow, cruel face, hard eyes watchful. Nabila slipped behind him, knife in hand. Others were becoming concerned. Djarka hurried up.

'Master?'

Again I pushed the ladle towards the cook's mouth. 'Drink,' I ordered. 'Drink!'

He refused.

Djarka summoned the guards. The man struggled, but I had his hands bound behind him. I made him kneel; a cord was put round his head, and at my instruction, Djarka looped in a stick and began to turn it. The cook screamed, and as he did so I poured ladle after ladle into his mouth, tipping his head back, forcing him to swallow. The rest of the camp was now roused, guards running from the perimeter, startled by what was happening. All the cook could do was groan and moan at the cord wrapped round his forehead. He tried to retch and vomit, claiming, as he spluttered, that he felt sick. I had him dragged towards the latrine pits and pegged out, then crouched at his feet, ordering the rest to go away. At first there was no sign of poison, but eventually I noticed sweat lacing his face, his eyes growing heavy. He moaned to himself as he stirred backwards and forwards, his stomach rumbled, and I drew away in disgust as he began to vomit. I ordered the cauldrons to be taken off the fire and had their boiling contents poured over him. I watched him scream for a while. Angry welts formed over his face, chest and belly. I crouched beside him.

'A quick death?' I whispered in his ear. 'For a quick death, tell me, who told you to poison us?'

'Kheb-sher,' the man muttered. 'Kheb-sher, he gave me silver.'

I nodded to Djarka, who hurried away. For a while there was some confusion, but eventually the man's personal belongings were found. Djarka brought them back: a battered pannier containing enough silver and gold to turn any mercenary's heart.

'Kheb-sher!' I muttered. 'Well, I'll send you to Hell before him.' Drawing my knife, I pulled back the man's head and slit his throat. I then ordered all the foodstuff to be checked, carefully scrutinised and examined, but nothing tainted was found.

We ate dry rations that night, drank water from the oasis spring and left the next morning, filing out across the grass-lands. Such a contrast to the valley we had left. Imagine meadows and fields where the grass grows to the height of a man's shoulder. The sea of green was broken now and again by clumps of acacia and tamarind trees, an ideal place for an ambush. The mercenary and his son, alarmed by what they'd witnessed in the camp, joined me at the front of the column.

'Why now?' I asked. 'Why do you think he tried to poison us after we left the valley?'

'Because those who hired him realised your task was done.'

'But,' I replied warily, 'I never led them to anything. They know nothing. You know what happened.' I faced the mercenary squarely. 'I mean, it was you who drugged our wine.' The man stepped back. 'But in doing so,' I grinned, 'you saved our lives.' I glanced back at Nabila, crouching in our chariot. 'Isn't that true, heart of my heart?' Nabila climbed to her feet and nodded. I was so worried, so agitated I hadn't even had time to thank her properly. I turned back to the mercenary and his son.

'So if I never led them anywhere, why now?'

The mercenary stared up at the sky.

'I too watched the cook. He didn't poison the pots.'

'What do you mean?' I asked.

'If he'd poisoned that food,' the mercenary replied, 'he'd have died immediately.' He grinned sourly. 'You poured enough of it into his mouth. He mixed in something to weaken our hearts, diminish our strength. What I think was planned is that we would have eaten and become ill, too weak to resist any attack. Most of us would have been killed. I suspect that you, my lord, would have been taken prisoner, to be closely questioned.'

'In which case,' I walked back to the horses pulling our heavy chariot and I grasped their halter, 'they will attack soon.'

'If they do, my lord,' the mercenary hurried up beside me, 'then you must fight and not be taken prisoner. The Vesper Bats have a cruel reputation. I have heard of one man whom they nailed to a tree and later beat to death. Another prisoner they disembowelled and ate his heart. The Kheb-sher has hired the filthiest scum from around the Great Green.' He looked nervously over his shoulder. 'If it comes to a fight, then it must be one to the death.' He gestured around. 'We have left the Barren Lands and are now on the moorlands, journeying south-west, which will bring us to the coastal towns along the Great Green. If the attack comes,' he glanced up at a buzzard circling in the sky, 'it will be here, you know that, my lord.'

Hefat: two-legged cobra

Chapter 6

I can still recall now, even though my memory is failing, how cool it was when we escaped the red-stone, sun-scorched valley and its meagre shrubs and little shade, moving through rolling plains of long grass which bent beneath a wind which sent the petals of the wild flowers fluttering. The grass would conceal the ambush; in some places it grew even higher than a man. I could visualise what had been planned: the Vesper Bats swooping in, hideous in their war paint and plumage, spears jabbing, curved swords and clubs lashing limbs and cracking skulls, and, of course, they had planned to attack men weakened by poison.

I walked away from the column, staring back: somewhere in the grasslands behind us, Mery-re was leading his column of Vesper Bats, crouched and swift like hunting leopards. They'd wait for dusk or dawn to plan that mad, savage, blood-spurting rush. A chariot would be of no use here; the long grass concealed all sorts of obstacles. I turned and gazed ahead at the oasis the mercenary had pointed out earlier, its blue-green-leafed palm trees soaring above the grasslands. I stared back down the column and ordered my men to quicken their pace and move immediately into the oasis. Once again I used the carts and chariots to form a circle. Luckily the trees which fringed the oasis helped close any gaps. I ordered the weapon stores to be unloaded, quivers to be filled, bows to be strung and distributed, small fires to be lit.

'What is it?' Djarka asked. 'Why are you so concerned? I can see nothing amiss.'

'We are the quarry, Djarka,' I replied, slapping him on the shoulder. 'Mery-re is the hunt master. Let us pray to Horus the Red-eyed, the destroyer of rebels, and Horus the Sly Crocodile that we be saved.'

'What are you saying?' Djarka snapped.

'We are meant to be lambs for the slaughter. We've been followed by Mery-re and all the scum he has collected. We will show him how the hunted can become the hunter. We will be the greyhounds of Horus,' I pointed at the soaring palm trees, 'and they can save us.'

I gathered the mercenaries around. I recalled how some of them had been used to guard the entrances to the Valley of the Kings and were skilled in climbing steep crags. I opened my small treasure chest and took out two debens of gold, which I held out before me.

'I want two men,' I declared, 'the best climbers,' I gestured at the palm trees, 'to climb right to the top and gaze out over where we came. We are being followed. We must find how many and how close.'

Mercenaries are used to danger, bloodshed and sudden death; that didn't concern them. They were pleased to be out of the dust in that place of coolness and shade, and eager to earn my gold. After sharp discussion amongst themselves, two men stepped forward. Though they declared themselves used to heights, they were slightly nervous at the prospect of the perilous climb before them. I gave each a deben of gold.

'If you come back safely,' I grinned, 'there will be more.'

The entire camp watched as the two men began their climb. One fell, bouncing like a stone, his scream cut short as his body hit the hard ground. The camp leech inspected him but shook his head sadly, so I ordered his throat to be cut and another man took his place. Eventually both men reached the top of the palm trees, which were swaying dangerously in the wind. They'd taken ropes and used these to lash themselves more securely, two black dots against the dark blue sky. They shouted and gestured to each other, then abruptly they began their descent. They reached the bottom breathless, arms, thighs and legs scarred by the rough bark of the trees.

'My lord,' one of them gasped, 'you are correct, we are being followed.'

'How far?' I asked.

'They could be here by nightfall,' the other replied.

'And how many?' I asked.

'It's hard to see – more like watching furrows in the grass. Perhaps two hundred in all.'

Mery-re planned for his hunters to be with us by darkness! They would either attack immediately or wait for that grey time between dawn and day. I tried to recall as much as I could about the Vesper Bats, the way they were armed, dressed in animal skins, those macabre shield-wings fixed to their backs. Some carried bows, most spears, swords or clubs, ideal for hand-to-hand combat, an ambush or a sudden sortie. I concluded that we could not move: to be caught out in the open would be fatal. The ring of trees forming the oasis was small and the best place to make a stand. I issued my orders. Quivers were emptied, bows prepared. I doubled the guard and walked into the long grass. It was dry and coarse, the ground hard and firm beneath. I returned to the camp trying to hide my sense of desperation and frustration. Nabila was already laying out my weapons; she had thrust a Babylonian dagger with a jade handle into her own waistband. Her hair was gathered back, tied tightly, her face hard and serious. I took out a phial of poison, one I always carried, and thrust it into her hand, but she threw it back at me.

'You mustn't be captured,' I whispered. I placed my hand behind her neck and, pulling her close, kissed her full on the lips. 'The Vesper Bats, you've seen their painted, cruel faces. They'll come swift and silent like the fluttering of leaves; you must not be taken prisoner!'

'I shall not be taken prisoner,' she smiled thinly, 'and neither will you. My lord Mahu, whatever the gods have decided, I do not believe they intend us to die out here.' She edged closer. Around me the mercenaries were already milling about, Djarka ordering the carts to be pulled in closer, an inner circle being formed.

'You are Mahu,' she pressed her fingers against my lips, 'Baboon of the South. You are cunning! Think, my lord!'

I did so, about those savages streaming through the grasslands towards us. I smiled at the thought of their bare feet. I stared at the grass and wondered if I should fire it, but there again, the breeze was fickle, shifting here and there, and could do as much damage as provide protection. The bare feet, however, were a different matter. I prayed to Sekhmet, the Lion-headed Devouress, the Bringer of Destruction and Devastation, then to Horus Who Burns Millions By His Gaze. I crouched down and closed my eyes. For a moment I was back in Thebes with its silver-capped obelisks, gold-corniced temples and sweeping avenues edged with red rock lions or gleaming black sphinxes. I thought of Ankhesenamun in her robes and oiled wig, sitting enthroned on a golden chair in some glorious chamber. I must return there!

I opened my eyes. The grasslands were bending under a stiff breeze, all around me the chatter of the mercenaries, whilst the bushes and trees whispered in the strong wind. The clatter of weapons brought me back to the harsh reality. Out there in the grasslands a legion of demons was pouring towards us, intent on bloody destruction. I gazed up. Against the light blue sky, the vultures, Pharaoh's hens, already sensed blood would be spilled and were now waiting for their moment.

I rose to my feet. I quickly armed and asked my mercenaries to bring as many empty clay pots as they could. I ordered these to be smashed into little sharp fragments and had them scattered between the oasis and the edge of the long grass. We ate and drank, then finished our inner circle of defence, the barricade where we would make our final stand. I moved amongst the men, giving the same message. We were about to be attacked; we could expect no mercy; we must either kill or be killed. We would either march out in triumph or our corpses would be left as a banquet for the vultures. I told them how we had no choice: if we fled, the enemy would catch up and annihilate us. The scribes, too, were brought into my council, the young and old, the strong and weak, they were given no choice: they must arm, and they must fight.

Darkness fell over the grasslands. We tried to distinguish the sound of the real night prowlers from our enemies edging closer. I thought they might come after dark, but they attacked at the grey time, when Red-eyed Horus sleeps and Ra has not finished his journey through the Am-duat. Feathered and painted, clubs raised, those hideous shield-wings giving off sinister, whispering sounds. We'd been alerted by our scout, a young mercenary who'd come dashing in, his sweat-soaked face gleaming in the torchlight. A short while later our assailants appeared. I laughed as I heard the screams as they trod upon the sharp pottery, then they were upon us, climbing over the carts, chariots and other impedimenta. They attacked from every side, so we soon withdrew into the inner ring. They were surprised. They thought we'd be a smouldering wick, a crushed reed. Instead they found us well prepared behind a makeshift circle of shields and barricades.

Our archers loosed feathered shafts, death-bearing arrows streaking through the air. In the first rush we beat them back. I heard the crack of whips as their captains urged them on, and in they came, spears jabbing, clubs whirling, axes falling, a vision of snarling dog faces. Now Mery-re may have been a high priest of this or that, but he was certainly no soldier. Fierce looks do not snuff out feelings of courage or, in my case, the sheer terror which can turn a natural coward into a fighting man. Mery-re's troops, despite their appearance, were mere mercenaries, the scum which drifts around the Great Green selling their spears for a few deben of copper, a handful of grain and a jar of beer. They expected, as such jackals do, an easy killing, only to be met by all the furies of the underworld. We fought like prisoners under sentence of death; even Nabila was armed with a bow.

I was confronted by one of the enemy chieftains, face gleaming with paint, copper rings, bracelets and necklace shimmering in the torchlight. He was a man of *netut-aaïut*, boastful words, his grinning face and thick black hair enclosed by the head and pelt of a jackal. He was armed with a heavy axe and war club, and he drove me back, knocking my curved sword aside, kicking up the sand, trying to blind me. I tripped, rolled and grasped a blazing brand from the fire. I half rose, jabbing this at him, and he moved aside. His hideous shield-wings made him appear like some angel of death spat up from Hell. I don't know what happened next. He parried but missed, and the fire brand caught him on his side, brushing the dried papyrus fringes of the shield. In an instant they caught alight, the flames leaping up, and the man's swift movements only fanned the fire, the flames coursing up as if through a field of stubble. He screamed, forgetting me, scrabbling at the cords that secured the shield, desperate to escape the fiery agony. I leaped forward, snatching my knife from my sweat-soaked waistband, and plunged it deep into his belly, turning the point upwards before pushing him away.

At last the attack broke off, and our assailants fled. We moved amongst the wounded, looking for our own. Two of the old scribes had been grievously wounded and there was nothing our leech could do, so he gave them a cup of mercy, telling them to look away before he slit their throats. As for the enemy, I severed the heads of two prisoners and had their corpses impaled on horn bushes on the edge of the oasis. The rest I stripped of all their possessions; then, forcing them to kneel whatever their condition, I walked along the line of prisoners, club raised, and dashed out their brains. I had their corpses thrown into the long grass, shouting abuse at the enemy hiding only a few yards away. The Vesper Bats moved in again, wings hissing, only this time they broke off their attack just before they emerged from the long grass.

An eerie silence fell, broken by the occasional taunt. I thought about that chieftain, whose blackened corpse had been dragged by its heels and tossed out with the rest. I quickly ordered oilskins to be brought, our carts and chariots to be drenched with their contents. We fell back to our inner ring and waited for the attack. The enemy came late in the afternoon, conch horns wailing, followed by screams and shouts. They climbed the carts, only to slip on the oily barricade. In any other circumstances I would have laughed. As the enemy regrouped, I ordered the archers to loose their fire arrows. Their targets were packed so close we could not miss, the oil which smeared their bodies and stained their armour turning them into flaming human torches.

This time they never reached our barricade. I have served with mercenaries all my life. There is a point to which they'll fight bravely, but when they realise they are going to lose their lives, and therefore any money, they simply melt away. The Vesper Bats, despite their hideous appearance, those awful wings and the crack of their captains' whips, were no different. They melted back into the long grass to regain their courage. I ordered my men to stand down, water to be brought from the wells, food to be distributed, and went to see Nabila. Her face was all flushed, eyes gleaming, and she was chattering like a child to Djarka about how many shafts she had loosed. I watched them curiously and suppressed a pang of jealousy. Nabila glanced up and smiled at me.

117

'Will they return, my lord?' she asked.

'They'll return,' I declared. 'They are like a river: sooner or later they know the obstacle which impedes them will break up. They'll be here, and they will show no mercy, not after the losses they have suffered.'

I expected a fresh attack before nightfall, but it never emerged. I walked to the edge of the oasis, straining my eyes and ears, wishing I could see what was happening. I offered gold, and again a scout climbed the palm tree, a small black figure swaying in the breeze against the darkening blue sky. At first I thought he'd fallen asleep as he just crouched there clinging on for dear life, then he made a gesture indicating that something was happening out in the grasslands, though I could hear no sound. I beckoned the man down. He returned swift and nimble as any monkey, body all bruised and scarred, hands chapped but eyes bright with excitement. A farmer's son from the land of Punt, he jabbered in his own tongue, and I had to slap him round the face before he recollected himself and answered in the lingua franca.

'There's another force,' he whispered. 'My lord, I cannot believe my eyes. Men dressed in white like sand dwellers.' He indicated with his hands. 'Faces hidden. I saw both the enemy and this new army.'

I felt my stomach pitch 'Are they Hittites?'

'No, my lord. They are moving swiftly, as if they know where the Vesper Bats are.'

'Are they coming to help?'

The man shook his head. 'I do not know what is happening, my lord.' He took a stick and squatted down and drew an arc in the dust. 'This is the edge of the oasis,' he explained. He moved the stick and drew a second arc. 'These are the Vesper Bats, and here, my lord,' he moved the stick even further back and formed a third arc, 'are the strangers moving in.'

'They wear no armour?'

'Nothing glints. At first I thought my eyes were playing

118

tricks. All I glimpsed were the white head-dresses. I saw no spears; perhaps they are carrying bows?'

Mystified, I left him and the oasis, going out into the grasslands, wondering what was happening. At last I caught it, a distant scream and yell. I immediately ordered my small force to arms and we fell back to the barricade. We stood, arrows to bows, weapons ready, pots of fire smouldering. I never knew what truly happened. How our mysterious rescuers trapped the Vesper Bats out in the open, driving them forward, bringing them down with feathered shafts or the thrust of a knife or sword. The sound of the battle grew louder and nearer. Occasionally a Vesper Bat, eyes terror-filled, came running in, seeking sanctuary, only to be brought down by one of our arrows. The sound of the conflict drew closer, though fewer and fewer of the enemy appeared. I concluded that the Vesper Bats must have been surrounded, cut off. From the dreadful sounds echoing across the grasslands, the shadows racing out under the setting sun, they were being massacred one by one.

The sun sank in an angry fiery glow. The grasslands shifted as if they had life of their own under a strong breeze which brought the rain clouds closing in. Darkness fell. The hideous screams stopped, followed by silence, broken by the rain, hard and pelting for a few hours. The clouds broke yet still we dared not move, but crouched, tense in anticipation. Eventually a conch horn wailed, and a fire arrow streaked out of the darkness and thudded into one of the palm trees.

'Lord Mahu, Baboon of the South.'

I recognised that voice; how could I forget it, as it once thundered out its hymn, its prayer of praise to the Aten.

'Lord Mahu, Baboon of the South, there is no need for you to fear. Your enemies are dead.'

I stepped over the barricade and walked to the edge of the oasis. They came out from the long grass, ghosts, visitors from the Land of the Dead. The central one was armed with a bow. I wondered if he was Akenhaten.

119

'Who are you?' I called, even though I knew the answer.

'We are the Accursed, the Hidden Ones from the Hall of Shadows,' the voice replied. 'Lord Mahu, tomorrow you must travel on. Move south-west, meet the power of Egypt and tell them to be prepared. As for your enemies, you have no further reason to fear them.' He tossed something which rolled to my feet. I glanced down and picked up the severed head. Even in the poor light I could make out the streaks of war paint, the glitter of the half-opened eyes, the fresh blood on the severed neck. I threw it into a bush, wiping my hands on my gown.

'Why have you come?' I shouted, but they'd gone, like flames into the darkness.

We waited another hour. I asked for volunteers. Of course no one came forward until I offered gold, then three of my mercenaries slipped like hunting dogs into the grass. They came back, eyes bewildered, shaking their heads. In the poor light of the moon they'd come across corpse after corpse of the Vesper Bats, some with their throats cut, others like porcupines, so many feathered shafts were embedded in their flesh. We feasted that night, happy and merry as men are when the harvest is over or the spoils of battle are being distributed.

Once first light had broken, I too went out into the grass-lands. Now, I have visited many battlefields; I have seen corpses piled higher than a man, but there was something eerie about what I discovered that morning. The Vesper Bats had been surrounded, broken up and hunted down one by one. They'd been shown no mercy, their throats cut, their heads severed. On two occasions corpses had been impaled, thrust belly down on to pointed stakes. Only once did we find the corpse of one of our saviours, overlooked by his companions. It sprawled close to the oasis, almost shrouded by the thick grass. One of my men turned it over, pulled the white mask from its face, screamed and ran away, hurtling like a dog back to the oasis to wash his hands. I edged closer: the face beneath the mask was truly hideous, the skin scaly and silvery; the leprosy had already eaten away both nose and upper lip. I gave him honourable burial, taking rocks, stones and dirt from the oasis to cover his corpse. I sprinkled some incense and, extending my hands, prayed to the cooling breath of Amun that this brave warrior's soul would find its way to the Fields of the Blessed.

I returned to the oasis, washed my hands and told Djarka and Nabila what I had found.

'Akenhaten's people,' I whispered. 'Probably sand dwellers, mercenaries or desert wanderers, men who contracted leprosy and were cursed. They came together and lived in that devil's valley we passed through. They must have picked up the trail of the Vesper Bats and followed them here. They showed no mercy. Anyway,' I sighed, 'what we saw this morning, what I have told you, is for no one else's ears. Let's journey, and journey fast.'

We travelled on, the mercenary and his son calling out directions. We turned slightly west, through the river valleys, and descended from the high ground, passing by empty villages, their inhabitants long fled. We soon found the reason why. We breasted a hill and there beneath us stretched the power and glory of Egypt. I could only stare in astonishment. The camp was sprawling, protected by a palisade and narrow ditch. The tents and bothies of the troops, the animal skins which served as covering rippling in the breeze, were organised neatly into squares, dissected by paths. The chariot park, the picket lines and the latrine pits were all distinguishable, as was the cluster of imperial standards.

My mercenaries and scribes, bruised and wounded, shouted for joy. We'd lost at least ten in that hideous fight at the oasis. Some of our younger comrades ran ahead, to be met by scouts, so by the time we reached the camp gate, Horemheb in all his glory and Rameses, his thin, vicious face bright with its usual smirk, were waiting to receive us. You'd think we were old friends. They clapped my back, shook my hand, congratulating me on reaching them. They asked question after question, Rameses, his lower lip caught between sharp white teeth, glancing appreciatively at Nabila. Only when I introduced her as my wife did he look a little shamefaced and glance away. When we were boys in the Kap, chasing the kitchen maids through the palace, we'd taken a solemn oath never to interfere with or entice another's woman.

Both questioned me about what had happened at Suppiliuma's camp. I told them what I wanted them to know – that the Hittites were sheltering Mery-re – as well as expressing my anger that our warship had left and we had been forced to travel over land. Horemheb, his square military face soaked in sweat and oil, just shrugged. He glanced at me, shook his head and turned to Rameses; that viper in human flesh merely grinned, as if enjoying our discomfort.

'It had nothing to do with us,' Rameses hissed, head forward, face a mask of false concern. 'I assure you, my lord Mahu, the war galley was under the direct orders of Lord Ay. You should take your complaint to him.'

'And you?' I asked Horemheb. 'You moved swifter than I thought.'

'I always do.' Horemheb stood back. He did look magnificent in his gold-edged leather breastplate with matching kilt, the field general's blue and gold sash tied tightly round his bulging waist. Of course, being Horemheb, he had had his head shaved completely, and his neck and chest were festooned with the gold collars of bravery and the silver bees of valour. Rameses was dressed no differently. For a short moment I realised how little we change; they were the same in the Kap, glorying in military valour and all the insignia of war, Horemheb always standing forward, Rameses slightly behind him. A man and his demon, a soul and his shade, those two were as inseparable as fingers on one hand. They asked me questions. I replied as evasively as they did to mine. Eventually Horemheb laughed, tiring of the game, and, gesturing me forward, led me into the camp.

It was all well organised: the imperial regiments grouped under their standards, the Horus, the Isis, the Ptah; the mercenaries in all their gaudy finery, watched carefully by Egyptian officers. Horemheb loved all things military and gloried in showing off his management and organisation. I was pleased. It was good to be back in the heart of Egypt. The troops looked well fed, confident and ready for war. They grouped round campfires or sprawled in whatever shade they could find, to share a beer jug and play those games of dice and knucklebones so common to soldiers wherever they go. Of course, the camp followers and the merchants had soon discovered the army, and everything was for sale. Fruit and vegetables from the farms, prostitutes from the towns, tinkers and chapmen; anyone who thought they could make a quick barter had clustered in. A corps of Medjay police moved amongst them, enforcing discipline. We passed the prison stockade where roisterers, those guilty of infringing military discipline, were locked in cages to roast under the sun. Everywhere Horemheb went, heralds would appear, proclaiming him to be the brave warrior, weighty of arm, declaring there was no one like him, that his strength was so much greater than any other general who had ever lived, that he raged like a panther who would tear his enemy to pieces on the battlefield. Oh, Horemheb was in his element, strutting about receiving the applause of his troops.

Only when we entered the imperial enclosure at the centre of the camp, guarded by Nakhtu-aa and Maryannou in their striped blue and gold head-dresses, did Horemheb relax, though I caught his look of worry. He stopped before the altar of Amun-re, a makeshift pile of stones with a slab of wood across the top, on one side the imperial Horus standard, on the other that of Amun-re. In the centre of the altar was a small tabernacle of polished sycamore wood, its doors slightly open. The priest had already laid gifts of bread and wine before it, and incense billowed profusely from pots. Horemheb put his face in his hands, bowed his head and prayed. We were then taken into the imperial tent under red and gold cloths stretched out over tent poles. It smelt fragrantly of acacia and frankincense, dark and cool, reminding me of Suppiliuma's pavilion.

Horemheb led us to the far end where cushions were piled around small wooden tables. Servants came in carrying platters of freshly killed quail, cooked to perfection over a charcoal fire and basted with herb juices. It tasted delicious, as did the bread, soft white and flavoured with honey. Goblets of white wine were thrust into our hands as Horemheb chattered, Rameses beside him, staring across the table at me with Djarka on my left and Nabila to my right.

'What news from Thebes?' I interrupted.

Horemheb shrugged. 'We are now in enemy country,' he declared. 'Our scouts cannot reach us.' He took another deep drink.

Horemheb's face had grown fatter, his paunch more pronounced. I recalled our days in the Kap: when Horemheb was nervous, he always ate and drank to excess. A good general, a man popular with his troops, he had the whole glory of Egypt's army with him, yet he seemed anxious, agitated.

We ate mainly in silence after that. Now and again Horemheb would cock his head slightly to one side and look at me from under his bushy eyebrows. Beside him Rameses ate sparingly. Occasionally his gaze would slide to Nabila, then back to the platter of food before him. Outside echoed the noises of the camp, the neigh of horses, the creak of wheels, the clatter of arms, the shouts and cries; despite the perfume, the camp smells drifted in: sweaty leather, charcoal, burned meat and horse dung. In the far corner of the imperial pavilion a blind harpist thrummed at the strings lacklustrely. Horemheb opened his mouth to speak, but Rameses nudged him and he fell silent. Only when the general's pavilion was cleared of servants, the blind harpist included, did Horemheb seem to take on a new lease of life. He bit deeply into a piece of succulent melon, staring across the table at me aggressively as he used to when we were in the refectory of the Kap.

'Why were you sent to Suppiliuma?'

'You know why: to buy you time, to create a diversion.'

'Well, you didn't,' Rameses intervened.

'How do you know that?' Djarka taunted.

'I took the risk,' I declared. 'I visited the Hittite camp even as you prepared for war. Suppiliuma knew we did not want peace.'

'Do you know who the Watchers are?' Rameses' question cut the air like a whiplash.

'The Watchers?' I shrugged. 'I'm not too sure what you are talking about.' I lowered my hand and brushed Djarka's thigh, a sign he was to remain silent.

'You've been very busy, General.' I bit into my own piece of melon. 'Busy amongst the Apiru, the tribe of Israar, inviting them into the Delta, learning about their traditions. Where did you hear about the Watchers?'

'Here and there,' Rameses smiled, 'here and there. Did you meet him?'

I glanced at Horemheb.

'Mahu, did you meet Akenhaten? Is he still alive?'

'I think so,' I replied, 'and so is Mery-re. He hunted us, hoping we would lead him to Akenhaten.'

'Where *is* Akenhaten?' Rameses asked softly.

'Where is he?' I teased back. 'So you can visit him, Rameses, you and your assassins?'

'He is a threat to Egypt.'

'He is a threat to no one,' I replied. 'General, what are you here for?' I leaned across the table and put my hand over

Rameses'. He didn't withdraw it. 'What are you *really* here
for: to fight Suppiliuma or search for Akenhaten?'

'If necessary, both.'

'But why are you worried?' I withdrew my hand. 'Why is
the Great General of Egypt, the Mighty of War, Pharaoh's
Sword, his Shield, his Bulwark, sitting in a tent staring at
Lord Mahu as if—'

'It's the Hittites,' Horemheb retorted. 'We thought they
were still in the north, in the Amki region; that we'd
advance, choose our ground, bring them to battle and defeat
them.'

'And?'

'Quite honestly, Mahu,' Horemheb replied wearily, 'we
don't know where the Hittites are or what they are doing.
They seem to have disappeared.'

I recalled Akenhaten's warning about the dangers threatening Egypt but I dared not speak for fear Horemheb and
Rameses would become suspicious. After all, how could I,
fleeing through the grasslands of Canaan, know about the
movement of enemy troops? Yet I decided to try my best.

'What? I saw the Hittite army,' I replied. 'They were camped
at Lachish, a sprawling horde, they can't be missed. You have
been misled. Perhaps they've slipped behind you?'

'Nonsense!'

'We've sent our fastest scouts,' Rameses intervened, 'north
to the Vermin Lords, but they too have no knowledge.'

Djarka moved restlessly beside me. Again I put my hand
on his thigh.

'Are you saying that Suppiliuma and his army have simply
vanished? Are you looking in the right place?'

'We are supposed to advance north,' Rameses explained
slowly, 'link up with our Assyrian allies and bring the Hittites
to battle. I have sent merchantmen up the coast, but they
report no Hittite army. I have dispatched scouts and spies to
the Vermin Lords; again, all they can say is that the Hittites

have marched east, but where?' He shook his head. 'They cannot be moving west!'

'And Thebes?' I asked, determined to change the subject so as not to arouse suspicion. 'What news from Thebes?'

'The Divine One,' Horemheb answered slowly, chewing on a piece of melon, 'the Divine One seemed in fine health when I left. He has sent us his good wishes, but since we crossed the Horus Road, there has been nothing.'

I knew then that something was hideously wrong. Horemheb wasn't worried only about the Hittites, but also about what was happening back in Thebes. Our conversation then turned to minor matters. Horemheb and Rameses complimented Nabila and asked about our journey, assuring us that we would be given comfortable quarters, which we were, a splendid pavilion not far from General Horemheb's.

For the first two days we simply rested, moving our possessions, taking account of everything we had. Nabila, pleased not to be travelling, unpacked coffers and caskets, gently bemoaning what we had lost. I opened my treasure chests and searched out my mercenaries and scribes to reward them lavishly. At night we joined Horemheb and Rameses in their tent to feast and recall the old days. Rameses was particularly interested in Mery-re; he laughed when I told him about the Vesper Bats. I had kept the identity of our rescuers in the grasslands secret, telling my mercenaries they were outcasts whom I'd bribed and who had no love for the Vesper Bats. I told the same to the two generals. Yet even as I spoke, I observed both men, those fighting hawks of Egypt, watching their eyes drift to the tent flap as if they were expecting news. They'd grow disappointed and drink more deeply after darkness fell and the possibility of any messages reaching them had receded.

On one thing I had sworn Djarka and Nabila to silence. They were never to mention my meeting with Akenhaten, his help against the Vesper Bats or the startling news that

Tutankhamun was dead. Such information was too dangerous, and I wanted to wait and watch.

Hefau: cobra, snake

Chapter 7

We must have stayed there a week.

I went out to admire the chariot squadrons. I visited the physicians and apothecaries for various creams, potions and powders to mix up for our men, as our own leech had been killed at the oasis. Of course, there was Nabila: I praised her lavishly for her courage and fortitude during our march south.

'You shall be always my precious olive,' I smiled, touching her cheek, 'and my love for you shall be like the ever-green cypress.'

We began to tease each other. I was about to fasten a cornelian necklace around her neck when I heard a shout, a trumpet blaring the alarm. I scrambled out of the tent and hurried down to the gate of the camp. Horemheb was already there, surrounded by his lieutenants; Rameses, slightly ahead of them, was staring down the track at a cloud of dust moving swiftly towards us.

'Is it an attack?' Rameses shouted up at the guard on the makeshift tower.

'Hardly, my lord,' the man shouted back. 'Four or five chariots travelling fast; their horses are wearied.'

The cloud of dust approached, horses emerging; they were indeed dropping with exhaustion. There were five chariots in all, the first one travelling much faster because it carried only two men, the rest containing four or five people each, some of them badly wounded, others hanging on grimly. The chariots stopped and were surrounded by Horemheb's personal guard, their spears lowered. The driver of the first chariot threw his reins down, jumped out, and staggered towards Horemheb, falling on his knees before him.

I shall always remember that occasion, the beginning of the time of the terror, of the world being turned upside down, of night becoming day and day night. All of Egypt was to be stirred and princes were to be cast down from their thrones. Looking back, yes, it all began there with that wounded, tired man, staring up at Horemheb, hands raised in a beseeching gesture. Horemheb grabbed a wet cloth and wiped the dust from the man's face, the mud from his caked lips, and pushed a wineskin to his mouth, urging him to drink. The man did, gulping and coughing, then he went down on all fours and began to speak.

His news was terrible. The Hittites hadn't disappeared. They had marched east, brought the Assyrians to battle and utterly destroyed them. Even worse, Suppiliuma was now heading west, intending to cut across the southern part of Canaan and block Horemheb's return to Egypt. The Great General was beside himself with rage. Forgetting all courtesy, he knocked the leather helmet from the man's head, grabbed him by the hair and, forcing his head back, ordered him to repeat the message. The man did so, eyes begging for mercy. Rameses whispered into Horemheb's ear, and the general let go of the man, walking away to compose himself.

Horemheb eventually summoned a council of officers, sitting himself down before the gate like some ancient king. He ordered the messenger to draw close, allowing him to rest his hands on his knees. He fed him a cup of watered wine while all the hideous details spilled out. How Suppiliuma had moved swiftly, advancing between the great rivers; he had caught the Assyrian army by surprise, attacking it just after dawn, annihilating our Assyrian allies. The officer, an Egyptian, maintained that Lord Ay had sent him to advise and liaise with the Assyrian princes. He explained how he had received the news of the disaster from a spy and barely escaped through the encroaching Hittite lines. Horemheb ignored all this. What he wanted to know was how swiftly Suppiliuma's army was moving. He was shocked by the reply. Even before he attacked the Assyrians, Suppiliuma had detached part of his army under Prince Zananza, sending him as an advance guard to trap the Egyptians in Canaan. This time Horemheb bawled for wine for himself, a deep-bowled cup. He drank greedily, then, throwing the bowl to the ground, tipped his stool over and strode back into the camp, followed by his officers.

A short while later Djarka, Nabila and I were invited to the general's tent. Cushions, coffers and chests had been pushed back into the shadows, and long tables had been laid out, covered with maps and charts. Horemheb squatted, dressed only in a leather kilt, surrounded by his officers, sturdy fingers poking the maps, muttering and whispering amongst themselves. Horemheb looked up as I entered, his swarthy face laced with sweat.

'Tell me, Lord Mahu, bearing in mind your earlier warnings, did you know any of this?'

'Tell me, Lord Mahu, did you know any of this?' I mimicked back. 'Of course I didn't, I just guessed!' I came forward, pushing the officers aside, and knelt opposite him across the table. 'Don't you see what's happening, Great General?' I taunted. 'Suppiliuma is marching swiftly west!'

'We know that!' Rameses snarled. 'He'll try to block our path back into Egypt.'

'Block it?' I retorted. 'Do you think, General Rameses, that the Hittite army will wait for you to return? Think, man!' I gestured. 'You are the defence of Egypt, what other troops are left in the Kingdom of the Two Lands? Some garrisons in

Lower Egypt, and Nakhtimin's army around Thebes.' I enjoyed the surprise in Rameses' face. Horemheb gulped noisily, sitting back on his heels.

'What are you saying, Mahu?' he whispered.

'Great General, Suppiliuma will not wait for you. He is the fox; the hen coops have been left unguarded, the dogs gone a-wandering. The Hittite will be in Avaris and boating down the Nile before you even realise it.' My remarks caused consternation amongst the staff officers, but from Horemheb's face, he knew I had spoken the truth. He sat, fingers to his mouth, chewing on a nail, eyes like black pebbles glaring at me.

'Then what do you advise?' Rameses asked.

'My advice is this: tomorrow morning, as soon as the tents and awnings are dry, break camp and march south, across the Horus Road, back into Egypt. If we move fast enough, we may outstrip Suppiliuma; his chariot squadrons advance more slowly. He's uncertain of the roads and tracks, and, of course, he'll expect resistance from our garrisons in Sinai and at Avaris.' I paused. 'You must return to Egypt' I declared abruptly, determined to convey Akenhaten's warning. 'Forget your dreams of conquest, General, that's for another day.'

Horemheb agreed; after all, he had no choice. An Egyptian army cut off in Canaan whilst the Hittite horde rampaged down the Nile would have ended all his dreams. He rose to his feet and went out to the altars. He sacrificed to the Seven-Faced Seth, to Amun-re, and to any other god he could summon to assist with the dangers confronting him. Towards evening he ordered rations of wine and beer to be distributed, as well as any food that couldn't be kept. Afterwards heralds walked through the camp declaring that, at first light, once the dew had dried, the army would return to Egypt. The news was greeted with a mixed reaction: on the one hand, like troops anywhere, the soldiers were homesick and wanted to leave; on the other, as rumours began to seep through the camp and gossip fanned the flames, the mood of the army changed, its exuberance and confidence giving way to anxiety and confusion. Believe me, the sorcerers and conjurers, the scorpion men and sellers of sacred amulets and scarabs did a roaring trade that night.

Horemheb realised the dangers: one thing you never allow soldiers to do is chatter and gossip. Even before the sun rose, and Horemheb made sacrifice to Ra in the cooling breath of Amun-re, heralds strode through the camp blowing on conch horns whilst officers hurried along the narrow tracks between the tents, loosening ropes, kicking men awake. As dawn broke, the camp became a hive of activity and confusion. Horses were hitched to chariots; donkeys rolled in the dust, braying noisily; trumpets called, drowning the shouts and cries of the officers. We stayed in the imperial enclosure watching the Danga dwarfs, whom Horemheb always kept around him, being loaded into a cart. The Great General took considerable care to ensure this stayed in the centre of the column and was well protected. Horemheb liked his dwarfs; ever since I'd known him, he'd always had these small creatures, with their tousled hair and beards, dancing attendance on him. Strange, he'd married Ay's second daughter Mutnodjmet, who also had her own retinue of dwarfs; no wonder the mutual attraction, they were truly well suited. I had words with Nabila in our tent, enjoying its cool darkness before the heat made itself felt. I embraced her gently, kissing her on the brow, lips and neck.

'Stay in the centre of the column,' I warned. 'This fight is not yours. Stick close to the dwarfs,' I grinned, 'and well away from danger.'

Horemheb waited until the noonday heat had passed, that devil which prowls at midday, that hideous, enervating heat which saps morale, dries the skin and fills the mouth with sand and dirt. Only when the sun began to dip was the order issued, and our column, now well prepared, left, following the twisting road towards Sinai. Djarka and I were made *tedjen*, officers in charge of a chariot squadron on the right flank. Chariots were provided for us, not ornamented with electrum, their javelin and quiver pouches embroidered, but plain battle carts of hardened wood and leather, pulled by small wiry horses, the best Horemheb could provide.

How can I describe our swift retreat through the river valleys of Canaan, aiming like an arrow for the Horus Road across Sinai? Suppiliuma, that crafty jackal, must have known that we might be warned, and had already sent his own representatives to stir up the Vermin Lords, who harassed us during the day with their sand rovers, desert dwellers and other mercenaries, anyone they could hire with Hittite gold. We marched in the late afternoon, our flanks being attacked by bowmen and spearmen, who'd appear from some clump of trees to inflict as much damage as they could before disappearing. Nightfall provided little relief. The coughing bellow of the lion, the roar of the hyaena and the insane song of the jackal were made more terrifying by figures slipping through the darkness armed with sword or dagger to attack our picket lines and horses, hamstringing, injuring, inflicting as much destruction as they could.

The Hittite lords had also sent advance guards to seize the main roads and passes. We brushed these aside; our light chariots were swifter, our men better trained and skilled. Nevertheless, it was one bloody affray after another, squalid, vicious fights at the mouth of some valley, lonely glade or rocky outcrop. The Hittites never used their chariots to try and smash our battle line, that would have been foolish, but their carts were big enough to carry men whom they could deploy for an ambuscade or sudden sortie. Time and again Djarka and I were involved in these hideous mêlées, men clutching at the rails of our chariots trying to drag us out or hamstring our horses. We fought back furiously. In truth, the Hittites knew they'd lost the element of surprise, and underestimated our determination. Speak to any Egyptian – ah yes, I can see the scribe sitting with me nodding in approval: other tribes and nations may wander the face of the earth, but try and prevent an Egyptian from returning to his homeland and that is incentive enough for him to fight. Horemheb's heralds and officers had instructed each unit about what lay ahead. If we were blocked from crossing Sinai into Egypt then what hope did we have? Desperation makes warriors of us all.

The bloody affrays continued until we reached the main routes across Sinai. The Hittites themselves knew what was at stake: if they reached Egypt before us then the Nile and its cities would be open to attack. Not even Ay and his brother Nakhtimin, for all their cunning, could offer stout resistance to such an invasion. Yet, at the time, that truly puzzled me – hadn't Ay and Nakhtimin realised that too?

In the end we broke through; we were ruthless, devoid of mercy or compassion. No prisoners were taken: those captured were immediately impaled on sharpened stakes as a warning to the rest. The enemy wounded had their throats cut and were left as fodder for the hyaenas and lions. Soon we were into Sinai, with its blistering rocks, its sand dunes rolling like a savage sea under a relentless sun. Here Horemheb displayed his true genius, his ability to organise, manage and lead men; above all, he kept his nerve. A few chariot squadrons were left to defend our rear, but now the Egyptian army came into its own. We were marching across land which was ours, armed with accurate charts and maps which showed the various oases and their deep-dug wells, constructed by earlier Pharaohs and overlooked by granite stelae boasting about the exploits of their founders. The greatest casualties were due to burns and sunstroke. For this Horemheb offered incense and wine to Amun and to Horus of Henes, the god of his own native town in the Delta. Djarka and I were of more practical help, using resin, weathered pancake, carob beans and bitter apples mixed together and boiled as salve for wounds, binding them with leaves of castor oil and, when these ran out, linen strips. I was surprised at how few leeches, apothecaries and physicians had accompanied the army. When I asked Horemheb the reason for this, he just shrugged, spat and said that God's Father Ay had promised him a medical corps but this had never materialised so he had left Egypt without it.

Now that we were safely back, heading like a spear towards To-Mery, Horemheb and Rameses were already planning and plotting. I was too tired and confused to reason what had happened and why; that would have to wait until safer times. At last we emerged from Sinai, a long but tightly organised column of men, horses, chariots, carts and sumpter ponies, shadowed by a great moving cloud of dust as if the gods themselves had come down to protect us. We had sustained casualties, injuries, wounds, but the horses were in good heart and our courage quickened as we followed the gravel-shaled track towards the city of Avaris. Lightly armed scouts were dispatched to the rear of our column to recall the chariot squadrons which served as our shield; these returned and informed Horemheb that the enemy was still following but not so swiftly.

One evening, when the stars hung heavy and the desert winds wafted in fresher smells than those of the Redlands, Horemheb invited me and his senior staff officers to a feast of freshly killed gazelle and quail meat in his pavilion. He dispensed with his servants except for a Danga dwarf crouching on either side of his cross-legged camp chair. He summoned us up one by one, filling our goblets with special wine, thanking us and thrusting into our hands a small silver brooch, shaped in the likeness of a falcon and studded with precious stones. Rameses went first and took up the position of honour behind the Great General's chair. I was last, but Horemheb intended no offence; he gestured me to stand a little to his right before clambering to his feet and raising his cup.

'Gentlemen,' he declared, 'our scouts have returned. The enemy are in retreat; they've withdrawn into Canaan.'

'Do we pursue?' an officer asked; his question was greeted with good-natured laughter.

'No,' Horemheb retorted, 'but we are only two days from the Delta, gentlemen, and have you noticed something?' He brushed the sweat from his cheek with the edge of his fly whisk. 'Nothing!' The smile faded from his face. 'No messengers to greet us! No supply columns; even more surprising, have you noticed, no merchants, no travellers?'

I gazed around at the ring of surprised faces. They were like me, dusty and very tired, too exhausted to reflect, yet Horemheb was correct: the approaches to Avaris lay suspiciously silent.

'Which means,' Horemheb spoke all our thoughts, 'Egypt's borders have been sealed.'

I was glad I was standing in the shadows where no one could read my face, for I suspected the reason.

The following morning we continued our march on to the green plains of the Delta. Oh, it was so beautiful to be approaching the Black Lands beneath a blue sky where swallows, sparrows, quail and geese flew above acacia, palms, sycamore and holm oak; to feel the coolness of the grass and the fresh tang of the great rivulets. Our pleasure was soon cut short by a scout hurrying back to inform us that the great crossroads ahead were blocked by squadrons of imperial chariotry, a wall of bronze between us and Avaris. Horemheb immediately deployed in battle formation, lining his chariots in serried ranks, archers to the front, spearmen placed between the squadrons as well as protecting the rear. The imperial standards and regimental insignia were uncovered and our battle line cautiously advanced, squeezing on to the broad thoroughfare, the great avenue which snaked through to Avaris.

We had hardly moved three miles when a cloud of dust

appeared and a squadron of chariots emerged under the insignia of Khonsu, the son of Amun-re: the emblem of General Nakhtimin. This crack corps of gleaming chariots and plump swift horses hurtled down towards us, stopping and fanning out in a long, threatening line about the space of two bow shots from our line. This stood, an ominous, gleaming wall, no sound except for the creak of harness and wheel, the horses clattering nervously, impatient to charge. Horemheb grasped the reins of his chariot, telling the driver to stand down, and shouted at me to accompany him. I climbed in beside him.

'In the name of all that's holy,' he whispered, 'what is happening? Why is Nakhtimin here?'

'I don't know,' I lied, 'and if I were you, General, I would go no further.'

I was about to continue when two priests emerged from the opposing line of chariots. They were dressed in white gauffered robes, panther skins draped around their shoulders. They walked slowly towards us, preceded by acolytes carrying bowls of smoking incense and jars of milk and wine, which they used to bless the ground before them, the usual insignia heralds carried when they wished to mediate between two armies. I recognised the taller of the two priests as Anen, Divine Father Ay's kinsman, a high priest of the temple of Amun-re. He now lifted the olive branch he'd kept concealed by his side, stretching out his right hand, a temple sistrum in the other which rattled ominously. He stopped a few paces before Horemheb's chariot and bowed.

'Great lord,' his voice carried, 'I bear messages from General Nakhtimin. He must talk to you.'

'He seems to want to fight with me,' Horemheb bellowed back. 'What is happening?'

'He wishes to talk.'

Anen's face, dried and lined like a desiccated olive, remained impassive, but his voice clearly betrayed his nervousness. Perhaps the Land of Ghosts is never far from us; the dead do not just look on but touch our hearts and can send our blood racing. That was a day of night, a curtain which finally dissected one part of my life, and the history of Egypt, from the rest. I recall it so vividly, the glory of Egypt divided. War chariots of the imperial squadrons ready to charge and crash against each other in the dusty, bloody din of battle, a portent of things to come. I sensed the danger, the sinister threat. I stood next to Horemheb in that creaking chariot, the wheels grating as they moved backwards and forwards, the horses' nostrils flared, plumed head-dresses nodding in the breeze, hoofs scraping the ground. The animals sensed the danger and were eager to escape from it by breaking into a savage charge. It was a cool day, the green of the Delta stretching out before us beneath a blue sky, the day's heat tempered by the wetness of the earth. Yet that day concealed secret terrors, something sinister, all conveyed by that middle-aged, hard-eyed priest, standing without any weapons, the symbols of peace in his hands.

'Speak to Nakhtimin,' I urged. 'Here, between the armies.'

Horemheb needed no second urging. He dropped his fly whisk and drew his sword, pointing to a stretch of lush meadow-land on a slight rise above the rivulets shaded by outstretched date and palm trees.

'Tell my lord Nakhtimin,' he shouted, 'to set up his pavilion there. He may serve us food. He is to bring only two companions, as I will.'

Anen bowed and withdrew. Horemheb dismounted. We stood under the shade of an acacia tree while the preparations were completed.

'You are to come with me, Mahu,' Horemheb grunted. 'You are Children of the Kap, you and Rameses.'

A short while later we took our seats on cushions in the pink pavilion Nakhtimin's men had erected. Before us on a small table of sycamore were palm-leaf platters heaped high with melokhia, lamb mixed with onions, garlic and pepper. It smelt delicious, whilst the wine of Canaan, bubbling invitingly in earthenware goblets, was almost irresistible. We came armed, as did Nakhtimin. He lifted up the far tent flap and swaggered in, accompanied by Anen and a staff officer I did not recognise, a soft-faced, dreamy-eyed young man with girlish features and effeminate ways. I recalled the stories about Nakhtimin's preference for male lovers. Both soldiers were dressed in full battle armour, gleaming ornamented breastplates and leather-striped kilts over white tunics, marching boots on their feet, their necks, arms and wrists gleaming with jewellery. They ostentatiously took off their swords and placed these on the ground beside them as Anen lowered the olive branch. Nakhtimin carried a pair of blood-red gloves, the sign of Pharaoh's personal favour; these he dropped in his lap, a blatant symbol of his own power and importance. He nodded imperceptibly at Horemheb, totally ignored Rameses, but turned and winked at me, his face breaking into a smile.

A wolf of a man, Nakhtimin! Sharp-featured, with the coldest eyes I have ever looked into. Ay's younger brother, Nakhtimin adored the Divine Father's very shadow. On that day, at the Oasis of the Sycamores, he was very much the soldier, garbed in all the regalia of a commander-in-chief. Horemheb noticed this and tensed. Rameses hissed like the cobra he was. I lifted the cup to toast Nakhtimin, but Horemheb caught my hand.

'Change,' he declared, gesturing at our tables. 'You eat what we were to eat; drink what we were to drink.'

Nakhtimin shrugged and whispered to his staff officer, who hastily complied. Only then did Horemheb, without waiting for any of the courtesies or for Anen to intone some boring prayer, shuffle closer to the table and eat hungrily and noisily, slurping from his cup, an open insult to Nakhtimin, who replied in kind. When he had finished, Horemheb leaned back, belching noisily.

'How is my lovely wife?' he asked, not waiting for Nakhtimin to finish his own food.

'The Lady Mutnodjmet is in good health,' Nakhtimin retorted, his mouth spluttering food. 'As are her dwarfs.' The staff officer immediately lowered his head and sniggered to himself.

'And Thebes the Victorious?'

'The city lies quiet; I have had little to do.' The false smile disappeared from Nakhtimin's face. 'Now all the caracals are dead.'

Horemheb twitched. Rameses coughed on something he'd eaten.

I wondered then what Nakhtimin was referring to. The reddish-brown caracal cat, with its short tail and tufted ears, was hardly the quarry for such a great man as himself.

'And the Divine One?' Horemheb asked.

'He, Blessed of the Two Lands, is why we are here.' Nakhtimin's words came out like a cat's purr, a soft but threatening reply, a sign of the impending storm. He turned to Anen. 'Make the proclamation.'

'In the eighth year of his reign,' the high priest intoned, eyes closed, 'in the third month of Akhet, in spite of all the knowledge of physicians, sorcerers and magicians, the God entered into his Double Horizon; King Tutankhamun soared into the sky. He has taken the likeness of the Sun Disc and the limbs of the God are absorbed by him who created them. The palace fell silent, hearts were in mourning, the Double Great Doors were sealed. The courtiers remained lost in their grief, their sorrow went throughout the city and along the great river. Pharaoh Tutankhamun,' Anen opened his eyes, 'has died.'

'Dead!' Horemheb and Rameses gasped in horror. Both men recollected themselves, and immediately took off their collars, sprinkling the dregs of their wine on the ground. They bowed down, scooping up handfuls of dirty sand, and sprinkled these over their own heads. I sat like a man taken down to the Land of Shadows, gripped by the silent horrors of the underworld. Out in the Valley of Death that cowled shadow had told me the same, but I had not really believed him. I'd hoped it was rumour. Now it was truth. My heart was seized by unnamed terrors, my eyes desperate to look once more on that sweet, youthful face, those eyes gentle as a doe's, his touch like the wings of a dove, the voice lilting and clear. Never again! Now I knew what those shadows in the valley near the Dead Sea had been referring to. Akenhaten's son was truly dead. He had gone into the Far West, to sleep in the long, evergreen grass of the Fields of Yalou. I would never see him again, never hold him; never watch him play, never sit and listen to him or be called Uncle Mahu.

Nakhtimin was talking; his voice was distant, hollow and incomprehensible. I heard the words 'fit' and 'fever'. He was describing a sudden illness which no physician or exorcist could prevent; the burial, the days of mourning. Such words caught my heart. If the seventy days of mourning were over, then Tutankhamun must have died at least three months ago. I tried to shake off my feeling of cold dread. Rameses had risen to a half-crouch, shouting across the table, demanding why he and Horemheb had not been informed by the fastest courier. I knocked my table aside, shouting for silence. The staff officer's hand fell to the hilt of his dagger. I yelled threats at him; the clamour subsided.

'Who has the regency?' I asked. 'Who supervises the Great House?'

'Why, Pharaoh does.' Nakhtimin's reply created an uneasy silence.

'And who is Pharaoh?' Horemheb's voice was harsh, strangulated.

'Why, the Chosen One of Horus, the Fitting of Forms, the Beloved of the Gods,' Nakhtimin chanted back. 'Divine Father Ay has assumed the flail and the rod, on his shoulders hang the *nemes*, his feet are shod with God's slippers, his head wears the double crown of Egypt, his brow protected by the lunging *uraeus*. He is—'

'No!' Horemheb knocked his table over and lunged at Nakhtimin. I threw myself in between them. The staff officer sprang to his feet, drawing his dagger. With one hand on Horemheb's chest, the other extended in the sign of peace, I screamed for calm. Rameses had the sense to help me, and we pulled Horemheb back, the Great General's chest heaving, his face saturated, mouth uttering wordless curses. Nakhtimin took his seat on the cushions as Anen handed across a silver-chased box. I knew what it contained: the Divine Cartouche of Egypt, Pharaoh's personal seal. Nakhtimin opened the little casket, whispered a prayer, took out the cartouche, kissed it and offered it for us to do likewise. To accept would mean we were loyal to Pharaoh; to refuse would mean civil war.

'We must withdraw,' I gasped. 'My lord Nakhtimin, so much has happened.'

'You may withdraw,' Nakhtimin agreed, 'but if you retreat it will be war, if you advance, war, if you stay still, war. Peace,' he lifted the cartouche in both hands, 'will only come if you accept this.'

We left that pavilion, or rather scrambled from it in a most undignified way. Horemheb was shaking with fury, not helped by Nakhtimin's subdued laughter and the giggling of his staff officer. Rameses and I, taking Horemheb by the shoulders and arm, led him back across to the shade of the acacia tree, forcing him to sit down. Staff officers, curious, drifted towards us. Rameses shouted at them to keep their distance, bellowing at a servant to bring wine as quickly as possible. We spent the rest of the day, late into the evening, beneath that acacia tree. I kindled a fire, Rameses brought food, bread and dried meat. At first it seemed that the Great General was going to drink himself into a drunken stupor, but that was Horemheb: fury first, followed by an icy calmness. He squatted, chewing his food, eyes half closed; now and again he lifted his head to stare across at that gorgeous pavilion.

'What has happened?' He took off his armour and, using a bowl of water, cleansed the dirty sand off his hands and face. 'Tutankhamun has gone into the Far West, the Divine One has left us. I will grieve for him, as you will, Mahu, as we all will, but that is not the problem.'

'The problem,' I replied, 'is that Divine's God's Father Ay is now Pharaoh of Egypt. He must have been accepted by the Royal Circle, by the temple priests, Nakhtimin's troops and the Medjay. For us not to accept him will mean civil war! We have to plot. Now is not the time for brave words and dramatic flourishes of the sword.'

We all agreed. Under the shade of those trees, with the shadows lengthening around us, we three hyaenas twisted and turned as we tried to follow the mongoose mind of Pharaoh Ay. Rameses left Horemheb sucking his teeth, a common gesture when the general was agitated, to issue orders to the rest of the army. Horemheb became lost in his broodings and mutterings. I was so tired I just lay down on the cool grass and slept. Djarka aroused me when the sun was setting. Rameses had returned with servants to screen those trees where we sat with coloured cloths stretched out over poles. Other servants laid out wooden platters heaped with strips of grilled goose and onions.

'Rameses has told me,' Djarka whispered, his face lined and drawn, 'how Pharaoh has truly gone into the Far West, and what happened afterwards.' He shook his head. 'I have told no one else.'

I rubbed my own face and cleared the sleep from my eyes. Images came and went; glimpses like you have in battle when you see a man's face, then another. Memories, like sparks of fire, coursed through my soul: Tutankhamun sitting on his stool by his pool of purity and laughing at the ducks; Ankhesenamun beside him, one hand on his thigh, those beautiful sloe eyes glancing over her shoulder at me; Lord Ay with his narrow, handsome, patrician face, his hooded eyes, those lips which could turn into a snarl or be ever so smiling and charming.

'Let us decide swiftly.' Horemheb drained his wine cup and held it up to be refilled. Rameses ignored it. 'This is the situation.' Horemheb cradled his empty cup. 'You, my lord Mahu, were sent to negotiate peace, I was dispatched to prosecute war whilst Lord Ay stayed at home and pursued his own path.' Horemheb breathed out noisily. 'He doesn't deserve the Double Crown.'

'Who else has a right?' Djarka smirked. 'You, General?'

Horemheb wagged a finger. 'You were asked to join your master,' he said through clenched teeth, 'because Lord Mahu would not speak without you being present, but watch your tongue! I have no right to the throne,' he continued, 'but neither does Ay; he is not of the Tuthmosid line.'

'He is grandfather to Ankhesenamun,' Djarka remarked, unabashed by Horemheb's hostility.

'And I,' the Great General replied, his voice rich with sarcasm, 'am the Lord Ay's son-in-law!'

'You could marry Ankhesenamun!' Rameses uttered those words in that lonely place, with the insects swirling in the grass, the sky turning blood-red, the vultures, like birds of omen, floating above us. Rameses had put his finger on the knot of the problem: Egypt had no true Pharaoh. Tutankhamun had left no heir. Lord Ay had once remarked how, in such circumstances, the Double Crown of Egypt would go to the strongest. He had succeeded, but would he keep it?'

'So you do dream dreams of empire?' I smiled. 'The Great Horemheb! Do you see yourself carrying the flail and the rod, ruler of the Two Lands?'

'Dynasties come and go.' Horemheb smiled thinly. 'After all, what was Ahmose, the founder of the Tuthmosids? Nothing more than a successful general.'

'More a lucky one!' Djarka snapped.

'So there you have it!' Horemheb smiled dazzlingly at me.

'The crown of Egypt is in the marketplace and who will wear it?' I gestured round. 'And, I suppose, General, how I reply will decide whether my friend and I leave this place alive.'

'It is the time of settling,' Rameses declared, 'of choosing sides, of taking oaths, of standing in the truth.' He glanced sharply at Djarka, who snorted with laughter.

'A time of truth?' my companion scoffed. 'Why should we trust you, Rameses? What plans do you have for my people; why are you gathering them in the Delta? You are no friend . . .'

'A time of truth,' Rameses had lost his cynical look. 'Is it not, Mahu, a time for us to exchange secrets? But first, are you with us or not?'

I gazed at these two warriors: Horemheb, with his square peasant face, his stubborn chin, his balding head shiny with oil and sweat, still obviously shocked by the news; next to him Rameses, with his lean, sinister features and watchful eyes, his lips nothing more than bloodless lines. I had to choose, the lesser of two evils. Ay could, would, never be trusted.

'It depends,' I prevaricated. 'It depends on what you intend.'

'It is not what we intend,' Rameses declared, 'but what has already happened. If we discover that Tutankhamun was murdered, that Ay deliberately dismissed us from Egypt so that he could remove Pharaoh from life, then it will be war, and war to the death.'

'And if not?' Djarka asked.

'Then, once again, it is the time of waiting.' Rameses shrugged. 'We shall see what the fates bring, but you must choose. Just because Ay has usurped the crown does not mean we have to fall on our faces before him. We are not just talking about the present, but the future. Are you with us, or are you not?'

Heftchet: the eternal cobra or snake

Chapter 8

What choice did I have, sitting in that lonely oasis, surrounded by Horemheb's troops, cut off from Egypt, not knowing what had truly happened there or what the future might bring? That is how Mahu, Baboon of the South, has survived over the years: by making the right choice, at the right time, in the right place. I stretched out my hand; Horemheb, followed by Rameses, clasped it, as they did Djarka's.

'Fine.' Rameses sighed deeply and glanced at Horemheb, who nodded. 'I've been talking to your mercenaries.' Rameses chewed his lower lip. 'I understand the scribe Huaneru was sent by Lord Ay to Tyre. Do you know the reason why?'

I shook my head.

'He carried a great deal of gold. Where is that now?' Rameses asked, all innocent.

'At the bottom of the Great Green,' Horemheb scoffed. 'He was carrying gold, Lord Mahu, to bribe the Vermin Lords to have you murdered.'

'Who told you that?' I tried to shake off the fear tingling my skin. I thought of Nabila's beautiful face; was she party to what this precious pair knew? 'Who told you?' I repeated.

'Spies in Thebes.'

'Which spies?

'I don't know. I truly don't,' Rameses replied. 'He, or she, simply calls themself the Oracle. The Oracle informed us that some of your mercenaries may have been suborned.'

'I believe they were,' I interrupted. 'One tried to poison us.'

'Don't take offence.' Horemheb smirked. 'The same happened to us. Two cooks, undoubtedly in the pay of Lord Ay, tried to poison dishes meant for me. We impaled them on thorn bushes. After listening to their screams for a day I had the bushes soaked in oil and set alight.'

'If the Oracle told you all this, why didn't you warn us?'

'We didn't know where you were,' Rameses replied, 'and we had no evidence, no firm proof. We've been waiting for fresh news from him,' he smiled. 'or her.'

'Ay certainly sent me into Canaan,' I replied, 'to negotiate with Suppiliuma; perhaps also to show the Vermin Lords that Egypt still has a presence in their land. I also suspect he needs to know if Akenhaten is still alive. If he is, he would probably reveal himself to me, and that's what Ay wanted.'

'And did he?' Horemheb asked.

'What do you think?' I teased back.

'If Akenhaten is still alive,' Rameses jabbed a finger in my direction, 'if I could find him, I would kill him. You know that, Mahu. Alive or dead, Akenhaten is still a great threat to the peace and security of Egypt, a matter we shall come to by and by.'

'So,' I peered up through the dusk, 'Ay hurries me out of Egypt and plans to murder me; he gets you out of Egypt and tries to kill you.' I breathed out. 'Only Amun-re himself knows the fate of Maya, Huy and the remaining Children of the Kap.'

'And Pentju?' Rameses declared. 'Don't let us forget Pentju, though he is such a lover of wine, so inebriated, he scarce knows his left hand from his right.'

'Pentju the physician is my friend,' I snapped. 'He'll hold the key to all this.'

'Which is?'

'Were we all sent out of Egypt so Ay could kill

Tutankhamun and usurp his throne? Tutankhamun left no sons. I heard a rumour that Ankhesenamun was pregnant, but her child must have been stillborn or died shortly afterwards.' I shrugged. 'Otherwise Ay would not be Pharaoh.'

'Was the child Tutankhamun's?' Horemheb asked. 'Or Lord Ay's? Rumour has it he slept with his own daughter, Nefertiti. Did he wish to continue his line and, when that failed, he murdered Pharaoh?'

'Impossible!' Djarka murmured. 'Pharaoh's flesh is sacred: if he lifted his hand against Pharaoh, Ay would be guilty of the most horrid blasphemy. If others knew that, they would not support him.'

'It's what he now intends that matters.' Horemheb intoned the words as if singing a hymn. 'Mahu, Baboon of the South, we have told you about the Oracle, though,' he lifted his hand as if about to take an oath, 'the Oracle told us nothing about Pharaoh's sickness and death.'

'Pentju will know the truth,' I said. 'Despite his drunkenness, he will speak honestly. You,' I gestured at Rameses, 'you talk about a time of truth, but you still haven't answered Djarka's question. Why are you so interested in the people of the Apiru, the tribe of Israar?'

'To speak bluntly, Mahu, because Akenhaten drew his heresy from the Apiru, his belief in the Aten. He turned the gods of Egypt on their heads, closed their temples, nearly destroyed Thebes and almost lost an empire. Can you blame me, or General Horemheb, if we have, how can I put it, a lack of trust in such people? I've heard about their legends despite your attempts to hinder me. How one day the tribe of Apiru, the clan of Israar, will produce a Messiah, a great leader, who will gather all the Apiru up and lead them out of Egypt into Canaan. No Egyptian soldier, no true subject of Pharaoh, can allow that to happen, which is why Akenhaten is still dangerous. I mean no offence,' he glanced sharply at Djarka, 'but until proven otherwise, your people in my eyes are suspect. I have heard,' Rameses continued, glancing at me out of the corner of his eye, 'that before Akenhaten mysteriously disappeared, he entrusted certain writings to people he called the Watchers. I ask you again. Do you know of these writings, Lord Mahu, or of the Watchers?'

'No,' I lied, 'but if I did,' I caught that shift in his eyes, 'I would share it with you. However,' I was determined to reassure these men, 'what use are such secrets now? Tutankhamun and Akenhaten are gone. True, Akenhaten did come from the tribe of Apiru: his mother, Great Queen Tiye, was of their blood. She raised her son on the visions of her people; he didn't need much urging. Because of his appearance, Akenhaten was rejected by the temple priests, who advised his father to have him drowned immediately after birth. Queen Tiye, however, pleaded successfully for the child's life. The rest,' I sighed, 'you know. As you put it, General Rameses, the world was turned on its head. Egypt was shaken to its very foundations. Temples were shattered, sanctuaries violated, but now Akenhaten has gone,' I continued hurriedly, 'into the West, he shall not return. What worries me is not Akenhaten or Tutankhamun, but the Lord Ay. Now, Akenhaten was married to Ay's daughter Nefertiti. She produced six daughters, one of whom, Ankhesenamun, survives. However, Akenhaten had a second wife, the Mitanni Princess Khiya. Thanks to Pentju's help, Khiya's womb was cleared of the poisons and potions which Nefertiti had fed her to keep it closed. Khiya conceived; Tutankhamun was her child. What Ay did not know is that Khiya and Pentju also had a relationship. Khiya became pregnant with a second child.'

'What?' Horemheb dropped his empty wine cup, which smashed on the ground. Rameses just sat shaking his head.

'This child,' I continued, 'was smuggled out of the City of the Aten by a Mitanni nobleman and his wife and taken back to their country. Lord Ay later heard of this. He had the young man tracked down and brought back to Egypt, where he died. Ay took an oath that it was due to natural causes; Pentju

154

always suspected that Ay had him murdered. His body lies somewhere out in the Valley of the Kings. What I'm saying,' I held my hand up for silence, 'is did Ay always have a blood feud against Tutankhamun? Did he see him as the reason for his own daughter's downfall, because, as you know, Nefertiti refused to accept Khiya and tried desperately to kill the young Prince Tutankhamun.'

'And you're saying the blood feud continued?' Horemheb asked slowly. 'That Tutankhamun's death, in Ay's mind, was justly merited?'

'It's possible,' Rameses murmured.

'Lord Rameses, let me speak your thoughts for you,' I declared. 'Did Ay see Tutankhamun as a usurper? If Khiya could carry one child of Pentju, why not another? What proof do we have that Tutankhamun was of Akenhaten's flesh? Did Ay,' I continued hurriedly, 'decide to kill him and so dispatched us all out of Egypt? Which brings me to why I shook your hand, General Horemheb. I want to live. I want to survive. I am not interested in the parentage of Tutankhamun, but in the young man himself.' I kept the tremor from my voice. 'I loved him as a son, I gave my word that I would protect him. If his blood is on Ay's hands, Ay's blood will be on mine.'

'If he survives,' Horemheb grated.

'What do you mean?'

'If Ay tried to kill me,' Horemheb smirked, 'I also tried to kill him. There will never be peace between us. He knows that. You've heard General Nakhtimin talk about the Caracals he's been hunting: they weren't the four-legged variety, the wild cat which lurks in the desert rocks. These Caracals were a guild of assassins in Memphis, the White Walled City, my garrison town. They were very skilled former soldiers, a good dozen in number. I hired them to kill Ay.'

I stared coolly back even as suspicion pricked my mind. Had Lord Ay sent that scribe to turn the Vermin Lords against me? Or was it General Horemheb? And the same for that poisoner: what proof did I really have for who was truly responsible? I felt as if I was being carried by the flow of some unseen river. The most important thing was to keep my head above the chaos and survive. I had to return to Egypt.

'Lord Nakhtimin said the Caracals were all dead,' Djarka observed.

'I doubt it.' Rameses shook his head. 'The Caracals move in two packs, not one. Nakhtimin killed one group, so he believes the problem is resolved.' He squinted up at the stars. 'The remaining Caracals might still be in Thebes; they could still carry out our orders.'

'That is how it's going to be, isn't it?' I murmured. 'We're turning on each other; it will be war.'

'Oh yes.' Horemheb smiled. 'This will end in blood.' He rose swiftly to his feet. 'But come, gentlemen, we have no choice. Let's sleep tonight and tomorrow we'll kiss Nakhtimin's arse!'

We met Nakhtimin just before dawn, when the sky was seared with pink and the Breath of Amun ruffled the palms and whispered amongst the bushes. Horemheb would have choked on the words, so Rameses spoke for all of us. We accepted Lord Ay as the Living Incarnation of Horus, Lord of the Two Lands, Wielder of the Flail and Rod, Owner of the Great House. We kissed the hieroglyphs on the cartouche so like those of Tutankhamun. The sun rose; we sprinkled water and wine and burned sacred incense to Lord Ra, emerging from his nightly journey through the underworld. I always loved such moments, even though I believed in nothing, hoped for nothing, looked for nothing. Afterwards we sat and shared a dish of fish, white and firm-fleshed, under a cousbariea sauce, and we all drank from the same jug of white wine. Nakhtimin was polite, tactful but cold. He made it very clear. Horemheb's troops would return to their garrisons around Memphis whilst we would be allowed to continue south with a retinue each but no troops. We agreed. Horemheb grew puce-faced, clenching and unclenching his fists, but Rameses had the measure of his friend and persuaded him to keep quiet.

The meeting broke up, Nakhtimin's troops drew apart and we continued our march into the Delta. I returned to my own men. They were pleased to be going home, but of the mercenary and his son there was no sign. They'd fled like ghosts out into the desert of Sinai. Nabila, however, was delighted to be back in Egypt, excited at the prospect of returning to Thebes. I rejoiced at the happiness in her beautiful face and felt guilty about my earlier suspicions. Nabila was pure of heart; she was to be trusted. It wasn't her past which concerned me, but the future.

Horemheb and Rameses immediately went into council with their own officers. Horemheb informed them how we three had accepted Ay as Pharaoh, but that if anything happened to either himself or Rameses while they were in Thebes, or if they were summoned, they were to march south immediately. Heralds and trumpeters spread the news through the camp: that Tutankhamun had joined his father in the Far West and that Ay was the new Pharaoh. The troops accepted this news reluctantly. Even the common soldiers realised the throne of Egypt was up for grabs, and that their master Horemheb was as wise and as strong as any other contender for it.

We finished our preparations outside Avaris. Nakhtimin, true to his word, had a galley prepared for us, *The Joy of Hathor*, a warship with a long hull: it had a projecting ram from the bows and a raised stern which curved outwards, surmounted by the huge head of a sacred falcon, gilded and polished. We left just before dawn, the rowers chanting their song:

> *My beauty's arms are soft and tender,*
> *They draw me into her secret garden.*
> *My beauty's arms are golden cords.*
> *They bind me . . .*

Djarka and I, sitting outside the gorgeously decorated cabin, joined in so lustily even Horemheb and Rameses could not resist. We sang as we used to in our small choir of the Kap. The captain rattled out orders and the *Hathor* reached midstream, her great blue and white sail unfolding to the creak of ropes. The warship turned to catch the wind, and so we began our journey.

Nakhtimin, of course, joined us. Our relationship was formal but friendly. He knew that we had no choice but to accept his terms for the time being; the future was another matter. Nevertheless, it was glorious to be back in Egypt. The Inundation had just finished and the cool breeze made for delightful sailing. Ay must have been relieved, for the flooding was full and strong, deepening the rich black earth, soaking the ground, turning the fields either side of the Nile a delicious fresh green. The villages and towns we passed were busy and contented, their quaysides lined with barges, skiffs, grain boats and merchant craft stuffed to the rails with trade goods for Egypt: wood, resin, gum, ivory, skins, fruits and cereals. The Nile had broken its banks, pouring into the adjoining broad, low basins and canals so its freshness reached the very edge of the Redlands, where peasants, small black figures against an arching blue sky, pushed the thick mud as far as they could to extend their fields before sowing. Cows, sheep and goats stood in this fragrant freshness, lapping at the water, searching for succulent fresh shoots and roots, disturbing all kinds of birds which clustered to prod at the silt. Cranes and herons were plentiful; their harsh cries as they scattered evoked memories of my youth, when Aunt Isithia, that terrible woman, would take me down to the Nile to wait for the white ibis to arrive.

Our journey was serene, disturbed now and again by a child, or a peasant riding a cow at the river's edge. They'd shout and scream as they glimpsed the majestic might of *The Joy of Hathor*. The river surface bobbed with the bloated carcasses of animals caught by the flood; vultures circled and swooped around these,

only to be disturbed by the ever-present menace of the croco-
diles who nosed in, drawn by easy plunder and fresh food. Such
scenes were a welcome relief from the horrors of the desert.

When I wasn't with Djarka, Horemheb or Rameses, I would
stand by the rail, one hand clutching the polished wood, the
other arm around Nabila, listening to her memories of her childhood in Thebes. It was a time of peace, of gentle recall, before
we plunged into the morass of intrigue and treachery at Thebes.
I informed Nabila exactly what dangers faced us and what
choices we had to make. She, Djarka and myself made a pact
with Horemheb and Rameses that we would not discuss what
had happened or what was to be done. *The Joy of Hathor*, with
its crew and river scribes, was an imperial warship where spies
might cluster as thick as flies on a drop of honey. Instead we
relaxed. It was a time of reflection. Horemheb was solemn and
withdrawn; despite his peasant face, his brain was probing
which road to take, what chances could be risked. He tried to
hide his shame at not achieving a great victory in Canaan, so
his cruel-faced shadow kept whispering a litany of his past
achievements and what glories the future held.

The river grew busier as flotillas of grain barges floated down
to Thebes and its imperial granaries, the Houses of Eternal
Plenty. Eventually we rounded the bend of Dendera and were
joined by an escort of imperial barges manned by Nakhtimin's
troops. One more night on the Nile, then, as dawn broke and
we cleared the reed mattresses from the deck, the lookout
standing high in the mast shouted that Thebes had been
sighted. We gathered by the rail, watching the gold-, silver-
and electrum-capped obelisks and temple cornices flash back
the light of the rising sun. We glimpsed the plumes from the
morning sacrifices and caught the flavour of their scent on
the breeze: fire, blood, burning meat and incense. On our right
rose the Necropolis beneath the peak of Meretseger, the Silent
One, which broods over the sprawling dusty City of the Dead,
its quayside already busy with its macabre trade of death. The

thick clumps of palm trees on our left abruptly thinned and the Great Mooring Place of Thebes, in all its bustling glory, came into view.

Of course, the court knew we were coming. Temple choirs, dancers, hesets and musicians greeted us with a fanfare of sound, singing, dancing and chanting. The quayside was a vivid stream of colour, with courtiers, priests, fan bearers and dignitaries in their costly robes, gleaming animal pelts and shimmering collars, necklaces and bracelets. Huge pink flabella, fashioned out of ostrich plumes and soaked in the most exquisite perfumes, sent out gusts of fragrance to hide the odour of oil, dried fish and human ordure and the hideous stench from the monkey and giraffe pens further along the river. Trumpets and conch horns brayed, sistra rattled, and as a chant to Horus of the Secret Flame rose to its climax, our barge turned sideways and edged alongside the quayside. Ropes were thrown, the great plank was lowered, and we came ashore to be greeted with a shower of lotus petals and garlands of flowers, and cups of brimming wine and sugared sesame cakes which none of us dared drink or eat.

An escort of officers, dressed for war and carrying their cruel-looking flails, ringed a group of courtiers, sheltering under parasols and gold-edged fans. The soldiers withdrew so that Huy, Maya and Sobeck could approach us to offer the kiss of peace. Huy was tall and urbane as ever, his calm dark eyes and serene noble face concealing his seething ambition. Maya, smiling and plump, shimmering with oil, reeking of perfume, his wig decorated with dashes of coloured ribbon, his fat, fluttering fingers glittering with rings, his small eyes almost disappearing in their folds of fat, came tripping up towards me in his high-heeled, gold-decorated slippers, robes ruffling, a decorated sash around his waist. Maya, the brilliant financier, the man who desperately wanted to be a woman. Beside him was Sobeck, more plump and calm than in his glory days as the Lord of the Slums. Now he was Mayor of

East and West Thebes, Chief of Police, husband of an even plumper wife and an adoring father of two fat children. Poor Sobeck! The leopard had become a lamb and he later paid the price. Sobeck, former lover of one of the Divine Ornaments of the Imperial Harem, had been condemned to a prison oasis for his impertinence, only to escape and, like the fighter he was, conspire, plot, betray and kill to reclaim his place as a Child of the Kap. On that particular morning, however, he looked as happy as if he'd reached the Far Horizon and was assured that he'd live for ever. He was resplendent in his gauffered robes, badges of office and cornelian necklace. I embraced him as I did the rest; glimpsing Maya's glance of jealousy, for Sobeck was still his great hero, the love of his life. The shrewd financier, the cunning plotter, had never forsaken his childhood friend; Maya still loved Sobeck beyond all things.

Ah well, the past! On that morning they gathered around us, these gorgeously plumed peacocks. In truth we were hyaenas, savage and merciless, bound by common ties with a sharp eye for personal gain. Of course, they fussed over Nabila, congratulated Djarka on his safe return and welcomed Horemheb and Rameses as conquering heroes. We milled about, Ay's spies busy amongst us, but we were the Children of the Kap, avengers of blood, the survivors of the crack of the whip, the thunder of chariots, the charging horse, the flashing sword, the gleam of spear. We were the Immortals, the Hyaenas of the Royal Circle, may the Blessed Ones forgive us, men whose past lives were littered with a mass of wounded, hosts of ghosts and countless corpses. More blood was yet to spurt, but that was for the future, the time of slaughter.

On that day, eager to avoid Ay's spies, we moved, one to the other, whispering and chattering, and unbeknown to our watchers, our time and place to meet were chosen. Today we would go our separate ways, but tomorrow, before dawn, we would meet for the hunt. I looked round for Pentju. I wanted to kiss that wine-drenched face, hug him close and hear him whisper the truth, but there was no sign of him.

Horemheb and Rameses elected to go immediately to the Malkata Palace. I decided to return to my farm, the House of the Evergreen Cedar, that garden-circled mansion on the outskirts of Thebes where Ay had banished me some years before. I wanted to be away, to be lost in my paradise with its pools of purity, gleaming ribbon canals, lush lawns, fruit orchards and black-soiled plots where I grew my plants and herbs. I was so pleased to reach it, to sit in the garden pavilion, its inside painted a restful green with pretty paintings of ducks and quails. Djarka and Mert joined me, she of the lovely face made even more beautiful by motherhood. Djarka could only sit and stare round-eyed at her. He loved this woman who, by her very smile, took away the lines of worry from his face, turning him back to that smooth-skinned young man with his shock of night-black hair who'd rescued me so skilfully from assassins so many lifetimes away.

Of course, I took Nabila on a tour of the mansion. Djarka and Mert withdrew to their own quarters to be by themselves with their children before formally greeting Nabila and welcoming her into the house. The day passed quickly. Mert and Nabila took a liking to each other. Mert braided Nabila's hair, painting her face, placing small flowers in the tresses of the oil-drenched wig so she looked as beautiful as the night, magnificent as the dawn and calm as the gentlest dusk. We ate and drank lightly, aware that the servants hurrying backwards and forwards might well be Ay's spies. We then withdrew to my private pavilion. The Golden Calf, that's what it was called. I had built it in a lonely part of the garden on a small man-made island which kept it free from eavesdroppers. The only approach was across a bridge which creaked deliberately; I'd arranged it so. We sat in a circle on our cushions, bit at sugared dates and almond cake, sipping wine, waiting for my guest to arrive.

The bridge creaked, and a dark hooded shadow slipped

through the doorway. The striped cloak was removed and Sobeck moved into the circle of light thrown by the translucent oil lamps placed in crevices around the wall. I rose to greet him, and we kissed and clasped hands. Then Sobeck settled himself on the prepared cushions, accepted a goblet of wine and raised it in toast. He helped himself to a piece of almond cake, studying me and Djarka; he winked at us, then stared at Nabila.

'Can we trust her?' he asked.

'With your life, Sobeck,' I snapped.

He laughed softly. 'I didn't think I'd ever hear the Lord Mahu, former Overseer of the House of Secrets, say that.' He lifted his cup in my direction. 'Welcome back, friend.'

I was impatient. Sobeck and I were old friends, but it was not the time for pleasantries.

'The Great House?' I asked.

'Firmly under the thumb of the Divine One.'

'Are you not going to ask what happened to us?' I enquired.

'I think we already know.' Sobeck grinned. 'But wait until dawn and tell the rest, that's what I agreed with Horemheb as he and his shadow were escorted to the Great House.'

'Will the Divine One see them?'

Sobeck cocked his head as if listening to the croaking of the bullfrogs, which cut like a horn blast through the constant whirr of insects and the chatter of birds as they settled for the night.

'Perhaps,' he replied. 'But your lovely wife?' He gestured at Nabila.

'The time of fire is here,' I retorted. 'Sobeck, this is not a dinner party, to talk and dream about the glory days of our past. By the way, where's Pentju?'

Sobeck pulled a face.

'Where's Pentju?' I repeated.

'He is hiding somewhere in the Necropolis,' Sobeck sighed. 'A secret place.' He fingered the gold ring in his earlobe. 'He's hired a fortified room somewhere near the Square of Foreigners. He has chambers above a Mitanni brothel.'

'Mitanni?' I asked, remembering Khiya, Akenhaten's second wife.

'What on earth is our good physician doing there?' Djarka asked.

'What do you think?'

'Did he attend the Golden Child?'

Sobeck lowered his head; a warrior, a rogue, a villain to the bone like myself, he was still touched by Tutankhamun's gentle ways.

'He did.' Sobeck lifted his face, tears in his eyes. 'I know the path you are treading, Mahu, but . . .' He shook his head. 'Pentju believes he's accursed by the Great House; they blame him for the death of our Golden Child.'

'What?'

'It happened so quickly,' Sobeck continued, as if talking to himself. 'The Divine One was always shy and withdrawn. Oh, I know about his fits, his abrupt changes of moods, his return to acting like a baby, but the Great House was firmly in the hands of the Lord Ay. We did not think anything amiss and did not learn about Tutankhamun's death till the twentieth day of mourning. Oh yes,' Sobeck smiled thinly, 'not until three weeks after he had first gone into the Far West was the proclamation issued and the official mourning begun. I have few details, I don't even know where his tomb is, though Maya probably does.' He sipped his wine, smiled and winked at Nabila. 'Think of two horses,' he declared, 'the fastest mounts pulling a war chariot.' He put the cup down and used his hands to demonstrate. 'Tutankhamun's death, the ritual of mourning, the preparation for Osiris is the horse on the left; Ay's ambitions the horse to the right. Ay himself guided both horses so expertly. The news was proclaimed that Tutankhamun was dead. There was no Wearer of the Double Crown, no Owner of the Great House. A meeting of the Royal Circle was convened. Ay, Nakhtimin and Ankhesenamun had prepared well. They gave their reasons for what they'd planned. Pharaoh was dead, and confusion must be avoided. Egypt was at war. A firm hand was needed, so on and so on. What could we do?' He pulled a face. 'The palace was ringed by Nakhtimin's troops, mercenaries gathered at every doorway; we all wanted to leave alive.'

'Did you try to consult with me? Horemheb, Rameses?'

Sobeck snorted with laughter. 'What could you do, Mahu, hundreds of miles away in Canaan? We didn't know if you were alive or dead.' He shrugged. 'What would you have done in our place? I have a wife and children. I recognised the threat, as did Huy and Maya; we all acquiesced.'

'You never met secretly together?'

'We thought we'd wait until you returned, *if* you returned.'

'You thought we might not?'

Sobeck spread his hands. 'Lord Ay always resented you, Mahu.'

'And he did not care about Egypt's army in Canaan?'

Sobeck glanced at the ceiling and shook his head. 'You know the answer to that as well as I do. He was only too pleased to have Horemheb and Rameses out of Egypt, chasing the Hittites round Canaan. Ay is shrewd. The Hittites cannot keep an army in the field for ever and they are more disliked in Canaan than we are. More importantly, Ay has resumed the tradition of sending Egyptian gold to the Vermin Lords. They'll turn on the Hittites and keep them occupied until Ay himself takes the field. Oh yes,' Sobeck pursed his lips, 'Ay has no intention of allowing our two Great Generals to gain all the glory. He'll collect that for himself, some time in the future.'

'You do know,' Djarka declared, 'he tried to kill all of us?'

Sobeck's smile faded. 'All of you?' he exclaimed. 'Yes, he would try that! After all, Mahu, you were the Divine One's guardian, while Horemheb and Rameses are Ay's rivals.'

'But he never moved against you!' I pointed a finger.

'Perhaps he intended to. Ay can wait like a cat, deep in the shadows.'

I half closed my eyes, rocking backwards and forwards on

the cushions. Flies buzzed noisily around the oil lamps, torn between them and the almond cake on the silver plate. I glanced round the semi-circle. Djarka squatted, hunched like a hunting dog, awaiting orders. Beside him, Mert had removed her garland of wild flowers and sat hand to her mouth. She had no love for the Lord Ay. Nabila was calm, staring into the middle distance as if absorbing everything she'd heard, unaware of the perfumed oil running down her face. Absentmindedly she rubbed her stomach, and my heart leapt: was she pregnant? Nabila caught my glance, smiled shyly and shook her head.

'And Ankhesenamun?' I murmured. 'We were only away a matter of months, but she conceived?'

'Twice.' Sobeck's eyes never left mine. 'One after the other, but they were both premature, stillborn, buried with the Divine One.'

'Were they truly his children?'

'Who cares, they are dead! Pentju will know the truth about that.'

'The truth!' I murmured. 'The goddess Maat! Tell me, Sobeck, the Divine Child: how did he die? What do you really know?'

Sobeck joined his hands together, peering through the darkness. For a moment his face lost its fatty creases, becoming lean and hard as in his youth, cruel-eyed and harsh-mouthed.

'They said he had a fit,' he whispered. 'If it was murder, the work of Red-handed Seth, then Lord Ay and I have a blood feud.'

'As shall we all!' Djarka's voice cut like a lash.

'Are we in danger?' Mert asked. 'If Lord Ay tried to kill you once, why not again?'

'You are – we are,' Sobeck replied, 'in no danger as long as we accept Ay as Pharaoh, Owner of the Great House. Falter in that,' he gestured, 'and all of us could die. There's other news.' Sobeck had a glint in his eye, a sign he was up to mischief. 'An old friend has returned.' He gazed in mock solemnity at me.

'Who?' I shook my head.

'Haven't you noticed? I have not asked about him.'

I gazed back in puzzlement.

'Akenhaten? You were sent to Canaan, Lord Mahu, to flush him out. Did you?'

I raised a finger to my lips.

'Whatever,' Sobeck moved his head from side to side, 'I couldn't care. He doesn't concern me any longer. You see,' he peered at me, 'Ay knows the truth, the rumours are all over Thebes. Akenhaten is dead of leprosy.'

'Where did you hear that?' Djarka asked.

'Your old friend has returned. Mery-re.'

'Mery-re!' I half rose. 'Mery-re and his vile Vesper Bats hunted us the length and breadth of Canaan.'

'I've heard something about that,' Sobeck agreed, 'from Mery-re himself.'

'He's a traitor.'

'Not now. He is shaven and oiled, elevated to be Chief Chapel Priest to Pharaoh himself, perfumed and robed in all his new-found glory.'

'Has he been pardoned?'

'No need,' Sobeck retorted. 'He's done no treachery. The song he sings is this: he was Egypt's spy in the Hittite camp.' Sobeck ignored Djarka's snort of laughter. 'He misled Suppiliuma with wrong advice and counsel. He claimed to have sent those couriers to Horemheb and Rameses, informing them what Suppiliuma intended.'

'I don't believe this!' I breathed.

'Mery-re also claims he met people who told him the truth about Akenhaten. How, after he left his city in the north, he contracted leprosy and died in the hill country of Canaan. Is that true, Mahu?'

I just gazed back.

'But he tried to kill us,' Djarka protested.

'No.' Sobeck picked up his wine cup. 'According to Mery-

167

re, once you'd left the Hittite camp, so did he, moving fast by a different route. The Vesper Bats were no longer under his control. He claims they were sent after you by Prince Zananza, Suppiliuma's son. Mery-re argues that once he heard about the Hittite plans to trap Horemheb and Rameses in Canaan, he realised he was of no further use. You fled, he fled. He has now returned to the bosom of his family, the Royal Circle, a hero, a sacred man, dedicated to the Lord Ay, supportive in every way.'

I closed my eyes and breathed out noisily. Of course, it made sense. It was all a dream, an illusion. Nobody could prove anything. Mery-re could spin his web, tell his lies and who could challenge him? True, he'd been High Priest of the Aten, Akenhaten's close confidant in those turbulent years, but that was true of all of us. He'd sheltered with the Hittites but now he could pose as Egypt's friend, a man who had carried out a very dangerous task, and of course, he and Lord Ay were of the same soul and heart. He'd tell Ay what Ay wanted to hear: that Akenhaten was no longer a threat, that he was a leper, rotting away in some lonely cave. The more I reflected in that Pavilion of the Golden Calf, the more my sense of danger deepened. What did Ay really intend? I glanced at Djarka. Ay was also of the tribe of the Apiru. Did he mean to return to Akenhaten's ways, bring back the worship of the One God, or something else? Would he try to found a new dynasty? I recalled Horemheb and Rameses instructing their officers: that was prudent advice. For Ay to succeed, Horemheb and Rameses would, eventually, have to be removed. Nakhtimin could do that, though he'd need our support, which was why we were being greeted as friends and allies for the time being.

'A time of treachery,' I whispered. 'But we've talked long enough, Sobeck. Where do we meet?'

'At the Oasis of Sweet Palm on the edge of the Redlands. Be there before dawn.'

Nes: to devour, consume

Chapter 9

Later that night, after Nabila and I had made love, I lay beside her, drenched in sweat, staring up into the darkness, listening to her gentle breathing. I turned over, running my fingers along her naked back, brushing the sweat beads, snuggling close to smell her perfumed body, her breath still sweet with the taste of wine. I wondered at her beauty, and pulling myself up, sat on the edge of the bed, dragging aside the gauze curtains and staring into the night. My agitation, despite the lovemaking, with its sweet words and soft kisses, still remained. Something about Sobeck, his manner! Suddenly I put my finger on it. Sobeck didn't care. What was it to him if Lord Ay ruled Egypt? Sobeck was the last person, now married with children, prosperous and powerful, to be drawn into a civil war. We all had so much to lose: why bother? Why question? I rose and walked to the corner, a place where I used to sit and write. I lit the lamps on either wall, took a writing tray with papyrus, ink pots and pens, and sat down. The plaster was cool; the oil lamps threw a pool of light which drew away the buzzing flies.

I smoothed out a piece of papyrus and tried to collect my thoughts. Moving right to left, I made my first symbol: Akenhaten. There was no doubt that my former master, the Veiled One, the accursed Great Heretic, was now a recluse, possibly a leper, a hermit in that sun-scorched valley in Canaan. He was no longer a threat to Egypt, there would be no return. Akenhaten, alive or dead? Ay and Mery-re no longer cared and would lie to suit themselves. Life had moved on. If Horemheb and Rameses learned this, they too would accept it. I made the second sign: Mery-re. He was astute and cunning. No one could disprove his story that he'd been Lord Ay's spy amongst the Hittites, deliberately misleading them, sending information to Horemheb and Rameses of what Suppiliuma intended. As for the attack by the Vesper Bats, Mery-re would wash his hands, wipe his mouth and protest his innocence, and who could prove to the contrary?

I dipped my quill pen back into the blood-red ink and watched a drop fall off. I made my third sign: To-Mery, the Kingdom of the Two Lands, Egypt. Sobeck was correct. Tutankhamun was dead and there was no heir apparent, so why shouldn't Lord Ay claim the crown for himself? A shrewd politician, a cunning warrior, a man of experience, a firm hand to guide the ship of state. I would accept that; the only real dangers were Horemheb and Rameses. I dipped my quill pen and made the fourth sign: the Hittites, the foreigners. Again Sobeck was correct. Ay had resumed sending gold to the Vermin Lords. Suppiliuma would soon be embroiled in countless attacks and skirmishes. He'd eventually withdraw and Egypt would regain full control over that land. So what did Ay intend?

I threw the pen down in exasperation. What were the obstacles to his power? I picked the pen up and wrote the names of Horemheb and Rameses, powerful generals. Yes, I tapped the parchment with the quill, they were Ay's real danger, so which way should I go? I recalled Tutankhamun's face, soft and gentle, his trusting eyes; and Pentju, my old comrade. I made my decision. If Tutankhamun had died of natural causes, if his life had been cut short by the gods, then I would accept it. If not . . . I closed my eyes. I'd taken an oath to

Akenhaten to protect his son. If Tutankhamun had been murdered, then my oath still stood. Ay, Pharaoh or not, would have to pay the price.

We met, as agreed, the following morning. Chariots milled about, horses snorted, the gleaming harness and carriages catching the first rays of the morning sun. We surprised a herd of wild asses and pursued them, the dogs streaking through the lush grass, scattering the flowers. We followed in pursuit, Horemheb and Rameses in the leading chariot, Sobeck and Maya behind, Huy guiding his own, then Djarka and I swaying through their dust. We had gathered at the appointed time, solemn-faced and apprehensive, unwilling to talk. There was none of the camaraderie of yesterday; only suspicion and sharp glances. Huy worried aloud if Lord Ay might learn of our meeting. Horemheb snapped back that he didn't care. Both he and Rameses had been fêted as heroes, but Pharaoh had not granted them an audience; instead he'd proclaimed that he would meet all his old friends in the Dolphin Chamber after sunset on the day after tomorrow.

At noon we ended our hunt and sheltered against the heat beneath the palm trees whilst our servants prepared food over fires. The game we'd brought down was skinned, gutted and stretched out over a grill, turning the air sweet with the smell of its cooking flesh as the servants basted it with herbs and oils. We chattered about the hunt, the lions we'd seen, the speed of the wild asses, yet we all knew what we were waiting for. Once the meal was ready, the servants withdrew. We sat in a semi-circle in the shade. Djarka acted as our guard, ensuring that no one came within earshot, and so the debate began. At first we allowed Horemheb to rant about how he'd been dishonoured, insulted and shamed by not being immediately received by Lord Ay. We all nodded wisely, letting him vent his rage, and at last he stopped, breathing heavily, slurping from his cup.

'We are to meet the night after tomorrow.' Rameses turned the conversation skilfully. 'The Royal Circle is to gather in the Dolphin Chamber, when I suspect Lord Ay will confirm us all in our offices. He'll praise us and proclaim his trust in all of us. What we have to decide is what we are going to do.'

'What *are* we going to do?' Huy asked, biting into a piece of quail. 'Lord Ay has been crowned Pharaoh; to resist his authority is treason, and treason means death and dishonour.'

'So why have you come here?' Rameses smiled back. 'Why don't you get into your chariot, gather the reins and drive gently back to Thebes?'

'We can all go back to Thebes and kiss the Lord Ay's arse,' Huy countered briskly. We became children again, squabbling and trading insults. Sobeck clapped his hands and cried for silence.

'We are not here . . .' He glanced up, peering through the palm fronds at the swooping buzzards. 'We are not here,' he repeated, 'to let the Redlands hear our woes. We have to face a choice – do we accept Ay as Pharaoh, yes or no? If yes, then let us feast and return to Thebes. If no, then what shall we do about it?'

'He tried to kill me,' Horemheb protested.

'You've no proof of that,' Sobeck replied. 'And the Caracals?'

Sobeck, as Chief of Police, must have heard something about the assassins who had slipped into the city to carry out bloody murder. Horemheb dropped his gaze, smiled, shrugged, and bit noisily into a fig. Sobeck stretched out his hand, fluttering his fingers, inviting Horemheb to confess. I wondered again which way the Chief of Police of Thebes was going to jump.

'It's quite simple,' I intervened. 'It depends on two things.

First, the past: how did Tutankhamun die? If Ay had a hand in his death then we must invoke the blood feud. Ay took an oath; we all took an oath to protect Tutankhamun, to be his men in peace and war. Secondly, the future: what does Ay intend? To take Egypt back to the days of Akenhaten?' I shrugged. 'Then we would all have to go our separate ways.' I glanced at Maya, squatting as genial and rubicund as the god Bes, nibbling at his meat, painted nails tapping the side of his goblet as if he was half listening to some music. I pushed my face close.

'Maya,' I whispered. 'Treachery's little turd! You are Overseer of the House of Silver,' I continued. 'You must have the list for the Royal Tomb, for Tutankhamun's funeral goods, the embalmment of his corpse?'

'Oh yes, I have.' Maya lifted his head. 'No insults, Baboon! Come to my office, or better still, I'll send you copies. Scrutinise the documents at your will.'

'I shall!' I hissed. 'I also want to see his tomb. Was it the one being prepared in the eastern valley?'

Maya shook his head.

'Where's Pentju?' I asked.

'Drinking and fornicating in his own private brothel.'

'Did he attend the Divine One in his last days?'

'Yes, he did, but then he disappeared, going back to his lust, like a dog to its vomit!'

I raised a fist; Maya stuck his tongue out.

'Don't bully me, Baboon! I simply paid the bills and escorted the Divine One to his House of Eternity. You were Pharaoh's guardian, not us.'

'Tell us, Maya,' I said. 'What truly happened? I mean,' I taunted, 'you are as much a stranger to Maat as any of us. The truth lies awkwardly on your tongue, as it does in your heart, but at least try!'

Maya made clicking sounds, eyes bright with mischief. He glanced slyly round at his companions. I recognised it then.

The past was over. We were all Children of the Kap, but Tutankhamun had been the clasp which kept us together. Now he was gone. I understood, as did Maya and Sobeck: like the hyaenas they were, they were forging ahead of the pack, ready to reach an accommodation with anyone over anything as long as it suited them. It was time for me to catch up.

'What truly happened?' I repeated.

'As I've said,' Maya replied cheekily, 'I was informed like the rest of Thebes that Tutankhamun was dead. Ay held enough power to ensure he could proceed for as long as he wished without telling anyone. I was given orders to prepare a tomb, not the one Tutankhamun had been building, but a different one, sheltered and hidden.' He pulled a face. 'Like you, I followed orders. Strange,' Maya mused, 'Tutankhamun had prepared a tomb positioned so the rays of the sun could invade its rooms and corridors, so reminiscent of the tomb his father Akenhaten had built in the City of the Aten. Anyway,' he sniffed, 'that was all pushed aside. Tutankhamun's death was declared and Egypt went into mourning. The decree went out that Horus had gone away to the Globe. The Great House was shrouded in lamentation. All rejoicing was forbidden. Ankhesenamun keened. Ashes were distributed. Ay and the rest did not shave.' Maya grinned and rubbed his smooth olive-skinned face. 'The orders came through and the workshop in the Necropolis became busy. The Divine One's possessions were taken from the palace. Pentju especially ordered the *shabtis* to be sent to the tomb.' (I kept my face impassive at that.) 'You remember those life-size figures? Pentju claimed Tutankhamun always treasured them.' Maya spread his hands. 'Tutankhamun's corpse was taken to the *wabet*, the place of purity in the Temple of Anubis, to be embalmed; the ritual was followed. The funeral cortège sailed out across the Nile, accompanied by choirs and dancing girls, and that was that.'

He spoke so glibly, I realised he was lying, concealing something. I knew Maya as we all knew each other. We had been raised together, forced to live cheek by jowl. Maya was gabbling out the official story and didn't care. He drained his wine cup in one gulp.

'I will show you the tomb. I've everything prepared,' he smiled, 'as well as someone to meet.' He paused. 'Let him tell you!'

The hunt broke up. We journeyed back down across the Nile. Our chariots were left in the care of my captain of mercenaries and we boarded the imperial barge Maya had prepared, a long, square craft flying the golden falcon standard. Maya must have had Pharaoh's permission for this, as the craft was manned by sailors and marines wearing the blue and golden *nemes* of the Great House. I was sure Ay must have known about our hunt. We crossed to the mooring place of Isis and Nepthys where chariots were waiting under the command of the Royal Chapel Scribe, Amendufet, a man I'd bought, or thought I had, body and soul. I was very surprised to see him there and dared not meet his eye lest I betray myself. Amendufet looked older, with a scrawny neck and wrinkled face; he was an official who acted full of his own importance. With anyone else it would have been a dreadful mistake: hyaenas do not recognise such arrogance. For me, for them, the things that mattered were life and death, whilst one's fortune could change in the twinkling of an eye. Amendufet, however, was different, more certain of himself: when I could, I glanced up quickly, winked and looked away. The scribe had done very well, trusted first by Lord Ay and now, apparently, by Maya.

The day's heat was dying as we moved out towards the Valley of the Kings: six chariots in all going up the dusty track which wound through the sandy crags up to the plateau then down into the Royal Valley. We passed imperial guardhouses and troops of mercenaries who patrolled the Mountains of the West, those sacred paths and caves beneath the peak of Meretseger. The guards did not hinder us but crouched in the dust as the Great Ones passed into the Mysterious Land where the Houses of Eternity, with their blind windows and sealed doors, faced the Immortal Sunset, the Far Horizon across whose gold-blue border the Fields of Yalou stretched to eternity. The Valley of the Kings is usually a bustling place, but on that day it lay silent under a blazing sun and clouds of dust. Very little greenery sprouted except for hardy thickets and bushes clinging to the thin soil which covered the rocks and escarpments. The path began to zigzag dangerously, yet we had all been in the Land of the Dead before and knew the route. We entered the main valley, sombre and menacing, the shadows of its craggy walls soaring above us as the sun began to sink.

At last we crossed the threshold into the gloomy amphitheatre which housed the royal tombs. We followed the track along the valley side and stopped before a stony cleft jutting out between two rocks, pointed, stretched out like a spear. Because of the poor light and the way the gap was concealed, we would have passed it without noticing had Maya not pointed to the steps leading down to a sealed entrance. The walls on either side were covered with inscriptions not yet faded by the dust-laden wind:

Alas, alas, raise, raise ceaseless laments. Order downfall. Fair traveller, you have departed to the Land of Eternity. Here he is captured. Thou, who had many people, art gone into the earth which loves solitude. Thou, who moved thy legs and walked, art wrapped and firmly bound. Thou, who had many garments and loved to wear them, lies in yesterday's worn linen . . .

It was a dramatic, mournful dirge, and we all read it as we knelt or crouched at the top of that gloomy staircase. Maya had brought a basket and a flask of oil and milk. We scattered their contents along with olive leaves, blue lotus petals and cornflowers. Amendufet broke the seals of a red earthenware jar and shook out its contents, then smashed the jar and lit small incense lamps, which he placed further down the steps. I knelt and chanted the funeral prayers, yet like the rest, I was astonished at this humble tomb with its undressed walls, rough steps, the door below ill-cut and badly formed, the seals of the officials peeling off like the sores on a beggar. Was this the last great resting place for the son of Akenhaten, the grandson of Amenhotep the Magnificent?

My eye caught the Horus names of Tutankhamun carved on a stela beside the door – Strong Bull, Fitting of Created Forms, He of the Two Ladies, Dynamic of Laws, who Calms the Two Lands, who Propitiates all the Gods. He who Displays the Regalia of King of Upper and Lower Egypt, Living Image of Amun. I also realised that behind that door were the two statues, the Watchers, containing the prophecies about the tribe of Apiru and their future in Egypt. Did they foretell a Messiah, an albino with blue eyes who would deal out judgement to the gods of Egypt? Had Ay, Pentju, Maya or Huy found those documents? If not, how could I read them now, sealed as they were behind the walls of eternity?

'Why the haste?' Horemheb's grating voice shook me from my reverie. I became aware of the hard pebbles biting into my knees and the silence of that eerie amphitheatre broken by the creak of wheels and the whining of our horses pawing the ground, ill at ease in this place of death. We were all alone, except for Amendufet standing so silently behind us.

'It was all done in haste,' Maya sighed, getting to his feet. We all followed. He gestured round. 'The tomb-quarrying had already begun, so we finished it and filled it with treasures. Ay determined the time: the sooner Pharaoh was buried, the sooner the new Pharaoh could reign. He collected the grave goods as swiftly as he could.'

I recalled the plunder ripped out from the City of the Aten, and gazed round the sombre limestone valley, its rocks changing colour as the sun set. Darkness would soon fall; the veil separating us from the land of ghosts was thinning. On the breeze echoed the coughing roars and snarls as the night prowlers greeted their feasting time. This valley was honey-combed with caves, caverns and pits for such beasts to lurk in. An army could be concealed there; even more so the treasure from Akenhaten's once glorious city in the north, now rotting under the sun, the home of the bat, the owl and the jackal. Ay would have seized such treasure in his haste to bury Tutankhamun.

I rubbed my face, trying to break free of the spell which seemed to bind us all. We stood at the top of those steps, staring down at the door to the other world. Cursing quietly, as if to confront my own feeling of hovering menace, I went down the steps. I reached the bottom and pressed my face against the cold plaster, fighting back tears. I whispered a prayer, letting my heart sing its own hymn of deep grief for that beautiful boy.

The joy of Amun is in your heart, you went through life with joy until you reached the bliss.
Your lips are now healthy, your limbs are green. Your eye sees far.
You will dress in fine linen.
You shall ride on a two-horse chariot, a golden spear in your hand, a whip with you, driving teams of Assyrian stallions.
Your slaves run before you doing your will.
You shall go upon your boat of cedar, high at the prow and stern.
You will come to that excellent abode which you have made yourself.
Your mouth will be filled with wine, beer, bread, meat and cakes, oxen are to be sacrificed for you.

Jars of wine will be opened, sweet music will be sung
before you.
Your chief perfumer anoints you with essence.
Your director of wine is there with your garlands.
Your steward of country people brings you geese.
Your fish man brings you fish.
Your ships, which will go to Syria, are laden with all kinds
of good things.
Your barns are full of cows and your fields are flourishing.
You are stable and your enemies are overthrown.
What is said against you does not exist.
You go into the presence of the gods clean in heart,
You come out just in voice.

I don't know where the prayer came from; I just uttered it as if Tutankhamun was still alive, about to revel in the glory he experienced so rarely in his life.

'Mahu, Mahu!' I opened my eyes. Djarka was standing behind me. 'Master,' he whispered, 'look at the seals.'

I studied the hard waxed impressions and recognised the Sun Disc of Tutankhamun.

'Ay was in such a hurry,' Djarka whispered, 'he used Tutankhamun's seal.'

I stared unbelievingly. The new Pharaoh always used his own cartouche to seal the door to his predecessor's House of Eternity. Why all this rush? Why such haste? I strode back up the steps and confronted Maya.

'The truth,' I demanded.

'The truth, Mahu?' That fat, cunning, brilliant little man adjusted his ridiculous wig and peered up at me. 'What you want to know is why Tutankhamun was sent so hurriedly across the Far Horizon. I've told you what I know. The next question you want to ask is was it the will of the gods or the doing of Lord Ay. Amendufet!' he called over his shoulder. 'Please join our council.'

The tired-eyed priest, now a little fearful of being in such a sombre place, stepped forward. 'Tell them,' Maya declared. 'They want to know the truth!'

Amendufet's hand went beseechingly to his lips as if he was about to cry. He glanced quickly at me.

'Tell us,' Rameses ordered.

'I was Chief Priest at the House of Purification,' Amendufet babbled, but paused in a fit of dry coughing. I made him drink from Djarka's wineskin. He thanked me with his eyes. I could see he was wary. 'I was Chief Scribe of the Wabet, the Holder of the Ethiopian Knife.'

'Yes, yes,' Horemheb interrupted testily. 'Tutankhamun, may the Lord Osiris receive him, has died. Why was he rushed to his grave? What is the mystery about his death?'

'My lord,' Amendufet whispered, 'he may have been murdered.'

A jackal further down the valley yipped. I felt the first chill of the evening breeze and noticed how the shadows were lengthening. I did not know what path Amendufet was following, why he should make such an honest declaration in such a lonely place. I glanced up. The sky had taken on a strange colour, dark-blue, scored with red.

'What makes you think that?' I whispered. 'Quick, man, tell us.' I stared hard at the scribe. Was he telling the truth? Amendufet's eyes flickered towards Maya. I realised he had no choice.

'The Divine One's corpse was brought in and laid on the Table of Anubis,' he explained. 'His flesh was still fresh, his face serene, as if his *ka* had just left. I stripped the Divine Body of all its ornaments. I undid the collarette: flowers soaked in magic potions which the physicians had tied around his neck to drive away the demons. My fingers . . .' Amendufet turned his own head, pressing his hand to the base of his skull just beneath his right ear. 'I felt it here, a swelling, a contusion, hard and angry. I turned the body over. I did not

182

wish the others to see me. I peered closer. The swelling could be detected by the eye.' Amendufet was now trembling. 'Then the Book of the Gates and the Book of the Dead were brought, and the ritual began. I was to answer to Lord Ay, but,' he gestured towards Maya, 'I had to tell someone what I saw, what I felt . . .' His voice trailed off. Amendufet I knew, as I did the hearts of many men and women whom, down the long passage of the years, I had interrogated. I knew he was not making this up, he was not lying – he was too frightened for that – though I sensed he wasn't telling the complete truth.

'Did anyone else see this?' Sobeck asked.

Amendufet shook his head.

'But there must have been other physicians who attended Pharaoh?'

'There were no other physicians,' Maya intervened. 'None except the Lord Pentju. Apparently when he was summoned to tend Tutankhamun during his last illness, Lord Pentju insisted that he, and he alone, be responsible. Lord Ay had no choice but to agree.'

I glanced up at the darkening sky, where a buzzard, black feathery wings spread, floated like a sinister spirit. Maya had spoken the truth. Pentju was Tutankhamun's personal physician. Ay would have no choice but to accept him. If Tutankhamun had been murdered, Pentju would have been the first to discover it and Ay would never have allowed him to live. Perhaps I should seek out Pentju immediately. I glanced at the faces of the others; they must have been thinking similar thoughts, yet we all realised that would be highly dangerous. Ay would be waiting for us.

'Is there anything else?' Rameses was now standing slightly behind Amendufet. 'Is there, priest?' he added menacingly.

'No, no, my lords.' Amendufet's voice was dry.

I gestured to Djarka to hand him the wineskin again. Amendufet slurped greedily and handed it back. Then, lunging like a snake, Rameses slipped a strangle string over the priest's head and whipped it around his throat. Amendufet screamed, an eerie sound in that haunted place, and fell to his knees, fingers scrabbling at the string, eyes beseeching.

'Please,' he gasped. 'I tell the truth, I know nothing else.'

'Think,' Rameses urged.

I glanced around: the rest of the hyaenas were cold; I could read their hearts. Amendufet was not of our coven. If he babbled once, he'd babble again. They did not know the full truth about the man. Maya showed no pity, more interested in his hennaed fingernails than in this ageing scribe pleading for his life. Horemheb crouched down beside Amendufet.

'Are you sure there is nothing else?' he murmured soothingly. 'Just tell me and your life is spared.'

'I can tell you nothing,' Amendufet spluttered. 'I saw what I did. I thought I was doing right. I told no one except the Lord Maya.' His eyes pleaded with his protector, who pulled a fan from his sash, snapped it open and vigorously wafted his face to cool the sweat.

'Nothing?' Horemheb asked.

'Nothing, my lord.'

'Kill him!'

'Ah . . .' Maya raised a hand, then let it fall. 'I suppose so.'

Rameses tightened the string; Amendufet screamed, begging for his life.

'I have a wife, two sons, mere boys!'

Sobeck walked away. Maya's fan fluttered faster. Horemheb still squatted, watching the man's eyes. Rameses, smiling thinly, tightened the cord.

'My lord Mahu,' Amendufet gasped, 'for pity's sake!'

I looked down those grim steps leading to that dark doorway. Tutankhamun lay beyond, his gentle eyes closed for ever in eternal sleep. Amendufet was spluttering, face red, eyes protuberant. Rameses was enjoying himself. Amendufet was crying. I made a hideous mistake, one I'd regret for the rest of my life. I sprang forward, pushing Rameses away. Amendufet fell forward, and Rameses whipped out a knife, his lean face twisted in fury.

'Don't!' Behind me Djarka had strung his powerful bow and notched an arrow to the cord, pulling it back. 'My lord Rameses,' he repeated, 'don't.'

Horemheb, still squatting in the dirt, squinted up at me. Rameses stood, knife at the ready, eager to lunge. Horemheb smiled at Djarka and waved at Rameses.

'I agree, let him live.' Horemheb got to his feet and kicked Amendufet, kneeling before him, who collapsed coughing and crying as he grasped my ankles.

'So do I.' Huy came out of the shadows.

'As you wish,' Maya simpered.

Rameses resheathed his knife, Djarka lowered his bow.

'Come, come,' Horemheb acted all genial, 'we are the Children of the Kap, we are united as one.' He urged Rameses and myself to clasp hands, yet I recognised, outside that lonely tomb, how the bond was truly broken, the tie which held us had slipped. Each soul would now sing its own song. Rameses was still glowering at me as Amendufet crawled away to recover. I gestured at the priest.

'Maya,' I declared, 'let him enter my household.'

'As you wish.'

Amendufet reached a rock and turned to lean his back against it. Djarka crouched down, coaxing him to drink from the wineskin. The priest was still wild-eyed, but I'd chosen well. Amendufet winked quickly at me before glaring venomously at Rameses. Djarka got up and came back towards me.

'He's all right,' he whispered, 'acting as usual. He'll survive. Just distract them, my lord.'

'The tomb.' I returned to the top of the steps. 'Maya, describe it.'

'I was the architect.' The treasurer looped his shawl over

his head, forming a cowl to shield his face. He gestured with one hand. 'The limestone was easy to quarry; it had already been started, I just finished it. Sixteen steps leads down to an antechamber. There's an annexe to the burial chamber and a treasury room beyond.'

He spoke like a scholar repeating something by rote.

'Scarcely a tomb for a prince!'

'That's been said before,' Rameses jibed.

'Tutankhamun's death was sudden and unexpected,' Maya declared. 'I carried out my orders.' He fluttered his fingers at Amendufet. 'I have the accounts; your creature can take a copy.'

I wondered then, just for a while, if Maya suspected Amendufet was really my spy, but immediately dismissed it. If he had known, Amendufet would have been sent into the Far West long ago.

'Ah well,' Maya squinted up at the sky, 'we should return to Thebes. I've had enough of rock and dust. The day after tomorrow we meet the Divine One.'

The rest were only too willing. We returned to the chariots, each going its separate way.

That night proved to be a beautiful one, the second of my return to Thebes. I arrived at my country mansion acting all excited, chatting to Djarka and Mert as if I was full of happiness at being home, looking forward to the forthcoming audience with Pharaoh: a fine display of lies and deceit for those servants who would undoubtedly report back to the Great House. I played senet and stick-throwing with Djarka's children and showed them the golden carp nosing amongst the lotus on the artificial pond. Afterwards I ushered them to the herb garden, teaching them the names of various herbs before rewarding them with honey cakes. Oh, it was' Uncle Mahu' this, and 'Uncle Mahu' that. Even as I played like a jackal amongst the lambs, tears stung my eyes: the children's voices echoed that of Tutankhamun.

When they had left, I sat beneath the willow tree and grieved for my golden boy. I kept recalling Amendufet's description of that contusion at the back of Tutankhamun's lovely egg-shaped head. I hit the ground with my fist and cursed Ay to be hunted and haunted by all the demons and devourers of the underworld.

'Master?' I glanced up. Djarka was standing there, a shifting shadow amongst the trees. 'Master, the Dog Man of Lower Thebes is here.'

'Bring him in!'

Djarka disappeared into the night and returned with the Dog Man, one of the best amongst the professional beggars, pimps and scorpion men who flourished in the Am-duat, the seedy, sprawling underworld of the Necropolis. By profession he was a cat lover; he mummified the creatures for those who wanted to make votive offerings to Bastet either in Thebes or elsewhere. He was Kushite by origin, black-skinned and shaven-headed. He could roll his eyes and act the fool with the best of them, but his wits were sharp as any knife. He was dressed, as usual, in the skin of dogs, hence both his smell and his name. He was my spy in the City of the Dead, one of the few who had survived Ay's searches through those fetid holes of the underworld.

He sat opposite me, his painted face grotesque in the light of the oil lamp Djarka had placed between us. He gobbled a plate of spiced meat, filled his mouth with soft bread and talked, oh how he talked, in his high-pitched voice! I sat cradling a goblet of wine as the Dog Man told me all the chatter of the Necropolis. I shivered as I listened, not because of the night breeze, but at the unnamed fears which sprang like leopard spirits from the darkness. Ay had certainly planned well, and whatever path he was following, he was much further along than any of us realised. He now controlled the temple priests, the police, the city and the mob. Tutankhamun's death had been proclaimed, but any grief the city felt was soon forgotten as the imperial granaries, the Houses of Plenty, were opened and the grain and foodstuffs poured out to feed the city poor. The Dog Man chattered on about how Ay's influence had been felt along the quaysides and through every quarter of the city. He had even reached agreements with the desert wanderers, the sand dwellers and the travelling merchants.

'Not to mention the Hittites,' The Dog Man declared between mouthfuls of bread and meat.

'Hittites?' I asked.

'Yes, Hittites.' The Dog Man smiled. 'Hittite merchants come and go into the Great House, or they used to; now they have stopped.'

'You don't know why?'

The Dog Man shook his head and continued his declamation. Tutankhamun had been a recluse, so his death was only marginally noticed by the city mob. It was business as usual: Pharaoh had died, gone into the Far West, but a new Pharaoh, a strong ruler, had emerged. The city would be kept peaceful, trade would flourish and the old ways continue. At last the Dog Man's voice began to falter. He told me nothing new, and I wondered if I should question him about Pentju, but there again . . .

'I know who you're thinking about.' The Dog-Man peered at me. 'Your friend the physician, Lord Pentju.'

I smiled in agreement.

'He is supposed to be sheltering in the Mysterious Abode, guarded by mercenaries, but more than that . . .' The Dog Man seized the wine jug and gulped greedily.

I realised he could tell me no more. He made to rise.

'And the Caracals?' I asked.

'Wild cats?' the Dog Man declared. 'Never touch them.'

Ni: *the poison of a snake*

Chapter 10

The Dog Man thanked me for the good silver I paid him and slipped through a postern gate, calling down all the blessings of the gods upon me. Oh, that was a busy night, just before the blood-letting began. Djarka and I were sipping wine in the Pavilion of the Golden Calf when Amendufet, his wife and two children arrived. I went out to greet them and assign them quarters. Later I introduced Amendufet to Nabila and Mert in the garden pavilion.

'One of my best spies,' I declared. 'Amendufet, scribe, priest, formerly in the service of Great Queen Tiye. He comes from the outskirts of Akhmin.'

'But not of the Apiru tribe,' Amendufet intervened. 'I loved the Great Queen Tiye, but Lord Ay, and his brother . . .' He turned and spat into the darkness. 'We had a blood feud over a temple appointment Ay wanted for Nakhtimin. I appealed to the Lord Mahu for help but it was too late. Now,' he felt his throat, still marked from the strangle string, 'now I have a grievance against them all.'

Djarka shifted his knees on his cushion. I stared at this sombre-faced scribe. Amendufet was a proficient spy. He worked for money, for honours, for protection, but also out of hatred. If Ay and Maya were friends, then Maya would certainly be Amendufet's enemy.

'I thought you'd contact me immediately.' Amendufet shielded the lower part of his face with his wine cup. 'You've been back in Thebes two days.'

'I have to move slowly and secretly,' I replied. 'Once I was guardian to Pharaoh. Now Pharaoh has gone, what am I? Just one citizen amongst many. So, Amendufet, what do you know?' I filled his cup.

'What do I know?' Amendufet once again touched his throat. 'You certainly took your time.'

'If I'd acted immediately, Maya would have been suspicious. Compassion amongst the Children of the Kap is rare. Do you think Lord Maya suspects?'

Amendufet shook his head. 'He dismissed me from his service like wafting a fly. He is pursuing greater things.'

'Is he with Pharaoh?'

'Lord Maya is with everyone. He supports Ay but, as you know, sows suspicion about him. He has already sent presents to Horemheb and Rameses and tonight he dines with Lord Sobeck, whilst he and Huy,' Amendufet lifted his hand, fingers entwined, 'they think as one.'

'Ah yes,' Djarka intervened, 'but is he privy to Ay's secret councils? Does he, do you, know anything about Hittite messengers?'

Amendufet shook his head and glanced uneasily at the two women.

'They are blood kin,' I whispered. 'Their lives, like yours, are entwined with mine.'

'I know nothing about Hittites,' Amendufet smiled slyly, 'but I do know of the Caracals, the assassins from Memphis. I listen at doors, Lord Mahu, as you told me to. Sobeck is Chief of Police, Mayor of Thebes; he knew all about General Nakhtimin's search for a secret group of assassins who had slipped into the city to wreak damage.'

'Does Sobeck know who sent them?'

Amendufet hunched his shoulders. 'Some people say Lord

Horemheb, others Rameses, others even you, my lord. Maya found out about them. He told Sobeck, who, in turn, informed General Nakhtimin. Anyway, the assassins were caught and impaled.'

'Did they confess?' I asked. 'Did they say why they'd come to the city, against whom they were going to strike?'

'From what I can gather,' Amendufet sipped from his cup, 'they went to their deaths silently. They did not break, but the suspicion is that they intended to strike at Lord Ay.'

'Now there's a second pack in the city? Come on!' I urged. 'I know about the Caracals.'

'Yes,' Amendufet agreed. 'According to Sobeck, the second group arrived individually, pretending to be merchants dealing in gum and resin. They've hired a house on the outskirts of Thebes, just beyond the Lion Gate. The mansion stands in its own grounds. They call it the House of the Sycamores, because of the trees which cluster around its gates.'

'And Lords Sobeck and Maya have not informed Pharaoh?'

'They dare not.'

'Of course.' Djarka softly clapped his hands. 'If they inform Ay, they might lose Horemheb's friendship. Telling Ay about the first pack, but not the second, allows Maya and Sobeck to balance between the rival factions.'

'Lord Sobeck,' Amendufet declared, 'does not even keep the House of the Sycamores under scrutiny, lest one of his own men betrays such knowledge to General Nakhtimin. The situation is one,' Amendufet raised his eyebrows, 'which nobody controls. Sobeck believes the first group of assassins were brought in to remove Ay as chief adviser and counsellor of Pharaoh. Now Tutankhamun is dead and Ay is Pharaoh, Horemheb probably wishes he had never gone down that path.'

'Do you know why,' I asked, 'Horemheb and Rameses should strike at Ay?'

Amendufet pulled a face. 'My lord, your explanation is as

193

good as anyone's: Horemheb has no love for the Lord Ay. If he'd removed him then, Horemheb might have become Tutankhamun's principal counsellor as well as leading general. In other circumstances Horemheb might be wearing the Double Crown.'

'There's something else, isn't there?' Djarka asked. 'This is not just about who governs Egypt.'

Amendufet wetted his lips. 'I agree.' He nodded his head. 'We've all heard rumours about General Rameses' interest in the Apiru tribe and the Israar clan. Rameses firmly believes your people, Djarka, were the cause of Akenhaten's Great Heresy. If General Rameses had his way, he would find out everything he could about your people, about what they intend, their prophecies, their dreams. Yes,' he nodded slowly, 'if General Rameses wielded full power, the tribe of the Apiru and the clan of Israar would be either wiped out or expelled for ever from Egypt. Lord Ay knows this. On the one hand he tries to keep the tribe of Apiru quiet, as one would try and brush dust under a cushion, but at the end of the day,' Amendufet peered at Djarka, 'Lord Ay, like you, is a member of the Apiru. Will he wait until the nightmare is forgotten, the Great Heresy a matter of fable, the City of the Aten fully crumbled, and then begin again? Many of his mercenaries are from your tribe.'

I was surprised by Amendufet's declaration and wondered if Ay had already reached a decision about the future. If so, sooner or later, he and Horemheb would fight. Civil war would rage.

'We're all spectators, aren't we?' Nabila spoke up. 'Sobeck, Maya, Huy and us. We've withdrawn from the game, waiting to see which way it goes. Who will be victorious, Ay or Horemheb? That's what it has come down to, hasn't it?' Her beautiful face was troubled, the flickering light emphasising the dark shadows under her eyes. For a brief moment I regretted drawing her into this. 'I have made my choice,' she murmured. 'Who knows,' she grinned, 'maybe the Mongoose Lord will try and see if my soul is up for sale.'

'Is it?' Mert asked teasingly.

'Already sold a thousand times over to my husband,' Nabila retorted. The smile faded from her face. 'I, too, know the Lord Ay. He's probably now discussing how he can bring about our deaths at the hands of assassins, or publicly on the hanging wall or stakes out in the Redlands. No wonder Pentju is hiding in the Mysterious Abode.' She gestured at Amendufet. 'But these Caracals, the second pack?'

'According to Lord Maya, the second group is about six in all – one woman and five men.'

'What are they waiting for?' I asked.

Amendufet spread his hands. 'My lord, I don't know. According to Lord Maya, these Caracals will now act not just because they've been hired by Horemheb, but because they have a blood feud with Ay and Nakhtimin. I suspect they are waiting for their opportunity. Pharaoh must travel through Thebes . . . go down to his temple to worship – a sudden attack . . .' His voice trailed off.

'Leave them,' I muttered. 'What do you know about Lord Pentju?'

'He's hiding in a fortified house in a square known as the Foreigners; it used to serve as barracks for the Medjay police.'

'Is it well guarded?' Djarka asked.

'By hirelings,' Amendufet replied. 'Lord Pentju has sold all his treasure and turned it into debens and ounous of gold and silver, as well as pouches of jewels and precious stones. He's even taken Amenhotep the Magnificent's Cup of Glory with him. He lives in an upstairs room served by Mitanni whores. He seems . . .' Amendufet paused, 'He seems very fearful.'

'About what?'

Amendufet shook his head. 'He tended Tutankhamun of Blessed Memory, he was present at the Pharaoh's going forth into the West, then he disappeared. He has even hired the

195

Khsru . . .' He paused at Djarka's sharp intake of breath: the Khsru, or Banished Ones, were temple boys, lady-men, rejects of society, one of the most vicious gangs prowling the Necropolis. 'They guard the entrances to the Square of the Foreigners.'

'And Lord Pentju left me no message?'

'He would not come here.' Mert spoke up. 'I issued invitation after invitation. He sent a boy with a stark reply. "I am Khakhu, the accursed!"'

'Why should he call himself that?' Djarka murmured. 'Does he believe he failed Tutankhamun?'

'He came to me,' Amendufet declared, 'at the Great Going Forth. He whispered one message.' Amendufet closed his eyes. '"If the Lord Mahu returns, and I am still alive, tell him not to approach me. Say I shall speak to him from across the Far Horizon."'

Somewhere in the gardens a bird chattered noisily, then a dog howled ominously from a house further along the river.

'I am not to approach him,' I whispered. 'Amendufet, what truly happened?'

'I don't really know,' he confessed. 'The proclamation was made that Pharaoh Tutankhamun had gone to meet Osiris; his corpse was brought to the Wabet. I felt those contusions but saw no other mark of violence. Yet there were rumours.'

'Of what?'

'What I've already told you: of great haste, of the tomb being hurriedly prepared, secret treasure hoards ransacked for funeral goods, of the . . .' he paused, 'of the Divine One's flesh being purified in an unseemly way, but, my lord, these are just rumours, gossip.'

I quietly cursed Maya: he must have known all about this but only told what he wanted us to know.

'Everything was chaotic, no one dared send messages to anyone else. I didn't know if you were alive or dead, or where you were. Nakhtimin's troops were all over the city, guarding the Great Mooring Place and the quaysides. War barges patrolled the river, chariot squadrons controlled the approaches to the city, going far out even into the Redlands. Gifts, bribes and promises poured out of the Great House to the noble and good. Envoys were dispatched to mayors and nobles throughout the kingdom. Ay's orders streamed like arrows out of the city; swiftness was the order of the day. The Divine One's corpse was handed over to the Wabet, and the seventy days of mourning was curtailed.'

Amendufet continued his description of what he called the last days, but I only half listened. Eventually I asked him to retire, informing him that my stewards and chamberlains would take care of him. Nabila appeared distracted. She and Mert wiped away the perfume oozing down from the small cones they'd fastened in their wigs. Nabila said something about how she must visit members of her own family in Thebes, and that she intended to do so tomorrow. I grunted absent-mindedly in agreement. Both women left. I sat in that pavilion, squatting on the cushions, peering into the darkness which grew deeper as the oil lamps guttered out. Images came and went, flitting like fireflies: Ay when I first met him, charming but treacherous, beside him his glorious daughter Nefertiti. The various Children of the Kap playing as boys, Pentju and Mery-re teasing each other, Horemheb and Rameses skulking in the shade, Huy ever alone, Maya and Sobeck always together, bittersweet memories from those glory days.

'We are in great danger, aren't we?' Djarka put his wine cup down. 'Shall we flee, master? Ay no longer has any need for us. He has what he wants. He has tried to kill you; he may do so again. Nabila is right, it is now war between Ay and Horemheb. We could choose sides, but even then we might not be safe.'

'I don't really care,' I declared. 'Ay, Horemheb or fat Maya – he could have told us so much but, as usual, he is treacherous

197

to all. What concerns me, Djarka, is one question: did Ay, or his friends and allies, murder Tutankhamun? If he, or they, did, then we must act. In the mean time,' I chose my words carefully, 'we must protect our lives, we must buy the time to live and hunt for the truth.'

'You mean Pentju?'

'No, not for the moment. Pentju is correct, we must not approach him, that would only alert Ay and Nakhtimin. We must show our good faith. We must win the favour of Pharaoh. We must make it very clear that we support him.'

'How?'

'The Caracals.'

'Do we tell Nakhtimin?'

'No, that will only alert Maya and antagonise Horemheb. We must kill them ourselves.'

'Master!'

'If the Caracals succeed it will be war; if they fail it will be war. Horemheb hired the killers thinking he was removing Pharaoh's minister, not Pharaoh himself. Now the situation has changed. Horemheb probably can't even control his own killers.'

'Which means?'

I lifted my wine cup and quietly toasted Djarka. 'If we kill them, Horemheb might well be relieved.'

'Who'd be blamed?'

'Why, everyone and anyone.'

Djarka smiled.

'They'll all be relieved. In fact,' I clicked my tongue, 'yes, it's the best step to take. It's an offering to Ay, proof that we have looked into the sacred smoke and discerned the forms yet to come. We must do something to placate and distract him. We must do it immediately.'

Djarka and I laid our plans carefully. We snatched a few hours' sleep and chose those mercenaries we could trust. We were awake before dawn, our men filing out through a side gate down to the barge Djarka had brought into the nearest quayside. Above us the stars were fading like flowers, the eastern sky turning slightly pink, though the cold breeze still lingered and the river looked fearful in that half-light, alive with the roar of a bull hippo and the constant chattering calls from the papyrus thickets. Fishermen were bringing in their catches; the air smelled of brine and wet cordage. Across the river, lights glowed from the sombre City of the Dead. Now and again a shout or scream carried across the water; but I couldn't decide its source. We kept to the bank, our rowers silent as they pulled against the river. City troops were out but they did not accost us; we were not going towards the city, but further north, to the sprawling farms and houses on the far side of Thebes.

The light strengthened. We passed under the towering mass of Thebes' walls and gates, the wealthy mansions of the nobles and on towards the less fertile lands, where houses stood bounded by mud-clay walls and undecorated gateways. All lay silent except for the bray of some animal and the bells of donkeys being driven by pedlars and traders towards the city gates in anticipation of a day's trade in the markets. Eventually we pulled into a narrow quayside where a lone skiff bobbed on the water and ragged fishermen were sharing out their meagre catch. We left one man to guard the barge. Our heads cowled, our faces masked, we slipped ashore with our weapons and hurried up the dusty track edged with lime trees.

At first I panicked that we'd arrived at the wrong place, but Djarka knew Thebes and owned the finest collection of charts and maps. We rounded a bend and I raised my hand. A short distance away, a clump of sycamores sheltered the high battered wall of an ancient mansion. A guard or porter crouched, head down, dozing outside the black double gates. Djarka crept forward as far as he could, unslung his bow and edged a little closer. I heard the whip of the cord, followed by the whistle of Djarka's arrow, but it thudded into the gate. Djarka cursed, grasped another arrow and loosed again. This time he hit his target, and the porter half jumped only to sprawl flat on his face. We hurried forward, loping like hunting dogs towards the mansion. We scaled the walls and dropped into an overgrown garden where the undergrowth grew tangled and thick, the pools of purity and small canals, choked with weeds, smelled dank and fetid. Disused pavilions and derelict outhouses stood around.

We crossed the garden. One of the Caracals must have taken to sleeping outside; he sprang up like a deer flushed out by the hunters. He was half asleep and wine-soaked. Djarka cut his throat. We continued at a half-crouch towards decayed wooden steps which led to a door with flaking paint. I kept my eyes on the pillars on either side, the plaster all chipped and stained, and failed to notice the door open abruptly and two savage dogs come bounding out, teeth bared. They charged straight towards us even as arrows whipped the air above us, clear indication that the Caracals were now alerted. The dogs were cut down and we hastened towards the doorway. I glimpsed movement at an upstairs windows and above the parapet which bounded the flat roof. I sent Djarka and the mercenaries to circle the house.

'All the outbuildings are empty,' Djarka reported when they returned. 'Everyone is in the main house, but,' he turned and snapped his fingers, 'I found this.'

One of the mercenaries brought forward a skin bulging with oil.

'There's more,' Djarka smiled, 'in one of the outbuildings.'

The Caracals had been clumsy and lazy. They had not prepared for an assault or become aware of how vulnerable they were. We cut dry bracken and gorse and piled it through the downstairs windows and up against the doors. The oilskins were brought, slit and thrown in and Djarka ordered fire arrows to be loosed from every side. The Caracals were too few; they'd trapped themselves in the upper storey whilst the wood of that old house, its doors, lintels and outside stairs, was like kindling to the flame. The fire caught hold. Pungent black smoke curled out as the flames roared up. It was if Horus, He Who Devours Thousands by Fire, had entered that dwelling. The Caracals had no choice but to flee. They came tumbling out of doors and windows to be killed and their corpses flung back into the inferno. In all we killed five males and a black-haired young woman. We sat and watched the house burn, and when we were satisfied, we slunk back to the barge, dragging the corpse of the porter with us. We threw that into a crocodile pool, embarked and made our way back before the alarm was raised.

On our return to the House of the Evergreen Cedar we paid our mercenaries, swearing them to secrecy. They were veterans who knew me of old, and pouches of silver, warm quarters and plenty to eat were sufficient guarantees of their loyalty. They knew the price of betrayal: hideous death. Djarka and I washed and changed, and broke our fast on the flat roof, relishing the morning breeze. As we watched the sun rise we reminisced about such mornings in the City of the Aten. Whilst we talked I studied my friend and companion of countless years, my shield-bearer in so many bitter fights. He had, in his youth, been so handsome, with his ringlets of black hair, his dark eyes, smiling mouth and olive skin. Now he looked old and tired, his hair flecked with grey and white, his skin lined and furrowed, his eyes, ringed with dark shadows, no longer bright and merry.

'You are worried, Djarka,' I said gently. 'Last night you asked if we should flee. Why?'

'Akenhaten was of my people,' Djarka replied, so quickly I could tell this was a theme he'd turned over in his heart many times. 'You know the story,' he added hastily. 'How the Apiru are to become a great nation, while the tribe of Israar will produce a Messiah, a saviour who will lead such a nation to outstanding greatness.'

201

'An albino,' I interjected, 'pale of skin, with hair white as the finest wheat.'

'Yes.' Djarka smiled dreamily. 'Do you know, my grandfather was an albino. A source of great shame to us; he was nicknamed "the Leper". Anyway . . .'

Djarka shifted, turning his head to catch the breeze. I watched, and wondered why he wanted to flee. Was everything breaking up? Was it really each soul for itself? Even amongst friends?

'Are we finished, Djarka?' I forced a smile. 'Tell me how it is, not how it should be.'

'For truth's sake,' he replied, 'I shall be honest. The future isn't planned; the past, however, still holds us. What binds us, Lord Mahu,' he struck his breast, 'is the pact of friendship, comradeship; common dangers, yet we are both growing older. I have Mert, two children.' He coughed and blinked. 'Now,' he whispered, 'let me tell you what you are, let me explain that first. You say you have no soul, no friends, no kin accept Nabila.'

I felt a prick of alarm at the way he pronounced my wife's name. Djarka caught my look.

'No, no.' He lifted his hand. 'I shall explain that. You, Lord Mahu, like me, were raised with no brother and sister, no one except your aunt Isithia, and she was full of hate and hurt. Look at you, Mahu, a lord of Egypt, an intriguer, a warrior, an assassin, an atheist. You have supped and dined with the greatest, you have wallowed in the bed of luxury, but you have also eaten the hard black bread of exile and rejection.'

I sat fascinated at this friend, usually so taciturn, now eloquent, pouring his heart out.

'Yet,' Djarka continued, eyes half closed, 'you are still a little boy, lonely, wanting to be loved, to be cherished; that's why you loved Akenhaten, Nefertiti, the Children of the Kap, even Lord Ay. They became your family; you never betrayed them, even when they betrayed you. You kept faith as you have with me. Tutankhamun was, in many ways, your son also. I recognise you do not care for Ay and the rest, that's all in the past, but you have a duty to discharge. If Ay is innocent of Tutankhamun's death, what would you do? Seek high office? I doubt it. Retire here to the House of the Evergreen Cedar? Fine. However,' Djarka wiped his mouth on the back of his hand, 'if Ay is guilty, then blood must be spilt and I am bound to help you.' He stared full at me. 'I have to keep faith with you, whatever the cost.'

'Except,' I whispered, 'for Mert and your children.'

'Precisely, my lord Mahu, I will not cross that line. I beg you not to ask me. If I have to choose, it will be them before you. There,' he shrugged, 'you have it.'

I sipped my watered beer and watched the sun rise in a glorious blood-red glow. Djarka had told me where he truly stood: one of the few people in my life who ever had.

'Do you think I will settle down to be a farmer?'

'Don't joke, my lord Mahu! Ay is of my people; that makes him dangerous. We are driven and racked by dreams and prophecies; Ay is no different.' His voice dropped to a whisper. 'Ay knows all the secret history of the Apiru; he is just as dangerous as Akenhaten. What if, Lord Mahu, Ay sees himself as the Messiah, the Saviour?'

'He is many things,' I joked, 'but not an albino!'

'No, but he could see himself as the herald of the new era. Ay nourishes his own vision of grandeur and splendour. Believe me, it will not be the way of Egypt. Horemheb and Rameses have recognised that themselves.'

'In the end?' I asked.

'In the end,' Djarka confessed, 'Ay will try to give flesh to that vision, whatever it is, and that will cause bloodshed and chaos.'

'Let us support Horemheb and Rameses.'

'Nonsense.' Djarka rose and stretched. 'Rameses is no

different from Ay. If he had his way, every Apiru, every member of the clan of Israar, would die, to kill the dream, to remove any future danger.' He came over and squatted before me. 'Master,' his eyes pleaded with mine, 'master, we are finished, it is finished. Let us do what we have to and let us be gone.'

I was about to reply when I heard a sound on the steps. Nabila came up, escorted by two of my mercenaries, one holding her parasol, the other her basket and walking stick. I rose to greet her. She was cool and fragrant, smelling sweetly of the perfumed water she'd washed herself in. She was dressed in white robes with a coloured tasselled shawl about her shoulders; her faced was painted, black kohl rings round her eyes. She smiled at me, brushed my lips with hers, then, lifting the fringed shawl up, covered her head and told me that she was going to visit her kin.

'I have to,' she teased. 'They are waiting for me. I will tell them all that has happened, then you must welcome them here, Mahu. Feast them, for they will be your kin as well.'

In view of what Djarka had just said to me about being lonely, I burst out laughing, Nabila looked puzzled, but I kissed her again, and told her to be careful and that I looked forward to meeting my new family. She left. Djarka followed her to the top of the steps; he watched her go, then returned.

'The Caracals were expecting us, master.'

'Nonsense! That guard would not have been asleep, nor would the porter.'

Djarka crossed the parapet, his back to me. I felt a shiver of fear.

'What is it?' I asked.

'Nabila,' Djarka replied. 'Master, is she what she claims to be?'

'Djarka!'

My hand went to the knife concealed beneath the cushions.

'Strange, isn't it,' Djarka mused loudly, 'how we met her.'

'She didn't arrange for those pirates to attack her ship,' I protested, 'or know that we would rescue her.'

'Peace, master, and take your hand from your knife.' Djarka turned and squatted down, his back to the parapet. 'She saved us in Canaan,' he repeated. 'She also seems to know a great deal about that country.' He lifted his head. 'Only the Invisible One truly knows,' he continued, 'but, master, I think she is one of my people. She certainly knows more than what she has told us. Do you remember that conversation last night: she talked of Pentju being in the Mysterious Abode. No, master,' he held a hand out, 'the Dog Man told only you and me that, as did Amendufet out at the tomb. Last night Nabila referred to the Mysterious Abode before Amendufet ever discussed Pentju's whereabouts. Even then he did not mention the Mysterious Abode. So,' Djarka leaned forward, 'how did she know?'

Nifi: the breath of a serpent or cobra

Chapter 11

The Dolphin Chamber in the Malkata Palace had never looked so splendid; the blue ceiling with its spangled stars brilliantly reflected in the shiny marble floor. The rows of pillars were painted a restful green with gold and red acanthus leaves at the top and base. The walls were a cobalt blue with paintings of golden dolphins, silver porpoises and other sea monsters leaping in eternal joy. Jars of the purest alabaster, in a variety of gorgeous colours, glowed in their countless niches around the walls like a myriad of summer flowers come to full bloom. At either side of the great chamber were wide windows overlooking the imperial gardens, where the rich black soil of Canaan allowed every fragrant flower to grow – the jonquil, the rose, lilies and hyacinths, their fragrance wafted into the chamber by the late evening breeze to mix with the *kiphye* from the lotus floating on the pools of purity as well as the sweetness from ornate baskets filled with crushed perfumed cakes of frankincense and sandalwood.

At the far end of the chamber stood a huge marble dais of cobalt blue edged with gold and silver, its front studded with precious stones. On either side of the dais rose stucco pillars of the same colour connected by an arch of sea-green cedarwood from which lunged golden cobras, the protectors of Pharaoh. From an adjoining chamber, music from the court orchestra of Kush, the lilt of the five-string lyre mixing with that of the thirty-two-string harp, swelled to a climax. Deeper down an adjoining passageway echoed the sound of sistra and the bellowing of trumpets and conch horns; incense smoke billowed in, a gong boomed and a herald's voice intoned Pharaoh's titles: the Living Image of Amun, the Fitting of Forms, Horus in the South. Trumpets brayed, and the great double doors to the right of the dais opened with a crash. Priests of the stole, the chapel and the sanctuary entered carrying censers and bowls of rose petals; they were followed by the fan bearers and Nakhtimin and his senior officers.

I knelt on my purple gold-fringed cushion and glanced slightly to my left. We were all there, in our fine gold robes and thick oiled wigs. Huy was decorated with his chains and medallions of office. Maya, painted like some high-ranking whore, moved in a shimmer of jewels, necklaces and costly rings. Sobeck was wearing the panther skin of the Chief of Police across his shoulders. Further along, in white linen robes, knelt the great generals Rameses and Horemheb. They had deliberately garbed themselves simply, with no medals or medallions, silver bees of courage or gold collars of valour.

Ay now appeared in a gust of gold dust, flower petals and incense. He swept in through the lapis-lazuli-edged portal, as magnificent as Horus in robes of pleated linen with a jackal tail hanging behind and an apron of gold and enamel over his stomach and groin. Gold-edged sandals adorned his feet, and on his head was the red and white crown of Upper and Lower Egypt, its gorgeous ribbons, displaying sparkling gems, fluttering in the breeze. He carried the flail and rod across his chest. To cries of: 'He is like the sun when it rises in the morning on the eastern horizon, he floods the world with his light . . .' Ay took his place on the splendid golden throne, the ends of its arms, carved in silver, portraying lunging leopards, its feet raging bulls. Above the throne floated a canopy of cloth of gold stiffened with brilliant diamonds. On the floor before the throne stood a matching footstool carved out of electrum and studded with flashing filament of gold.

As Ay sat down, he rested his feet and deliberately pushed the footstool forward. I heard Horemheb gasp, and looked a little closer. The footstool was ornamented with silver leaf depicting Pharaoh punishing his enemies, the coloured head-dresses and long hair of these foes revealing them as Hittites. Ay was making his point: if a victory was to be won against these new People of the Nine Bows then it would be his, no one else's. Horemheb ground his teeth; Rameses muttered to himself. Others entered. Ankhesenamun, lovely in her lush opulence, seemed slightly plumper. She looked resplendent in her snow-white robes and thick-heeled sandals, and her beautiful face, with those seductive eyes, high cheek bones and sensuous mouth, was framed by a splendid wig cascading down to her shoulders and decorated with ribbons of gold. Mother-of-pearl bracelets circled her wrists; a necklace of gorgeous cornelian her lovely throat.

Ankhesenamun sat down on the small throne to Ay's left, hiding her face behind a fan of the purest ebony. On her right, her fellow conspirator, the lady-in-waiting Amedeta, looked so much like her mistress I wondered if she was some bastard child of Ay. Amedeta was not dressed so magnificently but squatted on cushions, fan open, peering across the rim, her eyes glowing like those of Ankhesenamun. She was openly laughing at us. Oh, they were two minxes who shared lovers as well as their own love, spoilt, pampered bitches but still very dangerous. I stared back at them as insolently as I could. On the day of reckoning, I reasoned, these two would pay. Ankhesenamun certainly did not look the grieving widow but sat with one hand holding the fan, the other, with its long hennaed nails, resting on the arm of her grandfather's throne. She reminded me of some resplendent, ferocious cat, claws bared, beautiful but cruel. Ankhesenamun's eyes caught mine, just for a heartbeat, and that impudent smile faded.

I glanced away and stared malevolently at the figure on Ay's left: Mery-re. No longer the chief of the Vesper Bats or the Kheb-sher of the Hittites, but now Chief Priest of the Red Chapel, leading prophet of the royal retinue. Mery-re's small face was round as an apple, plump and satisfied, eyes all innocent, mouth as smug as ever with that look of deep piety which deceived no one. He was garbed in all the glory of a high priest, robes white and soft, gold and silver decorating his fat neck and wrists, a leopardskin draped across his shoulders. He carried a pomander which he sniffed every so often before raising his eyes heavenwards as if in constant prayer. I could have killed the smug little bastard on the spot!

The end of the procession had reached the Dolphin Chamber: the Director of Pharaoh's Cabinet, the Keeper of the Plume, the People of the Circle, the Men of the Rolls, the Lords of the Secrets of Heaven, the Prophets of the Royal Court. Nakhtimin stood behind the throne, the only armed man present. We'd all been searched at the Great Gates, our retinues, including Djarka, told to wait in the courtyards near the Avenue of the Sphinx and the Ram. Ay now gathered us together. The great double doors were closed and we immediately prostrated ourselves as an unseen herald began to chant Ay's praises. This was followed by the longest silence of any prostration. Ay was making his presence felt. Matters were not helped by someone, I am not too sure if it was Horemheb or Rameses, belching long and telling, as we had all done as children at the Kap to annoy our teachers or scribes. I pressed my face to the floor, body shaking, until I recalled Djarka's advice. He had spelled out the threat very clearly. The Children of the Kap were now engaged in insult and baiting. They were at war with each other, but we were not, as yet, at war with any of them. Djarka had pressed his fingers against my lips.

'Smile and bow low until we know what path we must take.'

I would heed that advice, and not be drawn or provoked.

At length the herald announced that we could look upon the face of the Living Horus. I knelt back and stared at that swarthy, sinister, handsome face with its knowing look and smiling mouth. Ay stared back, his heavy-lidded cobra eyes black and implacable. He raised one hand. Mery-re fell to his knees and, in a nasal high-pitched voice, intoned a long prayer. I stared at that malevolent little turd masquerading as a priest.

Once Mery-re had finished his gabbling, Nakhtimin came and knelt on the cushions at his brother's feet so that he faced us. He was dressed in all the regalia of Commander-in-Chief, as well as Chamberlain. His proclamation hardly surprised us. Huy was confirmed as Overseer of the House of Envoys, Maya the House of Silver, Sobeck Chief of Police in Thebes. Then, raising a hand, Nakhtimin snapped his fingers. Scribes hurried forward with little coffers and chests. Nakhtimin took out scarlet gloves, silver beads and collars of valour which he handed to Ay, who, in a ringing voice, proclaimed how Horemheb and Rameses were his close friends and favoured clients; they were 'Braves to the King'. The two rogues were summoned forward to receive lavish praise and all the marks of Pharaoh's honour. Horemheb was declared to be Chief Scribe, General of the Army of the North, Commander of all Egyptian forces across Sinai, as well as Governor of Memphis. Rameses was proclaimed to be his lieutenant.

There was nothing for me. Ay had only given what people already possessed. I had been Guardian of the Prince; now he had gone, so I had lost any reason for being there. Ah well.

Once all the hypocrisy was finished, Nakhtimin ordered the hall to be cleared, leaving us, the Children of the Kap, the hyaenas, with their Pharaoh, his brother and Ankhesenamun. We brought our cushions closer in a semi-circle before the throne. One of the guards, a Kushite, brought in a tray with a silver flagon and gilt-chased goblets. Ay filled his cup and drank greedily, smiling at us over the rim. The wine was shared. I was suddenly aware of how that marble chamber, with all its beauty, was where the dreams of empire had flourished, being given flesh by the Great Amenhotep. Now it was silent as people took goblets of wine and glanced slyly at each other. The years had changed us all. Once that same group, with the exception of Ankhesenamun, had sat and plotted against all others; now that game had ended.

'My friends.' Ay removed the Double Crown and handed it to Nakhtimin, a gesture not lost on us. 'My friends,' he purred like a cat, 'welcome to Thebes the Victorious! We are friends, we are here to discuss common problems. Grievances can be resolved, questions answered, then we can feast and rejoice in our friendship.'

Mery-re smirked. My anger boiled over.

'Why, my Lord Mahu,' Ay had caught my change of expression, 'is there something amiss?'

'I received no office.'

'That will come in time.'

I gestured at Mery-re. 'But not as soon as for traitors and assassins.'

'Mery-re has always,' Ay pursed his lips like a master scribe lecturing a not so intelligent pupil, 'had the interests of our house at heart. He kept us informed about those zealots who still pursue the crazy ideas of the Great Heretic.'

'As we all once did.'

Ay ignored Nakhtimin's sharp intake of breath.

'The past,' he smiled, 'lies behind sealed doors; a glorious future beckons us on.'

'Mery-re tried to kill me!' I shouted. 'He and his loathsome Vesper Bats pursued me the length and breadth of Canaan.'

'Not my doing!' Mery-re's high-pitched voice cut like a knife. 'I was sent by the Lord, the Divine One.' He hastily corrected himself. 'To search out the followers of Akenhaten and learn the counsels of our enemies. I used my position to befriend the Hittite princes and serve them with ill advice. Never once,' he pointed at me, 'did I hurt or threaten you, did I?'

I glared back.

'I was a spy.' Mery-re pouted. 'I worked for the interests of Egypt. I had to pretend, I had to act, and in the end, I had to flee. I had to warn Lord Horemheb how the Hittites planned to slip by him into Egypt.' He hitched the leopardskin higher about his shoulders. 'The Vesper Bats were not under my control. They were mercenaries taking their orders from the Hittite court.'

I turned to Horemheb.

'We were warned,' Horemheb conceded. 'All I can tell you is that we were advancing north from Sinai when we received information that the Hittites were moving fast, intending to get behind us, cut off our route back into Egypt.'

'Enough,' Ay hissed. 'The past is the past. What we need now is friendship, that is what is important.'

'Divine One,' Rameses glanced scornfully at me as if my concerns were petty, 'God's Father Mery-re now enjoys the peace of the Great House, yet,' he sucked his lip, 'we were absent when Tutankhamun went into the Eternal West. There is the question of succession, the right . . .'

Ay nodded solemnly, as if this was a weighty matter which often concerned him. Beside him Ankhesenamun sat regally, her left hand now resting against her grandfather's thigh.

'The young king,' Ay intoned, face all sombre and mournful, 'suffered a fit and died. Lord Mahu, you witnessed such fits. The Divine One was rendered speechless, inert.' He spread his hands. 'We did what we could but he slipped into death.'

We all sat silent.

'True,' Ay nodded slowly, as if answering an invisible question, a sign he'd rehearsed this speech many times, 'true, the burial rights of Tutankhamun were hasty, but what could I do? Egypt was at war; there was no true successor. The good of To-Mery is what matters. I was hailed by the priests, the troops and the court. Most reluctantly I assumed the burden of the Great House . . .'

As Ay warbled on, I recalled the question I had once posed to him: if Tutankhamun should die without an heir, to whom would Egypt go? Ay had replied quickly, fiercely: 'To the strongest!'

In truth that had happened, and on this particular evening, Ay made it very clear to all of us. Once some troublesome issues had been cleared, at least to Ay's satisfaction, we turned to other matters: the strengthening of garrisons along the Horus Road, the defence of the diamond mines across Sinai, and a projected military expedition into Kush. Ay pursued these matters deliberately, boring us all to silence.

Eventually the meeting ended and we were invited to a splendid banquet in the Hall of the Eternal Sun, which stood in its own gardens at the centre of the palace. This was a beautiful hall of audience, though smaller then some others, its walls covered with miniature suns, interspersed with *ankh* and *sa* signs. Its columns were painted red, with golden vine leaves curling from base to top. Large open windows breasted three sides, with glistening pools beneath to provide an atmosphere of coolness. In the centre of the hall was an extended dais of polished cedarwood beneath a rounded wheel which could be ingeniously lowered so that its rim and spokes served as holders for glowing alabaster lamp jars. The dais had been arranged for a banquet: cushions, stiffened to take our weight, formed a circle around the polished acacia tables. Musicians of Kush gathered in the doorway whilst choirs in the gardens beyond sang soft hymns. Ay, the great host, summoned us to sit, and we feasted royally, on red mullet and tajines of beef, lamb with chickpeas and other vegetables, whilst various wines, rich and strong, brimmed our goblets.

At first we ate and drank self-consciously, but the fragrance of the wine and Ay's lavish hospitality induced us to relax. Amedeta returned to dance sinuously and sensuously; a trained temple heset, she whirled and turned to the soft rattle of the sistra and tambourine. She was clothed only in a tasselled loincloth, her exquisite coppery body shimmering in the light of jewels, bracelets and rings. She danced to celebrate the joy of the goddess Isis' victory over the murderous Seth, and was watched hungrily by Horemheb and Rameses. Once her dance was finished, the formal part of the banquet ended. Guests left their tables to mingle, either going over to the cushioned seats or out into the cool of the garden. I found myself sheltering against the glare of the setting sun under the shade of an outstretched sycamore, staring, as if fascinated, at a clump of wild herbs planted in large rounded tubs of black earth. As I bent and sniffed their perfumes, I heard a chuckle. I turned: Ankhesenamun stood behind me. In the fading light she was so reminiscent of her mother, Nefertiti, in the way she stood, one foot slightly forward, head tilted back, watching me languidly.

'Welcome home, Uncle Mahu,' she slurred, swaying slightly from side to side. 'Did you enjoy Amedeta's dance?'

The lady-in-waiting came forward. The two minxes stood, arms round each other, clasped close as if they were lovers. I didn't like the smile on Ankhesenamun's face or the smirk on that of Amedeta.

'Mistress . . .' I bowed, now distracted by the sight of Ay and Horemheb in close discussion on the steps leading up to the hall. 'Mistress,' I repeated, 'my condolences on the death of your husband, not to mention those of your two children.'

For a moment the bitch's smile faded, her lovely shoulders sagged, and a brief look of sadness showed she still had a heart.

'I . . .' She broke away from Amedeta, kicking at the ground with the toe of her sandal. 'Uncle Mahu,' she whispered, 'he fell into one of his fits.'

'Did he . . .' I kept my voice composed, 'did he ever talk of me?'

She smiled, and her next words sealed her fate and that of her house, I swear that by the living Horus! 'Uncle Mahu, he never stopped talking about you. He pined for you; he'd sit and say, "Uncle Mahu would say that or do this. When will Uncle Mahu return? Why did he leave, will he bring me back a present?" He fell ill, he lost his speech. Pentju came, but there was nothing he or anyone could do.' She chattered on like a child, until I could take no more. I pressed a finger against her mouth and stared into those lying eyes.

'Enough,' I hissed, and walked away. Someone called my name, but I walked on deeper into that exquisite garden until I reached a T-shaped pool protected by a pergola covered with vines. I went round through the entrance. The entire pool lay under the shade of a huge sycamore tree; around it flowers bloomed, their perfume mingling with that of the water lilies. Ducks swam lazily around the edge of a papyrus thicket. The garden had changed, but that pool evoked memories. I had once walked there with Akenhaten, Nefertiti and Ay as we plotted against the power of the priests. And hadn't Djarka and I brought the young Tutankhamun here to teach him how to fish?

I sat on a wooden bench and wept for our golden boy. Thoughts came and went. I grew sleepy-eyed, and dozed for longer than I wished. When I awoke it was growing dark. I startled at a sound and whirled round. Mery-re stood in the entrance to the pergola, dressed so elegantly in his white robe, a garland of flowers around his neck. Behind him was a row of dark figures. I glimpsed the gold and blue *nemes*, the head-dress of Pharaoh's own bodyguard.

'Why, Mahu, you look startled.'

'It's dark,' I snapped, 'and I don't like you standing behind me.'

'The guests are leaving. The Divine One wishes to see you.' Mery-re waggled his fingers. 'Come.'

I had no choice. I was not taken to the Hall of Eternal Sunlight but across the garden. Mery-re scurried in front, preceded by torch bearers, the flames sparkling and spluttering in the windswept darkness. On either side of me strode Nakhtu-aa armed with shields and curled swords. We entered a deserted and neglected part of the gardens and reached steps leading down to an underground cavern. Perhaps it had once been a cellar, I don't really know. I was ordered to stay at the top, while Mery-re scurried down like a monkey. Time passed. The guards gathered around me, hard eyes in scarred faces. I recognised one of these, a companion from a campaign years earlier. For a few breaths his face relaxed, and he shifted his eyes as a warning to me to be careful. The door at the bottom opened.

'Come!' a voice ordered. The guards escorted me down the steps and pushed me through the half-open door. Beyond stretched a low-ceilinged chamber vividly lit by torches. Ay and Mery-re squatted on a pile of cushions, behind them two slabs slightly tilted like those in a mortuary room. On one of the slabs sprawled a corpse. The hair and beard had been completely shaved, but due to the tilt of the slab I recognised the scarred face of the mercenary, our guide from Canaan, who had mysteriously disappeared when we'd met Horemheb's army. On each corner of the slab a fiery torch glowed. In the dazzling light, the savage wounds to the chest looked all the more grotesque. The eyes, despite the scarabs placed there, were half open, as if the mercenary was watching me, his blood-caked lips ready to whisper some secret.

'Come in, Lord Mahu.' Ay gestured to a stool a few paces in front of them. I obeyed. The door closed behind me and I heard the shuffle of feet. The Nakhtu-aa were guarding the entrance. I fought to remain calm. I stared round and noticed the terrifying pictures on the walls depicting demons from the underworld: a large vulture, bright blue with ochre wings; a hippo-headed beast holding two sharp knives, a red disc

219

above its head; an eerie-looking child with a misshapen yellow head and red body, wielding two swords, one blue, the other green. I recognised the Cell Keepers, the Demons of the Night, the Lords of Terrors with Faces to the Left. I had been brought here to be frightened; perhaps I should have been.

Years later, when I was hiding in Kush, I came across the guard who had warned me with his eyes. By then he was a standard bearer in one of the great forts beyond the Cataracts. He told me one night, as we shared a jug of beer, how Ay had turned to *stekhi*, malign magic, whilst Mery-re was truly a Kheb-sher, who had forsaken the path of the One and become a follower of the Shems, the Prowlers of the Dark. The guard confided that Ay and Mery-re would use the corpses of the unburied, such as that of the mercenary, to call on their spirits from the icy land of the dead to help them. It may have been true, though at the time it was the living who concerned me.

Ay was dressed in a simple robe over a loincloth, Mery-re the same, and both had strange markings on their faces. Ay gestured over his shoulder with his thumb.

'Nakhtimin's men caught him out in the Redlands.'

'Who is he?'

Ay laughed softly. 'He and his son.'

'Where is his son?'

'Dead in the Redlands.'

'Why didn't you bring him back as well?'

'He lies in the sand near the Oasis of the Vulture God.'

I recalled the place: a small enclosure of palms about two miles into the desert east of Thebes.

'He was your guide through Canaan, Mahu.' Ay's voice grew brusque. 'He was coming to see you, he and his son; they were bringing messages from Akenhaten.'

My heart fluttered but I kept my face impassive. Mery-re was watching me intently.

'What messages?' I asked.

220

Mery-re closed his eyes. '"To my friend Mahu," he intoned. "The Veiled One, for the last time but in all friendship, sends greetings and bids him farewell. I shall not speak any more until we meet in the Groves of Osiris as we did on that first day when the light was first born. Seek out the Watchers. Farewell, Mahu, Baboon of the South."'

'You have no proof,' I retorted.

Mery-re opened his eyes. For once in his awful, terrible life, I recognised the little turd wasn't lying. Maat had brushed his tongue with her feathered wings. He was telling the truth. Akenhaten had referred to that first morning we had met in the groves of the Malkata Palace. I also understood why Nakhtimin had not brought the mercenary's son in: they had probably tortured him to extract the message. I experienced a deep sadness, a feeling of desolation in my limbs. Akenhaten was truly gone. He would walk no more with men. I felt tired, and for a brief moment I realised why Akenhaten had grown so exhausted, so sick of the cup of power. Yet for me there was still Nabila, Djarka . . .

I gestured at Ay. 'I thought you said Akenhaten had died some time ago.'

'He did,' Mery-re smirked, 'for all he mattered. Now he's truly gone.' He squirmed with delight. 'But let's talk about the living.'

'You are married, Lord Mahu, congratulations! A beautiful woman. You are most fortunate – as was she, to be rescued.' Ay beamed at me.

'Why did you send your scribe,' I accused, 'to plot my death?'

'Nonsense!' Ay smiled, his lying eyes bright with excitement. 'We are pleased you have returned safely, Mahu; we just wonder at whose campfire you now sit.'

'Pentju,' Mery-re declared. 'Has Pentju spoken to you at all?'

'You know he hasn't.'

'How can we trust you, Mahu?'

'You can't, as I can't you. Judge me by my actions,' I continued. 'The Caracals you hunted?' A sharp intake of breath behind me meant Nakhtimin the assassin was present. 'You did not kill them all, so I did it for you. I have friends in the city who told me everything. Go to the House of the Sycamores. Search amongst its ruins: the Caracals are dead, a gift, O Divine One,' I tried to keep the sarcasm from my voice, 'from Djarka and myself.'

'There was a fire,' Nakhtimin said behind me. 'Who hired the Caracals, Mahu?'

'Divine One, if I knew . . .'

Ay laughed and turned to the small ebony-inlaid table beside him. He picked up an exquisite jewel-encrusted goblet and sipped from it. I recognised the cup with its motif of lions' heads, its blue cobalt rim and stem: the Glory Cup of Amenhotep the Magnificent, a sign of majesty, the personal property of Pentju. Ay toasted me with it.

'So you have not spoken to Pentju?'

'You know I have not.' I gestured at the cup. 'He hides in the Mysterious Abode. He is frightened.'

'He is certainly frightened.' Ay lifted the goblet, eyes greedily examining it. 'He sent me this as a gift, or a bribe. What does he fear, Mahu?'

I stared back, genuinely puzzled. Pentju was hiding, protecting himself, and, knowing my old friend, for a very good reason. But why send the Glory Cup to Ay?

'Who are the Watchers, Lord Mahu?' Mery-re demanded.

'By the Lords of Light I wish I knew,' I stammered to cover the lie.

'Can we trust you?'

'As much as I do you.'

'Do you know,' Ay smacked his lips, 'Horemheb has asked for the hand of the Lady Ankhesenamun in marriage.' He laughed drily but he was throbbing with rage. 'How dare that peasant from the Delta,' he hissed, 'who has my feckless daughter already sharing his bed, now ask for my grand-daughter, the Queen Dowager? He dreams his dreams of glory, Mahu! One day I must test those dreams, then you must decide.' He toasted me once again and flicked his fingers, a sign that I should withdraw.

I left the palace shortly afterwards, collecting Djarka and my two mercenary escorts. We passed the marble gate, one mercenary walking in front with a torch, the other behind. Djarka stumbled beside me, half asleep. He told me how he had carried out my orders to inform Sobeck about our destruction of the Caracals.

'He was surprised,' he muttered, 'and he'll undoubtedly tell Maya, who will inform Horemheb.'

'And you told him the reason why?'

'Of course,' Djarka scoffed. 'We did it to help Horemheb. If the Caracals had struck, Horemheb would have been blamed.'

I stopped and stared up at the full moon riding across the meadows of heaven.

'Akenhaten is truly dead,' I murmured. 'I know he is. He is gone into the Eternal West; either that,' I added bitterly, 'or into eternal oblivion.'

Djarka walked on a little further and fell to his knees, face in his hands as he muttered a prayer in his own tongue. He rocked backwards and forwards then, wiping his eyes, rose to his feet. I told him about the rest: the death of the mercenary, Horemheb's desire to marry Ankhesenamun. Djarka grasped my wrist, pulling me close.

'It's over,' he whispered, his breath hot against my face. 'Master, it is certainly over. We should flee. The day of the Great Reckoning is close, and this will all end in blood . . .'

Neb-t Kheper: snake goddess

Chapter 12

I rose early the next morning. Djarka's warning, like the memory of a nightmare, sobered my mood. The sky was still dark. I sat on the roof terrace and, in the half-light, watched the mist swirl and curl through the palm trees down by the river. The breeze was bitterly cold, as if carrying a warning of what terrors that day would bring. I sat on reed matting in the corner of the roof wall, sipping watered wine mixed with honey. The events of the previous night coursed like sparks through my soul. Ay had threatened me; Mery-re was as sinister as ever. I watched the eastern sky tinge with red as the sun began to rise. It reminded me of the scarlet cuts on the mercenary's corpse. Ay did not trust me. I would be given no high office, and they would wait for any sign of treachery. The only reason Ay did not move against me was that I was a Child of the Kap: an attack upon me might provoke the hostility of the others or signal that they too were marked down for destruction. It was a matter of waiting, but waiting for what? Akenhaten was dead. He and his dreams were dust. I wondered why the mercenary had been sent. Undoubtedly he carried more detailed messages, but what? Perhaps Djarka was right. It was time to flee, but where to? Memphis, or beyond the Horus Road?

I fell into a daydream, almost unaware of the sun strengthening and the onset of the first prickly heat of the day. I wondered about my treasure. There were merchants in Memphis and the Delta with whom I had reached secret agreements. Djarka came up and asked me if I was going into the city. He whispered something about Pentju but I wasn't listening, so he glanced at me strangely and left. Servants brought food and beakers of ice-cold water. The children ran out to play in the garden, chasing each other around the Pool of Purity. Mert and Nabila, together with the maids, came to join them. Someone had brought a bag of the fine gold dust which is sprinkled during processions. The children chased Nabila and Mert, throwing handfuls at them. I watched this scene of domestic contentment and wondered how long it would last.

Later Nabila came up to see me, escorted by a servant carrying her fan and parasol. My wife hadn't changed her robe, but she had brought a gauze linen shawl, fringed with silver tassels, to protect her against the sun. She said she wished to visit certain markets in the city, and before I could ask, she gestured at the servant, who had a leather money belt strapped across his shoulder, saying she had sufficient debens of silver and ounous of gold. She kissed me softly on the lips; her eyes were black-kohl-ringed, bright with life. She was nervous, but I was too distracted to notice. She walked to the top of the outside stairs then turned, glanced directly at me and smiled. A beautiful gesture! I thought she was going to walk back to me but she shook her head as if talking to herself and went down. I listened to the patter of her reed sandals, the chatter of the servant and then she was gone.

That was the last time I ever saw Nabila, my beautiful wife of a few months. I have searched everywhere. I have bribed where I could. I have begged where I could. I have bullied where I could, but no one knows where she is. Only Ay and Nakhtimin know the truth, and they took it to the grave; that and all the other hideous, bloody secrets of their vicious struggle for power.

I have always thought of that day as the time of silence, of secret terrors and hidden danger, yet it was so quiet to begin with. I stayed on the rooftop. A servant brought up a parasol, then another one to protect the dishes of fruit. I drank too much and woke heavy-eyed and thick-tongued. The house and garden were peaceful. The children had withdrawn from the day's heat. The only sounds were the call of a bird, the constant whirring of insects, until I heard the cries of servants hurrying to a side gate. I immediately grasped my war belt, strapped it on and hastened clumsily down the steps. Djarka was already in the hall of audience. He'd kicked a table and stool aside, walking up and down, gesturing at a dust-stained Sobeck.

My old friend did not look so plump or genial as usual. He was dressed in the gleaming leather kilt and belt of office, a panther skin about his shoulders, leather guards on his wrists and stout marching boots on his feet. In the doorway thronged members of the Medjay in their fringed skirts of tanned leather, their black hair crimped. The officers sported vividly coloured feathers pushed into the knots of hair at the back of their heads. Around their necks hung pendants of the vulture goddess, the insignia of the elite police corps which patrolled the Necropolis, the City of the Dead. Djarka fell silent at my approach. Sobeck strode towards me, grasped my hands and pulled me close to exchange the kiss of peace. One hand went behind my head so I couldn't withdraw.

'Pentju is dead!' he whispered. 'Be careful what you say and do.'

I stood in shock. Pentju, my drunken friend, the once elegant court physician, the boy whom I'd teased in the Kap, the sharer of so many of my secrets! It truly was the Day of the Night God, the Season of the Dark! Pentju was a link to the past. I tried to control my breathing.

'Prudence,' Sobeck whispered. 'I cannot trust all my men.'

I pulled myself free. Sobeck stood, eyes red-rimmed; I'm not too sure whether it was from dust or tears.

'How?' I asked.

'You'd best come,' he replied. 'I have not moved his corpse.'

I told Djarka to guard the house. He wanted to accompany me but I shouted at him to stay. I remember taking a pair of sandals and a walking cane surmounted with the head of Anubis from a reed basket near the doorway. Strange, isn't it, how you remember such petty details?

I left my house, hurrying along well-shaded roads, past gilded mansions and stately residences, into the city through the majestic Turquoise Gate. I remember the din, the dust and the smell. Such a contrast to the peace of my own mansion, past temples and palaces ablaze with gold, silver, electrum and lapis lazuli, along avenues fringed by snarling human-headed lions of black granite which glared across the avenue at sphinxes hewn out of roseate stone. We reached the Great Mooring Place along the Nile, a porticoed quay-side, the pillars decorated with the exploits of previous Pharaohs, showing them victorious over the People of the Nine Bows. We had to wait for a war craft. Sobeck refused to talk to me, shouting orders, demanding people stand aside for the officers of Pharaoh. At last a craft displaying the standard of Horus came alongside and we clambered aboard. The Nile was still swollen and fast-moving, and the oarsmen had to fight against the swift current whilst our lookouts on the prow blew wailing blasts on conch horns, warning other craft to pull aside. We were no respecters of persons. There was a funeral barge carrying an ornamented coffin casket escorted by boatloads of mourners and singers: this, too, was peremptorily told to let us by.

We came in like an arrow to the Place of Osiris, the great quayside of the City of the Dead dominated by towering statues of the gods: the human-faced Osiris and the dog-featured Anubis. More of the Medjay were waiting for us along with a standard bearer carrying a stiffened pennant displaying a broad-winged vulture. We hastened through the

City of the Dead up narrow tracks and along stinking streets where the dirt was piled high and naked children searched with their fingers and red-rimmed eyes for dry dung for their households. The smell of rotting vegetation competed with the ever-pervasive odours from the shops of the dead, the embalming houses where the People of the Tombs did a brisk trade in gutting corpses, cleansing them in natron and packing the cadavers with a range of products, from smelly black rags to costly unguents and perfumes. Casket sellers, coffin makers, sculptors and carpenters shouted for trade. Raggedly dressed scribes advertised that they could write any letter. A group of temple heralds stood on a corner preparing a stake for the impalement of a tomb robber. The felon stood bound and tied in his own doorway, shivering with terror as he waited for sentence to be carried out so that people in his own street could witness what happened to those who plundered the dead.

Life swirled around us in the City of the Dead. Someone once told me that the Necropolis had forty thousand inhabitants and every day something like two thousand embalmings took place. Little wonder the beer shops and drinking houses did a roaring trade, whilst the seething, smelly streets were full of prostitutes from every country. They all scattered at the approach of the Medjay, entire streets emptying before us. The Vulture Men were well known for their use of the club and sword. We crossed the great Avenue of the Embalmers and up through a maze of runnels into the heart of the Necropolis. The houses here grew more dingy; there were not so many children or pack animals, just dark shadows in the doorways which retreated at our approach. At last we entered the Mysterious Abode, a sinister, eerie place, a market square bounded on each side by houses: in the centre, ringed by dusty sycamore trees, stood the fortified house where Pentju had decided to hide.

It was the type of place you see in a dream. Once built as

231

a fortified block house or fortress for the Medjay police, it was fashioned out of grey limestone, with narrow windows on each of the two storeys. It boasted a small garden at the back, a main doorway approached by steps, and side doors at each end. More of Sobeck's men were waiting here. They had cleared the square and now crouched, bows unslung, in the shade of the sycamore trees. Sobeck explained how the downstairs chambers served as drinking rooms and bartering places, while the upstairs rooms were a brothel where Mitanni prostitutes plied their trade.

When we burst through the front door, all the customers had fled. A group of whores, thick oiled wigs almost hiding their faces, naked except for braided girdles, huddled in a corner. By their glazed look and slurred voices, they'd apparently decided to drown their sorrows, being offered generous bowls of wine by the greasy, fat-faced owner. Another chamber, its doorway guarded by Medjay, housed a different group. At first glance I thought they were women, with their long wigs, painted faces and embroidered robes. The stench of perfume was so heavy you could almost taste it.

'By what right,' one of them shouted, trying to force a way past a guard, 'are we held here?'

The voice was deep and masculine, with a slight lisp. I noticed the line of grey stubble on the upper lip. All those paints and cosmetics couldn't hide a male face.

'Lady Boys!' Sobeck whispered, gently pushing me on.

I remembered what I had been told: how Pentju had hired this gang of transvestites to guard him. Despite their feminine ways and painted faces, the Lady Boys were one of the most savage gangs roaming the City of the Dead. Prostitutes and catamites, pimps and procurers, they specialised in selling human flesh and did not care about the age or sex of their victims.

We crossed the shabby hall of audience, the fire hearth in the centre full of grey ash. Crude paintings on the wall depicted temple girls – hesets and prostitutes – in every pose imaginable. The place reeked of burned food and stale wine. We climbed the staircase to the second storey. Pentju's chamber was the central one, on a needle-thin gallery which stank of cheap oil and animal fat. The heavy door to the chamber had been broken off and hung askew on its leather hinges. The inside bolts at the top and bottom had been wrenched away. The chamber itself, however, was surprisingly neat and clean, the floor of polished wood, its walls limewashed. The pillars down the centre had been discreetly painted in a refreshing green and blue. Embroidered cloths hung against the plaster. There were two pots of incense, blackened and burned, and, on the eating table, a row of jars filled with crushed herbs. The gauze sheeting around the bed was lily white; the coffers and chests unbroken.

Pentju lay sprawled on cushions along the dais just beneath the shuttered window at the far end of the room. I went across and knelt down. My friend had certainly aged: his sparse hair had turned white, the stubble on his mouth and chin was like that of an old man. He wore little jewellery except for a bracelet which I recognised as a gift from Tutankhamun. His tunic was well laundered except for the front, which was now stained with wine and vomit. His face was a dull grey, heavy-jowelled, mouth gaping, eyes rolled back in the full anguish of death, and he seemed smaller than I remembered. I pulled back his tunic. The loincloth beneath was stained, and a dark, mulberry-coloured rash discoloured his stomach. I smelled his mouth: very sweet, as if he had chewed on crushed raisins; his tongue was coated with a yellowy-white skin, as were his lips, as if he had drunk the richest milk. I picked up his hand: its flesh was ice cold, the muscles hard. Sobeck crouched beside me.

'It's not a seizure,' he whispered. 'When we arrived here, some of the customers had not yet fled. One of them was a physician from the House of Life at the Temple of Meretseger.'

'Poison?' I asked.

Sobeck nodded. 'I told the physician to check him carefully. He thinks it was some herbal potion mixed in wine, and yet . . .' Sobeck rose to his feet, wiping the sweat from his face. He pointed round the chamber. 'There are two jugs of wine and five cups. I found no trace of poison in any of them.'

'And food?' I asked.

'Pentju was in the best of health this morning,' Sobeck replied. 'Our physician never ate until sunset.'

I asked Sobeck to wait for a few moments and knelt by the corpse, trying to rearrange it as best I could. I wanted to shut those eyes, but the muscles of the corpse were hardening, so I took a strip of linen from one of the bed sheets and placed it across my friend's face. Then I closed my own eyes, and tried to recall a moment when Pentju and I had laughed, joked, drunk and celebrated. I don't believe in the Far West. There is nothing beyond the Far Horizon. If the gods exist, they don't care, and if demons prowl, they are not half as fearsome as many of the people I have met, fought and struggled with over the years. In the end I recited a poem about friendship, about days in the sun and perfumed evenings when the food was rich and the wine flowed like water. Then I sat back on my heels and glanced over my shoulder. Sobeck and his officers were now opening coffers and chests. I rose, went to a window and glanced down at the dusty square. The shadows were lengthening. I called Sobeck over and asked him what had actually happened. He wiped his face with a napkin, threw that over his shoulder and leaned against the wall.

'Pentju was hiding, from what I don't know. I can get little understanding from the proprietor or the Queen of Delights.' Sobeck smiled thinly. 'That's the name given to the brothel keeper. She manages four Mitanni girls; Pentju appeared to have taken up with them.' He sighed. 'They're not the prettiest of girls but, apparently, Pentju relaxed in their company.'

'You know the reason why,' I replied. 'Khiya, Tutankhamun's mother, she was a Mitanni princess. She and Pentju were very close. The Queen of Delights must have brought back memories.'

'Well, they certainly looked after Pentju. They brought him food. He tended their ailments.' Sobeck pointed with his thumb towards a chest. 'Pentju brought his treasure with him, and before you ask, none of it has disappeared. Our physician was well protected by the Lady Boys. They patrolled the house and kept a guard outside his chamber. Despite their appearances, they are as nasty as any snake, and as dangerous. No one was allowed in without their permission.'

'And today?' I glanced to the window and wondered idly where Nabila could be.

'Pentju rose this morning and, as usual, walked around the Mysterious Abode and drank two cups of wine. According to witnesses he was sleepy-eyed but merry. He then adjourned with two of the Mitanni girls. They left him shortly before noon. He would usually sleep during the heat of the day, but,' he sighed, 'today's routine was different. Pentju had two visitors, both of them women, masked and cloaked, though the guards claim that they were both young and smelt fragrant, like ladies of the palace. Each gave a scroll to one of the guards, who then gave it to Pentju.'

'Have you found these?'

Sobeck pointed to a small warming dish on a table almost hidden by the broken door.

'The charcoal's still warm,' he declared. 'Perhaps the papyri were burnt there. The first woman left after about an hour. A short time later the second woman arrived but did not stay as long.'

'And the guards have no other description?'

Sobeck shook his head. I noticed one of the Medjay

emptying a coffer on to the floor. He began to sift through its contents, an intrusive gesture which I resented. I shouted at him to leave it alone. The man glanced at Sobeck, who nodded, ordering him and the rest to leave. Sobeck and I then searched the chamber, a soul-wrenching task. Pentju had moved most of his personal possessions here, bittersweet memories of his past. He had even kept his writing pallet from his days as a scholar in the Kap, as well as the embroidered sash and stole bestowed on him when he became a physician in the House of Life at the Temple of Isis. There were presents from Akenhaten and other members of the Royal Circle: a statue of a Mitanni god, undoubtedly a gift from the Lady Khiya; a locket of hair in a leather bag inscribed with the throne names of Tutankhamun; caskets of jewellery containing cornelian necklaces, bracelets of glittering faience, silver and gold rings, a jewelled pectoral and a gorget with a medallion in the centre depicting Hathor, the Lady of the Sycamores. There were debens and ounous of silver and gold dust in calfskin pouches.

One strange thing I noticed immediately. Pentju was a great writer. He prided himself on being a scribe, a disciple of Thoth, yet I found no letters, no rolls of papyri, only a few medical treatises, one on the left ear and another on the ailments of the anus, as well as a scrap of a temple hymn, a song of praise to the glories of Osiris. I was mystified by this. The more I searched Pentju's possessions, the more certain I became that he had destroyed anything which could threaten him or anyone else. It was as if he expected to be arrested or summarily executed: nothing incriminating, nothing to indict either him or anyone else. The only document Sobeck discovered was in a secret compartment of a jewellery casket. It proved to be Pentju's last will and testament, drawn up by some temple scribe. The opening prayer to Osiris was long-winded, as is the custom of such documents; it revealed only that he'd left everything to the Mitanni courtesan, the Queen of Delights.

'She'll be pleased,' Sobeck muttered. 'Her heart will sing with delight.'

He stood swaying, hands on hips. I studied him closely. Everything was breaking up, draining away. Yesterday's brothers and allies could be today's opponents and tomorrow's enemies. Where did Sobeck's loyalties lie? Could he be trusted? Had he had a hand in Pentju's death? He certainly seemed genuinely puzzled by it. He nervously fingered the gold ring in his earlobe, sweat glistening on his bald pate.

'Here is a skilled physician.' Sobeck walked back towards me. 'Pentju may have been a toper, but he knew his wine and was very wary. He definitely drank poisoned wine, yet there is none to be found in this chamber. So how did it get here and leave no trace?'

'Except on poor Pentju.'

'Except on poor Pentju,' Sobeck agreed. 'He drank it and died alone.'

'Could anyone else have come in?'

'And forced Pentju to drink poison?' Sobeck laughed. 'I doubt it.' He walked over to the windows. 'These were shut. The outside is guarded, as was the door, which was bolted and barred from the inside.'

'So how was he discovered?'

'One of the Lady Boys became concerned and began to hammer on the door.' Sobeck shrugged. 'There was no answer. Pentju had left strict instructions. If anything mysterious happened to him, they were to seek you out urgently.'

'But they didn't.'

'Ah yes.' Sobeck glanced at me out of the corner of his eye. 'And if you were dead, they would look for me.' He spread his hands. 'You've been absent from Thebes for some time. I'm well known in this squalid hole. After all,' he added drily, 'I am supposed to be Chief of Police.'

'Supposed to be?'

Sobeck gestured towards the door with his head. 'Some of

them I trust, but I suppose most of my men are in Nakhtimin's pay. The palace will certainly know about this by now.'

'And don't you want to know?' I asked, grasping his arm. 'Sobeck, are you so full of the good things of life that you have forgotten the past? Pentju was our friend, our comrade; he has been murdered!' I tightened my grip, digging my nails into his flesh. 'I want to know why.'

Sobeck agreed and shouted for his officers, ordering them to bring up the guards. He and I sat on reed-matted stools and questioned the Lady Boys. I still recall them – bullies, assassins, men with no heart or soul, dead eyes in hard faces, made all the more sinister by the way they dressed as hesets, with heavy oiled wigs, eyes ringed with green kohl, cheeks carmined and lips rouged. muscular bodies draped in gauffered robes of the purest linen. They wore earrings and necklaces; one even sported a gorget around his slender throat. They walked like women, swaying slightly in high-heeled patten shoes, amid gusts of cheap perfume. Yet they were truly dangerous. The affectation, the fluttering eyelids, the feminine gestures and lisping voices were only superficial. These were killers to the heart. Assassins, hired to protect a man, they had failed and so wanted revenge. Time and again Sobeck had to threaten them as they tried to question us. In the end we told them nothing, whilst they gave very little in return. Pentju had been in good spirits. He never left the Mysterious Abode. He liked to drink and consort with the whores. He was generous in payment and fearful of the outside world.

'And the two visitors?' I asked. The leader of the Lady Boys, who rejoiced in the name of the Golden Heart of Isis, moved on his stool, daintily sketching the air with his hennaed fingernails.

'One came after the other,' he lisped. 'Cloaked and cowled. The first one brought a scroll in a leather pouch. I took it in to the master. He seemed pleased and told me to bring her in. She must have stayed for about an hour and then she left. We think she was young. She smelled of perfume. A short while later, the second one came.'

'Do you think these strangers knew each other?'

'I don't know.' The Lady Boy pouted. 'But there was gossip in the alleyways that a group of mercenaries were seen close to the Mysterious Abode.'

'Whose mercenaries?' I asked.

'I don't know,' he screeched. 'Mercenaries are common around here.'

'And this second woman?' I persisted.

'Again, young and perfumed. She climbed the stairs with ease. She must have stayed half the time as the first and then left. She brought a piece of papyrus, closed and sealed.' He shook his head. 'And before you ask, I don't know what it contained.'

'Was either of them carrying anything else?'

The fellow shook his head again.

'Did your master,' I asked, 'have many visitors?'

'Oh yes.' The Lady Boy fluttered his eyelids. 'It wasn't the first time a woman had visited him, but always secretly.' He gazed round the chamber. 'Ah well,' he whispered, 'the day's work is done. We still have to be paid.'

Sobeck ordered him to go back downstairs and the Queen of Delights was brought up. She waddled into the chamber, a grotesque sight: eyes almost hidden by rolls of fat, cheeks glistening with oil. She was dressed in a swathe of linen, and the way she moved reminded me of a ship in full sail. She owned more jewellery than a princess. Precious stones winked at ear, throat, chest, ankle, finger and wrist, and she wore a necklace of little bells which tinkled at every movement. Despite her size, she had a grace and a calmness which reminded me of Khiya. Once she had sat down, enthroned on a camp stool, I studied her more closely. Appearances are deceptive: her twinkling eyes and merry mouth demonstrated a complete disregard for Sobeck and the Medjay, whilst the way she dismissed the Lady Boys, with a contemptuous shrug and a stream of obscenities, showed a courage which must have appealed to Pentju. She also had an infectious laugh. She praised Pentju, and clapped her hands greedily when Sobeck indicated that all her former lover's possessions might now be hers. She then cried a little, tears rolling down her fat cheeks, shoulders shaking, before dabbing at her eyes with the back of her hand. She gestured at Pentju's corpse.

'He should be moved: the day is hot, he will begin to smell.'

She then lapsed into her own tongue, a high-pitched nasal chatter, rocking backwards and forwards. I suspected she was praying. She answered most of Sobeck's questions but could provide little information: Pentju had moved into the Mysterious Abode. He had hired her and her girls. The proprietor brought food and wine and through him the Lady Boys had arrived. She told us how Pentju had informed her that he loved Mitanni women and wished to hide from the cruelty of the world.

'He ate and drank,' she exclaimed, then gestured towards the bed, 'and sometimes we would all join him there.'

The thought of Pentju being lost in folds of fat with the Queen of Delights, not to mention what she grandly called her 'ladies-in-waiting', was extremely comic and I tried not to laugh.

'Did he talk about the past?' I asked.

'No.' She leaned forward and tapped me under the chin with her finger. 'You are Lord Mahu.'

There was a shift in her eyes, a quick glance away. She was warning me to be wary of Sobeck; that perhaps she had something to say for my ears alone. For the rest, she gossiped like a monkey on a branch. She knew nothing about the mysterious female visitors, Pentju's past, or his days as a physician. I bided my time, allowing her to bore Sobeck.

Eventually I asked him to question the properietor and he swaggered out. I moved the stool closer.

'I am Mahu, Baboon of the South,' I whispered.

'So you are.' She leaned closer. 'You understand the Mitanni tongue. Pentju told me about Princess Khiya.' She lapsed into Mitanni, speaking slowly, carefully. 'This is all I know. The master was very frightened. He claimed to have seen great evil – the murder of a god.' She raised her hand, gesturing me to remain quiet. 'He was very fearful of Lord Ay, yet also very angry; he never told me why. He said his days were numbered. He would not survive the year. I think he sent a precious goblet to the palace as a bribe.'

'Who took it?'

'I don't know and I don't care. He told me that if you never returned, the gods would intervene, but if you did, the truth would lie with the Watchers. He claimed to have looked into the visions of the night but he said the secret was now with the Watchers, the *shabtis* who guarded his master. I can tell you no more.' She pointed to the corpse. 'For pity's sake, I must remove it.'

She went and called up some servants. I heard her arguing with Sobeck on the stairs, but eventually she had her way. I moved to the bed and sat down. Sobeck shouted for me. As I got up, my foot caught on the folds of the sheet. I had to crouch down to free it and my hand brushed the fine gold dust lying on the floor: not the thick grains used by the money changers and merchants, but that fine dust, like sand, which children use in their games. I recalled Nabila being chased around the garden. I crouched, staring at my hand. It was no coincidence. I remembered Djarka pointing out how Nabila knew where Pentju was. She must have been one of the women who visited him today. But why? Where was she? What in Maat's name had she been doing here? Why hadn't she told me? Was she a friend of Pentju?

'Are you well?'

I glanced up. The Queen of Delights was standing there, staring curiously down at me. Servants were carrying the corpse to the door. I clambered to my feet. She came up and grasped my hands, speaking again in Mitanni.

'I remember something,' she murmured. 'Pentju mentioned it last night.'

'What was it?'

'Great evil was done and the Realm of the Dead must be entered for the truth to be known.' She turned and waddled away.

Sobeck came up. For a while, because I was so distracted, I didn't understand what he was talking about. He grasped me by the shoulders.

'Mahu,' Sobeck's face was only a few inches from mine, 'Djarka told me that you massacred the Caracals. I wanted to ask you why, but all this,' he waved a hand, 'distracted me.'

'I had to,' I hissed back. 'If they'd struck, bloodshed would have followed, Horemheb knows that. As it is,' I added bitterly, 'blood will flow.' I gestured with my hands. 'Just go away and leave me for a while.'

Sobeck pulled a face, made a rude gesture with his fingers and walked down the stairs. I sat on the floor with my back to the bed and tried to organise my chaotic thoughts. Outside, the sun began to set. The Mysterious Abode was coming to life, preparing for the night. I watched the doorway. Sobeck reappeared and I made my decision.

'Mahu, what is it, what is wrong?' I rose and told him quickly about Nabila. I could see that the news shocked him. He bit the quick of his thumb and stared longingly towards the window as if he wished to be gone.

'Sobeck!' I urged. 'It's true what I say: soon everything will fall apart. Choices have to be made.' I grasped him by the shoulder. 'Years ago, I pleaded for your life, I saved your life.' He broke free from my grip, cursing under his breath. 'You must help me,' I urged.

'Why?'

'First because of friendship; second because you have to make a choice; third because Pentju was murdered; fourth, I do not think Tutankhamun died a natural death.'

Sobeck swore under his breath. There was a sound in the corridor. Sobeck strode across and shouted at the officer who must have been lingering there to go away.

'Not here,' he muttered.

I followed him down the stairs, back through the narrow streets, past squalid houses, their fronts like secreted faces, with only a few windows set high in the walls and low doors opening on to passageways which stretched into the shadows. Women and children, standing or squatting outside, shouted obscenities at the traders and merchants struggling to get their pack animals to the nearest market-place.

Followed by a few hand-picked Medjay, we hurried along needle-thin, slanting streets, across squares where the dust hung in the air like a heat haze. Sobeck was agitated, ordering his men forward to clear a path through the noisy throng of sheep, geese, caged pigeons, goats, horses and cattle. Even so we were shouted at by the tradesmen kneeling in rows behind their big grass baskets, trying to entice us with jewels and perfumes – all the tawdry items of the marketplace. On the corners confectioners baked their sweet bread, butchers offered goose leg, all hot and spiced, travelling barbers gestured with their stools to the dusty shade of doorways or that of some palm tree. As I passed, I wondered how long such life would continue. If these people knew the truth, or could sense the nightmare in my own heart, would they be as agitated as I was? Would they even care? I was tempted to turn and flee but that is the trap which closes around you. If you enter the double doors of the Great House to play the game of power, you can't walk away as if it were some cock fight, a contest of wits or a song which is finished. The game has to be played out. Nevertheless, I was torn by anguish at what I had learned, and growing acutely anxious about Nabila.

Rehes: *fierce-mouthed, like a cobra*

Chapter 13

Sobeck took me deeper into the Necropolis, to a dingy, foul quarter where he had once worked as a dog skinner, a place where he was still so feared he could depend more on the loyalty of the scorpion men who swarmed there than on his own police. At the corner of a crooked alleyway, he told his men to rest at a beer stall set up under an acacia tree. He led me on, down a dark tunnel, to the House of the Lady of Happiness – a sprawling wine booth with an image of the goddess Hathor above the doorway. The inside was surprisingly clean, its walls painted and limewashed, and furnished with soft reed matting, comfortable stools and polished low tables. On the walls were inscriptions; I remember them still, exclamations such as: 'Drink till you're drunk, and don't stop enjoying yourself'. A large sign boasted that the house sold every type of wine, that of Avaris, Buto, the Star of Horus, the Lord of the Sky, wines of Kush, as well as beers of every variety. Sobeck took me over to a far corner behind a screen, clicking his fingers at a servant, ordering honeyed wine and strips of fillet beef. We both ate hungrily.

'What is it you want?' Sobeck asked.

'I want the city searched for Nabila. Only when I find her will I discover who she really is and what she has done. I want you to send out your best men. I also want a messenger to be sent to Djarka. Ask him to use everyone he knows to search for Nabila.'

Sobeck nodded. 'And?' he asked.

'Tell Djarka to dismiss the servants and to hide, if possible, in some secure place. Tell him to take great care'.

Sobeck looked puzzled. 'What is the matter with you, Mahu?'

'It's very dangerous,' I replied. 'Pentju has been murdered. Lord Ay knows I have visited the Mysterious Abode; his spies must have told him.'

'Perhaps Ay has problems of his own.' Sobeck sipped from his cup. 'There were rumours this morning that he had fallen ill.'

'Knowing Ay,' I sneered, 'I'm sure it will be nothing malignant, but if his belly is sore or his head heavy, it might only distract him and perhaps assist us.'

'To do what?'

'To break into Tutankhamun's tomb.'

Sobeck's jaw dropped. 'Impossible!' he stammered. 'By all that's holy, why? If we are caught, it's impalement, death without trial!' He pushed the table hard against my chest. 'I asked you why!'

I was tempted to tell him everything, but Sobeck could only be trusted once he was implicated.

'The tomb contains the truth,' I replied, 'and I can't tell you what that is until I discover it myself. As for the danger,' I pushed the table back, 'it must be done tonight. No one will suspect: his tomb lies deserted in a secluded part of the valley. It must be done quickly. Once it is finished, either way the truth will be known.'

Sobeck leaned back against the wall, wiping the sweat from his throat.

'I know what you're thinking,' I urged. 'You're wondering, Sobeck, whether you should betray me to Ay, but it's too late: he doesn't really trust you, that's why his spies watch you.

He'll wonder about the Caracals. Did you know about them and refuse to take action? Above all, he knows you have spoken to me. Pentju is murdered,' I continued remorselessly. 'I now know, don't ask me how, that Our Lord's tomb contains the truth about many things.'

'And Horemheb?' Sobeck asked.

'I prefer him to Ay.'

Sobeck stared for a while into his wine cup. Then he grunted something, rose to his feet and left the wine booth. I stared at one of the paintings on the wall and drank greedily. If Sobeck returned, then he had made his choice. If he didn't, the alleyway I was hiding in would be the place I died. An age seemed to pass. Memories came like bats winging through the darkness. How close I had been to the land of ghosts. How I had often lived my life in the shadow of the noose, the sword, the dagger, the club, the poisoned cup. Faces thronged through the darkness to greet me: Akenhaten in all his arrogance; Nefertiti with her gorgeous red hair and heavy-lidded blue eyes; Amenhotep the Magnificent, being fondled by one of his daughters; the men I had killed, the women I had taken. Finally, Nabila, with her lovely face and calm eyes. Even then I knew a sense of loss; deep in my heart I recognised something heinous had happened. Yet at the same time, I was certain she had not been a traitor. I drank more wine, aware of sounds around me but still concentrating on that door. Sobeck appeared, slipping in as he once was, lithe, swift and deadly as a leopard. He seemed to have lost the burden of the years, and was once again narrow-faced and bright-eyed.

'It's done,' he whispered, and stretched his hand across the table. 'I've dismissed my men. I'm with you, Mahu, to the death.'

I clasped his hand and we left the wine booth. We were no longer the Lords of the Things, Leaders of the Circle, Masters of the Secrets. We were brigands, Sons of Seth, speeding like darts through the darkness. We reached the outskirts of the Necropolis, pausing only at a shabby beer shop where Sobeck picked up a sack and slung it over his shoulder. Before we left the city, he led me to a disused well which concealed one of his secret caches of weapons. He took out a sword, a heavy Syrian bow and some arrows, and we continued. We left the murk of the city, travelling through the icy darkness to the edge of the Redlands. Above us, the sky was pitch black, the stars hanging heavy like glowing lamps. The whipping wind brought in sand and the sounds of the night prowlers. A bird hooted long and mournfully.

I felt a speedy release as I ran beside Sobeck: all the tension and resentment spilling out in that hasty, sweaty run. We were children of Thebes. As members of the Royal Circle, Guardians of the Secret Places, we knew all the turning, twisting secret ways that would lead us into the Valley of the Kings. We were aware of the dangers: the approaches to the valley were guarded by units from the crack regiments – the Nakhtu-aa and the Maryannou, veterans of foreign battles. On the clifftops above us we glimpsed pinpricks of light which betrayed the presence of chariot squadrons, fanning out through the darkness to guard the Houses of Eternity.

We slipped and slithered and then, like the moon breaking free of clouds, we arrived in that lonely valley. We crouched at the top of those steps stretching down into the darkness, inviting us on to cross the threshold into the land of the dead, the final resting place of Tutankhamun. We left our weapons in the shadows and crept down the steps. Using the tools Sobeck had brought, we hacked away at the bottom left-hand corner of the doorway. The plaster was weak and thin so the doorway proved no obstacle. We managed to excavate a hole and wormed our way through into the freezing-cold passageway beyond. Sobeck hastily filled the gap with some of the rubble. Then he took from the sack an oil jar and two cresset torches coated in pitch. Using a flint, he fired one pitch torch, then the other, and gingerly lit the lamp. The light flared up, driving back the darkness.

'We are safe,' Sobeck muttered. He pointed to the rubble in the doorway. 'That will block the light.'

'It's not guarded,' I replied. 'So few know it's here.'

I lifted the torch. The passageway was sombre, the walls undressed. The floors sloped slightly downwards as we hurried to the next wall. I was confident there would be no traps as the burial had taken place so swiftly. We hacked away at the second doorway and in a short while were through, pushing the torches before us. We lifted the light and gasped at the treasure hall before us. The antechamber was full of precious items: voluminous bales of cloth, beautiful state beds shaped like mythical animals and studded with precious stones. I recognised one of them as Akenhaten's bridal bed, fashioned out of ebony and ivory with statues of Bes and Hathor carved at the foot. Along the walls were golden chariots with wheels of silver and spokes of gold over which were slung harnesses of blood-red leather adorned with coloured glass set in delicate gold network. In the corners stood golden hawk standards. There were chairs and thrones finely worked in silver and lapis lazuli, caskets and coffers, stools and ornaments.

I glanced to the right and saw the sealed doorway to the burial chamber, before which stood the Watchers. Lifting my torch, I walked slowly towards them. They faced each other upon papyrus mats in characteristic pose: left leg forward, holding a staff in one hand and a mace in the other. They were over two yards high, carved from wood and plaster, the flesh parts covered with a shiny black resin. The head clothes, broad collars, kilts, armbands and bracelets were overlaid with gold. On each statue's brow was a lunging Uraeus with diamond eyes. I recognised both *shabtis* from the royal palace.

Sobeck and I forgot the danger which confronted us. I examined each statue carefully. Both effigies had extended flared kilts. I felt along the rim of one of these and groaned with disappointment. At the base, just near the wooden legs, holes had been bored then covered with plaster. This had been pulled away, and the holes, hollowed out to contain papyrus rolls, were empty. I moved to examine the statue on the right. Again, in the front of the triangular kilt I found two holes hollowed out. This time the plaster still held fast. I took out a dagger and chipped away at it, crumbling it to dust, and from each hollow pulled a roll of papyrus. They were both still smooth and soft. I had what I searched for.

What more can I say? Some scenes stay fresh and fertile; others grow stale. I was greedy as any robber. I clutched those papyrus rolls and glared fiercely at Sobeck, warning him not to ask, claiming the precious parchments as my own.

All around me in that gloomy torchlit chamber lay the junk of empire, statues and thrones which had once adorned the beautiful sun-filled palaces of Akenhaten now sealed in darkness. Ay must have stripped his treasure hoards, tossing in precious goods as though to appease the spirit of the young Pharaoh. If I have ever entered a hall of ghosts, that was one. They call them the Houses of a Million Years, yet that antechamber was as sombre as a tawdry tomb shop. I felt a deep rage at the way my young prince had been sent into the West.

Sobeck was eager to go, plucking at my arm, his face and chest drenched in sweat. Yet I couldn't leave like that. I had to say something. I had to make a formal salute to a young man I had loved as dearly as any son. Sobeck was frantic, begging with his eyes for us to flee, but I pushed him away and squatted on the ground, pressing my hot face against the cold plaster of the door leading to Tutankhamun's burial chamber. I sang softly under my breath a verse from the Funeral Hymn of the Great Kings. Surely you know it? 'To the West, to the West'. Now, how does the next verse go? Ah yes. 'He has come to thee, my Lord, to see thy beauty. He has not done evil. He has committed no violence. He has not stolen. He has not caused any man to be killed. He has made no one weep. He has not despised the gods in his heart. He is pure. He is pure.'

Only then did I leave, following Sobeck back through the battered doorways, filling in the gaps with rubble, then out into the freezing desert air. We raced like shadows, darker than the rest, into the gloom of the Necropolis. Sobeck would not let me go but took me to a house of fragrance, where the loveliest whores plied their trade, and we were offered baths in cool, fragrant water, washed, dried and anointed by the ladies of the night. I did not need these, just a chamber made sweet by baskets of flowers, a writing table, a palette of pens and fresh rolls of papyrus.

There I read, studied and wept over Pentju's confession, written out so carefully on those two rolls. I have them still. I kept them safe over the years in a copper container. The scribes of the Divine One can have them now. I have read them so many times, I could quote them word for word, as a blind harpist recites the words of a hymn. The confession was transcribed on the two scrolls in temple hieroglyphs, the handwriting neat, the letters well formed. Pentju must have been sober when he wrote it. It was directed towards me but it was really written as if I was a chapel priest, or a priest of the ear. The scribes have a word, *ab*, which means 'to speak directly from the heart'. I immediately sensed Pentju was doing this. His confession read as follows:

Pentju, royal physician, to Mahu, Baboon of the South, health and greetings, life and prosperity. You may read this on your return or, if you are dead, I shall tell you all in the Halls of Eternity. I shall not live long. My days are numbered. The spinner of time will cut the flax and I shall go into the dark. I write in the hot season whilst all of Egypt awaits the Inundation. Our Divine Lord,

Tutankhamun, lies coffined, hastily prepared for his journey into the Far West. How the gods will rage! How his mother will weep! How his father, if he knew the truth, would utter vile curses. The wheel has turned, the seasons have come and gone. I know the truth. Akenhaten, a leper, now hides in the Valley of the Sea of the Dead, deep in the heart of Canaan. The princes of that land are no longer Egypt's friends. They no longer kiss the cartouche of Pharaoh. They seethe with rebellion.

You have been sent north to the Hittites to negotiate a peace which does not exist, to whisper honeyed words to the Vermin Lords who regard such words as chaff in the wind. Horemheb and Rameses (aren't they just like boys?) have gone marching north with all the massed might of Egypt. How Ay must laugh to see us all dance to the tune he pipes. He wanted you out of the way. Only the gods know if you will return. Ay secretly deals with the Hittites. He weaves sinister designs and may use them to destroy Horemheb. You are not to live. If the Hittites don't kill you, Ay's vile sprite Mery-re will do the task for him, but not before you lead him south. Ay wishes to know if Akenhaten still survives, and if he does, Mery-re will try to kill him too. But if you are reading this in some secret place, then I'm only telling you what you already know.

I have prayed for you constantly. I do not believe in falcon-faced gods or those who look like a jackal or have the wings of an eagle. I do pray to that One whom Akenhaten worshipped, who sees all things and lives in all things. I pray He keeps you safe and brings you back to deal out judgement to the gods of Egypt.

Oh how I wormed my way into Ay's heart, ever ready to do his bidding. I scurried about like his little dog, yapping and licking his feet, but my ear was close to his heart. I learned about his secret designs and did what I could. If you must know, I was the Oracle. I warned Horemheb and Rameses when I could. I also knew the secret of Akenhaten's hiding place and used Apiru desert wanderers to keep him informed about everything. How I enjoyed that! Ay never suspected; in his arrogance he dismissed me as a drunken buffoon!

You left Avaris and Ay sent his creature the scribe to overtake you and arrive in Tyre before you. Only the gods know what secret messages he carried. I doubt if they were for your well-being. However, in every ball of dung there is an ounce of sweetness. If you survive, and if she survives, you will have met Nabila – she is the daughter of a close friend, a woman I trust with my heart. I knew her father very well in those golden, sun-kissed days when the blood ran like wine in my veins and my heart could sing. He was a member of Akenhaten's court, a scribe you would not know, a man of honour. He did me great service. When he died and I emerged, like a rat from a hole, I protected Nabila. She came to me before she left Thebes for Tyre. I swore her to secrecy. She was never to reveal to you, or to anyone, that she knew me. If she did, even by chance, she would render herself vulnerable. I know you, Mahu, cunning baboon, you'd think it strange. Certain things are best kept secret. She knows of you, she has glimpsed you from afar. I told her you have a good heart and speak words of truth. Above all, I told her you were my friend. I made her swear by the eternal flame and the unnamed god she and her people worship to do all in her power to bring Ay's evil designs to nothing and assist you in every way she could. Only the Lords of Light know what has happened to both of you.

What I have planned may now be dust in the wind, yet I did what I could. Nabila is of the Apiru. Her father worshipped the One. I recommend both of you to His care. I talked about you to Nabila and I made her laugh. I think she liked you even though she had not met you. So you see, Mahu, there must be some goodness about you.

Once you were gone, life became more serene. I dared not visit Mert lest I bring her under Ay's watchful gaze, I was too busy acting the inebriated fool. I was at the quayside to wave Horemheb and Rameses off to war. Afterwards I sat back and watched Ay the spider spin his web. Mahu, I confess this and we shall all pay the price for our failure: when we executed Nefertiti, we should have killed Ay. He is the canker in the rose. He has a mongoose soul and a heart given to intrigue as a buzzard is to flying. He has amassed treasure, raised troops, bribed priests and scribes. He sees himself as the embodiment of Egypt. Our Lord Tutankhamun was a mere speck in his eye.

So what shall I confess? I confess to murder, the death of two children. If you survive, you will have heard how Tutankhamun's lovely wife and queen Ankhesenamun conceived two children. Both were premature and stillborn. I killed them. I had no choice. Ankhesenamun is as vicious as her grandfather. She slept with Tutankhamun and practised her arts. Our Good Lord told me, in moments of lucidity, how he could not generate his own seed. Tutankhamun, may the Lords of Light cherish him, was impotent, barren, dry as a withered branch. He could not beget children, but Ay could. I suspected, and the Divine One knew, that Ay visited the bedchamber of his granddaughter and, with that bitch Amedeta looking on, pleasured her and made her fertile. Ay dreamed dreams of fathering his own line through his own flesh, an abomination in my eyes. Such children would have been cursed. They would not have brought light and peace to the Kingdom of the Two Lands.

So, secretly, I fed Ankhesenamun potions to bring such life to an end. I have no regrets. Let Maat weigh my heart on the scales of truth: those children could not be born. Perhaps Ay and Ankhesenamun suspected, but they had no proof. Two cobras lusting for power! The evil they did possessed a malice all of its own, like some demon loosed to wander the corridors of the palace. Openly they cherished Tutankhamun but secretly they mocked him as the son of a Mitanni princess.

My lord's heart was disturbed. He grew more silent and withdrawn, a recluse, a hermit in his own palace. He would often lapse into trances, returning to being a mere child, as if he hungered for the days when his father ruled. I did what I could. On certain days Tutankhamun would emerge from such childish moods and talk about his parents and the worship of the Aten. I could do little to help him. I felt like a boat, without rudder or oars, bobbing on a fast-flowing river.

I recalled our conversations about the Watchers and the secrets they held. I came across the truth, as you do with such things, not by design but by accident. You may recall the statues, the guardians, the *shabtis*, brought into the palace from his father's treasure house: you used them to guard the Divine Boy's chamber. One evening, when Tutankhamun had returned to his childish ways, he crawled beneath one of these statues and, like the child he acted, began to pick at a piece of plaster under one of the kilts. I went to help him and noticed the piece of papyrus sticking out. There were four such hollowed holes. Each held a document, a prophecy written in Akenhaten's own hand about the things to come in Egypt. Mahu, friend of my heart, I have destroyed these. If they fell into the hands of Ay, or worse still, Horemheb and Rameses, the people of the Apiru would never know peace.

The prophecies talked of a time to come, when the unknown God will gather the people of the Apiru together and lead them with fire, sword and wondrous signs out of Egypt. How, in that time, he will make the sun go down at noon and darken the earth in broad daylight. How he will turn Egypt's feasts into funerals and their festivals into mourning. How the people of the Apiru will be led into Canaan, a land of milk and honey, at a time when Egypt, its gods and its armies, will glut on destruction. How the people will be led by a great leader, a man who will see God face to face, an albino with red-rimmed eyes, a mouth which stutters but a heart as formidable and as fierce as a raging fire. How Egypt has sown a tempest and will reap the whirlwind. Yet that will only be the beginning of a new world and a fresh covenant between God and man.

I read such words at the dead of night and was filled with unspeakable terror. It will happen, and the power of Egypt cannot prevent it, though how it will occur I do not know. I read these prophecies then burned them. I dared not tell any man what we, the Children of the Kap, have done to bring this about. I look back. It is as if we were all making a journey but we did not know the destination. We wove a tapestry but we were not aware of the story it contained. Don't you realise, Mahu, we are all trapped? Evil men though we are, God keeps us close to his right hand to use for his own secret purposes.

One trouble follows another. The prophecies were discovered and destroyed. Tutankhamun fell into a fit. I was present the night it occurred. I swear this, by the truth: Tutankhamun came into his own chamber, eager to speak to his loving wife, only to find her in bed with her grandfather. He whispered this to me before his heart drifted away and he fell into that sleep which is the brother of death. He survived many days, sometimes lying as if dead, other times shaking and convulsing, banging his neck against the headrest. I did what I could but I was alone. Ay was already lunging forward like a cobra, plotting and planning, scheming and lying, proclaiming himself Pharaoh. Even before Tutankhamun was dead, the priests of the Wabet took over, led by Ay's creature Amendufet. I was forbidden to attend upon the prince. I was told there was nothing else I could do. I had to agree. One thing I begged of Ay, as Physician of the Presence: when Tutankhamun's death was announced, that I be allowed to take out his heart and place it in the sacred scarab before the casket was sealed. That favour was denied me.

So I have told you this, and I swear by my own heart on any hope of entering eternal light, I believe Tutankhamun was murdered. He was hurried into the Far West. Ay grew tired of waiting, of allowing Tutankhamun to continue in a sleep which never seemed to end. Of course, my words will be rejected as those of a malicious heart, the utterances of a drunken buffoon. They will ask for proof, but the proof lies in that tomb.

If a man is murdered, as you know, Mahu, the assassin will remove the heart and not permit it to be buried with the corpse. I recall you telling me a story of a beautiful young widow whose husband had died suddenly of some strange infection of the belly. Months later his tomb was broken into, the outer casket ransacked and the Medjay summoned. The dead man's brother insisted the body be buried again. However, when the embalmers returned to the task, they found no heart concealed within the sacred scarab. If Tutankhamun's tomb is ever opened, and that will be one sacrilege upon another, no sacred scarab will be found containing his heart. That widow had murdered her husband and removed the heart to silence his spirit so it would not come back and haunt her. I believe Ay did the same with Our Lord. He was frightened Tutankhamun would linger too long. Such a simple act! A cushion across the mouth and nostrils, hideous murder, blasphemy, sacrilege! Afterwards Ay ensured the heart would not be buried with him.

I asked to see the list of funeral goods, the oils and perfumes used, the treasure Ay ransacked to fill Tutankhamun's tomb. I found no trace of a heart scarab. For the rest, it was one just abomination after another. Once the prince was dead, his body was soaked too long in the natron, the corpse dried so hard one arm became loose, as did part of the breast bone. The tomb was hastily prepared and painted. I heard they were in such a hurry, they cracked the lid of the sarcophagus, whilst the plates which were placed around it were so hastily put together and ill-fitted, the sacred symbols pointed in the wrong direction. Ay played with the Time of Mourning like a child does with counters in a senet game. Seventy days were supposed to elapse. In truth no more than forty did.

Ay is to be cursed! Tutankhamun must be avenged! I have no proof, just the singing in my heart and a deep feeling of desolation. Ay will not allow me to live much longer. Tutankhamun's burial is to take place tomorrow and the Watchers will be moved tonight to guard the tomb. I shall place this, my last letter, in one of those hollowed gaps and seal the opening with plaster. I shall keep sober until the plaster dries then I shall drink myself into oblivion. Tomorrow I will leave the Malkata. I will destroy everything Ay might seize, except my treasures, and I shall plan my revenge.

First I have great hope in you, Mahu, Baboon of the South. You are a born survivor. If you read this and have the will, the energy and the means, you shall be my vengeance. Secondly, I do not know the heart of Ay but

I think he nourishes great dreams of power. He is of the Apiru tribe and, in his twisted heart, he thinks he wears the mantle of the Messiah. He might try to turn Egypt on its head and destroy those who oppose him. I cannot leave things to chance. Ay sees himself as the greatest of Pharaohs; yet he is a little man with a malicious heart and a narrow soul. He sends one of his women to me – you know her well, the whore Amedeta – to stroke my groin and whisper in my ear. She has murmured how Ay lusts after the Cup of Glory, Amenhotep the Great's goblet. In time I shall give way to her and send the goblet to him, but only when I have finished with it. Do you recall your gardening days during our time of exile? You grew herbs and distilled poisons, concocting new potions. You showed me how to paint the inside of a cup, in truth, smearing it with a poison which gradually crumbles to a powder the eye cannot detect, so death comes slowly and the victim never suspects the source. I shall do that with the Cup of Glory. I shall take refuge in the Mysterious Abode and watch what happens, and if I die, and you read this, do what you have to. Do not trust Ay or Ankhesenamun. Strike, and strike hard! As for you, my old friend, soon all our glory days will be gone, lost like tears in the rain.

I sat, it must have been for an hour, staring down at Pentju's letter, the key to so many mysteries. I mourned him, but I knew, as Pentju would have realised, that his letter had taken me back to my early years, when danger was in the very air I breathed and to survive a day was a great achievement. Sobeck came in slightly drunk, a girl on each arm, laughing and giggling. He pushed his new-found friends away and took the first scroll. I have never seen a man grow sober so quickly. He shouted at the women to leave, slumped down on a cushion, read the first scroll and snatched the second from me. When he had finished, he sat for a while, face in his hands, groaning like some animal in pain. I took the scrolls back, rolled them up and hid them curled round my dagger in its sheath.

'If Pentju is lying . . .' Sobeck took his hands away from his face. 'But why should he? He must be telling the truth, so what is to be done?'

I stared coldly back. Sobeck grew agitated.

'I knew nothing of this,' he shouted, 'nor did Maya or Huy. We were not party to it,' he repeated. 'There is no blood on our hands.'

'We are all bloodied,' I hissed back. 'We are all guilty, me more than anyone! I took an oath to protect Tutankhamun. I understimated Ay.' I rose to my feet. 'Ay is dying; he does not know it, but Pentju will keep his word.'

'So the problem is resolved,' Sobeck replied eagerly.

I laughed and turned away. 'Do you really think so?' I glanced over my shoulder. 'What about Nakhtimin and his regiments? Ankhesenamun and her wickedness, Mery-re and his malice, the high priests, the scribes, the merchants?'

'Pentju could be lying.'

'Is he?'

Sobeck glanced away. 'What is to be done?' he muttered again.

'There is blood to be avenged. Nabila was Pentju's friend. She went to inform him that I had returned and tell him what had happened. Pentju probably swore her to secrecy.'

'And the second woman?' Sobeck asked.

'Amedeta! She was escorted by mercenaries, whom the Lady Boys glimpsed. Ay thought Pentju was besotted with her. She was his messenger, the one way he could keep Pentju under scrutiny: that's how the Cup of Glory was sent to the palace. Once I had returned, Ay thought it was too dangerous to allow Pentju to live.'

I came and sat opposite Sobeck. 'After Nabila left,' I

explained, 'Amedeta arrived. She asked to share a cup of wine with Pentju. When our good physician wasn't looking she secretly poisoned the cup. He would not suspect a shared goblet and the potion wouldn't act immediately. Amedeta left; Pentju continued to drink wine from the same goblet. Any trace of the poison would disappear. He bolted and barred the door after his visitor, then the seizure happened: perhaps a matter of heartbeats, and Pentju was gone.'

'And Nabila?'

I put my face in my hands. I had no tears left, so I couldn't cry.

'Ay and Nakhtimin would know about her. Perhaps they kept her under close watch.'

'But how would they know she was dangerous?' Sobeck protested. 'How would they discover when she left your house?'

I tried to control my panic.

'Mahu,' Sobeck insisted, 'she may be dead. Either that or kidnapped.'

I rose to my feet and glared down at him. 'Whatever the truth, Sobeck, we are both guilty of treason and tomb robbing. Go home,' I urged. 'Hide your treasure and your family, then wait for me.'

'No,' Sobeck rose to his feet, 'I'll come with you.' He rubbed his face. 'I mean, Nabila, you'll need help'.

When we returned to my mansion, darkness had fallen. I expected to find it deserted, but Djarka was waiting for me in our small hall of audience, sitting cross-legged beneath the window, head tilted back as if he was listening to the eerie sounds of the night. He was dressed only in a loincloth, but I glimpsed the bow and the decorated quiver close by. He rose to greet me, moving the cushions as he did so. I noticed a shield and sword. In the poor light he looked as if he had been crying, his eyes were so red-rimmed.

'Mert and the children?' I asked.

'Gone,' he whispered, staring over my shoulder at Sobeck standing in the doorway. 'They and most of the servants. I have sent my family north along the river. They are taking letters to friends in Memphis. I am frightened, master.' Djarka wiped the sweat from my chest. 'Not for myself, but for them.' He looked at me curiously, then at Sobeck, who still kept his distance. 'You've heard the news from the palace? Lord Pharaoh is ill – some complaint of the stomach.'

'Nabila?' I asked. Djarka refused to meet my gaze. 'You can't find her, you haven't found her?'

Djarka shook his head. 'But I have found someone,' he replied, brushing by me. 'Sobeck, it's good to see you.'

I watched these two clasp hands, though they were clearly wary of each other. I recalled the days, many years ago, when Amenhotep the Magnificent was plotting against his own son and no man dared trust another. I thought of the poet's line about the centre not holding: that was what we had become, an army in disarray, each man seeking his own safety. If Djarka distrusted Sobeck, the Chief of Police was equally suspicious.

'You have sent your wife and children away.' Sobeck tried to be friendly, grasping Djarka by the elbow, then he laughed. 'So have I,' he confessed. 'To one of the fortresses beyond the Fourth Cataract. I know the commander there.'

'Nabila,' I insisted.

Djarka spun on his heel and left the hall. I heard raised voices. He returned almost dragging a dirty, dishevelled figure dressed in a shabby leather kilt and top, a pair of sandals round his neck; in one hand a jug of beer, in the other a half-chewed lump of bread. Djarka would have forced the man to kneel but I gestured him to come forward. He stank of fish and oil, mud and slime, all the rank odours of the river.

'This is Frog-face'

'Who?' I asked.

'I'm a boatman.' Frog-face squinted at me while he hastily

cleared his mouth. He swayed slightly on his feet, being much the worse for drink. Nevertheless he was wary, hastily sobering up. Sobeck had taken off his medallions and badges of office, but Frog-face clearly knew who he was. 'I'm a boatman,' he repeated nervously. 'I know Djarka. I ply my craft from the mooring place of Isis. He came asking questions about your wife, the Lady Nabila.'

'And?' I grasped Frog-face by the shoulder and pulled him close whilst I opened the wallet on my belt. I took out a small deben of silver and held it up to catch the light.

'I saw Lady Nabila return.' Frog-face went to drink from the cup but Djarka snatched it from his hand.

'Tell my lord Mahu what happened.'

'Lady Nabila returned. I was sunning myself on the quayside. I like to catch the heat of the day, that's why they call me Frog-face.'

I raised my hand threateningly.

'I recognised your wife,' Frog-face hurried on. 'I'd seen her before. She left the quayside and went up the steps. There was a servant with her. A short while later she returned. She looked anxious, eager to hire a boatman. I wasn't quick enough, but I heard her say to Taswaret, another boatman, that she wished to take his craft. She said, "My lord has asked me to return to the city." Taswaret picked up his belongings and they left.'

'You don't know where?'

'No, lord, I don't. What is strange is that Taswaret never returned. There has been no sighting of him or his craft along the river.'

Sobeck muttered something under his breath and walked away to hide his agitation. Djarka was staring at me despairingly. I could read the thoughts of his heart. During my long and bloody life, many have tried to take my life and the river is the ideal place for an assassin, so easy for a barge to hit a punt midstream. The Nile is full and fast-flowing, the perfect shield to hide a murder. I abruptly felt sick, clutching my stomach, dropping the silver deben. Djarka seized my arm and helped me towards the cushions.

'Give him the silver,' I muttered, 'and let him go. Make sure he has told us all he can.'

Sobeck came over and squatted beside me. I could hear Frog-face, loud in his thanks as he was bustled into the night. Djarka returned with a jug of Charou wine and three cups. As I drank I thought of Ay and that poisoned goblet. I placed the cup down and put my face in my hands. Nabila was gone!

'You'd best tell him.' Sobeck pulled my hands away. 'You'd best tell him,' he repeated. 'Time is short. The hours are passing.'

Gerh en ahaa: the night of battle between the Apep, the
great snake of the underworld, and Ra

Chapter 14

I hid my own grief and talked. Djarka listened, tight-lipped, hearing me out. He asked me to repeat what Pentju had read from the prophecies taken from the Watchers, shaking his head in wonderment and rubbing his arms as if cold. He asked questions about the heart scarab and narrowed his eyes when I mentioned Amendufet.

'What is to be done?' Djarka echoed Sobeck's question.

'I've been thinking.' Sobeck glanced towards the door. I nodded at Djarka to close it. 'I've been thinking,' Sobeck repeated. 'Nabila went across the river. We know she visited Pentju. She was no traitor to you, Mahu, but a close friend of our comrade. She probably brought him news about you and all your doings. Ay saw her as a danger, either because of what she knew or because he had discovered her relationship with Pentju.' He paused and waited until Djarka had resettled himself.

'We know that Nabila came back across the Nile. She was about to return here when someone intercepted her and gave her a false message. Remember her words to the boatman. "My lord has asked me to return to the city." She can't have been talking about Pentju. The only other person whom she would call "my lord" is you, Mahu, but you never gave her such a message.' Sobeck stared at me. 'So whom would Nabila

269

trust? Me?' He shook his head. 'I was with you. Maya or one of the rest?' Again a shake of the head. Sobeck glanced out of the corner of his eye at Djarka.

'I gave no such message,' my friend replied coldly.

'Amendufet!' I exclaimed.

'Impossible,' Djarka breathed. 'He was across in the city.'

'Was he?' Sobeck lifted his cup.

'Get Amendufet,' I ordered. 'Tell him to bring his lists of the funeral goods in Tutankhamun's tomb, he knows the ones.'

Djarka brought the treacherous scribe back, heavy-eyed from sleep, a gauze robe thrown about his shoulders. He shouldn't have worn that. Nabila had given it to him as a gift.

'Master.' He yawned, handing across the papyrus sheets.

I looked quickly at these and stared at him. He was blinking and scratching, slightly apprehensive but still acting the faithful retainer.

'You don't ask why I summoned you?'

'Master, we live in stirring times.'

'Don't we just,' I retorted. 'You know the boatman called Frog-face.'

Amendufet licked his lips and shook his head disdainfully, as though such information was below him.

'He knows you,' I continued. 'Tell me, Amendufet . . .' I looked down the list detailing the treasures – the golden thrones, the calcite jars, the yellow alabaster pots, the coffers and caskets, the silver-gold bedsteads, the precious cloths, perfumes and oils – which had filled Tutankhamun's tomb.

'Yes, master?'

'Where is the heart scarab?'

Amendufet wasn't such a good liar. Just for a moment his eyes darted from the left to the right, tongue coming out to lick dry lips.

'The heart scarab,' I continued. 'Is it here? No matter,' I continued. 'Whom do you work for, Amendufet?'

'Why, you, master.'

'So where did you go in the city today?'

'Various errands.'

I lifted my goblet and pressed it against the side of my face, glanced at Djarka and nodded. Amendufet was now agitated. Sobeck was leaning forward, clicking his tongue.

'Do you remember this?'

Before the priest could turn, Djarka had slipped the string over his head and round his throat.

'Rameses was killing you when I intervened.'

Djarka went to tighten the knot, but I held my hand out.

'I promise you,' I murmured, 'you will leave this room alive if you tell me the truth. Call upon the Lady Maat! Lie and you will be dead, and by this time tomorrow, your wife and children will have joined you.'

Amendufet shook his head.

'Kill him!' I ordered.

Djarka tightened the string. Amendufet's hands fluttered like the wings of a bird.

'Please,' he begged.

'I shall make it easy for you, Amendufet. If you lie, Djarka will kill you, then he'll take our mercenaries and snuff out the lives of your family . . .' I leaned forward, wetted my finger and placed it over one of the lamps, watching it splutter out, 'as easily as that. So,' I warned, 'the game begins. Remember, lie and you die. You have become Lord Ay's spy. He must have heard about what happened out at the tomb? Correct?'

Amendufet nodded.

'You were supposed to be my spy, but of course, who is Lord Mahu? Correct?'

'Yes,' Amendufet spluttered.

'Our fat treasurer recognised you could be frightened; that is why he was content to see you die.'

Again there was a nod.

'Good.' I rubbed my hands together. 'Think of your wife and children. You are doing very well! Now tell me, you piece of dog-shit, when the Golden Child was buried, Tutankhamun, the Lord of the Two Lands, was he buried with his heart?'

Amendufet swallowed noisily. He clutched his stomach with one hand, the fingers of the other going to his mouth. 'I don't know.'

Djarka tightened the string.

'I truly don't,' he wailed, 'except for one thing. I asked Lord Ay if I should send the heart scarab to the priests of the Wabet. I was intrigued by his reply. He said he would take it to them himself.'

'And?'

'I later asked the chapel priest of the Wabet if he had received the heart scarab. He claimed to have no knowledge of it.'

'You must have wondered.' Sobeck spoke up. 'A man buried without his heart renders his *ka* powerless.'

'And Nabila?' I asked softly.

Djarka tightened the bowstring.

'Lord Ay feared her. He knew of the relationship between her and Pentju the physician. He said he wanted to see her.'

'Liar!' I shouted.

Djarka pulled the string ever tighter.

'You followed Nabila,' I accused. 'It was you who informed Ay that she was visiting the Mysterious Abode. You came back across the Nile and waited for her in the palm grove between the mooring place of Isis and this house. You told her that I wished to see her in the city, and she of course believed you. What happened to Nabila?'

'I don't know,' Amendufet stammered, 'I truly don't. I have told the truth.'

'Why did you leave the truth in the first place? Why betray me?'

'I had no choice,' he gasped. 'After the banquet in the Hall of the Eternal Sun, Lord Ay and Mery-re summoned me. They said you were finished, a dead man already.' He licked his lips. 'I had no choice but to betray you. I had to do what they asked. They wanted to know all about you, about Nabila. Master, I kept faith with you as long as I could. I've told the truth,' he wailed. 'You promised me . . .'

'You've told the truth?' I waved my hand. 'Ah well, good night, Amendufet!'

He clambered to his feet and staggered towards the door; he opened it and fled into the night.

'I gave my word,' I whispered to Djarka, 'he would leave this room alive, and so he has. Now hurry after him. Kill him! Let the river have its corpse.'

Djarka rose to a half-crouch. 'And his wife and family?'

'Leave them,' I replied. 'They have committed no sin.'

Djarka slipped from the hall. I never gave Amendufet a second thought.

'What now?' Sobeck urged.

'Amedeta,' I replied. 'We must seize Amedeta. She has Pentju's blood on her hands; whether she wants to or not, she will tell us what has truly happened.'

'Tomorrow morning,' Sobeck declared, 'Ay will move to the Temple of Amun to worship and make sacrifice. Afterwards there will be a reception in the temple gardens.' He paused at the heart-chilling scream which cut through the silence.

'Amendufet has paid for his sins.' I smiled. 'Tomorrow Amedeta will pay for hers.'

The luminous mass of the great Temple of Amun at Karnak was bathed in sunlight; its dazzling white columns, shaped like papyrus flowers, reflected the morning light. In the distance echoed the deep murmuring roar of the crowd massed along the Avenues of the Sphinxes and the Rams. Tens of thousands of Thebans had turned out to watch Ay, the Divine One, King of the Two Lands, process solemnly to make sacrifices. The massed squadrons of Nakhtimin's chariots led the processions, and in the dust following them came the leading officers of the army, flanked by servants carrying huge ostrich fans soaked in perfume to hide the stench. The military bands, with fife, drum and trumpet, echoed the marching rhythm of the men. Shaven-headed priests in robes, shoulders decorated with leopard, panther and jaguar skins, sprinkled sacred water and burned cups of sweet-smelling incense. Sweat and perfume, dust and smoke mingled.

At the heart of the procession was Ay, resplendent in the Double Crown, carrying the flail and the rod, the upper part of his body clothed in the *nemes*, the sacred coat of the Pharaoh, a beautifully embroidered sash around his middle. The lower part of his body was masked by folds of drapery. He wore the sacred gloves; on his feet were gold-edged sandals, which rested on a silver footstool carved in the shape of prostrate Nubians, Libyans, Kushites and other People of the Nine Bows. All around him clustered the divine aristocracy of the court, the Keeper of the Perfumes, the Holder of the Royal Sandals, the Chief of the Cabinet, the divine fathers and temple prophets, the scribes of the Inner Circle, all Ay's creatures. Of course we were present, the Children of the Kap, the members of the Royal Circle: Huy and Maya resplendent in their robes, Horemheb and Rameses glittering in their gold collars and silver emblems. I was also there, for the last time.

We passed through two soaring pylons on either side of the entrance to the temple and entered a vast area, sixty acres, a veritable forest of granite which included temples, pylons and courtyards. I followed the royal procession through the ebony-edged doors, going down to the Holy of Holies where the statue of the god waited in its enormous head-dress surmounted by ostrich feathers and gleaming enamel eyes. On such occasions

I always wondered if any of those around me truly believed in what they were doing. The temple choirs sang:

> All lands tremble under your fear.
> Your name is high, mighty and strong.
> The people of Punt and those of the East-land prostrate
> themselves before you . . .

I stood leaning against a wall and read the hymn inscribed there with the oft-repeated refrain, 'Egypt sets her frontiers where she will'. I tried not to catch Sobeck's eye. He looked exhausted and worried. Neither of us had had much sleep. We had assembled in the Great House shortly after dawn. Whatever happened, Ay would expect us there. Horemheb and Rameses looked disgruntled. Maya was agitated. He kept glancing at Sobeck, intrigued by his friend's haggard appearance. Of course, words of condolence were whispered about Pentju; even Nakhtimin swaggered up to reassure me that although he had heard about Nabila's disappearance, he was certain that nothing sinister had happened. I could have killed the bastard on the spot, grabbed a dagger and stabbed him, but every hunter has a time to slink and a time to pounce. I was hunting different quarry; Nakhtimin would have to wait.

Of course Ankhesenamun looked gorgeous in her head-dress, a pure gold gorget studded with precious gems around her throat, jewelled bracelets snaked round her lovely arms. I drew close to see her. She glanced across, then looked away. Beside her was the ever-present Amedeta, dressed like a virgin priestess, her exquisite high-cheekboned face carefully painted, composed into a mask of false piety. I kept watching her as much as I could throughout the procession, during the temple rites and the journey back to the palace. An occasion Ay used for the last time to emphasise his power and dignity, demonstrating to friend and enemy, to Egyptian and to stranger, that he was Pharaoh.

Once the procession was finished, Nakhtimin's guards led members of the circle and other chosen guests through the luxurious halls of the Malkata Palace, their gorgeous galleries and chambers flooded with light and adorned with exquisitely carved columns of wood painted in bright colours. It was the last time I ever saw such glory. My life had begun in the Malkata Palace; the final days of my greatness were played out there. I still recall its doors plated with gold and silver, the lintels flashing with malachite and lapis lazuli, the walls covered with a lacework of brilliant paintings; glittering pools of purity, exuberantly decorated porticoes, gardens which were a chequerboard of light and shade, coloured floors with intricate mosaics, pink-bricked fountains, narrow canals of filtered water, garden beds rich with black soil, shrubs, bushes and trees of every kind, where gloriously plumed exotic birds screeched and caught the eyes with flashes of colour. On that particular day all was peace and calm, though I noticed Nakhtimin's guards, hand-picked Nakhtu-aa, were everywhere, dressed in their blue and gold striped headdresses and their leather kilts, all armed with wickedly pointed spears and oblong shields displaying the Ram of Amun.

We dined in the Golden Vulture chamber, the beautiful mosaics of the floor being reflected in the brilliant, shimmering ceiling. The great doors to this chamber had been removed from their hinges so light and fragrance flooded in from the Water-Lily Garden. Small tables had been set up where guests could sit with their colleagues and friends, whilst Ay and his immediate entourage feasted on a grassy bank under a canopy of gold. My heart rejoiced when Ay raised the Cup of Glory to toast and welcome his guests. Now that I had the opportunity to study him closely, Ay looked distinctly unwell, despite the sacred paints which coated his face.

Sobeck and I shared a table with Maya. We tried to chatter

as if nothing had happened. My greatest pain came from acting as if Nabila was simply visiting friends, while the hate and the rage seethed in me like a bitter black bile. Ay scarcely ate. Now and again he kept touching his stomach, pressing his fingers against the cloth of gold as if to ease some pain. Ankhesenamun, sitting on his left, appeared distinctly uneasy. Only then did I notice one person absent, both in the precession and at that final feast: the round, treacherous face of Mery-re. While the feast was served – platters of various meats, roast geese and haunches of baby calves and gazelles, adorned with ham frills and served on a bed of lettuce, red cabbage, sesame seed and cumin, together with jugs of Hittite wine – I enquired of Maya where Mery-re could be. He tried to reply in an off-hand manner, but I knew he was lying, as he immediately turned the conversation to another topic.

The afternoon dragged on, Ay entertaining his guests with troops of acrobats and dancers. I ate well but drank sparingly, all the time watching Amedeta like a hungry lion would its chosen victim, waiting for it to separate itself from the rest. Shades and parasols were brought out against the heat of the day and the various groups began to break up. Sobeck nudged me. Amedeta had left the royal table, slipping through the hall to the latrines, a servant girl hurrying behind. Sobeck staggered to his feet, hand to his mouth, and swayed towards the door. He turned, shouted at me drunkenly and pretended to stumble into a table.

'Sobeck,' I called, 'you are a toper!' Acting as if I wished to help, I followed him out. We embraced each other, then walked tipsily past the alcoves and recesses where Nakhtimin's men lurked. The latrines were set in a small chamber specially built over a narrow canal used to wash the effluent away. Amedeta's maid was sitting crouched near the door, arms crossed. Sobeck playfully grasped her by the arms, pulling her up towards him. She was startled. Sobeck drew his dagger; she opened her mouth to scream, but he put his hand across her mouth and pushed her into the latrines. Amedeta was standing with her back to us, hands over a bowl of water. She turned and gasped as I pricked her chin gently with the tip of my knife.

'Don't scream, Amedeta, otherwise I'll have to kill you and your maid. You're an assassin! You have the blood of my friend Pentju on your hands.'

Those lovely eyes rounded in alarm.

'Don't scream,' I repeated. 'And don't tell lies.' I pressed the dagger tip a little more firmly until a bead of blood appeared. 'Don't worry either about the palace being guarded.' With my free hand I felt beneath my robes and drew out the small phial of poppy juice I had brought. Neither woman had a choice. They were forced to drink, crouching on the floor, their backs to the wall. They were wine-soaked already, and the poppy juice worked quickly. Both women slumped, heads to one side, mouths gaping.

Sobeck grew agitated. He muttered something about it all being finished, how he was worried about his wife and children, even regretting what he had done. By then I couldn't care. I felt nothing but an icy coldness which grips my heart whenever I confront an enemy to take his life. I snapped at Sobeck not to act like some frightened dog and to help me lower the bodies out of the window. I climbed out first myself. It was in a neglected part of the palace, overgrown and tangled with gorse. We placed both bodies beneath a bush. Sobeck squatted down to guard them while I pursued the rest of our plan.

I made my way back to the Place of Waiting, where the retainers and servants gathered for their lords. My trusted mercenaries were there. I had travelled to the palace in the biggest litter I could find, with long poles on each corner and screened by heavy drapes. To dull the suspicion of any spy, I acted now as if I was drunk, claiming my friend Sobeck could hardly stand. Shouting and cursing, I led my mercenaries, bearing the litter, round the outside of the palace, desperately hoping I would not become lost. At last we reached the place. Sobeck and I took the striped robes of two of the mercenaries and put these on. Amedeta and the girl were still lost in their world of dreams. We lifted them into the litter, Sobeck and I took our places among the bearers, and we left the palace without any trouble. The two mercenaries we had relieved went before us, forcing their way through the busy throng outside the palace, driving away the scorpion men, the traders, the purveyors of animal fat, the honey sellers and perfume makers who thought some great lord would be eager to make a purchase.

Strange, isn't it, that the last time I ever journeyed through Thebes, I plodded like a servant. I had a premonition that the end of a very long journey was in sight, though I tried to concentrate on what was to happen next. We were going to Sobeck's mansion, which lay along one of the great avenues shaded by palm trees just beyond the Sphinx Gate; Djarka would be waiting for us there. I just hoped he was. He was now truly agitated about his wife and children, begging me to flee. Sobeck had supported him. I had won the argument, not through reason but by declaring that if they did not help me, I would do it myself, and, if captured, what might I tell Nakhtimin's torturers in the terror-filled caverns of the House of Chains?

I gazed at the crowd as we passed, glimpsing faces and scenes. A Kushite with a pet mongoose which could perform tricks. Snake men with trays round their necks offering to sell philtres and powders to strengthen the body. A group of whores in garish wigs with vividly painted faces; they were trying to solicit the company, and silver, of some Nubian archers resting under a tattered awning drinking the cheap beer of a travelling merchant. A little boy ran by with a monkey on his shoulder and the bells on the creature's neck gave off a silver tinkling sound. The boy had a mop of thick black hair. He was stout, with a pugnacious face. I felt as if I was seeing a ghost of myself so many years ago with my favourite pet monkey which Isithia had cruelly killed. I blinked and, freeing one hand, wiped the sweat from my face. We crossed the Square of Perfume Makers, going down the Avenue of Lotuses, which is flanked by beautiful carvings of that exquisite flower; a place where the rich and powerful stroll, where they can sit in small gardens which ring the pools and are protected from the heat by large fringed canopies soaked in perfume. I kept my face down as the curious wandered up to pry on what was in the litter. The other porters drove them off.

At last we reached the Sphinx Gate. For a while we had to wait. A cart had overturned, and once that was cleared, a squadron of chariots from the Khonsu regiment came thundering in from a patrol along the Redlands. The horse plumes, the clatter of the wheels, the standard bearer in his heavily armed war chariot, quivers and javelin pouches resplendent in their red-gold, reminded me of something Sobeck had told me as we journeyed to the palace. How military activity outside the city had increased, whilst his Medjay scouts had reported that some units were leaving, heading north. Were Ay and Nakhtimin massing troops to oppose Horemheb's army in Memphis?

The chariot squadron clattered by. They were pursued by a group of Danga dwarves, naked except for loincloths, black hair and beards straggling down, eyes wild in their wizened faces. They had been celebrating at the Temple of Bes and were now indulging in one of their strange rituals where they would drink until intoxicated and dance until they dropped. I thanked the gods that they had not chosen to pursue us. I was fearful of the poppy juice wearing off. Then I heard shouts and we were moving in a cloud of dust through the Sphinx Gate, past the obelisks boasting of the exploits of previous Pharaohs and on to the broad shady avenue.

At last we reached Sobeck's house. The great mansion was now deserted. Sobeck did not even trust his own officers. The only people present were Djarka and a few of my mercenaries, burly, grizzled veterans, scarred and hard-bitten. I had told them they were part of the plot, and that if I fell, they fell with me. They had sworn an oath that they would stay as long as the gold and silver was paid; once that ran out, so would they. I respected such honesty. Djarka was still agitated. He said he would remain until darkness and do what he could, but then he must be gone. I screamed at him that I didn't care and sat down beside the litter, watching my mercenaries rouse Amedeta with jugs of water, laughing as they poured it over her painted face, soaking her robes. The servant girl I locked in a cellar with some food and wine. I told her I had no quarrel with her and that she was safe provided she stayed quiet. By the time I returned, Amedeta was awake, heavy-eyed, face paint smeared. She began to cry and threaten me. I slapped her face and dragged her from the litter, pushing her before me towards the garden pavilion where Sobeck and Djarka were waiting. I showed her the deep pit Djarka had dug near the irrigation canal where the clay was soft, the water seeping through.

We sat on stools in the pavilion. I told Amedeta she was going to die, and that the only choice she had to make was whether to have a merciful death, a cup of drugged wine, or be buried alive. I had no pity, no compassion for this beautiful woman I had once lain with. She had a cobra heart and was steeped in the wickedness of Ankhesenamun and Ay. I told her what I knew. How her mistress had become pregnant not by her husband but by her own grandfather, who wished to pass the children off as his own and turn the Golden Boy into a cuckold. I said I knew all about the games Ay used to play when Tutankhamun suffered one of his fits and Ay used to make the young Pharaoh bow before him. Eventually Amedeta stopped her sobbing, a calculating look in her eyes.

I told her about the death of Tutankhamun, or rather his murder: the absence of the heart scarab, the blasphemy and sacrilege Ay had committed. She did not confirm my suspicions, but neither did she deny them. Finally I described her visit to Pentju and his murder.

The more I talked and watched, the more excited I grew. Amedeta was staring at me as if she was almost impatient for me to end my litany of accusations. What, I wondered, did she have to tell me? I finished and sipped from the cup of wine Djarka had brought, then offered it to her. She snatched it and drank greedily.

'What do you want, Lord Mahu, Baboon of the South? If you have brought me here to try me, what defence can I make? Soon my mistress will know that I'm gone, so kill me if you must.'

'Nabila?' I asked.

'I know nothing of her.'

I slapped her face and threatened to turn her over to my mercenaries. She screamed back insults but still claimed she knew nothing.

'What *do* you know?' I asked, running my finger down her cheek. 'You know Ay is dying?'

Oh, I enjoyed that, the utter confusion in her face.

'Tell us, tell us that we lie.' Sobeck spoke up. Djarka lunged forward, slicing at her ankle with the small dagger concealed in his hand. Amedeta screamed and clutched at the blood bubbling through the cut.

'Life for life, Mahu,' she gasped. 'Promise me my life, and I will tell you.'

'Tell us,' I retorted, 'and I promise you a swift death.'

'Life for life,' she repeated. She ripped off a piece of her robe and used it to cover the wound. 'The day is passing, Mahu, soon it will be dark. How long can you stay here? They will find out. The bargain I'm offering is better than you will get from anyone else.'

'But if we don't kill you,' Sobeck declared, 'Ay certainly will.'

Amedeta forced a laugh, gesturing round the pavilion.

'This is your house, Sobeck, but why can't I hear any voices? Where are your wife, your servants, your children? They have fled, haven't they? What they have done, so can I. Egypt is changing.' She pointed to Djarka. 'And your wife, your children, your life? I'm offering my life for yours.'

Sobeck and Djarka muttered. She had convinced them, and they were more than aware of the hours passing.

'Tell us,' I lifted my hand, 'and your life is safe.'

'Ay, Ankhesenamun and Nakhtimin are bringing the Hittites into Egypt.'

She laughed at our gasps of disbelief. Sobeck went to protest, but I grasped his arm. Amedeta was staring at me coolly.

'Mahu, you great baboon. Why do you think Ay sent Meryre to the Hittite camp? He was to open negotiations for an alliance. You were supposed to die there, Horemheb and Rameses to be cut off and forced to capitulate.'

'But . . .' I interrupted.

'But?' she mimicked back. 'Matters have proceeded apace. Ankhesenamun is now a widow. They do not plan to marry her to Horemheb, but to Zananza – the Hittite prince. Meryre has been sent to the Hittites again, not just to negotiate, but to bring the bridal party into Egypt.'

'But what does Ay plot?' I asked.

'He intends to found a new dynasty. Ankhesenamun will marry a Hittite prince, Ay will marry one of their princesses. They will divide Canaan between them.'

'And Horemheb and Rameses will simply look on and clap?'

'They'll be dead, as you will be.'

'And their troops?'

'Think, Mahu. You remember Nakhtimin meeting you in the Delta at Avaris?'

'He left troops there, didn't he?' I whispered. 'They'll be the welcoming party for the Hittites.' I tried to imagine a map of Egypt, Thebes in the south, Avaris in the north, between them the garrison city of Memphis, the white-walled town, the home of Ptah – the god man.

'Of course,' I breathed. 'Horemheb and Rameses are in Thebes. They'll never be allowed to leave. Their troops are leaderless and they'll face an enemy on either front: Hittites and Egyptians coming from the north, Nakhtimin advancing from the south. They'll be divided.'

'Ay's agents are already busy in Memphis offering bribes. Every army has its grumblers. They'll also cut off supplies.' Amedeta laughed at my disbelief. 'Its already begun,' she hissed. 'Nakhtimin is dispatching troops to the north.'

'Where?' I asked.

Amedeta giggled behind her hand.

'Of course!' I exclaimed. 'Where else but Akhmin, Ay's home town!'

'This is what will happen,' Amedeta explained. 'The Hittite envoys are already in Egypt, camped outside Avaris. They will be joined by Prince Zananza and will travel down to Akhmin. People will think it is just another peace delegation. They will be joined there by high-ranking officers and the peace treaty and marriage alliances will be sealed. Zananza will then journey on to Thebes. Horemheb will find out and object but it will be too late, he and Rameses will be placed under house arrest.'

'And if Ay dies?' I asked.

Amedeta shrugged elegantly. 'Nakhtimin takes over, or Zananza.'

I stared at Sobeck and Djarka. Amedeta tended to the wound on her ankle. She was brave. Despite the mortal danger which faced her, she was humming gently under her breath.

'Does Maya know?' Sobeck asked.

'He may suspect.'

'When is this to happen?'

'Within the month.'

'Is there anything else?'

'No, except when can I go?'

I called in my mercenary captain and took Djarka and Sobeck out into the garden. A cool breeze now ruffled the trees. I noticed despairingly how the shadows had lengthened. A mongoose slipped from underneath a bush and scampered across to the lush vegetation circling Sobeck's fish pond. I gazed round that garden, with its pavilions and ornamental pools, its shaded paths, vine trellises, fountains and flowers. My own garden was like this, but what did it matter now? Within days it would all be shattered.

Djarka plucked at my arm. I shrugged him off, so he confronted me and I gazed on his face for the last time. I recalled the lithe, olive-skinned young man with his dark eyes and black ringleted hair, the side locks oiled and twisted, resting against each cheek. I remembered his speed and cunning and the unswerving loyalty he had shown me over the years. Now his eyes were red-rimmed, his cheeks furrowed, his hair cropped and dusted with grey. He stretched out a hand.

'Lord Mahu, I must be gone. Soon all the paths and roads, as well as the river routes, will be closely guarded. Nakhtimin's men will be swarming like ants. I must reach Memphis. I must take Mert and my children out of that city and go north to shelter amongst our people.' Djarka peered up at the sky. 'I'll like it there, in the open lush meadows of the Delta. You can hide there and, if necessary, escape.' He put one hand on my shoulder and stared sombrely at me. 'What does it matter if Ay wins or Horemheb? I'm tired, master. I too took an oath to Akenhaten. It's finished. I must be gone.' He raised his hand towards Sobeck. '*Ankh* and *sa*, life and happiness, for however long it may last.'

He walked away, but paused under an acacia tree and beckoned me over. In the shade of that tree I embraced my old friend for the last time. Neither of us had mentioned meeting again, but as I held him close, Djarka dug his nails into my back.

'Stay near and listen, my lord,' he hissed. 'I must go, not because of the danger to me and Mert, but because of my children. No,' he continued fiercely, 'listen. You remember the dark days of the great plague in the City of the Aten, when Akenhaten was purged, when he realised he was not the Saviour or the Messiah? He was tended by our holy men; I was present. Akenhaten asked them if the Saviour, the Messiah, would come from his line. "No," one of the prophets replied, "but from him!"'

I broke free. 'Who?' I asked.

Djarka was staring at me, a look I had never seen before. 'He was pointing at me,' he whispered. 'Don't you remember, Mahu? One of my ancestors was an albino. We carry the divine sign in our blood. No one else knows that! For friendship's sake I have told you. If you live, tell no one until the appointed time. If you die, take the secret with you.' He stretched out his hand. 'Just clasp it. We met as friends and we'll leave as friends.'

Qerra: a serpent-fiend of the underworld

Chapter 15

I clasped Djarka's hand. He smiled and was gone. I never saw him again. Sobeck was pacing agitatedly up and down. He too wanted to go, but I begged him to stay, to guard Amedeta until I returned. I left him with my mercenaries but took the captain with me, a tough, wiry little man with a scar which crossed his face from his left eye to his right ear. I informed Sobeck that I was going to the palace, but that was a lie and probably cost him his life. Using tracks and narrow paths, I skirted the city to my own mansion, so quiet under the late afternoon sun. We scaled the wall, dropping into the garden, an eerie experience, skulking like dogs, moving from one bush to another. The servants were all gone. I found the two mercenaries I had left dozing in the hall of audience surrounded by jugs of beer and soiled platters. I kicked them awake and told them to guard the gates, both the main and the side one. The captain lit a fire and I opened my secret places, chests, coffers and caskets. I burned papers and manuscripts, sheets of white papyrus freshly written and ageing manuscripts turning yellow and curled. All those documents collected over the years, a hoard of memories turned quickly to ash. I didn't want them to fall into Nakhtimin's hands. One thing I did save: my secret journals.

Next I opened my jewel store. Like any tomb robber, I took

the smallest and most precious items, the stones and rings, the bracelets, the pouches of gold and silver, throwing them into two leather sacks. When I was satisfied, I went down into the wine cellar. I remember how dark and cold it was. I hadn't grieved for Nabila, or Tutankhamun. I was still bitterly implacable. I had a grudge to finish, and the sooner the better. On one thing I was determined: the complete and utter destruction of Ay and his clan. I was like a servant with a list of tasks, finishing one and moving on to the next. My friendship with Sobeck, at that moment in time, mattered little; even Djarka's departure was simply one dark cloud massing with the rest. The storm had to break.

I picked up an oilskin and thrust it into the captain's hands; I drew my dagger and ripped another apart, watching the oil splash out. I went upstairs and did the same with a fresh sack, moving from one chamber to another, to pavilions, outhouses, even my herb garden. I removed the two sacks of jewellery and some weapons I had taken from the armoury, and called the two mercenaries over. I gave them each a brilliant amethyst, personal gifts to me from the Great House.

'Once we've gone,' I ordered, 'burn the place.'

'And then, master?'

'Flee,' I declared. 'Pray for all the speed of the cheetah. Put as much distance between yourself and Thebes as possible!'

The two villains agreed. I gathered up the weapons and the two treasure sacks, one of which contained my journals, and slid through the side gate, the captain following. We kept to the trees and vegetation which fringed the track leading down to the mooring place of Isis, following the paths around the city and back to Sobeck's house. The day was changing, the sun beginning to set, the sky turning a cloudy gold, the waters of the Nile darkening. Shadows raced across our path as if the day itself knew what was happening. On one occasion we paused and stared back: even though we had gone some distance, I could see the black plumes rising against the forbidding sky. The mercenaries had fired my house. We made our way back carefully, aware of the growing number of soldiers and patrols on the mooring path and quaysides, but we were two men amongst thousands. We approached Sobeck's house from the rear.

I suppose if you have lived your life in danger you become like any animal, haunted by a feeling of unease, the prickling of hair on the back of your neck, the tightness in your belly. Sobeck's house looked quiet but I noticed the rear gate was slightly ajar, yet the chief of police had closed it behind us. I turned to the mercenary captain. He too was wary, constantly blinking, head slightly turned as he strained to hear a sound.

'Leave the treasure,' I urged. 'Come with me'.

The mercenary made to object.

'Well, you don't think,' I joked sourly, 'that I would leave you to guard it?'

The man gave a crooked grin. We crept towards the wall. I helped him over and followed, slipping down, bruising my leg. I crouched, pushing aside a bush, and stared across. Near the acacia tree where Djarka had made his farewell, I saw something white flutter in the breeze. I picked up my bow, strung an arrow to the cord and loosed it towards that patch of white. Nothing happened. I scrambled forward, the mercenary following me. There was no need for caution. Nakhtimin's killers had been and left. Any friendship Ay had had for Sobeck had counted for nothing. My old friend had fought vainly for his life. I could easily follow the trail of destruction. The house and gardens held that sinister menace which always follows a massacre, as if the spirits of those so brutally slain still hover about, beating furiously, howling loudly, but unable to break through that invisible, impenetrable wall which divides the living from the dead.

The ancient scribes talk of destruction as the Night of the Great Ploughing, the Day of Fire. I understand what they mean. Sobeck's beautiful garden possessed all the horrors of a battlefield, as if that invisible wall I talked about had, for a short while, fissured and snapped open, so the demons, the devourers, the strange-headed beasts of the underworld could break through. The murderous god Seth, red of hair and with bloodied hands, had certainly left his mark. Sobeck and my mercenaries must have fought like men possessed. Corpses soaked in blood littered the grass. The assassins were all dressed the same, dark robes over boiled leather armour. Some wore military boots, others were barefoot, hardened faces made all the more grotesque by violent death. Some still grasped axe, dagger, mace or sword. One was pinned to a tree, like a fly, a spear piercing his body. He hung grotesque, arms splayed out.

I reached the pavilion where Sobeck must have made his last stand. He lay just outside the doorway, face resting on his hand, eyes closed. He would have looked asleep if it hadn't have been for the blood gushing out of his nostrils and mouth to form a dark pool either side of him. I turned him over. He had been cut in the neck but his death wound was a large, jagged gash above the groin. I brushed away the flies gathering to feast and glanced up at the sky. The vultures and buzzards which hunted along the wet banks of the river had smelled the blood and were beginning to gather.

Amedeta lay within the pavilion. They'd tied a rope around her head; it was still tightly bound. I wondered if she had talked before she died. Perhaps she had screamed, that's why the assassins had slit her throat and left her corpse sprawling on the floor. They'd made a mistake. Nakhtimin and Ay would not be pleased. They should have taken Amedeta back to the palace so they could discover what she had truly confessed. I turned the corpse of one mercenary over with my foot. I doubted if they were soldiers, probably a gang of professional assassins hired by Nakhtimin. I entered the house; the only time I felt a stab of pity was at the sight of the poor serving maid's corpse. The assassins had dragged her out, abused her, then dashed her head against the wall.

There was nothing to be done, no time to grieve. The gods know I have had many years to do that. The gods, if they exist, can be my witnesses. I have travelled the length and breadth of the Nile. I have even journeyed through the great forests to the south of Kush. I have stood on the sandbanks of the kingdom of Punt and stared out across that broad waterway which the spice ships use. I have travelled through searing deserts and stood on the cliffs overlooking the Great Green. I have seen every type of god and sheltered in the shade of every kind of temple. Oh yes, I have even been into the land of the Hittites and seen the standards of their storm gods. I have visited the western islands and moved amongst the tribes, strange-looking men and women with fair hair and blue eyes. I have spent tens of years hiding from the might of Pharaoh. However, one thing I have always done, if the gods care to listen, is make sacrifice and votive offerings to the spirits of my dead. Sometimes I can feel them all around me: Akenhaten, Nefertiti, Khiya, Sobeck, Pentju and, of course, always Nabila.

On that day of wrath, however, that day of anger, I had no time, no heart to mourn. I could not sit and enjoy memories of Sobeck or bemoan his death. We left that house, slinking like animals through the undergrowth.

'They must have come here first,' I declared. 'It took some time for Sobeck to die, then they went searching for me, but all they'll find is fire.'

'What now, master?'

For a while I squatted, wondering what to do. The mercenary sat opposite, watching from under heavy-lidded eyes. I knew what he was thinking, so I picked up my dagger.

'Lord Mahu has fallen.' I grinned at him. 'You must be looking at those treasure bags and wondering what to do next. Forget such thoughts. I am possessed by a demon. Whatever you think, whatever you try, there will be another corpse before sunset and it won't be mine.'

The mercenary rubbed the side of his face and grinned, squinting at me evilly. I patted one of the sacks.

'This is yours, if you do what I say. Nobody knows who you are. Hide yourself in a robe. Go and seek out the Lord Maya. Bring him here. Tell him to write out a pass allowing the bearer to go where he wants.'

'What happens if he betrays me?'

'He won't. Tell him Sobeck is dead and Lord Mahu has news. Tell him he has nothing to fear, nothing to lose and much to gain. He must come by himself.' I peered up through the branches. 'He can bring one guard.'

The mercenary chewed his lip.

'There is one other thing. Maya will be in the palace, and so will General Horemheb.'

I paused, thinking out the details of the plan, my mind teeming like a box of ants. Even before I left Sobeck's house, a path forward to my vengeance had been glimpsed.

'Yes, yes,' I added. 'Lord Maya must see Horemheb, who should give him a letter which declares I am acting on his authority. It is to be addressed to the colonels of his regiments at Memphis. It is to be written in his own hand, brief and succinct. It must describe me as his herald.'

'What happens if Horemheb refuses?'

'He won't, he has no choice. Let Maya whisper to him that Sobeck is dead.'

I made the captain of the mercenaries repeat my messages until I was satisfied, then he slipped like a cat into the night. I felt I was safe. They wouldn't think of returning to Sobeck's house, not until dawn. I crept back in for scraps of food and a jug of beer, then returned to the tangled undergrowth, curling up like a child, plotting for tomorrow.

*　　*　　*

I stared up through the palm fronds, watching the vultures swoop like lost dark souls against the sky. All around me echoed the sounds of the camp. We were sheltering in the Oasis of the Night God, a sprawling tangle of palm trees, gorse, and reed-fringed pools which lay on the borders of the Redlands, thirty miles south of the town of Akhmin. I shifted my head, scratching it gently against the roll of cloth which served as a head rest. I picked up the waterskin, sprinkling its last drops over my face. I calculated it must have been twenty-five days since I'd fled Thebes. Maya had come, weeping over Sobeck. The dice were thrown. He'd made his choice. He thrust the passes into my hand, cursed Ay and left. My mercenary captain, treasure in hand, disappeared shortly afterwards. I left shortly before dawn.

In the end there had been little danger. Nakhtimin didn't have time to impose the ring of steel which he had now thrown round Thebes. I had travelled quickly upriver, posing as a pilgrim going to visit the man-god Ptah, a pleasant experience after the horrors I had witnessed. For the first part of the journey I noticed the war barges on the Nile and the clouds of dust thrown up along both banks by the chariot squadrons. Now I knew why they were moving north. I had arrived at the quayside at Memphis, a bustling, colourful place where merchants travelling to and from the Great Green paused to rest or do business. The city thronged with people of various tribes and the marketplaces swarmed with beggars, itinerant traders and mercenaries selling their swords. I wondered how many of these were spies.

Once darkness fell, I slipped into Colonel Nebamun's house. The old rogue, one of Horemheb's most trusted commanders, was pleased to see me, greeting me as such veterans do by reminding me how we had both served against the Great Usurper. He knew a little about what was happening in Thebes and was growing concerned at Nakhtimin's troops still being present in the Delta, as well as the way the town of Akhmin was being reinforced. When I showed him Horemheb's letter and told him what had happened, his face turned an unhealthy grey.

We had been sitting on the roof terrace sharing a jug of Hittite beer, savouring the fragrance of the special flowerpots Nebamun's servants had brought up. Once he realised what was happening, Nebamun kicked one of the pots aside as he hurried to the steps, bawling for a messenger. The following morning, just after dawn, when the sky was grey and the breeze cool, I met Nebamun and his corps commanders on the roof terrace. Nebamun read out Horemheb's letter, which declared that its bearer would be Horemheb's herald and that what he did was for the good of Egypt. I stared round this circle of commanders. They had all been Maryannou, braves of the king, or Nakhtu-aa, strong-arm boys, warriors who had killed at least three men in hand-to-hand combat. Soldiers who had risen through the ranks, grizzled, hard-bitten veterans who had fought the People of the Nine Bows, on the river, on the Great Green, in the searing heat of the desert or in some desolate marshland. They were wounded and scarred but they were the glory of Egypt. I knew their allegiance to Horemheb was unswerving. They had no time for Ay, Nakhtimin or any of the Akhmin Gang. They hated the idea of the Aten and they rejected Nakhtimin's troops as bully boys, war dancers, not true soldiers of Egypt. They commanded four crack regiments which had recently been reorganised: the Ptah, the Horus of Henes, the Isis and the Nepthys.

They sat and listened as I described everything to them. The idea that their beloved Horemheb was a prisoner in Thebes made a few gnaw on their knuckles, and if I hadn't stopped them, some of the hotheads would have marched directly on the city. The news about the Hittites soon silenced them. They were quick enough to realise the dangers of being wedged between two armies, one in the Delta and the other in Thebes. In the end they accepted my solution. The Hittite delegates would leave Akhmin for Thebes; in fact, it would be a bridal party. We would have to wipe it out, massacre everyone, create a rift between Egypt and the Hittite Empire which could never be healed. We would destroy whatever army accompanied them and march on Thebes.

Secret preparations were drawn up, and everyone was sworn to silence, though the news we received from Thebes was not good. Ay, despite his illness, was massing troops outside the city, even drawing in garrisons from beyond the Third and Fourth Cataracts. More units were being sent north and a veritable army was gathering in the Delta. Nevertheless, we were just as secretive, a pack of hyaenas plotting the hunt. Nebamun sent spies into Akhmin, and one of these, an ugly-faced spice trader, reported that Nakhtimin had arrived there, as had Mery-re together with Prince Zananza. They were not planning to leave by river, but would start their journey by travelling through the Blacklands to Dendera, the great bend in the river, where a flotilla of barges would be waiting. Nebamun and I decided that they would never reach Dendera. To this end we had brought our army out into the Redlands, hiding in the Oasis of the Night God. Seven miles to the south-west, Nakhtimin's column was approaching the Oasis of the Jonquil. They would shelter there for the night and continue their journey the next morning. Nebamun and I had decided to attack just before dawn.

So there I was, sprawled beneath a tree, staring up at the sky, wondering if, at the same time tomorrow, I would be alive. I still grieved for Nabila. Sorrow for her held me fast. I wanted to kill and kill again. I was desperate to finish this business, but what then? Sobeck was dead, Pentju murdered, Djarka had disappeared. I fell asleep dreaming about the future, which, of course, is stupid: the present hour you can control, but the future is in the hands of others.

We marched the next morning, just as the stars began to

fade and the full moon lost its brilliance. The dark was still biting cold, our blood was sluggish, but eventually we were moving, chariotry supported by corps of Nubian footmen dressed in white-padded kilts, their wiry hair knotted. They were armed with shield and spear, axe, sword or mace. Behind these came units of Syrian archers in their leather garb, reinforced bows slung over their shoulders, quivers of feathered shafts slapping against their backs. Our main force was chariots, carriages gleaming in the dull light, embroidered quivers and sheaths packed with death-bearing feathered shafts. The light chariots, with their brood wheels and teams of specially selected horses in their gleaming leather harness, were ideal for desert warfare. Each horse was caparisoned with a body cloth bearing the colours of its regiment and a plume of the same hue. We advanced in three columns. Our scouts, sent out before us, came hastening back with the news: Nakhtimin still rested at the Oasis of the Jonquil.

We attacked just before dawn. I shall never forget that morning, the last time I ever took part in a charge of imperial chariots, the full glory of Egypt's power. The sky was beginning to lighten, and our three columns had re-formed into two lines of chariots, Nebamun and I in the centre of the first line. The old colonel moved his chariot forward; in niches either side of it were thrust the standards of Ptah and Horus of Henes, Horemheb's personal insignia. Beside me, my charioteer, a *tedjen* of the first class, grasped the reins, wrapping them round his wrist; he smiled at me and winked. I felt that thrill, the tingling in the stomach, the tightening of muscles, the shiver as the blood races under the skin like a swallow under the sky. Our horses caught the excitement, neighing and pawing the ground, nostrils flared. Chariots creaked and groaned as wheels juddered backwards and forwards. Behind us the Nubians and Syrians were already chanting their own prayers.

Nebamun's chariot moved forward slowly, the same pace

he would follow if leading a ceremonial parade through Thebes. We advanced, two long lines of chariots, the elite corps of the Horus regiment. Nebamun, resplendent in his gleaming corselet, was bedecked with all the medallions and collars of a renowned warrior. Like the rest, he was technically guilty of treason. He was attacking the power of Pharaoh, but in his eyes, Ay was a usurper. The old colonel had drunk deeply of Canaan wine, and his face was flushed for battle. I remember the hymn he sang as our war horde moved forward:

The glory of Ptah cannot be dimmed!
The majesty of Horus of Henes is wonderful to behold!

The refrain was taken up by his men, and the hymn was shouted for the heavens to hear. The verses continued, proclaimed by Nebamun, echoed by his warriors. Our pace quickened, Nebamun's horses breaking into a trot. Now the old colonel bawled out single lines:

'For the glory of Ptah!'

'For the majesty of Horus!' came the thundering reply.

Our horses broke from a trot to a gallop. We breasted a rise: beneath us lay the Oasis of the Jonquil, a mass of palm trees, around it Nakhtimin's camp with its horse lines and chariot parks, its camp fires still smouldering, smoke plumes rising. I heard the yap of a dog and glimpsed small figures moving. The breeze was behind us, the sky lightened, the sun about to rise. Nebamun's chariot broke from a gallop into a charge and so we came on, the power of Egypt sweeping down towards that oasis like angels of death. We were no longer part of the world. Our world had shrunk to galloping horse, streaming plume, rattling wheels and tightened reins, a long arc of charging chariotry heading like an arrow into the heart of the enemy.

We swept in like a pack of hunting dogs, brushing aside pickets and guards, losing ourselves in the bloodied frenzy of battle. What memories stay with you from such a bloody affray, so many, many years ago! Startled faces, human beings going down under galloping hoofs and crushing wheels; warriors flinging themselves at you only to be brushed aside. Our charge took us into the heart of Nakhtimin's camp, and then it became like any other battle, warrior against warrior, yet that charge had broken them. Many died only a few heartbeats after waking. Our chariots slowed, hampered by the bushes and brush, the ropes of the pavilions, all the obstacles of a camp. My *tedjen* was the best.

Nebamun and I had decided that he would strike at the Hittite, leaving Nakhtimin for me. We reached the royal enclosure, knocking down the meagre fence. Before us rose the altars Nakhtimin had set up: one to Amun-re, the other to the Hittite storm god. The resistance was stronger here, spearmen and archers being organised into ranks. Yet it was too late. Nebamum had struck like a hawk, his chariots coming in from every direction, now reinforced by ranks of Nubians and Syrians, panting and sweat-soaked but still eager for battle, hungry for the spoils. I glimpsed Zananza, dressed in a tunic, a flower wreath on his head; the sight provoked a momentary stab of sorrow as his long-haired bodyguard was cut down and the prince himself, surrounded by Nebamun and a ring of officers, was shown no mercy. A Hittite came screaming at me, face smeared with blood, but my *tedjen* clubbed him back.

Nakhtimin had decided to make his last stand before the altars. He and his officers, still wine-soaked, heavy-eyed and bleary-faced, hadn't had time to arm properly. Nakhtimin glimpsed me, and his face contorted with anger, mouth screaming his fury. I dismounted and we met in a clash of swords but his eyes already had the look of death. I shouted Nabila's name at him and we closed, sword and dagger skittering off each other. No finesse, no skill; I hacked and hewed, driving him back. A Syrian archer, following close behind, loosed a shaft, catching him in the thigh. Nakhtimin collapsed to one knee. I brought my sword down, slicing his neck just above the shoulder. He went down on both knees, eyes glazed, mouth coughing blood. I stood behind him, shouted Nabila's name again and sliced with my sword, taking his head in one furious, vengeful cut, the blood spurting up as an offering to the demons of the darkness.

The battle lust was on me, those furies which possess you when the carnage is at its height. The battle turned into a massacre. Every Hittite was killed. I found Mery-re in one of the pavilions. He still looked smug, face and body drenched in perfumed oil. In those few seconds, with the blood boiling within me, the years were forgotten. He yelped for mercy, kneeling, hands joined, shouting out memories. He was still crying when I crushed his skull. The camp was given over to slaughter. They had brought women with them, temple girls from Thebes as well as Hittite maids; these were ravished and raped and their throats cut, bodies piled in a heap as our men turned to looting the caskets and coffers.

By mid-morning the camp was ours. I had lost control of Nebamun. The Hittite officers, together with those of Nakhtimin, were made to kneel, hands bound behind their backs. There must have been forty in all. Nebamun showed no mercy. Leather corselet and kilt drenched in blood, he placed both his standards on the altar and moved down the long line of prisoners armed with a war club, smashing their skulls, a bloody sacrifice to his gods. We spent the rest of that day sheltering in the Oasis of the Jonquil. I drank deeply on plundered wine and had to be kicked awake the next morning. Nebamun had been ruthlessly cruel. The bodies of Nakhtimin, Zananza, Mery-re and at least four dozen others had been impaled on a long row of stakes. Later on, Nebamun dictated letters to garrisons in Akhmin and the Delta ordering them to make full submission or face devastation.

Three days later we moved slowly south by land and river,

the news of our great victory going out before us. Of course it was all over. Ay was dying, whilst in Thebes, Huy, and especially Maya, had been busy: that fat, wily treasurer opened the House of Silver and the House of Bread to all. Officers, priests and scribes were suborned or menaced, the merchant princes threatened or bribed, the city mob roused to proclaim the power of Horemheb. The Great General was freed from house arrest. He and his sinister shadow Rameses took a barge north to meet us at the House of Lebanese Cedar, one of those great waterside mansions with a gleaming hall of audience overlooking resplendent gardens. The Great General was hailed as a saviour by his men and so the game was over.

I knelt before him in the hall of audience, he and Rameses lounging on cushions, spitting out grape-seeds, slurping noisily from deep-bowled goblets of wine. They half listened to my story; Horemheb, drunk, gazed blearily at me, wagging one thick-set finger.

'Ay is dying,' he slurred. 'He is in the House of Kumes, only five miles down the road. You know,' he continued, 'I am married to his daughter, but you, Mahu . . .' He shrugged drunkenly.

'Visit him,' Rameses hissed, his soulless eyes glaring at me. 'Give him our best wishes and send him . . . no' He smirked. 'Tell him to embrace the Far Horizon.'

I found Ay resting in a garden pavilion at the House of Kumes. Most of his guards had long deserted. The sheets he fingered were soiled, the back rest he leaned against stained with sweat, the fruit in the bowl wrinkled and dried. He had lost weight: his handsome, narrow face, once so full of pride, arrogance and venom, was lined and sunken, those once life-filled eyes dark pools of despair, his mouth, which could spit out such malice, no more than dried, cracked lips. He was feeble and fretful, gasping for breath, and I wondered what poison Pentju had fed him.

He recognised me and forced a smile. He told me how much he hated me, for had I not killed his daughter Nefertiti? He cursed himself for not taking my head. I asked him what had happened to Nabila, but he just taunted me, so I sat and told him what I knew. He plucked a dagger from beneath the covers and flailed at me. I knocked it away and he began to cry, appealing to our glory days when he and I had sat and plotted. I asked him once again about Nabila. He sneered, so I picked up some cushions and held them over his face, pressing down even as his body jerked as he fought for breath. I cursed him with every text I could recall from the Book of the Dead. I was still pressing down on the cushions when I realised his moans had stopped and his body lay inert, lifeless. I took the cushions away and stared into his empty eyes, then pulled his head over, hoping his *ka* had not left his body, and whispered in his ear.

'Go down to the horrors of the underworld and tell them I sent you there.'

I looked around the room: no one was there, the passageway outside was deserted. Everyone had fled, except for a Saluki hound, a watchdog chained to a goat post. I returned to the death chamber armed with a sword and a small axe, and hacked at the corpse, plucking out Ay's heart. I fed it to the dog, then left.

I came across a wine booth set up under some palm trees a short distance from the House of Kumes, and drank myself stupid. Horemheb's guards found me there the following morning, nursing a sore head and a dry tongue. They arrested me and I joined the list of Horemheb's enemies. We were arraigned in front of the Great General and put on trial before a military tribunal composed of Rameses, fat-faced Maya and Huy. Most of the prisoners were Nakhtimin's officers. Some of these were sentenced to death, being taken to the House of Slaughter; a few were banished. Others had their barbaric sentences reduced to a speedy cup of poison in the House of

Chains. Ankhesenamun had also been seized. She had been stripped of her finery, her head shaved, her face washed, garbed like a penitent in a sheath leather tunic. She was accused of treason against the Kingdom of the Two Lands and its people, of bringing on to its sacred soil the People of the Nine Bows. Manacled and chained, waiting my turn at the far end of the hall, I watched that princess kneel and beg for her life. Rameses enjoyed himself, yelling abuse at her, lecturing her loudly.

'How dare you,' he screamed, 'sin against Horemheb, Mighty Bull, Lord of the Flame who Lives on Truth, He who Lights the Eastern Sky? So you wish to marry a foreign prince? Then you shall, far away from Egypt. Take her away.'

My turn came next. I'll be honest, I was courageous. I refused to kneel or recognise the authority of the court. Instead I shouted at Rameses about all I had done. He watched me, that cobra of a man, Horemheb's dark soul, and pursed his bloodless lips, nodding in agreement with what I said. Maya and Huy kept their heads down, refusing to meet my eyes. Eventually Rameses ordered me to shut up and cleared the court. He rose from his chair of judgement and personally unlocked my chains. He brought cushions for me to sit on and a goblet of chilled wine. I was tempted to seize him but Rameses kept looking behind me: there must have been a bowman, hidden away, arrow notched, watching my every movement. Rameses seized my face between his hands as he used to when he bullied me in the Kap.

'Come, come, Mahu,' he whispered. 'You broke into Tutankhamun's tomb. What did you find there? What did the Watchers hold? What is prophesied about the people of the Apiru?' I thought of Djarka, smiled and stared back. Rameses' grip tightened on my face. 'Life and peace,' he whispered. 'Wealth beyond your wildest dreams: just tell us.'

'Do you know, Rameses,' I replied, 'I have never decided what I dislike most, your looks or your stench.' He smirked, winked and took his hands away. I thought I'd be executed then, but Horemheb always did have a soft spot for me. Instead I was sentenced to perpetual banishment, under pain of instant death. I'd be allowed to take a small sack of treasure with me. The following morning sentence was carried out: Mahu, Baboon of the South, once Lord Mahu, Overseer of the House of Secrets and of Scribes, Friend of Pharaoh, Beloved of the Royal Flame, was turned out on the highway like a travelling tinker.

I have wandered the roads and the tracks of the world. I have gone beyond the Cataracts to the great jungles of the south. I have travelled north across the Great Green and met the blue-eyed ones. I have seen great cities go to war and be consumed by flames. I have seen armies, swarming hordes, move across windswept, grass-filled plains. I have talked to men who have travelled to the edges of the world. I have eaten strange foods, celebrated ghastly rites and slept with women of every type. I have searched for Nabila but never found her.

Fifty years have passed since the day I left Thebes. I did discover where Djarka was but never approached him, for he was hiding amongst his own people, the Apiru. I also know how Horemheb, Mighty Bull, had no heir but left his crown to Rameses' son, and how the offspring of the great cobra searched the length and breadth of Egypt, wiping out all memory of the Aten, the One. But it was too late. Djarka had a daughter and she had a son, an albino, Moses. He rose to become a great prince amongst his people and is now in fierce confrontation against Pharaoh, also called Rameses. Pharaoh doesn't know what to do. Should he let Moses and his people go, or annihilate them? He has searched the records, whilst the Overseer of the House of Secrets has alerted his Eyes and Ears all over Egypt in the hunt for Mahu.

Eventually they caught me, and have brought me back to Thebes to tell my story, give my advice, but what can I tell them? Nothing except the past, about the days of doom when Akenhaten turned Egypt on its head; when Nefertiti, the most beautiful woman who ever lived, ruled my heart; when Ay and the other hyaenas dreamed their dreams of glory. I am now old and toothless, wizened and bent. I need a young wench to keep me warm at night and a bowl of wine to gladden my days, yet they still come and ask me what they should do about the future. What can I tell them? Except to bend against the coming storm!

Historical Note

We know a great deal about Mahu from his unoccupied tomb at El-Amarna (the City of the Aten), dug deep into the ground against potential tomb robbers. The paintings in his tomb are hastily executed but do show Mahu's great achievement, the frustration of a very serious plot against Akenhaten (N. de G. Davies, *The Rock Tombs of El-Amarna: Tombs of Pentju, Mahu and Others*, Egypt Exploration Society, London, 1906). Archaeologists have also found both his house and the police station in what is now known as El-Amarna; even the fact that he kept an armoury close at hand (see Davies, above). The character, opulence and decadence of the period are well documented and accurately described by the historian Joanne Fletcher in her excellent book *Egypt's Sun King: Amenhotep III* (Duncan Baird, London, 2000). The rise of the Akhmin Gang is graphically analysed by a number of historians, including Bob Briers and Nicholas Reeves, as well as myself in my book *Tutankhamun* (Constable and Robinson, London, 2002). Queen Tiye's control of Egypt, particularly of foreign affairs, is apparent in what is now known as the 'Amarna Letters'.

The events of this book are grounded in firm scholarship so there is a great deal of evidence for what Mahu writes. Robert Feather, in his marvellous book *The Copper Scroll*

Decoded (Thorson, 2000), describes the link between Akenhaten and the caves around the Dead Sea. For the rest, the best witness is actually Tutankhamun's tomb, described so graphically by the man who discovered it, Howard Carter (*The Tomb of Tutankhamun*, BCA, 1972). A useful appendix for this is Nicholas Reeves' *The Complete Tutankhamun* (Thames and Hudson, 1990–1). I, too, have discussed the tomb and its contents, as well as the fate of Tutankhamun, in my non-fiction work mentioned above. The state of the tomb, the condition of Tutankhamun's corpse, the haste with which the tomb was prepared, the two foetuses found in the caskets, the ill-fitting sarcophagus, the cracked lid, etc. are all analysed by the above authorities. Tutankhamun did die mysteriously and he was buried very quickly. What is more curious is that, shortly after his death, his tomb was broken into at least twice; it was later resealed by Maya. Howard Carter, when he first found the *shabtis*, the Watchers, believed that those perforated holes in the statues had been burrowed out to contain documents which had later been removed.

Ay did seize power but his rule collapsed, though the actual details are shrouded in mystery. Ankhesenamun did open negotiations with the Hittites (we still have her letter inviting them in), and, according to my research, the Hittite wedding party was ambushed and wiped out. Horemheb, according to my book on Tutankhamun, later revelled in this and took responsibility for it.

The date of the Exodus has always been shrouded in mystery, but many commentators believe there is a link between the Aten heresy and the Egyptian attack on the Israelites. Chapter 1 of Exodus, Verses 1–22, graphically describes what we would now term ethnic cleansing by Pharaoh against the Egyptians. In the end, however, this stirring period of human history is shrouded in mystery which one day perhaps will be satisfactorily resolved.